W9-BUE-374

The Country House Courtship

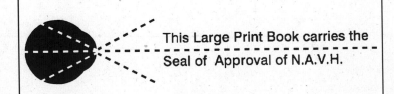

This Large Print Book carries the
Seal of Approval of N.A.V.H.

THE COUNTRY HOUSE COURTSHIP

LINORE ROSE BURKARD

THORNDIKE PRESS

A part of Gale, Cengage Learning

GALE
CENGAGE Learning™

Detroit • New York • San Francisco • New Haven, Conn • Waterville, Maine • London

GALE
CENGAGE Learning™

LIBRARY OF CONGRESS CATALOGING-IN-PUBLICATION DATA

Burkard, Linore Rose, 1960–
    The country house courtship / by Linore Rose Burkard.
      p. cm. — (Thorndike Press large print Christian fiction)
    (Regency inspirational romance series ; no. 3)
    ISBN-13: 978-1-4104-2760-1
    ISBN-10: 1-4104-2760-9
      1. England—Fiction. 2. Large type books. I. Title.
PS3602.U754C68 2010b
813'.6—dc22   2010009683

Published in 2010 by arrangement with Harvest House Publishers.

Printed in Mexico
1 2 3 4 5 6 7 14 13 12 11 10

To my husband,
Michael John Burkard,
without whom
I could never have pursued
the dream of writing
the way I have.

Special thanks to: Dee Hendrickson, for reading the manuscript and giving me suggestions and encouragement; Nancy Mayer, whose outstanding knowledge of the Regency is always helpful and reassuring (she, too, read the manuscript and gave me pointers). Debbie Lynne Costello and Melanie Dickerson, my daily goal-sharing writer friends who read parts of the manuscript and helped keep me accountable for my daily word counts! And Nick Harrison, my editor, who is always kind. I also want to thank Harvest House Publishers for another great book cover and their support. It's a pleasure to be a Harvest House author.

ONE

London, England
1818

Mr. Peter O'Brien felt surely he had a devil plaguing him, and the devil's name was Mr. Phillip Mornay. The paper in his hand should have made him happy. Indeed, it ought to have elicited nothing but joy. For after two years of holding a curacy that didn't pay enough to feed a church-mouse Mr. O'Brien was being recommended to a wealthy landowner whose vicarage had gone vacant.

The recommendation had come from the curate's previous naval commander, Colonel Sotheby, and the appointment was to a parish in Glendover — a prestigious position to be sure. In addition to having a decent curate's salary at last, Mr. O'Brien would have claim to a large glebe, a generous and well-built house, and, in short, would see himself by way of having enough to begin a family. (If he found a wife to marry, first, of course. O'Brien could just hear the Colonel's good-natured laugh ring out at that remark.)

But to the curate's consternation, the landowner's name was *Mr. Phillip Mornay,* none other than the Paragon himself. And Mornay, Mr. O'Brien knew, would never grant him the living. To do so would go against everything he knew to be true of him. After all, no man who had once overstepped his bounds with Mr. Mornay's betrothed, as Mr. O'Brien unfortunately had, would now be presented to the vicarage on the man's lands. *Of all the rotten, devilish luck!* To have such a letter of recommendation was like gold in the fiercely competitive world of the church, where there were more poor curates looking for a rise in their situations than there were church parishes who could supply them.

Therefore, instead of the boon from heaven this letter ought to have been, Mr. O'Brien was struck with a gloomy assurance that Mornay would sooner accept a popinjay in cleric's clothing than himself. Even worse, his mother agreed with his appraisal as she perused the letter while she sat at her breakfast.

"You do not wish to renew old grievances," she said. "Mr. Mornay is not, to my knowledge, a forgiving man. Shall you be put to the expense and trouble of travelling all the way to Middlesex, only to be turned down in the end? What can you possibly gain in it?"

Mr. O'Brien nodded; he saw her point. But he said, "I may have to do just that. The Colonel will never recommend me for another parish if he learns that I failed to apply myself to this opportunity."

"Write to him," replied his mama. "See if you can politely decline this honour, with the understanding that any other offer should be most welcome and appreciated!"

He doubted that any letter, no matter how "politely" written, would be able to manage his desire to avoid this meeting with Mornay, as well as secure the hope of a future recommendation. But he thought about it, put quill to paper, and sent the Colonel a reply. He asked (in the humblest terms he could manage) if the man might commend him for a living to be presented by some other landowner; indeed, *any* other landowner, any other gentleman in England than Phillip Mornay.

He could not explain the full extent of his past doings with Mr. Mornay without making himself sound like an utter fool; how he

11

had hoped to marry the present Mrs. Mornay himself, some years ago. How presumptuous his hopes seemed to him now! Miss Ariana Forsythe was magnificent as the wife of the Paragon! He'd seen them in town after the marriage, but without ever presenting himself before them. It appalled even him that he had once thought himself worthy or equal to that beautiful lady.

When the Colonel's reply came, there was little surprise in it. He assured Mr. O'Brien that his apprehensions were ill-placed; that Mr. Mornay's past reputation of being a harsh, irascible man was no longer to the purpose. Colonel Sotheby himself held Mornay in the greatest respect, and insisted that the Paragon had as good a heart as any Christian. In short (and he made this terribly clear), Mr. O'Brien had best get himself off to Middlesex or he would put the Colonel in a deuced uncomfortable spot. He had already written to Aspindon House, which meant that Mr. O'Brien was expected. If he failed to appear for an interview, he could not expect that another recommendation of such merit and generosity would ever come his way again.

Mr. O'Brien realized it was inevitable — he would have to go to Middlesex and present himself to Mornay. He knew it was a vain cause, that nothing but humiliation could come of it, but he bowed to what he must consider the will of God. He knelt in prayer, begging to be excused from this doomed interview, but his heart and conscience told him he must attend to it. If he was to face humiliation, had he not brought it upon himself? Had he not earned Mornay's disregard with his former obsession with Miss Forsythe, who was now Mrs. Mornay?

He no longer had feelings for the lady, but it was sure to be blessed awkward to face her! No less so than her husband. Nevertheless, when he rose from his knees, Peter O'Brien felt equal to doing what both duty and honour required. He only hoped that Mr. Mornay had not already written his own letter of objections to the Colonel; telling him why he would never present the living to Peter O'Brien. The Colonel was his best hope for a way out of St. Pancras. It was a gritty, desperate parish with poverty, crime, and hopelessness aplenty — not the sort of place he hoped to spend his life in, for he wanted a family. A wife.

Prepared to face the interview come what may, Mr. O'Brien determined not to allow Mornay to make quick work of him. He was no longer the youthful swain, besotted over

Miss Forsythe. A stint in the army, if nothing else, had hardened him, brought him face-to-face with deep issues of life, and left him (or so he thought) a wiser man.

Aspindon House, Glendover, Middlesex
Ariana Mornay looked for the hundredth time at her younger sister Beatrice, sitting across from her in the elegantly cozy morning room of her country estate, Aspindon. Here in the daylight, Beatrice's transformation from child to warm and attractive young woman was fully evident. When Mrs. Forsythe and Beatrice had arrived the prior evening, Ariana had seen the change in her sister, of course, but the daylight revealed it in a clarity that neither last night's flambeaux (lit in honour of their arrival) or the interior candlelight and fire of the drawing room had been able to offer.

Beatrice's previously brown hair was now a lovely luminous russet. Ringlets peeked out from a morning cap with ruffled lace, hanging over her brow and hovering about the sides of her face. The reddish brown of her locks emphasized hazel green eyes, smallish mischievous lips, and a healthy glow in her cheeks. Beatrice noticed her elder sister was studying her, and smiled.

"You still look at me as if you know me

not," she said, not hiding how much it pleased her to find herself an object of admiration.

"I cannot comprehend how greatly you are altered, in just one year!"

"I regret that we did not come for so long," put in Mrs. Forsythe, the girls' mother. She was still feasting her eyes upon Ariana and the children (though the nurse, Mrs. Perler, had taken four-year-old Nigel, the Mornay's firstborn, from the room, after he had spilled milk all over himself minutes ago). "We wished to come sooner, as you know, but Lucy took ill, and I dared not carry the sickness here to you with your new little one." At this, she stopped and cooed to the infant, who was upon her lap at the moment. "No, no, no," she said, in the exaggerated tone that people so often use when addressing babies, "we can't have little Miranda getting sick, now can we?"

Ariana smiled. "It matters not, Mama. You are here, now. I only wish Papa and Lucy could have joined you." Lucy, the youngest Forsythe sister, and Papa had been obliged to stay home until the spring planting had been seen to. Mr. Forsythe did not wish to be wholly bereft of his family, so Lucy, who was a great comfort to him,

15

had been enjoined to remain in Chesterton for his sake.

"I could not bear to wait upon your father a day longer," Mrs. Forsythe answered with a little smile. "They will come by post chaise after Papa has done his service through Easter. And then we will all be together — except for the Norledges. Perhaps when Papa comes, he may bring your older sister and her husband."

"I would want Aunt Pellham too, in that case," Ariana said.

"Oh, my! With your Aunt and Uncle Pellham, and the Norledges, even this large house would be filled with guests, I daresay!" said her mother.

Beatrice, meanwhile, was barely listening. She was still happily ingesting the thought that Ariana had evidently noticed her womanhood. At seventeen, hers was not a striking sort of beauty — one did not stop in instant admiration upon spying Beatrice in a room, for instance, as had often been the case for Ariana; but the younger girl had no lack of wits, a lively eye and countenance, and, not to be understated, an easy friendliness. Among a group of reserved and proper English young ladies, Beatrice would be the beacon of refuge for the timid; she was welcoming where others were aloof; inquisitive and protective where others looked away.

Nor was she the sort of young woman to glide across a floor, dignified and elegant. Instead, Beatrice was ever having to keep her energy in check; when rising from a chair (her mama had made her practice doing so countless times) she could appear as elegant as the next young woman. She ate nicely, even daintily. But left unchecked, her natural enthusiasm might propel her through a room with alarming speed. Her shawls were ever hanging from her arms, never staying in place over her shoulders; and her mother forbade her from wearing hair jewellery, as it tended to lose its place upon her head. Bandeaux were her lot — besides bonnets, of course.

"It is fortunate that I am only seventeen," she had said to her mama only last week, while the woman was draping a wide bandeau artfully around Beatrice's head. "Or I believe you would exile every manner of female head attire from this house, saving turbans! Although my hair holds a curl twice as long as Lucy's!"

Mrs. Forsythe had paused from her ministrations and met her daughter's eyes in the looking glass before them. "I daresay you are suited for turbans; perhaps we should shop for some. I believe they are very popular just now." Since the last thing in the world Beatrice wished to wear upon her head was a turban — no matter how many ladies in the pages of *La Belle Assemblée* wore them — she simply gave voice to an exasperated huff, evoking a knowing smile upon her mama's face.

"I should *adore* a full house of guests," Beatrice said, now. "Please do invite the Norledges, Ariana! Only think of the diversions we could have; play-acting with enough people to fill all the roles, for a change! Or charades; or even a dance!"

Ariana looked at her sister fondly. "Which dances do you like best?"

"The waltz!" she quickly responded, with a smile to show that she knew it was mischievous to prefer the waltz — the single dance which entailed more contact with the opposite sex than any other ballroom fare. Mrs. Forsythe clucked her tongue, but Beatrice blithely ignored this, taking a peek at her brother-in-law to gauge his reaction, instead. The host of the gathering was reading his morning paper, however, and not listening to the small talk between his wife and her relations.

And relations were virtually all around him. In addition to Beatrice and Mrs.

Forsythe, there was his aunt, Mrs. Royle-forst, staying with them at the present; and her companion, skinny, nervous Miss Blu-ford. These two ladies had not yet appeared for breakfast, which was no doubt on account of Mrs. Royleforst. She found mornings difficult, and either slept in or took a tray in her room.

"What do you think, sir?" asked Mrs. Forsythe of her host. "Shall my daughter invite the Norledges to join Mr. Forsythe and Lucy when they set out for your house? Or is your home already filled enough for your liking?"

Mr. Mornay looked over his paper enough to acknowledge that he had heard her question. "As it is your and my wife's family, I think the two of you must decide upon it. As long as there are bedchambers enough," he added, looking at Ariana, "you may fill them with guests as you please."

"Thank you, darling," she said, making Beatrice stifle a titter. Her sister and her husband were still inordinately romantic, to her mind. Good thing no one else was present save her mother! She would have been embarrassed for them in company.

"Shall I take the baby, Mama?" asked Ariana, for Miranda was beginning to fuss.

"I suppose she wants to be fed," agreed

her mother. Ariana nodded to a maid who was seated against the wall, who went and received the child from her grandmother and took her gingerly to her mama. Ariana's eyes sparkled with happiness as she took her little girl. She murmured to the baby, by turns picking her up and kissing her face, and then just holding her in her arms and gazing at her in loving adoration. "I shan't feed her yet," she said. "She isn't insisting upon it."

Beatrice's thoughts were still upon the diversions that would be possible with a large group staying at the house. "If they all come, can you and Mr. Mornay hold a ball, Ariana? Or, will you take me to London this year for the Season? Then I may go to as many balls as I like, and you will not have the expense of holding them!"

"If she takes you to London for the Season," put in her mama, "she will have a great deal more expense than just that of a ball! Besides which, you are too young for such."

Beatrice looked at her mama, her enthusiasm temporarily dampened. "But my sister sees I am older now," she said, looking at Ariana with a silent plea in her gaze. "And I am not too young for a Season, according to the magazines. Many girls my age do have their coming-out, Mama!"

"Many gels," she returned instantly, "have little sense, and their parents, no better; your papa and I did not allow either of your sisters to go about in society at your age. You have been already too indulged, if you ask me. London society is out of the question!"

Beatrice was now thoroughly dampened in her spirits, but she looked about and settled her eyes upon her brother-in-law. "I daresay Mr. Mornay has seen many a girl of my age — and younger — make their debut during the Season. And to no ill effect. Why, I am sure some of them have made the most brilliant matches! Many a man of good standing prefers a younger lady for his wife. You had ought to let me go while I am young enough to enjoy this advantage."

Mr. Mornay was frowning behind his newspaper. He knew that his young relation wanted his support in the matter, but Mr. Mornay was assuredly not in the habit of coming to the aid of young women, particularly regarding a London Season. So he said nothing, though an ensuing silence in the room told him the ladies waited for his opinion.

Ariana, who knew better, offered, "Let us discuss it another time. There are months, yet, before the Season. And with Miranda so young, I cannot decide at this point, in any case."

Beatrice, who had no idea she was treading on dangerous ground, said, "Only let Mr. Mornay tell us his thoughts! I know my mother will listen if you tell her, sir," she said directly to him.

He put his paper down reluctantly, and then looked at Beatrice. "I think Ariana was young to face society at nineteen. At your age, you need to be sheltered, not put forth among the wolves."

Her face fell so entirely, that he almost chuckled at it. "Why are you so eager for a Season?"

She smiled a little. This was better; he was inviting her to explain so that her mother could see the good advantage in it. "I have long lived with the memory of my sister's tales of her experiences in London," she said. "She met *you* there! Her coming out is what brought her to marriage, to Aspindon, to a better life! I have had my fill of Chesterton, I assure you! The prospects for marrying well in that region are as dismal as ever, if not worse," she said. (Ariana closed her eyes at this; she could hardly bear to hear her sister telling all the reasons Phillip would most despise.) "Why does it seem that all the eligible young men in the county are either in a regiment somewhere, or at sea, or in need of a fortune? I must go to London or Bath, where there are more men one can meet!"

She paused, looking at him earnestly. "I have no fortune, sir, as you are well aware. And with your connexions, I am certain to make very advantageous acquaintances! What could be more certain? I shall end up, no doubt, just as my sister has, with a man like you!" Beatrice evidently thought she was giving him a great compliment. She waited, expecting a gracious answer.

"Oh, Beatrice!" moaned Mrs. Forsythe. "You foolish gel!"

Mr. Mornay stood up, after folding his paper to a neat size. He said, "It takes more than wearing a corset to say a young lady is grown up, would you not agree?" He directed his remark to the whole room, but then settled his eyes upon Beatrice. He then gave a small bow to the women in general, and turned to leave the room.

Beatrice blushed slightly, embarrassed to be chastised by her brother-in-law.

Mr. Frederick met his master at the door, holding out a salver with a letter for Mr. Mornay, who took it but then looked curiously at the butler.

"It arrived in that condition, sir! I daresay it was lost in the mail or some such thing."

"Hmm, very good, Freddie." He held up a battered and ink-soiled missive for his wife to see, while eyeing it dubiously.

She looked amused. "Who is it from?"

He unfolded the paper, as the sealing wax was almost entirely worn off already, and scanned the signature at the bottom. "Colonel Sotheby. I'll read it in my office."

She nodded, and Mr. Mornay left the room.

Beatrice was still smarting from his earlier remark, and said, as soon as he'd gone, "How 'grown up' can I be, when I am forced to exist in a small country village, with no prospects, and genteel company only upon a Sunday?"

"You overstate your case! That is not true," answered her mama, disapprovingly.

"And as for wearing a corset," Beatrice continued, after taking a sip of tea, "I do not pretend that wearing one is what makes me of age for a Season. I have formed my principles upon sound reason. I have sat beneath the tutelage of my father and of Mr. Timmons, and of his curate, and I should say my principles are well-founded."

"We are glad to hear it," Ariana said, with great forbearance, "but really, you should not be setting your mind upon seeking a man like my husband; you should be intent upon finding the man that God has chosen for you."

"And so I am!" she protested, her eyes wide and laughing. "But look at the advantage He gives me in having *you* for my sister! Am I to ignore that? When it could be the very means of bringing me and my future husband together?"

Ariana played absently with little Miranda's blanket, tucking it in about her chin more snugly. She met her sister's eyes. "London is not the only place a young woman may meet a husband. And if you want *my* husband's approval of your plan, the last thing in the world you should tell him is that you want to meet a man like him! Or that you wish to marry above you in any way!"

"But is it above me? To marry well? When my sister is Mrs. Mornay of Aspindon House?"

"It is above you," said her mother, "because you are Miss Forsythe of Chesterton."

"I am a gentleman's daughter," she replied.

"With no dowry to speak of," said her mama.

Beatrice's cheeks began to burn. "With a

brother-in-law of great fortune and consequence!" she said, petulantly.

"That does not signify!" said her mother.

"It does to me!"

"It should not!" Mrs. Forsythe was quickly growing ashamed of her daughter, and she was relieved that Mr. Mornay had left the room and was not hearing Beatrice right now. Ariana's eyebrows were raised and she was doing her best to act as though she had no part in the dialogue.

"But it does, Mama!"

"Beatrice! You have already said far too much on this matter, which proves to me your great ignorance of the world." She held up her hand for silence as Beatrice was about to protest. "Not another word! I shan't have it, not another word." Mrs. Forsythe turned her attention to her elder daughter.

"I think I will visit the nursery to see how Nigel is faring. Do you mind?"

"No, indeed. He will enjoy showing you his toys," Ariana said as her mother rose to leave the room. "I'll be up myself, shortly, to feed the baby."

"Very good." She nodded to her daughter, and then her eye fell upon Beatrice. "I think it would be wise if you said nothing more regarding a Season. In fact, I forbid you to

26

mention it to Mr. Mornay again! Do you understand me?" There was a short silence.

"I do, Mama." Beatrice was not happy, but she recognized that particular tone of voice. She considered, moreover, that it would be a simple matter to keep from mentioning her hopes to the man, for he evidently would not encourage her in them. But as for herself, she would continue to think of the Season in London. She would continue to hope; and some other day, when Ariana was in a good disposition, she would prevail upon her to sponsor her in London.

Beatrice did not want to be disrespectful, but she knew that Mr. Mornay was quite in error regarding her. He did not know, for instance, that she was determined to make a good match, and recognized it as her lot in life. Every inch she saw of Aspindon just confirmed her sense that a rich life awaited her. She was born for it. And now all that was necessary was to meet her future husband — the man who could make it all happen. She had long prayed for just such a meeting and knew that it was bound to occur. All she had to do was be properly outfitted, and in the proper company, for it to do so.

All she had to do was change her sister

and brother-in-law's minds on the matter. How difficult could that be?

Two

Beatrice had a secret fascination for her brother-in-law, which perhaps did its part in fueling her resolve to marry a man like him. She had no romantic notions about Mr. Mornay, of course — that would be wicked! But she saw no reason why she could not get herself a husband of his ilk, despite anything her mama or Ariana had said. Twice already Beatrice had quickly stood aside when her brother-in-law was approaching so that she could watch him; he spied her by chance both times, caught her gaze, and both times had looked again at her, as though perplexed. Beatrice had given little smiles, and he nodded in return.

Little did he know that she was practicing upon him! If she could meet Mr. Mornay's dark eyes and handsome expression with equanimity, she felt certain she could do so when meeting other gentlemen whom she admired. Besides, it was becoming more and more clear to Beatrice that a man of means *must* be her object in marriage: Her sister's house and grounds were precisely the quality she adored. Not to mention, servants aplenty; a beauteous bedchamber all to herself with its own little sitting room; meals to delight in; yes, all was opulent, indeed. There was an enormous park and grounds that went on for near a mile, and actual tenants — to make one feel quite important!

The Mornays might just as well have been lord and lady, in Beatrice's opinion. Mr. Mornay was the sitting magistrate for the county; their estate was finer than Lady Middleton's, a thing Beatrice had pointed out on her last visit at Aspindon (and been roundly shushed by her mother for). Who, she asked herself, after experiencing this fine life, could be content with marriage to any mere mister? Was it not plain to see that Beatrice's family had been raised a notch in society by Ariana's marriage? And she, Beatrice, certainly deserved a union of equal advantage. By God's grace, it had become her due.

Mr. Tristan Barton entered his apartment on Brooke Street in London. It was a second floor flat, a rare find in the imposing neighbourhood where most townhouses were fully occupied by one person or family, not separated into flats like this one. It gave Mr. Barton the advantage of being a resident of Mayfair without the usual expense of a house. Since he lived with only his sister, he saw no reason to incur greater damage to his pocketbook by keeping an entire house.

After he'd given up his coat, gloves, and hat to their sole manservant, he pulled some bank notes from a pocket of his waistcoat and began to count them. Sometimes when gaming got hot and heavy, he lost track of how much he was winning or losing. Tonight, he'd come out on top, at least. As he stood in the doorway to the drawing room counting the notes from his pocket, he heard a low cough and looked up.

"Anne! Why are you not abed?" He was not smiling.

His sister compressed her lips with suppressed grief. His brows came together. "What is it, Anne? What has happened?" She had been standing against the fireplace, staring down into the flames until she heard him come in. She put a handkerchief to her mouth and turned away, making him enter the parlour. She let herself down shakily upon a sofa.

"For heaven's sake!" he said, exasperated. "It cannot be so bad as all that!" He had undone his neckcloth, letting the cravat hang untidily about his chest. Watching her, he sat himself in a chair and leaned back contemplatively. "His lordship has abandoned you, hasn't he?"

Her only response was to shut her eyes hard, as if she could block out the unwelcome words.

"Did I not tell you that family was too full of its own importance?" he continued. "I tried to warn you."

Anne's grimace deepened; but she cried, "Oh, if it were only that! I pray God it would be only that!"

He looked perplexed, but he sat back, watching her cautiously. "I, for one, am the bearer of *good* news." This drew her attention, and, through her tears, she looked at him expectantly. He saw her look and smiled. "The Regent needed a man to do him a personal favour, and I proposed myself — and, what do you think? He appointed me to it!" He waited for her reaction, but when there was none but a continuing look of questioning, he added, "He has put his trust in me for the thing! Do you not see how this signifies? If I can accomplish the deed for the prince, I will hereafter be a part of his set. No one will give me looks as though I am not good enough for them any longer!"

To her continuing silence, he added, "It would be a feather in your cap, dear Anne. Perhaps his lordship — if he is what is troubling you — will see you in a different light. If my consequence improves, yours shall too, it is certain."

When Anne's look merely darkened, he added, "Is this not what grieves you? That his family frowns upon you? If I succeed in my hopes for the prince, I may even be able to wriggle a recommendation for you from some great lady! Enough to burn the ears of the Countess and make them change their opinion of us! Enough to shut the mouths of those prigs, for sure!"

She turned sharply away at those words, and a small sob escaped her throat. His face darkened. "All right; out with it, Anne. Dash it, what has happened? Tell your brother while he is in a good humour over this stroke of fortune. I cannot think why you are not rejoicing at it as well. Whatever concerns me concerns you."

"That is precisely the thing," she said, raising her agonized face to his, "that worries me most!"

"What?" A look of dark suspicion entered

his eyes, and he stood and swiftly approached her where she sat. He sat down near her. Something told him that only gentleness would part her from her secret. "What is it? Tell me everything." His face and demeanour were grave.

She could barely stand to look at him.

"Does this concern his lordship?" His voice was disarmingly soft.

"Not any longer."

"Go on," he said, but his hands began to form a fist, though he wasn't aware of it.

"Promise me you shan't do anything rash; or refuse to see me."

"Good heavens, Anne! Do not say — it cannot be — you are not carrying that man's child!"

She nodded, gasping, and buried her head in her hands, crying heartily. He looked at her for a moment as though thunderstruck. After a few moments, he touched her upon the shoulder, and she looked up at him, hopefully.

"Is there anything you can do about it?"

"What . . . what do you mean?" A very pretty woman, Anne's large eyes glistened with tears, and then with dawning horror as she took in his meaning.

"Isn't there something women do — to get rid of — such a problem?"

Her eyes widened and she stared at him in silent horror. Finally she cried, "Do you think I could do that? Do you think I am so heartless that I could harm my own child?"

"What I think," he said, jumping to his feet in anger, "is that you are foolish, and thoughtless, and are *ruined,* if you do not!" He took a deep breath and looked at her with rage in his eyes. "You've ruined us both!" He paced in one direction, then stopped and turned back to her. "How could you let him — why? Why did you do it, Anne? When he might have married you!"

She shook her head. "No. He was not at liberty to. You know his parents forbade it!" There was silence a moment. "Perhaps if your friendship with the prince had come sooner, it might have been different . . ."

"My friendship with the prince, indeed!" He plopped back down upon a sofa. "And how long do you suppose I will be welcome at Carlton House if it — if you — become known to the world?"

She was trying not to cry afresh. "The prince is hardly what one could call free of scandal himself."

"And you think that signifies?" He was being rather vicious, but he could not help himself. "He is the prince! The Regent! He may do as he very well pleases! It is a deuced different affair for the likes of us!"

Again, a restless silence hung over the room, while Anne sat staring at nothing, holding a handkerchief over her mouth. She refused to meet his eyes. "I know I have disappointed you," she said in a hoarse tone. "But you must believe that his lordship cares for me. He'd marry me if he could."

"He *will* marry you, by Jove! Or I'll see him on the field!"

"No, Tristan! You must not challenge him! I cannot have either one of you hurt on my account!"

"I shall have to, I can see! There's no other reason for him to marry you now, Anne! You've already given him what he most wanted."

"That is not true! He *loves* me!"

"Love! Little good love is to us now!" Mr. Barton closed his eyes and lifted his hands as if he wanted to wring some sense into her, but he stopped before her, dropped his arms abruptly, and turned away in silent frustration. "I am going to proceed as I planned, only now you will have to accompany me. I cannot leave you in town where your condition will be noted. I'll put out word that I mean to issue a challenge just as soon as I return to town; only I cannot say why, and everyone shall want to know!"

She looked at him sadly. "I beg you, do not challenge him!"

He made a scornful sound. "If I do not, no man will think me honourable. If I do, the matter is bound to come out. You've got me blocked at both ends, Anne! *Well done!*" he said sarcastically. He hit his fist against the side of the sofa and turned his face away from her in disgust.

In a strong tone, he spoke again. "Where I take you, no one will know you; and no one, even there, *can* know of your condition. Do you understand?" He paused, looking back to survey her with different eyes. "How long until it will be obvious?"

"Not for many months. I think . . . I think my confinement will begin in August."

He jumped to his feet and turned on his heel. "Your confinement, dear Anne, will begin much sooner than that. You have made yourself a prisoner of the house, from the day you need to let out your stays; do you understand?"

She didn't answer, but slowly agreed, nodding her head. Then, looking up at him she asked, "What favour did you agree to accomplish for the Regent?"

He looked at her morosely. "Not that it

matters now, but he has learned that Lord Malcolm is letting his house to tenants, and will accept monthly terms. As Malcolm is neighbour to Aspindon House, he expects little trouble in renting the place year-round. I am to take the house for a month or two, on the pretext of trying life in the country to see if it suits; while in fact I must ply Mr. Mornay to sound the depth of his intentions concerning the prince. The Paragon has stalled on an offer of a viscountcy, and I am to discover the reasons behind it."

"A viscountcy! My word, why on earth would he?"

He looked at her gravely. "That is what I am to find out."

After a small silence, she asked in a low tone, "So I will go with you?"

"I have little choice about that, now, do I?"

His tone made her wince.

"But as I said, when your condition . . . worsens . . . you will retire from society. I will consider the arrangements that must be made at that time; this unfortunate . . . circumstance must not be discovered. By anyone." He paused, studying her face. "Does his lordship know?"

She shook her head. "Not yet."

"He'll know when I've issued my ultimatum. Pray God he doesn't let it out."

"Do you think he is such a fool that he would want it known?"

"Nevertheless, I'm afraid the only thing for it is to take you from London until after the birth of your bastard."

"Tristan!"

Her pained expression softened his a little. But he added, "Let us not talk of it! I'd like as few reminders of your condition as possible, if you don't mind. I am exceedingly grieved for you, Anne."

She studied his face. "You *are* grieved, but not for me. Let us be honest with each other. You are grieved that I have not married his lordship and become a lady, and you are further in horror that I may jeopardize your new friendship with the prince. Is that not closer to the truth?"

He almost smiled, but then his look became grave again. "You are my sister. I am grieved."

There was silence while they continued to study each other a moment. Then Barton said, "I charge you to not contact his lordship or tell him you are with me. He may discover my whereabouts, but I should prefer it if he did not learn of yours. You are not to be trifled with by him again!"

"He may call upon us. I told you, he loves me!"

"Well, we'll see about that, shan't we?"

THREE

Mr. Mornay could present the living at Glendover to whomsoever he chose, when and if it fell vacant. And Glendover was vacant; the last vicar had died unexpectedly two months since, and the Paragon still had not presented the benefice to a new man. He was considering the names of a few; he had held four interviews, and was happy with none of the applicants. He hoped, at first, that the Colonel had a good man to fill the situation, but when he saw the name of Peter O'Brien his face froze for a moment in disbelief. *O'Brien!* That man had plagued him throughout his courtship with Ariana.

O'Brien was not intentionally vexatious, but had managed to make a supremely heavy cart for the horse, so to speak. He was, in other words, burdensome. His actions in the past had resulted in Ariana's abduction, and he had been caught stealing a kiss from her — which Mr. Mornay had almost been in time to prevent, but had instead found his bride-to-be just recovering herself from the man's grasp. He felt an old stirring of irritation, and when his eye fell upon the date on the letter — 5 January — he felt a strong new one. *Why in blazes hadn't the letter reached him sooner?*

It was too late for him to write and prevent the interview. It was 24 February, and O'Brien would be arriving any time — if he had the pluck. (With any luck, he would not.) And imagine if Phillip had not got the news beforehand! He might have received him most ungraciously. In light of the hearty words of commendation from Colonel Sotheby (so the young man had done a stint in the army; that spoke well of him), he decided to make an effort at giving Peter O'Brien a fair chance at the living. Wait, no; that was asking too much. He could not purposely grant the man a place in their parish. He'd be in their lives forever. No one could be expected to be that forgiving! Certainly not he!

He would make an attempt at peace, however. Let O'Brien prove his mettle, if he could.

He wondered how Ariana would react when she heard. Just in case the man did not show up, he decided to say nothing to her at present. No sense putting her in mind of the uncomfortable events of the past. It was unfortunate enough that he had to think on them.

The next day, when Ariana and Phillip joined their guests in the drawing room, Ariana said brightly to her relations, "What do you think?" She took in the sight of her mother and sister on one sofa, both with canvases and needles in hand; her Aunt Royleforst, on an opposite settee beside Miss Bluford, who was helping the lady make out the illustrations in a fashion magazine; and made her announcement: "Mr. Mornay has just this minute got a note by special messenger — there is a curate en route this very moment to apply for the living! I do hope he is suitable! We have been without a vicar these past two months, and have gone to Warwickdon for our services. It is not too inconvenient to go there, only a short drive; but Mr. Hargrove (the vicar at Warwickdon) is very soon to abandon us for a new living *he* has got!"

Ariana did not know that the hastily written note which her husband had just received was from Mr. Peter O'Brien. He had wished to inform Mr. Mornay that he was, at that very moment, no more than four or so miles away, and desired to know if he was welcome at Aspindon House. Permission was granted — Mr. Mornay knew the man had travelled from London, and could guess at the trouble it had cost him. If only that deuced letter from the Colonel had arrived when it should have — none of this would be necessary. But he told his wife he was expecting a new candidate for the living, and now entered the room where the ladies were, to join them in waiting. Perhaps the "interview" would go quickly.

Meanwhile, the women in the room nodded their understanding. "And then you will have no man at all; that won't do, will it?"

"Indeed, no. Mr. Mornay and I should have to move to Grosvenor Square simply to attend service!"

Beatrice gasped. "You *will* take me with you? It is the perfect opportunity!"

Ariana took a seat on a wingchair next to the sofa and near the fireplace. "*If* we go, you are welcome to accompany us," she said with a smile. Her sister was so eager for a Season! Beatrice returned to her sewing but with a face of triumph. "Oh, splendid! Thank you, Ariana!"

Mrs. Forsythe's demeanour was barely patient of this enthusiasm, but she said, "Do not be overhasty. There are always an abundance of curates looking for employment. If this man does not answer the purpose, another will, I am certain. You have only to ask around and you'll soon have a list of candidates longer than your parish birth registry, I vow!"

Suddenly Beatrice hoped that the man coming would not be found acceptable. If no one filled the position before Mr. Hargrove took up his new living, the Mornays might remove to their London house! Which meant that she, Beatrice, would join them and live in Grosvenor Square. She had seen the magnificent house at the Square, but not spent more than a night beneath its roof. Just the thought of staying there again sent excitement through her veins.

"Shall we try to guess at the sort of man our cleric is?" asked Ariana. She had taken up her own bit of needlework — her perpetual project was to knit blankets for the poor, dropping them off in the village whenever she had more than one finished.

"Shall we all get to see him?" Beatrice asked curiously.

"I would very much like to, if I may," put in Mrs. Royleforst.

"You may all meet him," answered their host. "It will serve to demonstrate his manners in company," he added lightly. He almost smiled at the thought. Perhaps there would be some diversion in this after all.

Beatrice was proud to be among the family in the finely appointed room, with its dazzling furniture and decoration. And her new walking-out dress of green and pink flowered cambric, the finest winter gown that she had ever had the felicity of enjoying, was perfectly suited for receiving company. Never before had Beatrice felt so indulgent, so condescending, so perfectly at ease among such wealth. After all, she was family; the house belonged to her sister's husband. She was not timidly come to leave flowers for the lady of the manor (as she sometimes did at home), but now she *was* one of the ladies of the manor. At least she was sure it must appear so to the coming visitor.

By this time next year, she thought to herself, *I shall likely be married to a fine gentleman, and my house, if not quite as elegant as Aspindon, will be richly appointed and pleasing to anyone.*

"Will you play, Beatrice? Shall we try to guess at the sort of man who is on his way?" her mama asked her.

"By all means!" Beatrice smiled. "This will

be diverting." She loved a good game, but somehow had convinced herself that a calmness of manner was her trademark. She must not be thought of as a flighty young girl who grew excited at the least cause, or gave way to much mirth. Her nature could not be grave, but of a decidedly serious bent. She did, after all, read poetry and novels, and a few (a very few) other books.

Beatrice saw that everyone was looking at her, and she asked, brightly, "Shall I begin, then?"

"Yes, do," said Ariana, noting for the thousandth time how much the girl had grown. She was little Beatrice no longer! Ariana watched affectionately while her sister spoke, taking note of her sturdy eyebrows that matched the hue of her hair and the strong features that hinted at a boldness of character, vivid imagination, and mischievous bent that showed primarily in the sparkle of her hazel green eyes. Since childhood Beatrice had shown a propensity to enjoy social occasions, and Ariana marveled that she had not changed in that respect. She was smiling while she thought on how to characterize the mysterious visitor to come, and Ariana had to allow that when she smiled, Beatrice could be called beautiful. She was at the dawn of womanhood, her elder sister thought. And yet, so young.

Beatrice thought for a moment longer, and then said, "I think . . . it will be a man who has long been a curate, and will be hankering to become a vicar."

Mrs. Royleforst opined, looking around, "Well, yes, of course, they all do. Perpetual curates! No meaner prison in all Britain for a gentleman!"

"My dear ma'am," Ariana hastened to reply. "I should say not. That is, there are many curates who are happily situated —"

"And twice as many who are well nigh starving," the older lady added smoothly. "Curates are nothing but gentlemen in a respectable debtor's prison called the Church. Come, come, Ariana, even you cannot defend our religion in this case; it cannot be. Pluralism, you well know, is a direct result of too many curacies offering such mean stipends as no proper gentleman can live on! I quite sympathize with poor curates, you see."

Ariana had to smile. "I can see, and I commend it in you. Indeed, I too feel most strongly for the plight of poor churchmen, you must believe me."

Beatrice, meanwhile, growing bored, scrunched up her face and said, "You must let me finish my caricature: I think — he is poor, exceedingly thin, and exceedingly dull in his conversation." (The others chuckled.) "He will insist upon calling just when you are prepared to dine, will accept your gracious invitation to join you, and will afterward drink port or claret while he bores Mr. Mornay to distraction (She peeked at the dark eyes across the room and was pleased to find them upon her with a look of small amusement.) and refuse to play cards, or dance, or be amiable." She smiled a little smugly.

Ariana laughed. "You have painted an ogre! Why is your opinion of a stranger so decidedly gloomy? What is to answer for it, particularly when you have the agreeable Mr. Timmons as your model for a vicar?"

Mrs. Forsythe asked, "Do you despise the profession?"

"No!" Beatrice said, looking around innocently. "Only, now I think on it, a man must do very well in the Church if he is to live as a gentleman, as Mrs. Royleforst says. He cannot make his fortune so well as a soldier or military man, having no recourse to the opportunities that war and travel provide."

"Opportunites," said Mr. Mornay, "such as dying at the barrel of a rifle?"

Beatrice paused and pouted at him. "That was not my meaning, as you well know, sir!" But the humour was not entirely lost upon her and she ended upon a little smile. "I grant it is a safer profession; but many a man has been made by his military service, while many a parson must scrounge and take on more parishes than he can handle, merely to get by."

"It is a grave injustice," said Ariana, "but no reason to assume our cleric must be morose."

Beatrice, nonplussed, said, "I thought you desired an ogre — someone we could laugh at."

"What *do* we know of this man, truly?" asked Mrs. Forsythe. "Is he coming by recommendation? I am certain Mr. Timmons could advise you where to find a good man, sir, (this to Mr. Mornay) if you are in need of help in that regard."

Mr. Mornay spoke up. "He comes highly recommended. He would not be coming at all, however, I assure you, except that the letter recommending him was delayed. Lost in the mail, no doubt, so that I only received it yesterday. But he is wasting his time."

Ariana was surprised. "Have you presented the living to someone else?"

Her husband met her eyes. "Without your

knowing of it? No."

"But you said he is wasting his time. And that he would not be coming if you had notice. What are we to make of that?" she asked, curious at his mysterious air.

"When the man arrives, you will understand me."

"We do need a vicar at Glendover," she reminded him. "The people all feel the absence of poor Mr. Applegate."

"The people are managing to get themselves to Warwickdon. 'Tis but two miles, and their spiritual needs are being met thus. I should like to fill the position with a man of *my* choosing, if you must know."

"But of course you will choose the man. Only you can, my darling." Her face registered a momentary discomfort as she recalled that they were not alone — it was vexing to feel they must address each other formally in the presence of guests. Calling Phillip "my darling," was her habit — not easy to alter on demand. "But I do think you must give this man — whatever you know of him — a fair trial of your scrutiny; for the Colonel's sake, if not his own."

"Do you have aught against the Colonel?" asked Mrs. Forsythe. "For what reason are you so decided in your opinion against the man he recommends?"

"It has nothing to do with the Colonel," he answered.

"What is the curate's name?" asked Beatrice.

"Yes, give us the name, Phillip!" added Mrs. Royleforst.

"Yes, the name!" echoed her minion, nodding her skinny head. She liked to be included in as much of genteel society as possible.

"Perhaps we can conjecture better upon his character if we hear his name." Ariana looked at her husband. They all looked at him.

"Ariana, do you not know it?" asked her mama, a little surprised.

"Actually, no, Mr. Mornay has not told me." She looked back at her husband. "You evidently know the man, or something of him. Is this not so?"

"I could never forget it, I assure you. But since he is expected any minute, I think I shall leave it to him to make himself known to you."

Beatrice said, "You can never forget it? It must be singular, somehow!"

"I should say!" cried Mrs. Royleforst. "If you indeed know this fellow, Phillip, ought you not to tell us what you know? Should we be on our guard? Something is afoot in this business, I can smell it."

He merely gave that maddening half-smile, so Ariana said, "Never mind, let us devise our own little name for the ogre, then." She paused and fell to thinking, and then looked up with a rapturous expression for a second. In the next moment, however, her face fell again. "Oh, I can think of nothing. Beatrice, do you have something?"

To everyone's surprise, not least of all Mrs. Royleforst, her companion, Miss Bluford spoke up. "I — I think I can, if I may be allowed —"

"But of course, Miss Bluford!" cried her mistress, quite surprised.

The lady's lips came together in concentration, and she lifted her chin. The other occupants in the room were almost craning their necks, waiting, except for Phillip, who had crossed his arms and merely sat, watching her with not the least surprise or curiosity on his face.

"How — how do you like —" and here she paused again.

"Out with it, my dear!" said her mistress.

Miss Bluford swallowed. "How do you like this? Mr. *Frogglethorpe.*" All the females in the room chuckled in surprise that sober Miss Bluford would produce such a name.

"Very amusing, Miss Bluford!" gasped

Mrs. Royleforst approvingly.

With this encouragement, Miss Bluford gave a little wobbly smile and added, "Let us say, then, Mr. Frederick Frogglethorpe!" Her skinny shoulders shook as she quietly enjoyed her own mirth and gave little peeks at the others about her (except for Mr. Mornay. She was still wary of him.). She loved that she had amused everyone.

"I daresay Frederick shan't like it," replied the lady of the house, thinking of their butler, Mr. Frederick, whom her husband called "Freddy."

Little Nigel burst into the room at that moment, leaving the door ajar.

"Mama! Papa! Nigel is back!"

"Come to Auntie Royleforst," said the large older woman, immediately. Mrs. Forsythe had been just about to offer her own arms to the child, and frowned, but she said nothing.

Beatrice repeated, "Frederick Frogglethorpe. I believe it has a very proper ring to it — almost." And she laughed. "Ah, yes, 'Mr. Frederick Frogglethorpe at your service, ma'am,' " and Miss Bluford tittered the most of anyone. Ariana was smiling, enjoying that her sister found the little exercise diverting. Beatrice added, "I think he will bow timidly, with overarching propriety, and will offer you a great deal of flummery." They all chuckled, and Miss Bluford, nodding fervently, agreed, "Yes, flummery — indeed, indeed! The richest sort! The smoothest going down! Quite the vicar!"

Mrs. Royleforst continued to feel amazed and amused at how Miss Bluford was coming out of her shell of silence, but she was too busy allowing Nigel the pleasure of crawling all over her large person to say anything of it.

The clock ticked, and they all continued to wait.

FOUR

Mr. O'Brien, having accepted that his fate was to appear before his old nemesis, the Paragon, did what he could to ready himself. He knew the "interview" would be a hopeless affair, but he was properly resigned to this. The Colonel's honour was at stake; his own honour demanded his acquiescence, and so he set himself to making his appearance in the best manner possible.

He went first to his mother and suffered the humiliation of enlisting her support in the form of funds. She was reluctant to help him in the scheme, feeling there was a preponderance of certain doom attached to the venture. But sons have their way of finagling help from their mothers, and soon Mr. O'Brien was in possession of enough money to call upon his tailor.

He had his overcoat relined and cleaned; he did the same for his boots and shoes, getting new heels and paying extra for the very best polish. He even bought a new waistcoat, and would have ventured a shirt as well, but needed enough money for the post chaise to get to Middlesex. He made very sure to keep enough for the return journey, as that, he knew, would not be far behind his arrival. During a routine hair trim, the barber somehow convinced him to sport the very latest fashion of a slight "whip" above his forehead. His hair was the perfect texture, he said; his face had just the right shape to pull it off without a hint of dandyism; and so when the curate left the shop, he had a new wave in his hair, and could hardly suppress a slight feeling of glee when two young ladies sent admiring glances in his direction as he returned to the family carriage.

With this little boost to his confidence, and a very good shave, he packed his clothing (particularly his whitest neckcloths — this was, after all, Mornay he was to see), kissed his mother goodbye, and set off on his doomed journey. Oddly enough, he felt almost optimistic. At first. But during the two-and-a-half hours of the drive, he had time to consider his past sins — the very reasons Mornay would never present the living to him. It had been years now since his humiliation and defeat at that man's hands; years since he had fallen in love with a woman, only to have her choose Mornay instead of him. He bore no ill-will toward her; indeed, his feeling at the present time for Miss Ariana Forsythe — er, Mrs. Mornay — was nought but benevolent. He wished her every happiness.

But he and Mr. Mornay had never seen eye to eye, and now, all this time later, the man had resurfaced in his affairs! Why had it happened this way? He'd thought the Mornays were behind him forever. Not that he'd done anything more dishonourable than giving way to a few weak impulses, stealing a kiss from Ariana when he ought not to have. It was a sin he'd repented of, received forgiveness from God for, and put decidedly in his past. But the name "Mornay" now brought it all back again, rushing across his mind like a soldier reliving some great battle. Only this was a battle of the heart — and one he'd lost.

He understood Ariana Mornay enough to know that he had nothing to fear at her hands; she would receive him kindly, whether she wished for him to have the living or not; but her husband? Why had he not written to the Colonel, telling of his abhorrence for Mr. O'Brien? Or, why had he not written directly, telling him privately what he really thought, and that he oughtn't to waste his time calling upon them at Aspindon? It would have saved him this pointless trip.

When the chaise stopped at an inn to pick up more passengers, O'Brien hired a fast-riding messenger and sent an urgent letter to Mr. Mornay. If he was to be turned away at the door, let him say so now, before he arrived. He hoped this would give Mr. Mornay the time he needed to send a message back. "Go home, O'Brien," it would say. "You are not welcome here." And go home he would, with relief. But that message had not come, and now the coach was well nigh the vicinity of Aspindon House. Mr. O'Brien sighed. He did not relish the next hour.

Unfortunately, without their knowing it, and just when Beatrice had tried out the name of "Mr. Frederick Frogglethorpe" aloud upon her tongue, the butler was at the door with a guest, and both men heard her pronouncement. Nigel had exited the room just as swiftly as he had run in (at Mrs. Perler's calling for him) and left the door open. Frederick, just raising his hand to knock, heard the words coming from the room. He stiffened, and grimaced. Why was he the brunt of a joke? He took a breath, and again went to knock — when Beatrice's voice again rang out: "I think he will bow timidly, with overarching propriety, and will offer you a great deal of flummery." They all chuckled, and Miss Bluford, nodding fervently, agreed, "Yes, flummery — indeed, indeed! The richest sort! The smoothest going down! Quite the vicar!"

Now Mr. Frederick's eyes opened wide in comprehension, which turned to apprehension. They were not making fun of him; they were making fun of the man with him! Mr. Mornay had told him to expect the arrival of a curate. It did not take a man of brilliance to understand that the occupants of the room were jesting with regard to a churchman. He felt deuced uncomfortable, but there was nothing else for it, so he knocked and opened the door all the way, so that both men could enter.

"Begging your pardon!" he said, in a tone that was almost a scold, for he hoped to silence the room (and did); "Mr. Peter O'Brien!"

From his position near the mantel, for Mr. Mornay was casually leaning against it, he cracked the smallest smile at Freddy. The man had bottom.

Meanwhile, the effect of the butler's

unmistakably demanding tone was that the room immediately fell into an immense silence. It was either that, or the name of O'Brien, or the realization that their "Mr. Frogglethorpe" had arrived, and that he was nothing to snivel at.

Mr. Mornay's eyes flew to his wife. He was curious, no sense denying it, as to how she would behave with her old admirer. Ariana recovered her astonishment first, and cried, with delight, "Mr. O'Brien! Upon my word! Do come in, sir!" To the servant she added, "Thank you, Frederick; send in the tea now." The butler, with a mild look of reproval that he could not erase, bowed lightly and left the room.

Beatrice's eyes were round with surprise — nay — amazement. She remembered Mr. Peter O'Brien! She remembered him as a tall, kind young man who had indulged her when, at the age of twelve, she had promised to marry him, of all things! She was blushing lightly for having just mouthed the words "Mr. Frederick Frogglethorpe," realizing that the man might well have heard her; and now her blush deepened at this memory. She despised blushing, however, and set to reasoning herself out of it.

It had all happened when Ariana's betrothal to Mr. Mornay was established five years earlier. Mr. O'Brien had maintained his hopes for her sister's affection right up to the wedding. But on that day when Ariana and Mr. Mornay had fallen into each other's arms — right there in Aunt Bentley's parlour (for Mrs. Bentley hadn't married Mr Pellham, yet, though she was Aunt Pellham now) — Beatrice had seen the forlorn expression on the young man, and felt terribly sorry for him.

He had been speaking with her father, and she had every reason, to her twelve-year-old mind, to think him a worthy gentleman. So she had said, when her father introduced her, "I'll marry you," to the young man. The men had laughed, so she added, "But I shall, Papa, as soon as you give your leave!"

So, without his asking, and contrary to all propriety, Beatrice had proposed herself to be this man's wife! And now, five years later, here he was, standing before her. *What if he remembered? What would he think of her now?*

In the past, he had gallantly treated her fancy for him with the air of a fond older brother. He had never teased or berated her, not even when she stayed with his family on Blandford Street in London, and assured them earnestly that she would marry Peter as soon as her papa gave leave. Just the thought of these memories sent a little extra colour into her cheeks, and she suddenly felt as though she was at the edge of her seat. Of all the people in the world whom she might have run into at her sister's house, this one man seemed the most unlikely — and yet here he was!

His gaze fell upon her. He had very blue and intelligent eyes; eyes that were unlikely to have forgotten her youthful *faux pas* — Beatrice quickly looked away. Why was she feeling the least bit flummoxed over this meeting? She'd only been a mere child, she reminded herself, when she had rashly promised to marry him. Nevertheless, it was mortifying. She could barely take in his dignified appearance — the handsome demeanour and good manners he was displaying — for fear he would take one look more at her and at once remember her rash promise! She hoped it was the sort of thing a gentleman would not dream of mentioning.

Her thoughts were flitting rapidly through her head while Mr. O'Brien spoke to Ariana and her husband. It was difficult to comprehend that she was truly seeing Mr. Peter O'Brien again! He had always been handsome, in her memory, but seeing him now was like a jolt. Perhaps it was an air of

63

maturity he had gained, more than an alteration in his features; but whatever the cause, he looked exceedingly fine. If it were not for the dread which had come upon her, she would be proud of him, and pleased to make this reacquaintance.

His twin-tailed black jacket was well fitted, and just hinted at the latest fashion with a little bulge in the upper sleeves, and wide tailored cuffs at the wrists. His cravat was more voluminous than those her brother-in-law favored, but not unbecoming; a fine embroidered yellow waistcoat peeked out of his jacket, and breeches with stockings and black shoes brought the eye to the floor. A cane, and hat in one hand, finished the ensemble. His hair was neatly fashioned into a whip, and it gave him a sort of dash that she did not remember in him. And — wait — he had used to have blond hair. It had grown into a deep brown, with just a few streaks of lighter strands here and there. How unusual, and yet the colour, she had to admit, suited him.

In short, he was as neat and fine a gentleman as Beatrice had seen, though she could not be sure if his polished look was due to superior tailoring, or if he had somehow grown into wearing his clothing with more aplomb. The dark colours suited a clergyman, and the hint of yellow from the waist-coat lightened his appearance so that there was no sense of severity in it. Beatrice reminded herself that if she could meet Mr. Mornay's dark eyes without a single flutter to her heart, surely, the presence of a mere curate would do no worse.

Ariana, meanwhile, was making introductions. When it came to Beatrice's turn, she said, "Beatrice, you recall Mr. O'Brien; my sister, Miss Forsythe, sir." Mr. O'Brien had been looking with polite curiosity at Beatrice, but at Ariana's words he seemed to open his eyes wider somehow.

"My dear Miss Forsythe!" He recognized her. His tone was warm but not overdone.

"Has she not altered a great deal in her appearance since last you met?" Ariana was smiling proudly. Mr. O'Brien raised his eyes while completing a bow, and exclaimed, in his soft-toned voice, "Altered, indeed! Grown up, I should say. What a pleasant surprise to see you."

Beatrice replied, while impulsively thrusting out one hand, "Thank you, sir," and met his eyes. A flash of deep blue was in them, and something more; was it amusement? She blushed deeper. He took her hand and held it lightly, and even bowed over it again, but did not raise it to his lips. (*To her relief!*

What on earth had made her offer her hand to him?)

Ariana was smiling affectionately; Beatrice dared not look at her mother.

Now, when Mr. O'Brien had entered the room, it happened so that he came in facing the sofa where Beatrice and Mrs. Forsythe sat. His eyes fell upon Beatrice and inwardly he felt himself start; it was a pretty face somewhat like Ariana's, but not. She caught his gaze and hurriedly looked away. He had no time to think about it, but somewhere in his brain he knew it must be Miss Beatrice. The sight of her! She was a young woman, not the pretty child he remembered.

He had by now collected himself from the surprise. He'd been prepared to see Ariana Mornay but instead had spied a face that at once resembled hers, but was evidently not hers, and it had startled him. It was like seeing something that should be familiar, only it was also foreign. But now he was bowing to the real Mrs. Mornay, Ariana, who was reassuringly herself, lovely as ever; and then Mr. Mornay.

"Thank you for receiving me," he said to him, still feeling very much on his guard.

Ariana noticed that Mr. O'Brien retained the soft-spoken earnestness she had always liked in him, but without the air of timidity that used to accompany it.

Afterward, when he was seated, she said, "Sir, I am pleased to see you looking so well."

"I could say quite the same thing for you, ma'am." With a look to Mr. Mornay, he added, "Mr. Mornay evidently takes excellent care of you."

While the maids brought in the tea service and began to distribute cups, Ariana looked at her husband with eyes filled with surprise. Turning back to her guest she said, "Well! I must say, you are the last person we expected to see today! We are just now waiting for other company. Do tell us what brings you to the neighbourhood."

Everyone else in the room had assumed that Mr. O'Brien was no doubt come about the living. Ariana, so surprised at his unexpected appearance, did not think that her husband could have known about this and not told her.

Mr. O'Brien froze in his chair. He turned to Mornay. "What brings me? Did you not get a recommendation? From Colonel Sotheby?"

"Colonel Sotheby!" Ariana looked in amazement at him, and her look of confusion changed to one of understanding. *"You are the man he recommended! My word!"*

She turned to her husband and gave him a look as much to say, *"Why did you not tell me?"*

He could always read her thoughts and said, "Have I displeased you? I thought you would enjoy the surprise." He did not want to say that he had doubted the cleric would show.

"I am surprised, indeed." This explanation satisfied her so that she was not vexed. She turned to their guest with a smile. "I beg your pardon! My husband did not say who we were to expect, only that a man was coming. So you have taken Holy Orders, then?"

"Yes. Three years back, actually."

He was by turns addressed with a polite question from nearly everyone in the room, saving Beatrice and Miss Bluford. Beatrice was aware he was speaking, but hardly knew what of, for she was still reeling with the thought of her foolishness regarding this man, this one man out of all the curates in England! She had practically forgotten all about the incident; she certainly did not consider it binding in any way. But the fear nevertheless assaulted her mind forcibly: *What if he remembers? What if he makes mention of it?* She would die a thousand deaths in one moment, and then she would wish to murder him!

She tried to concentrate on the conversation, but found herself studying the churchman with curiosity. Beneath the stylish hair, his dark sideburns lay trim and neat. He was as fair-skinned as ever, but his features were somehow redolent, it seemed to Beatrice, of having suffered in life. This must be what accounted for the change in him. He had more presence than in the past. He did not wear a pained expression, but one such as a person who was accustomed to receiving bad news. It could perhaps be called a world-wizened look, as that of a man who knew of serious truths.

If he chanced to look toward her side of the room, Beatrice averted her gaze speedily. At one point she found Mr. Mornay eyeing her intently, which might have been disconcerting, except that she was too consumed by the fear of her childish promise being spoken of to properly take note of her brother-in-law. She rehearsed how Mr. O'Brien's eyes had met hers with polite curiosity, then surprised recognition. There was a flash of warmth in them — fondness as for a child — which would be exactly what he used to feel for her, for she *was* a child. That realization ought to have soothed her fears, but did not.

Her discomfort was increasing, the longer he sat and conversed. There was only one thing for it, to her mind. She made a decision: If Mr. O'Brien made the slightest reference to her childish fancy, she would feign ignorance. She would pretend *she* did not remember. It was not a wholly honest strategy, she knew, but her desperation to avoid embarrassment was severe enough to recommend her to the thought.

The tea cups were filled, and soon the room fell silent while everyone sipped tea or ate a sweet biscuit. Mr. Mornay had now opted to sit beside his wife. Miss Bluford scurried to get her mistress just the right assortment of biscuits that she liked; Beatrice ate hastily, hoping to fortify herself somehow with the victuals. Mr. O'Brien ate little, as though just to be polite.

Ariana asked, "Why do you not tell us about these past years? Where have you been situated? How has life treated you? Will this be your first vicarage? I can still hardly comprehend that *you* are to be our very own parson! I am —"

Mr. Mornay cleared his throat. When she looked to him, he said, "Mr. O'Brien is come only to explore the opportunity of this living — as we must consider whether he will fit *our* idea of what we must have in a vicar. We, both of us, must find it fitting, before anything is settled."

Ariana thought she could tell by his tone and eye that he meant not to approve of the man. Surely that was his meaning in saying such a thing. She was disappointed, for it had seemed so providential and comfortable an arrangement, having Mr. O'Brien here to fill the vacancy. Only, of course, her husband would not want it to be so. He had never felt the slightest regard for Mr. O'Brien, and, to the contrary, had used to call him "that endless pest." She would talk with him about the matter when they were alone; but for now, she turned a bright smile to the cleric and said, in her best hostess voice, "So — tell us what you have done since 1813."

Mr. O'Brien also understood Mr. Mornay's meaning as boding nothing good for him. Why had the man allowed him to come? Why had he not prevented the whole affair by means of letters? He was irked that it was happening so. That he had been put to the trouble and expense of this call when it was going to end as he feared. He would soon be back at St. Pancras's parish, as though the whole interview, the travel, the expenses, had never occurred. But he had no time to dwell further upon the subject. Mrs. Mornay had addressed him with a question.

He answered as best he could, briefly detailing his short stint in the army — with a look of significance to Mr. Mornay that no one but the two men understood the meaning of. Mr. O'Brien explained how he had received a sum anonymously, of sufficient size to purchase a commission.

"Anonomously?" asked Mrs Royleforst with astonishment.

"Yes." A short silence commenced, and so he continued his tale. How, during his first field assignment, he had injured his left arm during an action at Vera (in Spain, he explained) while defending the Bridge over the Bidassoa. It was a key structure and the French did lose it in the end; but 850 British soldiers were wounded or killed, and Mr. O'Brien was one of them. (He assured the room that over 1500 French casualties had been suffered, which was sufficient to underscore the English victory, and brought relief upon the faces of his audience.)

Since the bullet had narrowly missed a vital artery — which would have cost him his arm, if not his life, said the medical officer — Mr. O'Brien had been forced to consider his time on earth in a new way.

His narrow escape from death made him reconsider his motives. He had joined the army to avoid dwelling on pain (spoken carefully and without a glance in Ariana's direction), and yet it had brought only more of it into his life. Besides his own injury, he had witnessed death and brutality on the battlefield as he hoped never to lay eyes upon in this world again.

"By contrast," he finished, "even St. Pancras's parish seems tame in comparison."

They all nodded.

"That is my parish, you know; I am curate there."

"At St. Pancras?" Ariana asked. A flash of concern went through her. What a difficult place for a sensitive soul!

"Yes, ma'am. My injury was the thing that brought my attention back to God and the Church. It is my calling, and I had shirked it." He related how he subsequently sold his commission, and in six months' time had taken Holy Orders. A year after that he accepted the curacy at St. Pancras and had been there ever since. At Christmas past, his old friend Colonel Sotheby had sought him out, seen his condition, and vowed to do something for him.

"What *was* your condition, Mr. O'Brien, if you do not mind telling us?" Mrs. Forsythe asked gently; and soon the whole room was rapt, listening to tales of Mr. O'Brien having to go to his family's home on Blandford Street to eat a proper meal, as he had given his own away; of finding the most sorrowful pieces of humanity upon the parsonage doorstep, only to have nothing to offer them but water and an old cheese. It was an underprivileged area, and many a sad sight had he seen on the streets; many a sad plight (he said with a deep sigh) that he was unable to do anything for, other than pray. Even now, at the memory of how helpless he had been to help others, his hands balled into fists, though he had nowhere to lay blame unless he desired to take on the structure of the Church, and the reason why so many curates were underprovided for.

When they asked for particular stories regarding St. Pancras, he said, "I fear I have said too much already." To the chorus of objections which ensued, he added, "Were I to give you further details it would reflect poorly upon me as a gentleman; for ladies are not suited for such that I could tell, I assure you."

"Oh, do, I *beseech* you, Mr. O'Brien!" Beatrice had been listening with such a piqued interest that she had wholly forgot her earlier embarrassment. She tried not to reveal the least surprise at her own outburst, however, and noted that he eyed her appreciatively. Mrs. Forsythe added, "We are not the swooning type of females, sir, and we understand the evils of this world well enough." With a glance at Beatrice, she added, wryly, "I daresay the right tale from you may even prevail upon my daughter Miss Forsythe not to pine after a Season in London, yet."

"Oh, Mama!" Beatrice said, blushing. *Why was she embarrassed? It was perfectly understandable that a young lady should desire a coming-out in London.* But she added, "I am not *pining!*"

"My opinion, sir," said the mother, "is that Miss Forsythe is too young for that pleasure; she is but seventeen." To Beatrice she added, "We'll speak more of it later."

I wish you had not spoken of it at all, Beatrice thought. No need to tell a stranger — well, he was virtually a stranger, for it had been so long — about her hopes or plans.

Ariana rescued her from further embarrassment by turning back to the newest guest. "Tell us more of your experiences, if you please."

O'Brien sought the eye of Mr. Mornay, who nodded almost imperceptibly, but it was enough. Mr. O'Brien obliged them. He told of females who were mothers before they themselves had left girlhood; of men who were so lost upon that demon gin, that they spent every last shilling upon it, and slept in beds of garbage and filth. These same men had children and wives, but left them to fend for themselves. He told how children of three years of age and older were taught to pick pockets and nap handkerchiefs so their mothers could sell them to buy food. Abandoned women, mothers with no husbands, and children with no parents at all; infants left on the church doorsteps. It was appallingly sorrowful.

The company listened with great silence. Mr. O'Brien's steady, low tones brought the hardships of the London poor to such poignant light that even Mr. Mornay forgot that he disliked the man, and Beatrice forgot to feel wary of him. The tea in her cup grew cold; she never did reach for more biscuits. Only Mrs. Royleforst, though enraptured with interest at the images and scenes he conjured in his tales, kept slowly eating her plate of baked treats until it was emptied.

Beatrice was intrigued by the depth of feeling within the eyes of Mr. O'Brien. His voice was tender and yet full of pity, or grief, or anger, at the things he had seen. The earnest blue of his eyes became like a magnet to hers, and she could not be oblivious to his deep wish to be of help to such people as were in his parish; she began to feel the injustices of life for the poor in a new way. His points of outrage at society in allowing the existence of such hubs of sin and evil were so deeply experienced that his gentle voice was like the sharpest hammer, piercing to her soul. Ariana was no less affected, and held one hand over her heart as she listened.

Mr. Mornay took his wife's hand, knowing precisely what kind of thoughts she was no doubt entertaining. She, who had always wanted to do much for the poor, but had been content to give herself to her family and the village of Glendover.

"In short," Mr. O'Brien said, "the people of St. Pancras are starving, and yet they do not seek a life elsewhere, but remain in their little rat nests — forgive my language, but I have seen these places — and continue to live by thievery and whoredom. I think I have aged a decade in these past few years, not only on account of my time in battle at war, but in these constant battles against evil here at home. I am too young, or, I daresay, too witless (with a smile) to devise any answer for the great need of the poor of

St. Pancras, and as a curate I am virtually useless except in my capacity to pray and give sermons."

Could this account for his dark hair? Beatrice wondered. Did not people usually turn grey, or white, as a result of great difficulties? Perhaps; but Mr. O'Brien had turned brunette, strange as it seemed. Again she noticed that the change suited him quite well. It was too bad that he was not a man of independent means. As a curate, he was not the type of man (she knew in her heart) that she must marry. She felt a pang of unrest with the thought, but brushed it aside.

No unsuitable man would make her turn her head, not even an impressive curate with a heart of gold! She was determined to have her day in the upper-class society of the Season, and to see what would come of that. There had to be gentlemen aplenty there, and Mr. O'Brien was not the only man in the world with beautiful blue eyes and a big heart.

I may be young, she thought, *but I am no longer the child who would marry the first eligible young man she met just because he wanted a cure for being lovesick!* Mr. O'Brien had been utterly deflated in spirit upon losing Ariana to Mr. Mornay, and Beatrice had felt sorry for him. Now she was older and wiser. Now she understood life far better. And besides, he no longer seemed the least bit sick from love.

FIVE

Ariana was feeling a great heartache. Had not she herself wanted to turn her hand to helping the poor of London?

She and Phillip had been so happy raising their own little family that thoughts of the plight of the city's poor had utterly fled from her mind. It had been too, too long since she'd even considered it. Phillip had agreed to support many a city institution, and they had been faithfully contributing their help since; but still she suddenly felt far removed from it all. It did not seem enough — writing a cheque or sending a bank note. Such was not a sacrifice for them. It was nothing like being there first-hand as Mr. O'Brien was.

What a good, good thing it was that God had sent Mr. O'Brien! It was reawakening her heart to things she must do. Things such as reacquainting herself with the efforts of the latest societies and organizations that toiled on behalf of the poor. A trip to London could help immensely in that; there was nothing like visiting personally to know whether an institute or school was worthy of their funds, for instance. Someday, she dreamed, she would like to get involved in a practical way. Knitting blankets was too antiseptic: she wanted to get her hands dirty in the work, so to speak!

Like most women whose husbands owned a large estate, she had no hand in the financial doings regarding it. Other than informing their man of business when she wanted to support a charity (who, in turn, would clear it with Phillip, she knew) she did not even have a hand in charitable giving.

With difficulty, she turned her mind back to Mr. O'Brien, who was saying, "The devil of it is, if I were as wealthy as, well, as you are, sir (and here he turned to Mr. Mornay), it would only help for a short period of time! These people are not trained to look after themselves; they do not know the least thing about homesteading, or simple gardening — those who have a small plot of land, that is. Most do not. But it is appallingly — *mad* — their manner of life!" He stopped, catching himself giving way to helpless anger.

The women were eyeing him sorrowfully,

81

with understanding. Ariana looked ready to cry, and Beatrice was heart-stricken. Mr. O'Brien collected himself; he knew he had made his point, and now felt almost apologetic.

"Mr. O'Brien," said Ariana, preventing that apology from coming. Her large, pretty eyes, somewhat watery at the moment, peered up at him. "I pray you will dine with us. You have nothing prepared elsewhere, I hope?"

"I believe I passed a respectable-looking inn some miles back, and was going to return to it for my supper, ma'am."

"Oh, do not think of it!" she replied. "You will eat your meal with us."

"Your offer is very kind," he said with utter sincerity. He seemed to have found a much more agreeable reception than he had hoped for, and he was startled, but pleased.

As mistress of Aspindon House, Ariana delighted in any benevolent action she might take. She was not cognizant that her husband was standing now with his back to the room, and staring out at the prospect as though he had never seen it before.

The maids began cleaning up the tea dishes, and Ariana said, "Mama, why do not you and Beatrice accompany Mr. O'Brien for a walk about the house while

Mrs. Perler and I see to the children?"

"The children?" asked the cleric. His eyes had come alight. "I beg your pardon, I had completely forgotten! Allow me to offer my deepest congratulations. I understand you have just recently welcomed a new little miss into the household!" Even Mr. Mornay turned around for this, for he, like his wife, was inordinately proud of his offspring.

"Yes, our baby Miranda; I thank you," said Ariana, smiling with pleasure. "Our little boy, Nigel, is four; and our little girl, Miranda, is just two months."

"Two months! My word, you are just out of your confinement! I do hope I shall have the pleasure of an introduction," he said in a droll tone.

All the women were smiling. "But of course!" Ariana said. "You could hardly avoid it in this household, sir, for we allow our children a great deal of time with us."

Tristan Barton sat across from his sister in the morning room of the Manor House, while he finished his coffee and toast. Miss Barton was morosely stirring her chocolate, absentmindedly.

"Now we are settled," he said, "I should like to call upon Mr. Mornay. It's deuces there's naught else to do around here, in *the country!*" he snorted with derision. "However can anyone prefer it?"

Miss Barton raised her head enough to cast a glance out a window of the room, which overlooked the frontage of the estate. "I think it's lovely country," she said. "And not even that far from Town."

"Half a day's drive, you mean!" he returned. "Quite far enough. In any case, I'll have to take the carriage, but I do not imagine you were planning on using it. You look ill, in fact. Are you unwell?" His eyes had narrowed sharply upon really seeing her face.

"I am fine," she answered, looking down for a second.

When she did look up, he said, "But you are certainly not in your looks. I want you to rest while I am out." Anne's eyes had darkish circles, as though she had not been sleeping well, or felt ill.

"Tristan?" Her voice was low, and she paused, looking flustered.

"Yes?"

"You — you shan't forget to tell them your sister is with you?"

He grimaced. "I told you I mean to introduce you. I've decided that you can be of use to me, in fact. You will keep Mrs. Mornay in company, so that I may hope to get more of the mister to myself. I am determined to do my service for the prince as speedily as possible. It may be that I can procure some good for us from this before any . . . detrimental reports may reach the ears of His Royal Highness."

He was standing now, brushing off his coat, and he asked, "How do I look, eh?"

She glanced over him. "I do think breeches are formal for a morning call."

"This is Mornay I'm seeing, Anne! Can anything be too formal for such a man?"

"When meeting him with the prince, or at an affair, I suppose not; but here in the country?"

"I wouldn't be at all surprised if he keeps to London styles, country or no; I mean to be prepared."

"You will seem to be striving for their approval."

"But I am. I must have their approval, or my chances of doing anything for the prince are dashed."

"But do you not want to seem more confident? As though you have no reason *not* to be approved of? You should allow your good manners to speak for you. Not your attire."

He went up to her and stroked her cheek. Miss Barton was surprised, but pleased. He looked at her almost pityingly, however, and said, "Anne, Anne. If you knew how to dress properly for the right company, I might even now be addressing you as 'my lady.' You failed to impress his lordship's family, do you not see?"

"You do not know the least thing about it!" she cried, taking his hand and throwing it from her. She was already in tears. He stopped, a little taken aback by her passionate rebuttal.

"Do not try to tell me anything about a matter you are entirely ignorant of!"

"What do you mean?" he demanded. "What am I ignorant of?"

She turned and glared at him for a moment, silent with anger. "It was your decision to sell our family home that first made them question our respectability!"

"Yes, but what of Brummell? Do you recall? He sold his estate, and no one questioned his dashed respectability!"

"Brummell was an Original! And I daresay that the same people who paid him court would shrink from giving him a daughter in marriage! Respectability and good *ton* are two different things! No one questions whether you are fashionable, or agreeable — but *you sold our family house!* You threw away our ties to the land! You must know that a family estate means the world to these people! How can you have failed to understand that?" Her voice was cracking, and she could no longer keep herself from sobbing. She rushed from the room.

The next day, Mr. Mornay asked his wife to take tea with him and the children in the nursery — a startling request, but Ariana was delighted to comply. They liked to be together for bohea and biscuits, but lately the children joined them in the drawing room since the guests were there as well. It would be cozier upstairs, just the four of them and Mrs. Perler.

Thirty-five minutes later, Miranda had been fed with all the attentions due an infant (meaning she was burped, nursed on the other breast, burped yet again, and thoroughly adored, all while maintaining a complete oblivion to the squeals of delight and laughter around her) before Ariana asked her husband, "Do you wish to hold your daughter?" Coat removed, he had been playing upon the carpet with his son, letting the child climb all over him and giving him rides upon his back.

"By all means," he said, with a little smile, patting Nigel on the head before getting up to come and take the baby. Unlike the manner of his rough play with their son, Phillip took his littlest child gingerly into his arms, but without the great air of confidence that usually accompanied his actions. He sat down and studied her face, touched her with his finger, and let her little fingers clamp around one of his. Ariana came and sat beside them, after giving Nigel some tea and letting him pick what he wanted from the tray, which usually amounted to naught but biscuits.

"Isn't she lovely?" Ariana said, for the thousandth time.

"She certainly is," he murmured. "Just like her mother."

Miranda had been born with a beautiful silky layer of dark black hair, but at two months, it was already beginning to fall out, and, to his delight, was being replaced with the same light golden strands he loved on Ariana. He may not have been in his element holding an infant, but the miracle of this child being flesh of his flesh still astounded him, and he relished having her. At Nigel's birth, he'd felt awestruck that he had taken part in giving life; and that the life was part of him, part of Ariana, and something that, once there, he would never want to live without.

Until his children were born, he'd had a sense of needing an heir, but to actually have a child of his own in his arms was unbelievably satisfying. He had to conclude that it was a God-given desire, hidden within some people more than others, perhaps, but there just the same. He hadn't known that it was within him to feel so much love, to be fiercely protective of others the way he felt for his family. Not until Ariana, and then Nigel and Miranda came into his life. *What was life without them? How had he ever thought he was at all enjoying himself? God was so merciful to have given him what amounted to a new life! A family. A wonderful, precious family.*

After holding the baby until she slept (Ariana never grew tired of the sight of her strong, handsome husband cuddling a baby against his chest), he motioned to Mrs. Perler to take the child, but his wife said, "I'll take her."

He handed her over gingerly, but said, "A few more minutes; then, come with me so I can speak to you."

"I haven't done, Papa!" cried Nigel, his mouth full of crumbs.

Their visits were the highlight of his days, even more so than just having tea every early afternoon; Mr. Mornay's eyes softened at his son's words, and he sat back down. Meanwhile, a maid began refilling cups for the adults, including Mrs. Perler, who was always allowed to partake with the family. She knew to sit aside by herself in a corner of the room unless she was needed, however, and she did so now. Ariana often had her tell any stories of things the children did, or what new smart thing Nigel had said or accomplished in her absence.

Ariana would have transformed a parlour into a nursery so that she could have the children always near her; but Mr. Mornay insisted that she needed time apart, to rest for one thing; and to be available to him, for another. And so the upstairs nursery, which was really a small suite of rooms, was decorated and filled with the latest toys and furniture and engaged for their daily care.

Nigel crawled upon his father's lap, a biscuit in one hand.

Ariana, snuggling a blanket-wrapped Miranda against her shoulder, was grateful for this family time, perhaps as much as her son. Phillip was kept so busy with the estate or visiting his holdings, or engaging in sport such as hunting or shooting with London gentlemen who came to visit, that she enjoyed moments like this immensely.

In fact she had been amazed, at first, to

see how much of his time was spoken for. Especially after having her impressions of him formed in London, where he seemed like a typical upperclassman, with time on his hands. She had not expected to find an involved landlord. Had he been often shooting or hunting to dogs or riding, it would come as no surprise; but he paid attention to the tenants, knew the men in each family by name, even asked about their wives. He oversaw the accounts of the estate to the extent of regularly spending a few hours with his man of business, his steward, and even the housekeeper, each by turn, going over accounts. As if Ariana hadn't already been starry-eyed about her new husband, this side of him only deepened her admiration.

The Mornay estate would never fall prey to poor management or disrepair while Phillip was its owner. Unlike the properties of much of the nobility, nay, much of the landed gentry, too, his was neither entailed nor mortgaged. She began to understand why the prince should want him for his government. He was superb with the management of his affairs.

She took a sip of tea with one hand, while continuing to watch the two males she loved most in the world. Mr. Mornay was breaking a biscuit up and handing pieces to the child, who watched his father with rapt eyes, smiling while he ate. After the child had finished the treat, Mr. Mornay's eyes met those of his wife. Oh, yes — he wanted to speak with her.

"Mrs. Perler," she said, "take the children to their grandmother and aunt in the drawing room. We will be there shortly."

"Huzzah!" Nigel shouted. "The drawing room! Will there be more tea and biscuits, Mama?"

When she and Phillip were alone, she looked at him expectantly. He patted the space on his lap where their son had been only minutes earlier, and with a smile she got up and claimed it. He immediately drew her toward him and kissed her.

Afterward, he regarded her face, turned up at him. "You are enormously pretty," he said, making her smile.

"But you did not arrange tea with me to tell me that," she returned. "What is it? You have got me so curious!"

He moved a stray lock of hair from her face, curling it around one of her ears. "We need to discuss Glendover once more. I know that yesterday you thought it might be granted to Mr. O'Brien, and" — he held up a finger to silence her — "I need to be certain you understand that such a hope is impossible."

Ariana, studying his eyes, said, "Impossible? Or not to your liking?"

He chuckled. "In this case, one is equal to the other. If I do not like a man for the living, he does not get it. Surely you could not expect me to actually consider O'Brien."

"You once said yourself, Phillip, that if we could improve a man's life, that was good enough reason to grant him the living."

"That was presupposing the man to have met my full approval. I am responsible to the parish to make the best choice of vicar that I am capable of. Mr. O'Brien is not that man."

"But what are you basing this conclusion upon? The past, I daresay, for you have spent no time with him alone. You have given him no interview, nor seen him fulfilling his office. Let him preside for us this coming Sunday, here at Glendover, and base your decision upon his actual performance. Nothing from your history with him is worthy of consideration at this time. You must let the past rest with the past, and allow him to prove himself as he is, now."

"Nothing of my history with him?" he asked. "Then let it be his history with *you* that concerns me. Either way, he still fails to get the living." He smiled lazily at her frown.

"Only promise me that you will not interview another man until you have given Mr. O'Brien every chance that he deserves to win this situation."

"I will speak to him, then, and I will question his theology if it pleases you." He looked at her squarely. "Mr. O'Brien will dig his own grave, I assure you. I'll wait as long as you like. But you cannot expect him to stay in the neighbourhood past one Sunday. He has his own parish to attend to."

"I understand. But I think our curate has improved a great deal in his character. I believe he will *not,* as you say, dig his own grave."

"Then we shall see. I give him until Sunday to prove himself, or he goes back to St. Pancras."

"Sir, might I have a few words with you?" Mr. O'Brien's bold gaze met and held that of his host, Mr. Mornay, who had returned with his wife to the drawing room only minutes earlier.

"Certainly," replied Phillip. "Shall we remove to an office?"

"I would be obliged, thank you."

Mr. Mornay began to lead Mr. O'Brien from the drawing room, thinking to himself, *Here it comes. He will ask me outright for the living.*

But Mrs. Forsythe saw them and said, "Mr. O'Brien! You do still wish to accompany my daughter and me for a walk upon the grounds, I hope?" For yesterday they had shown the man about the large house, giving him a brief tour of the public rooms, which both women were still enjoying taking in themselves.

"In this weather?" asked Ariana, for the late February air was chillingly relentless, making all the chamber maids extra busy with filling up coal bins, stoking fires, and removing ashes. They were forever scuttling into and out of the drawing room and other public rooms to maintain the heat of the fires.

"I beg your pardon," Mr. O'Brien said sincerely. "I mean to keep my word, to be sure; but I shall join you afterward if that will be agreeable."

But Mr. Mornay said, "By all means, accompany the ladies. We can talk later. There's no hurry, I assure you."

Mr. O'Brien looked at him curiously. Did he already know what he wished to say to him? But how could he? He said, "Very good; I am obliged."

Soon the three of them, cloaked in coats and scarves and hats and gloves, had set out from the large front door, choosing to take the walk that led around the long house.

"We'll stay close to the house this time, and see if we can circle it before getting too cold," said Mrs. Forsythe. Beatrice was curious as to why her mother suddenly was in want of outdoor exercise, as well as why she had said, "this time," as if there were certain to be more such outings. But she merely nodded and drew her scarf about her tighter and went along.

They followed a paved brick walk, remarking about the beauty of the house and the grounds, and the prospect. In five minutes or so they reached one end of the structure, and turned and were out of sight.

About thirty minutes later, Mr. Barton let out a whistle to himself as his carriage came to a stop in front of the stately dwelling of the Paragon and his wife. The country house was impressive with its Georgian columns and Venetian-style windows. The sheer size of the place, and the neatness and formality of its grounds (not least of which began with a mile-long, tree-lined drive — or so it seemed) had brought his mission —

his reason for being there — strongly to mind. Aspindon House was certainly impressive enough to be the abode of a viscount. Even an earl, for that matter!

It did his heart good to see this firsthand evidence of prosperity in the world; it reminded him that there was always a great deal of money, somewhere, and that playing one's cards correctly might well result in ending up with a greater share of it. If he could succeed in influencing Mornay for the prince, he might well be on his way to a bit more of a fortune than he had at present. If more money was not given him, and it was unlikely it would be, he could at least be sure of a continued welcome into the circles of the upper class, and enjoy the bounty of others.

And Mr. Barton did have wealth. But his fortune was not endless, whereas his gaming habit was. He had discovered, moreover, that fortune alone did not always ensure acceptance in the *bon ton*. His sister was apparently wiser than he, for selling their family home had been a grave mistake, but one which he had willingly committed, thinking only of the assets it would give him to settle in Mayfair. His foolishness was evident to him now, but too late. Looking at Aspindon looming stately and elegant before him, he hoped his luck was about to change.

The groom finally appeared, allowing him to hand over the ribbons and head toward the great front door. His pulse quickened at the prospect of what lay before him. He hoped he was about to find the man at home. He hoped, more, that he would somehow gain his favour — a much trickier thing to procure than a mere audience with him. His sister might indeed be useful in that matter, however, for he expected that Mrs. Mornay was short enough of genteel company to be delighted to learn of her new neighbours.

He straightened his coat, checked his cravat with his hands, and reached up for the knocker. The next hour would no doubt be most illuminating as to whether his hopes had any chance of succeeding or not. He took a breath and rapped firmly on the door, twice. And waited.

Six

"A note, sir, by special messenger, from Warwickdon."

Freddie handed the missive to his master, and even Mr. Mornay seemed surprised to be receiving a second urgent letter in two days. He opened it right there in the parlour, letting Ariana read it with him, for they were seated side by side. Mrs. Royleforst's small eyes opened as wide as they were capable of while she waited, hoping to hear the contents.

Mr. Mornay's brows rose while he read, and he and Ariana shared a look of surprise.

"Upon my word!" she exclaimed.

Mr. Mornay looked at his aunt and explained, "Mr. Epworth, the magistrate at Warwickdon, reminds us that our neighbouring parish is going vacant of its rector, and a vicar is needed, directly. Mr. Hargrove is above anxious to take up a living in his town of birth in Yorkshire. He is the rector of the parish, you see."

Ariana exclaimed, "We knew he planned on leaving, but thought he had a replacement secure. It seems that arrangement has fallen through. Did you ever hear of such a thing? A rector looking for a clergyman just when we have got us one! And," she added, smiling, "if we grant Mr. O'Brien Glendover as well, he could hire his own curate for Warwickdon! That will put him in a splendid way to afford a wife and family, to be sure!"

Mr. Mornay held up one hand. "You run ahead of yourself, Ariana. I am perfectly happy to recommend O'Brien for Warwickdon, despite the fact that it means our endless pest shall be a mere two miles away at all times. ("I said that affectionately!" he assured her, when she rolled her eyes at him.) But keeping him on my own property is another thing, entirely. I should think you would welcome this news as a means of satisfying your hopes of doing him some good; he will be a vicar, have the glebe, a comfortable vicarage, and the lesser tithes."

"It is rather *extraordinary,*" put in Mrs. Royleforst. "That two neighbouring parishes should fall vacant simultaneously!"

Mr. Mornay was scanning the letter again. "And that Mr. Hargrove is anxious to leave his situation as soon as possible! He says here that he has had a 'flood of requests to perform baptisms, a few weddings, and that a funeral appears imminent, if he can make the move quickly enough.' Furthermore, his parish in the north is so happy of his returning that they are arranging a day of village festivities to proclaim his arrival." He looked up. "They want him directly."

"I daresay, he must be enormously pleased at that," Mrs. Royleforst said, shifting in her seat upon the sofa until she felt more comfortable.

"Mr. O'Brien's coming is providential!" exclaimed Ariana. Turning to her husband she added, "You are not willing, I see, to grant him Glendover, but God has provided for him, nevertheless!"

"Indeed He has," concurred Phillip. In fact, he quietly gave thanks for this unexpected boon. The timing of it was superb. Despite what he'd said to his wife about O'Brien, he'd had small misgivings. Now he could refer the man for an excellent situation without having to offer him his own parish. It was an act of Providence!

Mrs. Royleforst was closer to the mark than she could have known. Mr. Hargrove was more than enormously pleased at the thought of the enthusiastic reception awaiting him in the north — he was ecstatic. Suddenly the spacious parsonage at Warwickdon and all the accompanying comforts of the living was a millstone around his neck. He wanted a vicar to fill his shoes — now.

Perhaps it was a divine intervention that the Ordinary of the parish had inquired of Aspindon House — Mr. Mornay, that is — for the name of a suitable applicant, there being no great house in Warwickdon to inquire of. And Mr. Hargrove's conscience was sufficiently intact that he did not wish to abandon his current flock without ensuring that services would continue; but he wanted a good man, one who could do more than ride in upon a horse each week, say his service, and ride off again to the next parish! He disliked pluralism in the clergy.

In a moment of inspiration he had thought of Aspindon House, remembered that Mr. Mornay was very likely considering a list of candidates for his own parish at that very time, and felt surely this was his answer.

The question was, did Mr. Mornay know of a candidate? A man who was worthy and true in his religion? And most important to Mr. Hargrove: a man who could come directly?

Ariana came closer to her husband and

searched his face with her large eyes.

"Phillip, are you certain he is not seeking merely a curate? You know as well as I do that a curate's salary is bound to be a pittance."

"I can speak to Mr. Hargrove, if you like, and just my doing so is certain to secure a rise in the salary; but I gather from the note that our clergyman will shortly be vicar if he is acceptable to Mr. Hargrove and the Bishop."

But still she frowned. Her voice sounded pained. "When we have Glendover available, it does appear to be a slight to him!"

A look of resoluteness fell upon her husband's handsome face. "We are doing him a great service with my recommendation. He will get the situation based on my word, you know that. It is far superior to St. Pancras; he will welcome it, I assure you. And he will not feel slighted. The man can hardly expect me to love him so well that I should want him in my life perpetually. 'Tis hard enough that I must suffer to keep him within two miles of us. You must see the unreasonable nature of your hopes."

"I understand your feelings upon this, truly I do." Ariana had come and placed her hands upon his chest, smoothing down miniscule wrinkles in his silk waistcoat. "But please consider that he and Beatrice may find they suit one another." She could not help but to smile. "I did not want to speak of this too soon to you, but I do think you must hold in mind that if he and Beatrice were to . . . become better acquainted, you may have the opportunity to benefit your own family by presenting him with Glendover!" She hoped to find him amused but instead he grew impatient.

"Ariana, they have just met."

"No, she knew him in London. Do you not recall her promise to marry him?" She looked very amused, but he did not share her feeling. In fact, Mr. Mornay looked thunderstruck.

"What? Are you telling me they are *betrothed?"*

Ariana lost a degree of optimism at this reaction, admitting, "Well, no; he did not offer for her; Beatrice felt sorry for him for losing *me* to *you,* so *she* offered for *him!"*

He let out a breath of relief. "That's absurd. It isn't done."

"I know, but it happened. It may mean something, yet."

He was quiet for a moment, thinking. "This changes nothing. I have said I shall give the man until Sunday to prove his worth — and I shall. But he won't do it, mark my words. And I have no intention of holding this benefice until a romance *may* bud between two people who may well have other interests!"

"Beatrice has no interest more upon her thoughts these days but finding a husband, she has said so!"

"It was my understanding," he replied speedily, "that she desires a wealthy man; a man about town; not a country curate."

"Well, that is nothing!" said Ariana, wide-eyed. "She will change her mind if she falls in love."

"*If* she falls in love?" he asked dubiously. "I cannot conceive that I am having this conversation!" He kissed her on the forehead. "I must see to this business. I'll go to my office directly; send O'Brien to me, will you?"

Ariana's lips were compressed, but she said, "Oh, very well."

He started to move off, but noted her expression, and turned back to her, putting his hands upon her upper arms to face her. He was wearing a "patient" look and Ariana steeled herself for a mild combing.

"Have you forgotten his disregard for your betrothal? For your expressed wishes? After you'd refused him more than once, he had the audacity to take advantage of you! Do you think I could ever willingly bring him so much into our lives?"

"I am beyond remembering that at all!" she replied, heatedly. "Why can you not do as I have done?"

"If you are beyond remembering it," he said, as though it was hard to conceive, "I am assuredly not. A man does not forget an offence involving the woman he loves. Perhaps you have truly forgot how he lost his head, his manners, his honour — when he dragged you into his arms in his house that day in London! But I have not. I cannot."

She watched him with a silence that was born not of ease or agreement, but of disturbance. He had never spoken of that day since their marriage; how could it still be so engraved upon his heart that he could recite it like a favourite poem, memorized and cherished? She turned away from his eyes, though there was not overmuch of reproof in them. It was more like injury.

"Can you allow that he is a changed man, now?" Her voice was quiet.

"He has done some growing up, I grant you. But the man is still untested, in my opinion. I do not want to have to consider whether he shall stop to visit you on occasion; or whether I should arrive home to find him present. His own past behavior has merited my disapproval in this matter, and you must not pretend it did not happen, Ariana. I cannot."

She said, "Mr. O'Brien did behave badly, but he sent me — he sent *us,* an apology. And he has matured since then. His youthful passion is behind him."

She met his eyes, upon which he said, "Waiting only for the right time to sprout up again, like a dormant seed in winter." He moved her toward him and his arms about her were heartening. "You are more beautiful than ever, Ariana."

"Only to you, sir!" She was amused by this.

"No, upon my honour, no! Motherhood has brought more lovely a glow to your face than I've ever noted. Being twenty-four has agreed with you more than any lady of my acquaintance heretofore. He will fall right back in love with you, I assure you. It is his nature."

"You forget that Beatrice is here now. I am a mother; a matronly dame to a single man."

He had to laugh. "A matronly dame? Not you, I assure you." He had to plant another little kiss upon her face, too, for he loved her like this.

"Perhaps I was too friendly toward him! In the past, I mean. I will not make that mistake, again."

He paused, but, stroking her face and chin, said, "Let us have no more discussion of the matter. I hoped for us to be of one mind in this so that you say nothing to give him false hopes of Glendover. Mr. O'Brien may accept as many benefices as he is offered; only anywhere else in England, than on my lands."

She looked thoughtful a moment. "I do think you injure the man's character more than is warranted; and I must say, it would be kind in you if he were to be given one of the advowsons you own in the north or south; he could profit from the salary while living at Warwickdon."

He took a breath and thought for a moment. "You plead his case strongly. Your interest in his welfare begins to strengthen my resolve."

"Oh, do not say so! You cannot mean you are jealous of him?"

He paused. "All you do is support him! You wish to grant him a living on our property! To keep him near you, in other words."

"Phillip! I have told you my only design is to encourage a match between him and

Beatrice! How could you even think — I am astounded at you!"

"And I am disappointed in you." Their eyes met, but Ariana had to turn away. Her husband had never before said such a thing to her. But she pushed away the sense of injury, bit her lip, and said, in a small voice, "The parish has stood vacant for two months now. The people need and deserve a parson. When *will* the position be filled?"

"When I've found the right man. I'm still settled upon retaining the rectorship in case we have another son." He turned her about and kissed her lightly on the mouth. "Not all men wish to join the army or navy, you know." He was studying her face.

"Do not be out of countenance," he said. "I am about to do the man a service. You'll see; he will be greatly encouraged."

"I hope you are right," she said with resignation.

In one of the cottages belonging to Aspin-don House, a home of an agricultural worker and his family, the mother of the household was bent worriedly over the still form of her sleeping eldest child, a girl named MaryAnn. The father walked in, brusquely forcing open the hinged door with a blast of cold air, and coming in loudly, stamped his feet and moved quickly toward the fire. He was rubbing his hands and held them out now, over the coals. "It's taken a nasty turn out there," he said, turning his hands to warm them evenly.

"She's still sick, Giles."

He made no answer, didn't flinch, and finished warming his hands before turning to look toward where the child lay on a makeshift bed of straw. He walked over and peered down at the girl, who was red with fever, her blond hair clinging to her face and head in wet wisps. Beads of perspiration were on her skin.

"I don' like it," said the mother, a woman not much older than her landlady, Mrs. Ariana Mornay. She curled her hands beneath her chin, worrying. "I think we should call the 'pothecary! She's been like this for more'n a day, now!"

The man looked at his wife a moment, thinking. "C'mon, now, Mary; we agreed on this. We can't do that. If word gets out, I'll be taken off the job; we can't afford that. Not in winter!"

"*Why* would ye be? It's not you that's sick!"

"You know how it is! With this fever goin' round, if Mr. Horton gets a whiff o' this girl bein' ill, I'll be chopped off the work like that! They're right afraid that somethin' awful will 'appen to the little master, or the new lit'le laidy at the big house."

"But we'er not sending *'er* to work! If ye don' go see Mr. Price, she might die, Giles! Can ye live wi' that?" The mother's tortured eyes pleaded with her husband. They looked twice their normal size, being wild with fear. She grasped his arm tightly with one hand, for he had made a move to turn away.

"I'll ask ye again. Can ye live wi' that?" When he made no answer, she said, "Look at 'er! Look at 'er! She's your daughter!" He pulled his arm loose and turned his back, but he was thinking hard.

He went to the nearest window — there were only two — and looked out sullenly. Then he slowly circled the room, still considering what to do. He came back and stood, looking down at the sick girl.

"I'll see what's to be done," he said, in a gruff, low tone, and replaced his cap and left the cottage. His demeanor was grim.

His wife watched him go, frowning with worry. She turned back to gaze upon the still form of her daughter, and then went and checked on her other offspring, two young boys, who were both soundly asleep. She felt their foreheads and necks; no fever. That was a mercy, at least.

111

Beatrice, Mrs. Forsythe, and Mr. O'Brien spent the next hour sightseeing on the grounds that flanked the house, except that they did not enter the maze. Beatrice had a fright of mazes, she had to confess. She had heard a lady telling once of a terrible misadventure which occurred when she had gone into a maze, and got lost for nearly an hour. It had started to grow dark, and by the time she made her way back out, she said, she had been ready to swoon. It took her two days to recover her composure.

Beatrice had taken that tale as a warning. When she realized they were at the mouth of the opening to the maze, therefore, she had objected strongly, so that she had to share her story with her companions. Mr. O'Brien was most solicitous and understanding, and he moved them on.

"I believe my daughter means to remove the maze," said Mrs. Forsythe. "No one goes in it any longer, for Nigel once ran ahead of Mrs. Perler and that poor woman nearly had an apoplexy! It took her fifteen minutes to find the child, you see, who kept running ahead, and would not give an answer or make a sound, as he thought it a game. I daresay she felt just like the woman you told us of," she added.

They continued on, for it was a clear day, giving much to admire even in winter. Mr. O'Brien was courteous and entertaining, and had offered an arm to each lady, so that they flanked him on either side.

"How long do you expect to be staying with us, sir?" inquired Mrs. Forsythe.

Mr. O'Brien met her gaze with a curious little smile. "I am unable to answer that question, ma'am, as I hardly expected to be here this long."

"Sir?" she asked, smiling in return. "Can you explain yourself?"

"Well," he said, "as you know, I am come on account of a recommendation from Colonel Sotheby."

"Yes; so what is your surprise at still being here?"

"I assumed, based on my past experiences with Mr. Mornay, that he would make quick work of sending me back to London, ma'am."

"Indeed?" asked Beatrice. "On what account?" As soon as she asked, she suddenly remembered how Mr. O'Brien had tried to put himself forward at Ariana's wedding — to the point of standing in for the Paragon, who was late. It turned out that Mr. Mornay had actually been shot in the arm the night before, which caused his tardiness; but Mr. O'Brien had certainly not endeared himself to anyone by making a last, though hopeless, attempt at marrying Ariana Forsythe.

"I believe, if you must know, it was my ill-advised infatuation for your sister."

He had been honest and frank, and non-evasive, and Mrs. Forsythe was determined to be pleased with him in any case, so she said, heartily, "I understand, sir! Now you mention it, I recall some such thing; but there is no need for us to dwell upon the past. We are all aware, I am sure, of how much we learn as we grow older; and how much we regret our youthful blunders."

Beatrice was pleased to be included in this assessment of learning more and growing older and regretting youthful blunders as though they were assuredly behind her, so she said, "Amen to that!"

She was sorely tempted just then to raise the subject of her own "youthful blunder" when she had promised to marry Mr. O'Brien. If she did, particularly in the context of putting these things in the past, it would relieve her of the constant worry that the curate would speak of it. But she fell to thinking about it, and wondering how to begin, and the moment was lost.

Mr. O'Brien, for his part, was both pleased and surprised by their good will, and chuckled to himself at Beatrice's response. He saw that they were coming around another bend of the house, returning to the front, and said, "I believe I shall inquire of our hosts for a hot drink when we reach the drawing room. Who shall join me in it?"

"I will!" said Mrs. Forsythe. "A good hot cup of negus, I think."

"I will too," said Beatrice, peeking up at him from within her bonnet. "Although chocolate will suffice for me."

Her large green eyes made a pleasing contrast to the buff-coloured velvety hat she sported, the ribbons of which formed a large bow beneath her chin. Her scarf was flapping behind her, and small russet curls framed her face. Mr. O'Brien was aware, deep within himself, that she was looking lovely. But a major portion of his brain warned him against noticing her at all. She was a Forsythe. He would never make a cake of himself by admiring another Forsythe girl. It was utterly unthinkable. Particularly as he was waiting upon Mr. Mornay to determine his fate, as it were.

On an intellectual level, he knew that only God could decide his fate. And how he prayed He would! If God were to grant him the vicarage at Glendover — but no, he shouldn't even think of it. It was not going to happen. He saw it in every look of his host. It was a mystery to him why Mr. Mornay had not yet thrown him out on his ears, but that was probably because Ariana had spoken for him.

She had also insisted he stay to sup with them; and then she urged him to take a guest bedchamber in the house, so that he found himself now as a guest of the Mornays. He had no idea when the gavel would be dropped; when Mr. Mornay would impart the dreaded news and make him leave. He had come prepared for that to happen, but each delay of the business somehow upped the stakes for him. This was why he had requested the meeting with Mornay. He could not, must not, allow himself to hope. He would concentrate on behaving as any good curate should; on seeking to make amends for his past transgressions. He could at least return home, then, in the knowledge that this event had occurred for a worthy cause. If nothing else, he would be at peace with the Mornays.

It would be an unexpected boon. He suddenly realized that he should like very much to be on good terms with the couple. Even with Mr. Mornay. Astonishing.

■ ■ ■ ■

When Giles Taller reached the apothecary's, he hesitated a few moments, looked around warily, and then entered the shop. Another man was at the counter talking to the clerk and Giles settled himself to wait, standing with his arms crossed, and his head bent, as though lost in his own thoughts. But he was listening, and couldn't help hearing the conversation.

"Ay, that's right. If this don't work to bring that fever down, all ye can do is wait. There's a nasty strain goin' round over in Warmley. Some say it came from London. Warmley got it a fortnight since, and so far three 'as died. I don't right know wha' it is, until I see someone 'as got it. But this 'ere's the best I can do for ye; if'n your lit'le one don't improve afore mornin', best call Mr. Speckman."

The man paid for the mixture, handed to him in a glass vial. When the clerk went to put the money away in a back room, Giles slunk back out of the shop and started for home. He couldn't risk letting it be known that his little girl had a sickness that might be the very one which had already left three dead in a nearby town. He could lose his situation. If he was forced to stop working on the Mornay lands, he'd be looking for different employment for weeks; he knew it. His family needed his small income to survive. No, he couldn't risk buying the medicine, whatever it had been.

SEVEN

Mr. Mornay was not yet to have the pleasure of telling Mr. O'Brien the felicitous news regarding the living at Warwickdon. Instead, he was notified that a caller had arrived, a gentleman named Mr. Tristan Barton. His wife asked if he would receive the man, as she did not recognize the name when Frederick announced it to her.

On the way to the entrance hall to meet him, Mr. Mornay tried to determine if the name, which seemed to faintly ring a bell, was identifiably familiar. He drew a blank.

When they had come around from the east side of the house, Beatrice exclaimed, "Look, someone's carriage is here!"

"It no doubt belongs to the Mornays," murmured Mrs. Forsythe.

"I wonder," she replied. At that moment, a groom was just leading the horses and equipage away from the front of the house, heading for a portico that led around to the stables. They hurried forward.

"Whose carriage is this?" Mrs. Forsythe asked the man.

"A gentleman caller, mum, just arrived." He shrugged.

But the eyes of the three met, and there was some curiosity in them all. "A gentleman caller!"

Mr. O'Brien's only thought was that it might be a man who was his competition; another curate hoping to be presented with the living at Glendover. He was soon to be ousted, in that case. He sighed.

As soon as they had removed their outer garments, they made their way back to the drawing room. When they entered, Mr. Mornay and a young man of distinctly fine dress and bearing came rapidly to their feet. He had dark hair, tightly curled for a man. His clothing was extremely fine, in the style of Mr. Mornay's garments, snugly fitted. Beatrice wondered if he were a lord, for he had the countenance and posture of a pampered man, not timid in company, as her idea of bluebloods was. She felt an immediate awe of his presence. And a great deal of interest.

"Excellent, you're returned!" exclaimed Ariana. "We have a new guest, a new neighbour, in fact, from the Manor House.

"Mama, I bid you welcome Mr. Tristan Barton." The excitement in her tone was unmistakable. As the three came into the room she continued smoothly, making the introductions. "My mother, sir, Mrs. Forsythe."

He gave an infinitesimally small bow, but said, "At your service, ma'am."

She nodded, with the slightest curtsey. "I am pleased to meet you, sir." She then took a seat on a settee.

Beatrice also curtsied quickly upon his introduction, and Mr. Barton's eyes flickered over her with a studied air of politeness; but inside he felt a surge of interest in the fair young woman, and was able to take a quick appraisal of her appearance.

"And, Mr. Peter O'Brien, sir," she said, "who is a curate." The two men were not far in age and looked at each other pleasantly enough.

"Ah!" he said, having found a point on which to comment. "So you preside in this parish?"

"No, sir; Mr. O'Brien is a friend of the family," said Ariana, quickly. "He resides in London."

When Mr. Barton learned that it was Mr. O'Brien's first visit to Aspindon House, he said, "Then we are both new to the neigh-bourhood. Capital. I shan't be the only one who knows nothing of the place."

"Indeed, you are not, sir," put in Ariana, "as my mother and sister are only visiting, as well as Mrs. Royleforst and Miss Blu-ford." (He had already been introduced to those ladies.) "And what do you think?" Ariana asked the others, with a smile. "Mr. Barton has even done us the felicity of bringing with him a sister!"

"You have a sister with you, sir?" Mrs. Forsythe asked, smilingly.

"Yes, ma'am," he said, with a little smile. "I am afraid I had to leave Miss Barton home today, as she was feeling rather un-well, but I expect she will wish to make your acquaintance, indeed, all of your acquain-tances, as soon as possible. She is seldom indisposed, and I am sure she will ac-company me here as soon as Mr. and Mrs. Mornay will allow me to call again."

"May I ask the age of your sister, sir?" asked Mrs. Forsythe. She was endeavouring to ascertain what sort of company they could expect in this woman.

"My sister is younger than I am," he said, and with a sparkle in his eye, added, "if that is any indication."

"Oh indeed it 'tis!" she replied, with a

laugh in her voice. "I take it she is quite young, then."

"Oh, not so very young," he answered, cryptically. "She is indeed five years my junior, and might well have married by now, only I have not found a gentleman I can approve of," he said, eyeing Mr. O'Brien suggestively.

"In other words," said Mrs. Royleforst, "your sister is an intelligent young woman of marriageable age, and we should all look forward to meeting her."

"You have the right of it, ma'am," he said, smiling, and beginning to enjoy himself.

Mrs. Forsythe was happy to think that another young woman of gentility would soon be of their company, for Beatrice's sake; but she also grew aware of a slight caution within her. What if Miss Barton began to turn the head of Mr. O'Brien? It also occurred to her, on the other hand, that Mr. Barton might be a suitable prospect for Beatrice; she would have to learn more of his character to know.

"I do *so* look forward to making her acquaintance," said Ariana. Why do you not come by with Miss Barton on the morrow?"

He smiled. "I think I may speak for my sister in saying that we should be delighted to join you, thank you very much."

"And do you always speak so confidently of what your sister might enjoy?" asked Mr. O'Brien, but with a smile.

Mr. Barton hesitated, returning the smile. "Not always, no. But I think I am safe in this, for I see a company of lovely ladies in this room, all of whom she will be delighted to converse with. We have made no other acquaintances yet, you understand; so this will be just the thing to please her."

Beatrice was listening, but was equally busy taking in every inch of the fine Mr. Barton, from his breeches and pure white stockings and cravat, to a ring on his finger. My, but he was a fine figure of a man! She had thought Mr. O'Brien to be impressive when he first appeared in the drawing room, but next to Mr. Barton, his elegance paled. Then again, Mr. Barton was a smaller man; tall and lean, but with the easy slimness of youth. Whereas Mr. O'Brien, who was also tall, seemed somehow to be a more substantial man, more mature, perhaps. He was not large of girth by any means, but seemed more muscular beneath the dark superfine and cambric, than the young Barton.

The three gentlemen began to discuss the hunting and shooting in the area, so that Ariana came and sat with her relations. "Only think how amusing this shall be, to have new neighbours who are not only friendly, but of a comparable age to myself and Mr. Mornay."

"But you and Mr. Mornay are not of a comparable age," replied Beatrice, who was technically accurate, but Ariana shrugged this off. "I mean, who may prove to be like-minded people. If Mr. Mornay approves of them, we may even put up a party, perhaps a little ball."

"Oh, I should adore that!" cried Beatrice. But this reminded her of something. "I hope you are still considering a trip to London, though, Ariana. And that I may come with you."

"I may need to make that trip," Ariana replied, eyes alight. She was thinking of her plans to visit charitable institutions in the city. "But not until we are better acquainted with the Bartons."

From across the room, they heard Mr. Mornay say, "Now you must tell us what brings you to Middlesex. How did you settle upon the Manor?" The women all turned to face their guest, being desirous of the same information.

Mr. Barton stifled a surprising stab of fear. *Here it is! The question that would either pave his way or ruin his scheme.* It was bound to come up, and he had prepared to answer it.

"I am looking for an escape from Town," he said, with an easy smile. "I thought Lord Malcolm would have told you, actually. My father left the country when I was young, and now I wish to know more of it to understand his reasons. I have been disposed against it for all my life without knowing precisely *why* I am." (He smiled.) "I felt it was time to determine for myself whether country living is truly as vile as he presented it, or if I have been brain-addled by him for no cause."

This, of course, brought forth a barrage of support for country living, until Beatrice said, "I am, I fear, the only one here who will not encourage you in country life, sir." To his raised brow, she added, "I, for one, *abhor* the country!" Beatrice was delighted with Aspindon House and its environs, but this little fact did not seem to enter her brain at the moment.

"You enjoyed our walk just now!" exclaimed her mother, in amazement.

Beatrice's gaze met Mr. O'Brien's, who was listening with an intent expression. She felt suddenly a little abashed at her strong terms, and so added, "Well, Aspindon House is of course singular in its delights. If I lived here year-round, I daresay I could bear it well enough." (There were titters around the room.) "But we hail from Chesterton, sir, where all is provincial and dull, I assure you."

Mr. Barton said, "I can say nothing against your sentiment, ma'am, as I make it a rule never to contradict a lady," which brought forth more general gaiety. But Mr. Mornay had not done learning of his new guest. "But how did you come to this small hamlet?" he persisted, to the man. "Am I to understand that you have some ties to the area? A wife who is to join you here?"

"I?" He was greatly surprised. "No, sir! I-er, learned of Lord Malcolm's extraordinary terms in letting his house; that he would take a monthly lease, which suits me exactly. It allows me to test the country without the expense or commitment of buying a house. I have engaged the property for only a month, and I may renew it for another if I choose. His lordship even expressed a possible willingness to part with the place entirely if I find it agreeable." He paused, and scanned the faces around him and then smiled. "How could I resist?"

"How kind of Lord Malcolm," said Ariana, wonderingly.

Mr. Barton smiled. "Yes, ma'am. Most providential."

"It does seem hard on the neighbourhood,

though; taking the house for so short a period." Mr. Mornay's eyes were keenly watching the guest as he spoke. But he knew that no one in the village would be pleased about the Bartons — or anyone — coming to "try out" their village. They would be at a loss as to how to treat them, and resentment would soon win out. A man of means who meant not to stay might just be up to no good. Such men might alight upon a small town merely to search out a naïve young woman to form a dalliance with. It was known to happen.

"You will have no standing or place in the village," he said. "People will not trust you." When Mr. Barton had no ready answer, he added, in a small attempt to dilute the severity of his words, "It bodes well for you that you are at least not merely staying at the Inn. That would surely raise doubts about your character."

"Yes." Barton jumped at that straw. "I had hoped that leasing the house for a month, at minimum, would be indicative of both my means, and my intentions."

"Your means? Very many could afford a house for a month, with no real means at all. An annual lease might be far superior if you intend to tell the world you are a man of means."

Mr. Barton licked his lips. "I have brought my carriage and two servants; I should think that would help give the impression of my means, sir." The tension in the room had escalated swiftly.

Ariana did not know why her husband was being so hard upon the poor fellow, who seemed, to her eyes, an earnest young man.

He protested, "I am confounded, I assure you, that my object could be misconstrued as an evil one: I depend upon your friendship all the more, Mr. Mornay, and that of your lovely wife and family (with a nod toward the ladies) to reassure the people in this area that I have only the best intentions." He finished uncertainly, and Ariana was quick to smile at him reassuringly, but her husband only continued to eye the man with a probing stare.

"To *try out* the country," Phillip said, a little sourly. Mrs. Forsythe's hand took hold of her daughter's, for the tension was palpable.

"Ah — *yes*. The proximity to Town was a further incentive to me, as I do not relish travelling."

Mrs. Royleforst was watching and listening with great enjoyment. She knew her nephew well enough to suspect he had a reason for raking the young man through the coals, and therefore she did not question it. She almost tittered aloud when his face grew pale and he licked his lips.

Beatrice, however, knew only that her brother-in-law was making a new acquaintance downright uncomfortable — intentionally. It was unpardonable, to her mind.

At that moment Mr. Barton's eye fell upon Beatrice's, who had been listening intently, and he cracked a smile. He knew the look of compassion in a female when he saw it, and inwardly gave himself a point for dressing. His sister had been against his wearing breeches . . .

. . . "It is only the middle of the day," she had pointed out.

But at least he had been right about the matter of his clothing, and to him that was no small thing. He saw it in the eyes and manner of the ladies, though Mr. Mornay was proving to be devilish unfriendly.

Ariana decided she had to end this perplexing tête-à-tête, and said, brightly, "Well, sir, we are not the village, nor are we flummoxed by your presence." She looked at her husband: "May I ask our guest to stay and dine with us, sir?"

"If it pleases you."

Ariana smiled, saying, "I daresay even the state dining table shall be filled! Let us all dress for it!" In another minute, Mr. Barton was invited, and accepted, an invitation for dinner, once again congratulating himself on wearing breeches, as well as for navigating through the maze of sticky questions Mr. Mornay had thrown at him.

"Perhaps we could have dancing!" put in Beatrice. "We will have three men and three ladies!" She turned to Mrs. Royleforst, "And if you care to dance, ma'am, I will share my partner with you!" Her excitement was refreshing to Mr. Barton. Miss Forsythe seemed like a girl he could enjoy the company of. He would ask to be her partner after dinner. It promised to be most diverting.

Ariana smiled at her husband, surprised to find him wearing a scowl as he studied Barton. But she said, "Should we send to inquire of your sister, Mr. Barton? Would she wish to join us, do you think?"

Mr. Barton lost his amiable look as he thought on her question. "No, I thank you, ma'am. When Anne is unwell, dancing is the last thing she would enjoy, I assure you."

Beatrice laughed. "We shall have our own little ball. It shall be delightful!"

Mr. Barton was looking back at her and smiling in return. What an attractive, delightful girl. Things with Mornay were starting out on a deuced uneven keel, but here was an unexpected boon: Miss Forsythe, a family relation. It was something to think upon.

The dinner was not as splendid as Ariana would have liked, for their chef had not had the necessary notice to make it so. But it was nevertheless sumptuous to the minds of the guests, and satisfying. The state dining room, with its elegant chandeliers and satin-damasked table, its silver and crystal service, goblets and covers and napkins, were not put to shame by the many courses the kitchens served up.

Mr. Barton was clearly in his element, happy that the Mornays did not stand upon points and insist that one speak only to the person sitting next to one, as some people did. Instead, he spoke freely across the table, addressing first one, then another person, or being addressed by them in turn.

Beatrice was not shy; she did her fair share of conversation, and part of it concerned her hopes of the Season in London. Miss Bluford had clearly fallen into an awestruck silence by the finery around her, and stared often at her host, which was thoroughly out of character for her. She often looked from one gentleman to another, in fact, but never murmured a word. Ariana thought the poor thing was very admiring of the gentlemen, and wondered, for the first time, if poor little Miss Bluford was a lonely creature.

But there was much joviality at the meal, and she had no time to focus her thoughts on the paid companion. At any other state dining room, Miss Bluford's presence might have been snobbishly ignored — companions were allowed at table, unlike servants, but that did not mean that all people accepted them. But Mrs. Royleforst treated her companion almost as a sister (albeit a servile sister), and no one else in the room — with the possible exception of Mr. Mornay — treated her condescendingly. However, Miss Bluford was properly astonished to find herself at the finest table she had ever sat at.

Beatrice was enjoying the sheer power of Mr. Barton's presence. When he spoke, she found herself listening with pleasure. The only chink in the armour of his persona was if Mr. Mornay chanced to say something. He alone seemed to deflate Mr. Barton's confidence completely.

Mr. O'Brien was no longer a man to vie for a woman's attention, particularly when her surname was "Forsythe" — so he merely observed how Mr. Barton managed to monopolize Beatrice's conversation, allowing his own remarks to be brief and to the point. He was determined to remain dispassionate, aloof. He spoke when spoken to, not averse to holding conversation, but he was certainly not about to insist upon having Miss Forsythe's attention when Mr. Barton so evidently required it.

The thing upon his mind most (other than the striking appearance of Miss Forsythe, which he was obliged to ignore entirely) was the fact that he had still not had an audience with Mr. Mornay. The thing was becoming absurdly overdue, to his mind. He had come to Aspindon House to inquire about a living. He'd been sent by the recommendation of a man the Paragon could respect. He deserved to have this meeting, even if he was to receive an unapologetic rejection for his troubles.

He noted the spotless cravat on Mr. Barton and wondered if his own attire was up to snuff. But how could it be? He was surrounded by men who dressed to the nines. True, little Miss Bluford spent as much time silently studying him as she did the other two gentlemen at table; but he had no idea what her object could be, or what she was trying to discover.

Miss Bluford was actually astonished at

the fine figures all three men made in their evening wear. Not a one of them was unhandsome, each had thick strong brows, though of differing shades. Each man had a strong nose, a fine forehead. Mr. Mornay, she decided, was the most handsome. He had an aura of strength about him, whether it came from being the master of the house, or from the fencing and sparring he did often as exercise. But the other two, she could not decide between. Mr. Barton's ease of conversation lent him an air of urbanity and grace that did much to add to his charms. Mr. O'Brien, on the other hand, had a quiet dignity and serious depth in his looks that gave him the air of a brooding hero (almost in the style of Lord Byron).

Miss Bluford had read many romances, and, as Mr. Mornay was frightful to her at times (not to mention married), and Mr. Barton too sauve for her to imagine conversing with at all, she finally concluded that Mr. O'Brien was the man most worthy of admiration. From that point, she paid special attention to all his conversation. She laughed at anything with the slightest touch of humor; she quite amazed Beatrice by her attentions to the man, in fact, but it served to make Beatrice appreciate his presence more, oddly enough, no matter how much

Mr. Barton tried to monopolize her conversation.

When the meal was ended, Ariana rose to signal the ladies to leave for the drawing room. Frederick came in to announce that the small band of musicians had arrived, however, and so Mr. Mornay offered to forgo the customary male practice of remaining at table to enjoy a glass of port with conversation not deemed fit for women. His wife thanked him with a brilliant smile.

The dancing was thrilling for Beatrice, especially since the Mornays enjoyed waltzing with each other. The small trio which had been hurriedly called for from town were equal to the task of playing the music required for various waltzes, reels, and country dances. Beatrice enjoyed a waltz with both Mr. Barton and Mr. O'Brien, and found the latter man to be a much better dancer, to her surprise. Mr. Barton was so much more the cosmopolitan man. But Mr. O'Brien had a sensitivity to her movements that made him give her just the right amount of leading to perform the steps in a smooth rhythm that was as pleasing to the eye, she was sure, as to herself. Nevertheless, she felt more at ease with Mr. Barton, for his looks were simple and curious, nothing more. Mr. O'Brien had eyes filled with thoughts and sentiments that she could not guess at, and which made her uneasy.

"Are you just come from London?" Beatrice had asked Mr. Barton, at one point. She could not resist learning more of the metropolis, and perhaps the Season.

Mr. Barton looked at her expectantly. "I am. Have you been there of late?"

"No!" A smile. "No, though I should like to acquaint myself with the place. My sister is considering whether she will give me a coming-out this year."

"Ah. For the Season?" To her nod, he said, "Splendid idea!"

Beatrice was elated at this response. "My mother is old-fashioned, I'm afraid! She thinks I am too young. What do you think, Mr. Barton?"

A charming smile. "That depends on how old you are, Miss Forsythe. May I ask?"

"I am seventeen years, sir."

"Seventeen." He was still smiling. "I daresay girls as young as fifteen sometimes have their coming-out; and seventeen is by no means considered too young."

She laughed. "You are in all things a tonic to me, Mr. Barton!"

"I am honoured to be of service," he said, and his eyes sparkled with satisfaction.

Mr. O'Brien saw the two of them talking

and smiling with each other, and felt as though a little feeble candle of hope was being snuffed out inside him. But for what had he been hoping? That Miss Beatrice Forsythe would be smitten with him? It was perfectly understandable that Barton should have her. He was evidently of a higher class than Mr. O'Brien; he had wealth and social aplomb, and would no doubt fit in just right with the Mornays. He wished her well of him, he really did.

EIGHT

Mrs. Julia Forsythe was as pleased with her richly appointed bedchamber as anyone used to much plainer living would have been. But she could not sleep. She needed to speak to Ariana. Earlier, with Mr. Barton and Mr. O'Brien in the company, and then the addition of the children to the room, followed by dinner, she had found no chance to raise the subject that weighed heavily on her mind.

Wrapping herself in a robe, and stopping only to put her slippers on and grab a candle, she quietly left the room, shutting the door behind her with as little sound as possible. She stopped to peer down the dark corridor, lit only by a few lonely sconces along the wall at far intervals. Now, which way was her daughter's room? She should not disturb Ariana at this hour, for it must be the middle of the night, but somehow the thought of walking the corridor appealed to her. And she might as well do it in the right direction. It was dark and quiet, and she detested tossing in her bed when sleep evaded her.

Hearing a sound, she held up her candle, and peering into the darkness beyond, saw the shadow of a figure. "Who's there?" she asked.

"Mama?" It was Ariana's voice, coming from far down the corridor.

"Yes! So it is you! I'm glad! I wished to speak to you!"

"Now?" As Ariana came out of the darkness, a little candle in her hand flickering with the house breezes, she said, "Are you unwell?"

"No, my dear, I am fine, I assure you. Only I could not sleep for want of speaking to you." She stopped to appreciate how fetching her daughter looked in an embroidered robe over a nightdress that sported a great deal of lace at the throat and sleeves, and with a frilly night cap on as well.

"What is it, Mama? What did you wish to say to me?"

"How is it that you are come out of your room?" the mother asked first. "Are you unwell?"

"I often take a look at the children if I awake during the night, if you must know. I adore watching them in their dreams. Will you come with me?" Ariana had been moving them along as she spoke, for she was indeed eager to lay eyes on her offspring.

Mrs. Forsythe smiled, even as she scurried to keep up. "You are enjoying motherhood, I am glad of that."

"Did you not enjoy it?" she asked, surprised.

"I did, you know it is so; I still do. Of course the station does come with many cares attendant. In fact, it is my other daughter who supplies my errand tonight. I must speak to you of Beatrice."

"Oh! Of course, Mama." Ariana agreed. "Let us just peek on the children first."

"Yes." As they walked, she said, "Actually, there are two things, my dear." They were speaking in hushed tones, the darkness of the night making them feel as though quiet must be observed. That, and the short span of their tapers' dim glow added to the feeling of privacy. The floor was draped at intervals with long, narrow carpets, and both wore slippers, but the air was not warm.

"As you know, Beatrice hopes you will sponsor her for the Season this year."

"Yes. Do you really object to it?"

"She is but seventeen, and my opinion is

that she needs must wait. Another year or two will only add to her charms — and her sense."

Ariana grew thoughtful a moment. "Beatrice is rather sensible for a girl so young, though, Mama, do you not think so?"

"Not in this matter, my dear. She thinks she is entitled to a high match because of your success."

"I know," Ariana stifled a chuckle. "Well, it is true that I can help her in ways that I could not have, if it were not for my marriage."

"Yes, but even so, you know she is not well-heeled in point of fact. She has no more dowry than you did, and I daresay there are few Mr. Mornays about who will fall head over heels in love with a poor gel!"

"Yes; yes. I will speak of it to her, and set her straight, Mama, I assure you." They had reached the nursery, and Ariana put a finger to her lips, while hesitating, listening, outside the door. She quietly opened it, though it gave a little creaking that could not be helped. The first sound they heard when they entered was the snoring of Mrs. Perler, who slept in a bed in a small connecting room to the right.

Ariana held her candle higher and went

first toward a crib that was against the wall across the room. Upon reaching it, she smiled down at the sight of the infant, on her stomach, her little round face to one side so that one small cheek lay against the sheet. As if aware of her mother's presence, the baby stirred, and then moved again, instantly beginning to fuss.

Far from being disturbed by this, Ariana smiled and put down her candle, quickly taking the child in her arms. While she quieted the baby, she joined her mother, who was looking down at Nigel. She had found the four-year-old fast asleep, his legs and arms sprawled outwards, and no blanket upon him at all. Mrs. Forsythe had replaced the blanket which had been kicked off, so that he was up to his neck beneath it. "They are beautiful children," Ariana's mama murmured, smiling herself.

Ariana said, "I know! How could they fail to be, with such a handsome father?" She moved toward a chair, and sitting down, said, "I will feed Miranda and then have Mrs. Perler put her back to sleep."

Mrs. Forsythe watched her a moment and then said, "Your nightdress is made for nursing a child! How propitious! They did not have such allowances in my day!"

The young mother said, while putting the

infant to her breast, "Yes; Mr. Mornay bespoke my "mothering" clothes, as he calls them. He is so thoughtful!"

"Some men do not like their wives to nurse children."

"He is happy to let me," she replied. "He knows I prefer to." After a moment's silence, she added, "He did make me wean Nigel to a wet nurse, on account of my fatigue. The boy was waking up hungry every two hours and I must confess, it was wearing on me rather alarmingly. But I do enjoy nursing my babies!" And here she looked down to marvel at her little daughter who was sucking away quite contentedly. It took only a few minutes, and then she switched sides for the baby, but also had to keep giving her little pinches on her cheek, for now the child was falling asleep instead of completing her meal. Soon Mrs. Forsythe went and awoke Mrs. Perler, who took the infant sleepily into her arms. "I'll put dry garments on her, ma'am," she said, amidst a yawn.

"Thank you, Mrs. Perler," Ariana replied. When they'd left the nursery, she said, returning to their earlier conversation, "So, you desire me to discourage Beatrice from having a Season this year?"

"Yes. I prefer she waits a year or two."

"But I have decided I must go, myself,

after your visit is ended; I need to re-acquaint myself with the efforts on behalf of the poor. I am afraid Mr. O'Brien's descriptions of St. Pancras should haunt me, otherwise." She paused. "I would like to bring Beatrice to Grosvenor Square with me. It won't be for a whole Season, and I will require her to accompany me on my charitable missions. Will that suit you?"

When her mother only frowned, Ariana said, "And, I should tell you, Mama, that many girls do come out at her age."

"Yes, but those gels are not my daughters. However, with your promise not to give her all frivolity and nonsense, I will allow her to accompany you."

"Very good," said Ariana. "I think you are right in it."

"Now, the other matter," the older woman said, looking at Ariana plaintively, "is dear Mr. O'Brien."

"Yes?" Ariana wondered what her mother could have to say about this man.

"Can you prevail upon your husband to grant him the living here? He seems like such a deserving young man, and so good of heart! If you must know, I do hope to encourage your sister to . . . er . . . acknowledge his good character, and if he were to get both benefices, of Glendover as well as

Warwickdon, even she might be satisfied with his income."

Ariana had been suppressing her glee. "Mama! I have had the very same thought! But to find you a matchmaker as well! It is too amusing!"

"My dear, a churchman may make quite as good a husband as any gentleman! But better than many, for we know already that Mr. O'Brien has a true religion."

Ariana fell to silent musing for a moment. "I can agree with that. I do not know if Beatrice will; and I must tell you, I cannot press my husband in this matter. Not any more, for I have already tried."

They were back near Mrs. Forsythe's guest bedchamber and so the two stopped walking.

"My dear. I have seen how he defers to you, how he adores you. Why cannot you say a good thing in the curate's favour? I fail to see —"

"Mama, things that happened in London — concerning myself and Mr. O'Brien — predisposes my husband against him."

"Things in London? Between the two of you?" Mrs. Forsythe's tone revealed a note of anxiety. In fact, she forgot to keep her voice down, and this time Ariana held up her candle and peered into the darkness of the corridor for a moment. She saw nothing.

"Have I been mistaken in his character? Is he dishonourable?"

"No, Mama! It was nothing of significance! But only something a husband would dislike."

"If it was truly nothing of significance, then I daresay it ought not to be considered or held against him now."

Ariana sighed, "I am in agreement with you on that. But my husband is not. I cannot dare say another word, for he already feels I support Mr. O'Brien too much."

Mrs. Forsythe fretted, "I have no desire to plant a seed of disharmony between you and your husband, my dear. But if Mr. O'Brien had the living, it would benefit him, his future wife (who just could turn out to be your sister), and therefore the whole family."

"Yes, I know," the other said, unhappily.

"May I have your word that you will apply once more to Mr. Mornay? He has a great deal of sense regarding such things, and he knows that to keep these things in the family is always preferable to bringing in a stranger."

"The thing is, there is nothing at present to say that anything at all will spring up between Beatrice and Mr. O'Brien. And now with Mr. Barton . . ."

"That is precisely why I could not sleep!" cried her mother. "Mr. Barton!"

"But he seems a gentleman, and if there is anything of ill-repute about him, my husband will learn of it."

"My dear — I do not wish to speak against a gentleman without cause; I can only tell you that I am convinced" (and here she stopped to search her feelings and thoughts), "that Mr. O'Brien is the superior man, fortune or no fortune. I have formed the opinion that a match between him and Beatrice would be advantageous for both of them. And I do not call it a coincidence that the two of them are here at the same time."

"But Mr. Barton is too," returned the younger woman. "How do you discount that?"

Mrs. Forsythe looked lovingly at her daughter, so grown up now that she was more like a friend than her child. "My dear; wherever there is to be a move of God in a life, does not the evil one try and fill the place for it with a lesser substitute? Have you never noticed? He tries to get our eyes to see something other than what is best for us, as though *it* must be best; when in fact it is but a mere shadow of the far better thing the Lord has in mind for us." She stopped and searched her daughter's face, holding up her candle. "Mr. O'Brien is that good thing for Beatrice!" she exclaimed. "And Mr. Barton is the shallow substitute! And he is turning her head, I daresay!"

Ariana tried to grasp her mother's point.

But Mrs. Forsythe continued, "We must *wait* upon the Lord if we want His best. If Beatrice sees Mr. Barton as the answer for all her hopes — and fails to wait for that which is better to show itself — Oh! I dare not even think of her sorrow, later."

"But Mama, you and Papa can withhold your approval from the man."

"As indeed we shall!" she said, in a loud whisper. "But I pray it does not come to that."

Ariana was concerned that her mother had taken her ideas too far. "Mama — nothing has happened yet between Beatrice and Mr. Barton. Do not borrow trouble. Did you not always say that to me?"

Her mother saw that she had not convinced her daughter of the dangers of Mr. Barton. "Pray for your sister!" she said, turning to open the door to her bedchamber. "And speak to Mr. Mornay if you have the courage!"

Ariana was left in the hallway, and she bit

her lip with worry. She went to her own bedchamber, blew out the candle, and snuggled against her husband beneath the covers. But she didn't expect to sleep. Her mother had thoroughly transferred her worries onto her!

Mrs. Forsythe returned to her bed at ease and fell asleep at once. Ariana, on the other hand, remained awake a good while longer, her mind filling with ideas and imaginations, what-ifs and if-onlys.

How would Phillip react if she raised the subject again with him? She prayed that her husband would be fair and do what was right and proper. That he would not base his decision on past grievances or annoyances. If Mr. O'Brien were to show an interest in Beatrice, surely Mr. Mornay must lose the slightest remaining vestige of jealousy. Jealousy? No, it was not jealousy, exactly; it was more like suspicion. She remembered that at one time Beatrice had promised to marry the curate. She wondered if Mr. O'Brien recalled the event. Perhaps, if he did, and if he approved of the older and more grown-up girl that Beatrice had become, more would come of this time of proximity for the pair. Her mother was convinced of the merit of a match between them; imagine if, after all this time, they should turn out agreeable to one another? How comfortably things would be settled for everyone, then.

With that prayer on her heart, if not her lips, sleep came at last.

Mrs. Betsey Taller awoke from a short sleep when her head made contact with the wall. She'd been sitting by the fire, keeping it hot for her daughter, who still lay, unconscious, on the straw bed. Her two boys, to her horror, had started whimpering the night before, and they, too, now lay abed hot with fever. MaryAnn had been sick for three (or was it four?) days now, but today she had begun moaning and coughing in her sleep. Instead of the quiet exhaustion she had displayed earlier, she was restless, tossing and turning, and it was driving Mrs. Taller mad!

Giles had not brought any physic to give the girl. She was sure the apothecary would have offered them something. Anything that might help at all would be administered at once. If only he had done his duty and brought it home!

She reached over and wrung out a cloth, and for the thousandth time placed it upon the girl's forehead. Then she did the same for the boys, changing their old cloths for new ones. When she returned to her daughter, she noticed that MaryAnn was suddenly still . . . ominously still. *Had she died?* With a terrible gasp she fell upon her, and was prepared to wail to high heaven, but she felt some movement of the chest. It was shallow, but MaryAnn was breathing. When she sat up again, she reached a sudden decision. The scare had brought her to her senses, no matter what Giles said. He was wrong to try to hide the fact of their daughter's illness. It wasn't honest, and no good could come of it.

She crossed herself, and then put her hands along the side of the perspiring face of her child and gazed forlornly at the girl. Then she rose and pulled a shawl around her shoulders. On an impulse, she pulled down a beautiful lined bonnet, which had been given to her by the lady of the big house — Mrs. Mornay. It was her most prized possession. She had no money, but perchance the apothecary would accept it instead. She took one last long look at her daughter, and then the boys — all three of them were sleeping or unconscious from the illness, she did not know — and then slipped out the front door. She could walk to the apothecary's. It would take near an hour, but she would do it. Then another hour, back. Her daughter's condition hadn't changed for two days, but now seemed to be growing suddenly worse. It only made sense that the boys would follow the same pattern. She could not wait. She would have to risk leaving them all alone and go now, while Giles was still out.

It was Mr. O'Brien's third morning at Aspindon, and he was determined to get the attention of his host for the matter of the living. He was disappointed, when he went for breakfast, to learn from a footman that "the Master" had already taken his morning meal.

Did the man know where Mr. O'Brien might find him? Before he could answer, Frederick came up the corridor and asked him, "Are you quite done with your breakfast, sir?"

Mr. O'Brien eyed the butler with surprise. "I am."

"Would you be so good, then, sir, to join Mr. Mornay in his study?" Mr. O'Brien stared at the butler, first in surprise, and then relief. Like the well-trained servant he was, Freddy was not looking at the cleric, but kept his gaze steadily ahead of him as he spoke.

"I should be *delighted* to join Mr. Mornay

in his study!" he cried, giving Freddy quite a surprise. He did not move his head, but swiveled his eyes upon the young man, blinking in surprise.

"Very good, sir," he said, quite deliberately.

Mr. Mornay sat behind a large polished rosewood desk, from where he motioned Mr. O'Brien to a chair. Mr. O'Brien had tried not to gawk on the way to the study, but the more he saw of the house, the more awed he felt. He even began to think that he could better understand his host now, simply for seeing his home with his own eyes. It must engender a certain amount of pride to be brought up in such magnificence, he thought. Not that he was ready to excuse arrogance, but a proper familial pride was perfectly understandable.

Upon the desk was a stack of books, one of which was a large Bible. There were two framed pictures, though Mr. O'Brien could not see the portraits they contained; a small sand pot for blotting letters; an ink well; a quill holder; and a compass. There was more, and Mr. O'Brien would have liked to catalogue every item in the room suddenly, but he took a breath as Mr. Mornay put his hands together upon the desktop and looked at him squarely.

It was time. Here was the announcement he dreaded and yet knew must come. Mr. O'Brien would not be found suitable for Glendover, and somehow Mr. Mornay had wished to keep him waiting this long to hear it. He cleared his throat, and met the man's gaze head on. So be it. Mr. O'Brien was unafraid.

NINE

In truth, Mr. Mornay almost felt sorry for O'Brien. *Here it comes,* he thought, again. *He is going to ask me for the living.* He knew it had to be a deuced uncomfortable spot to be in. But the young man, after glancing about the desk, had leveled his gaze on Mornay, who recognized a maturity in that one gesture that had not been in this man upon their last meeting. He had become bolder, for sure.

"How may I serve you?" Mornay asked.

Mr. O'Brien's brows cleared in a sort of relief. This was a decidedly open and non-hostile way for the man to have begun the conversation, although it did seem to ignore the point.

"Well, sir, I must say that I ought to be asking you that question."

Mornay merely made a small smile, and then casually opened his snuffbox and took a small pinch. He offered it to O'Brien, who declined politely.

". . . As I am here on recommendation?" he added, hoping to jar the man's memory.

"Yes?"

"From the Colonel."

"Yes."

"You did get the letter?"

"Yes."

Mr. O'Brien was now practically at the edge of his seat. "I have to know! Forgive me for being blunt, sir, but *why* have you allowed me to come? I do not entertain the notion that you have wholly forgiven me for what has occurred in the past, nor do I expect that you shall. I cannot blame you; I was too much a fool, and I know it." His eyes had been roaming the tops of the walls, as he spoke, but once again he settled them upon his host, and there was nothing of hope in them. "Why have you let me come? I know what your eventual answer must be; you would sooner present your living to the pope than to me! Is that not so?"

Mr. Mornay hadn't expected to find O'Brien amusing. "I . . . do not think I could present it to the pope." But he smiled gently.

"Well, to anyone else in England, then, any other curate save this one!" and he hit his own chest with his thumb, in a disgusted manner. He looked at Mornay. "I need to know, Mr. Mornay, have you brought me here to amuse yourself? As a hoax? I cannot think you have any motive that would be for my benefit. So I beg you, be plain with me on the matter, and I may yet leave here with some semblance of my dignity intact, though I am the first to admit I have precious little of that when I am in your presence to begin with!"

"Slow down, O'Brien," Mr. Mornay murmured. "I did not summon you here; I did get the Colonel's letter, and, if you must know, I would have indeed attempted to discourage you from coming all this way, had I received it in a timely manner." He pulled a missive out of a top drawer of the desk, and unfolded it now. "It shows a date of five January, and states that you will arrive at my home on the twenty-fourth of February, if I have no objection, and will be in residence."

He looked up at the younger man. "The thing is, you see, I did not receive this letter until the day you arrived." He set it down again.

Mr. O'Brien looked thunderstruck. "What!" He shook his head. "I do not understand! The Colonel assured me he'd written to you last month! I tried to reason him into a different recommendation, sir, of anywhere and anyone else —"

Again the little smile. "I imagine you did," he said.

"He insisted I come for the interview, however, so, you see, I had no wherewithal except to appear. He would never agree to recommend me to someone else if I hadn't, and I am quite sure I shall need another recommendation, as you know only too well." His voice was growing quieter and more defeated by the second.

"So we, neither of us, wished to have this interview, and yet here we are." Mr. Mornay took the letter and placed it back in the drawer from which he had taken it.

Mr. O'Brien began to stand up. "I can be packed and on my way as soon as I can hire a post chaise, sir." He met his eyes. "I shall return to London, and we both may try to forget this happened." He paused, standing now. "If I might be so bold, however, as to ask that you will indeed tell the Colonel I did my part in coming —"

Mr. Mornay was watching him, looking almost amused. "Don't be in such a deuced hurry, O'Brien. My wife has asked you to be our guest, and as such, I cannot have you dashing off in a hired post chaise. As for the benefice," and here he met his eyes

159

head on, "I am afraid I cannot present it to you." There was an empty pause, a hollow moment for Mr. O'Brien, though it was just as he expected; but then Mr. Mornay went on, "but I have just received word that our neighbouring parish is in desperate need of a curate; Warwickdon. A very ample situation, vicarage, a hundred-and-fifty-acre glebe; it ought to suit you, and I know," he added, picking up a pencil and playing with it in one hand, "that it will provide a decent salary. There is no question but that it is far superior to your situation at St. Pancras."

Mr. O'Brien's brows went up while he heard this, and his mouth might just as well have dropped open in utter surprise, for that was how he felt. "Warwickdon! The very Warwickdon I passed through on my journey here? With the Gothic-style church that is visible from the road?"

A steady clear-eyed gaze met his. Only someone as familiar with the Paragon as his wife would know that he was suppressing a smile. "The very one, sir."

Meanwhile, Mr. Barton had come to make his second call upon the Mornays, and had his sister in tow. Miss Barton was decidedly not feeling her best, but he had insisted she come to meet the other women. Their hopes

160

of making her acquaintance had been too plain for him to ignore, and he wanted to do everything in his power to cement good relations between himself and the Mornays — while he could.

Anne was received warmly, and soon they were all lounging about the drawing room, where Mrs. Royleforst was playing with Nigel, and Mrs. Forsythe held the baby. Anne could not help herself — she had to go and sit beside the lady to see the infant. She had never cared for an infant in her life. After admiring Miranda for some minutes, Miss Barton gasped with pleasure when Mrs. Forsythe offered to let her hold the child. She looked to Ariana, who was watching, and said, "Oh, thank you!" when she smiled her assent.

Mr. O'Brien had not yet returned from the meeting with Mr. Mornay, and seeing an opportunity, Mr. Barton invited Beatrice to a game of piquet. They sat at a small card table on one side of the room, and Mr. Barton produced a set of playing cards from a pocket.

"You have cards upon you?" she asked, rather shocked.

He saw that it had been a mistake to have them, but he answered, "I was hoping to suggest a game with you today. I merely wished to come prepared."

She smiled. "I see." Glancing at the cards, she said, "May I?"

He handed her the deck, and she quickly started pulling out any card below sixes.

"You know," she said, while she shuffled the remaining thirty-six cards, "I have read that this is a popular game at men's clubs."

"And so it is," he answered, surprised that she would mention that.

"Do you enjoy gaming, sir?" She did not meet his eyes, and Mr. Barton had to smile to himself. Miss Forsythe was supremely easy to read; she wished to know if he gamed habitually. Easy to answer to her satisfaction. "Not at all, Miss Forsythe! It is a hazardous occupation, as you must know."

"Indeed, I do," she said, with a relieved smile. Mr. Barton relaxed in his chair, while she dealt out the hand. This was going to be an amusing diversion. He chanced to look up and saw that Anne had been listening to their talk, however, and she wore a look on her face that told him she knew he had purposely lied to Miss Forsythe. Her brother, in her opinion, was addicted to much gaming. He merely narrowed his eyes at her, and then yawned. Anne returned her attention to the baby in her arms.

Mr. Barton was happy to be occupied in

such a fashion that he did not have to give any of *his* attention to a child. He'd shrewdly caught on quickly that the Mornay children were welcome into the midst of the adult gatherings whenever Mrs. Perler or their parents seemed to feel it beneficial for them. If Nigel scraped an elbow, he was brought to his mother. If Miranda was unusually fussy, to Mama she must be brought. The Mornays never murmured a complaint at this practice, though Mr. Barton frowned upon it. He was wise enough to keep his sentiments to himself. The Mornays were not fashionable in their treatment of the children. Most upper-class houses acted as though youngsters were nonentities when guests were about. In London, one could almost come to believe that no one had any children. No one of the fashionable world, that is, and at least not small children. They were never in sight, never heard from, never spoken of. With the Mornays, it was an entirely different thing. The children must be considered in every decision.

It was an irritation he would live with. But he started thinking of how to broach the subject of the prince's wishes to Mornay. His safest course was to wait for a good moment and slip it into a conversation that could support it. But how long until that

happened? Anne was still as slim as a rail —
but her very thinness meant that her condition would likely show up all the more
starkly. He had best stop pussyfooting
around and get to the point. Soon.

Mr. O'Brien was still agog with his sudden
good fortune — such a blessing! "Is there
no curate in line, then?" he asked his host.
"Have no arrangements yet been made?"
He was as eager as a young cub, and his
words were spilling out faster as a result.

"I have been applied to," Mr. Mornay
said, "to give them the man to fill the
vacancy. I am happy to offer them you — if
you wish."

"If I wish?" He looked up at his host; the
man he had feared was his enemy, but who
now seemed to be doing him a favour.
"When's the last time you stopped at St.
Pancras's parish, sir?"

Mr. Mornay smiled. "I thought so." He
reached for a piece of paper. "I'll write your
recommendation this very moment, and
perhaps we can even squeeze in a visit to
the place this very day so that you can see
it. Mr. Hargrove — he is the incumbent —
cannot be off soon enough. He is above
anxious to take up his new living as soon as
possible."

He quickly penned the letter, and assured the magistrate that he could send a man that very day, whom Mr. Hargrove could interview personally for the vacancy.

"Where is Mr. Hargrove off to, do you know, sir?"

"Oh, somewhere in the dales, I don't recall, really. Apparently he has many relations in that area, and they are eager to welcome him. His new benefice shall supply him a surprisingly substantial income, which is good news for you, for he won't require any part or share in the glebe."

O'Brien watched while Mornay, his old nemesis, took out a crisp piece of foolscap and dipped his pen in ink. The man was behaving in the most disarming, generous manner imaginable. If he didn't know better, Mr. O'Brien would have had to admit that he was feeling downright friendly toward him. Only that couldn't be possible. Mr. Mornay had used to despise O'Brien.

"I'll suggest our visit later today, which ought to send him into raptures; he could not have imagined that we would just happen to have a curate in our midst." The little smile on his face revealed that he found the circumstance amusing. Mornay didn't look up, but spoke while he wrote. Mr. O'Brien was dazed with the unexpected benevolence.

"Later today!" he exclaimed, as one who might be dreaming. "Are you confident, sir, (I hope I may ask) that the Ordinary will approve me, then?"

Mornay glanced up only for a second. His mind was evidently on the paper before him, but he replied quickly, " 'Twas the Ordinary who asked me to see to the business. He apparently has a frightfully busy schedule as of his writing to me, and he is prepared to accept the man I choose." He laid down his pen, and while he neatly folded the missive, he looked into Mr. O'Brien's eyes.

"The magistrate of the village of Warwickdon and the Ordinary are one and the same man, you see." When he finished writing, he put down the pen and looked squarely at Mr. O'Brien. "I have one reservation which must be addressed."

Mr. O'Brien's heart skipped a beat. "Yes?"

Phillip's eyes looked hard at the young man. "I hope I can expect that your youthful infatuation for my wife has been fully resolved?"

Mr. O'Brien shut his eyes in a moment of horror, and then opened them wide. "Sir — if I only knew the words to describe to you the remorse I have suffered regarding your wife — the shame I have felt! The memory of my past behaviour is a constant reminder to me of why I must fall to my knees daily and beg God to use me as His minister! I am helpless to my own depravity, I am afraid."

Mr. Mornay was satisfied, and tried to stop him. "That will suffice," he said.

But Mr. O'Brien had not done reproving himself. "Just the thought of my . . . *infatuation* (he said the word with difficulty) — keeps me ever humble before God, sir."

Mr. Mornay's brows went up, and he was almost annoyed. "O'Brien, you needn't rake yourself over the coals! Receive God's forgiveness and be done with it, man! I only require knowing for certain that you are no longer harbouring any secret hopes of her."

"No, sir! Upon my honour! Upon my soul."

"Do not swear to me upon your soul!" He stood up, scowling. "Your soul is a business between you and God, and has nothing to do with me."

"Of course, sir, I know it." Despite his host's evident annoyance, Mr. O'Brien had to smile, for he was being encouraged in the faith by a man he least thought to find faith in.

Mr. Mornay lit the sealing candle and let a proper size blob fall upon the folded letter; he blew out the stick of wax, pressed his seal into the little blob after blowing it somewhat dry, and then stood up, signaling Mr. O'Brien to do the same.

The cleric felt awkward, but he said, "I don't know how to thank you. Your generosity to me is quite . . . quite remarkable!" Mr. Mornay listened with a peaceful silence and then nodded, but he went and rang the bellpull. He said, "I believe you have letters to write, sir."

Mr. O'Brien said, "Yes, of course!" He needed to write to the vicar of his parish, and give notice. He would send a letter to the Ordinary of St. Pancras as well; he started to say something, but took a step toward the desk, behind which his host was again seated. "I can't thank you enough, sir! I can't —"

"No need. Be off with you, then." He knew his wife would be grateful to see how happy the man was for this change in his situation, however, so he said, "You may announce your good fortune to the others."

"Yes, sir. Thank you, sir! My utmost thanks to you, sir!"

Mr. Mornay stood and turned to face his bookshelves, putting his back to the younger man, who was supposed to recognize his cue to be gone. Instead, from behind him, he continued to hear, "I shall never forget this kindness. It means a world of difference to me."

Mr. Mornay had taken a volume from his shelf, and now opened it as if to read a passage, but he looked at the young man enough to say (in a firm tone reminiscent of his old cutting replies), "Mr. O'Brien. Get yourself to the drawing room, *before I change my mind.*"

The cleric's eyes opened wide. "Yes, sir. At once." And he scrambled off.

When he joined the other guests, Mr. O'Brien's heart was lighter than it had felt for an age. He knew the warden at St. Pancras would be sorry to see him leave, but he himself could not be so. It had only been an irritation to feel so useless in the parish. When he walked in the room, Ariana chanced to look up, and she smiled. His immediate responding grin told her everything she needed to know, and she held out one hand to him, saying, "I must offer my compliments to you, sir, and my deepest congratulations!"

He bowed over her hand, and then straightened up. The room had fallen quiet at her words, so he looked around to include everyone in the happy news of his new appointment. He felt a small pang of concern when he saw that Beatrice was off to the side at a card table with Barton, alone, but he was too aloft on this cloud of his own good fortune for it to really plague him.

He noticed the presence of a new young woman, a pretty lady who was holding the baby; but the look on her face was one of deep disturbance. Mr. O'Brien, for a moment, was reminded of the faces of girls in his parish that he saw all too often; girls whose babies were the inevitable result of their working in the "skin trade." They did it to survive, but had no means to support the babies which often resulted from the business. He blinked and looked again, and recognized a sense of deep sadness afflicting the young woman — he would be curious to make her acquaintance.

Meanwhile, the others were delighted at his news. Beatrice asked, "I understood you were here to apply for Glendover's living. Was I mistaken?"

The man smiled ruefully. "No, you are correct; but Mr. Mornay has been so good as to refer me to Warwickdon, and I am much obliged to him, I assure you. I did not expect to fill the vacancy at Glendover."

"If you are content with Warwickdon, sir," said Beatrice's mother, "then we are indeed most happy for you."

"I hope you will all come to tour the vicarage with me, perhaps later today?"

"So soon?" Beatrice's mama was all surprise. "How delightful!"

Anne looked up and her face registered only concern. She was sick to her stomach almost every day lately. She was sure it was due to her "condition," and therefore did everything in her power to hide her complaints. But she did not relish the thought of the outing.

"Astonishing, is it not?" Mr. O'Brien replied to Mrs. Forsythe. "The vicar is champing at the bit to be off, and he will welcome me just as soon as I can make the proper arrangements. I shall ask to borrow pen and paper from the Mornays and send my resignation to St. Pancras's directly."

"Miss Barton," said Ariana, realizing belatedly that an introduction had yet to be made: "May I have the honour of presenting Mr. O'Brien to you? He is to be the new curate, as you have just learned, of our neighbour village of Warwickdon."

"How do you do, sir?" When she spoke, every vestige of sadness or trouble fled from her expression, and Mr. O'Brien thought he must have been mistaken. She smiled calmly and then properly averted her eyes to the baby on her lap.

"Mr. O'Brien, I present Miss Barton, the sister of Mr. Barton."

"Miss Barton; I am honoured," he said, with a light bow. She nodded shyly, and that was all. But again Mr. O'Brien felt sure they had a troubled young woman in their midst. Unfortunate as it was, he knew the look.

With that done, there were little pockets of chatter regarding when they would know if the tour was to occur this day or not. Ariana was happy when her husband returned to the room, and eager to know of any news. First, of course, he had to greet his exuberant son, who had run to him with a shout of, "Papa! Papa!" He held him easily in one arm, ignoring the hands that were touching his face and neckcloth as though they were curiosities in themselves, and told his wife, "We should hear shortly from Mr. Hargrove, as I've sent a good rider." He took a seat in a chair off to one side of the room, just as Mrs. Perler arrived to take her charges to the nursery.

Ariana accompanied her to feed the baby with privacy; Miss Barton had given Miranda up with a word of thanks for the pleasure of holding her, and a sigh, which amused the mama. "You are fond of children, Miss Barton." She waited to hear the response.

"I hope so, Mrs. Mornay."

Mr. O'Brien did not blink, but he heard her response and mulled it over with interest.

On the way upstairs, Ariana, too, was musing upon the very pretty sister of Mr. Barton. She was quiet and reserved, in the way of one who had known sorrow. Mr. Barton was far more gregarious and good-natured, but there was an air of thoughtfulness in Miss Barton's silence that made Ariana feel nothing but warmly toward her. She hoped, given time, that she would be trusted with the secrets of the lady, and that they would become very good friends, indeed.

Back in the drawing room, Mr. Barton asked amiably if there was anything of interest in *The Chronicle,* which was open before Mr. Mornay, upon his lap.

After a pause, Mr. Mornay said, "There is an outbreak of the influenza," he said, "which appears to have originated in the metropolis, but is slowly spreading to outlying areas."

"I heard something of that before we left Town," said Mr. Barton. "It is chiefly among the poor, who do not know enough of sanitary practices to keep their homes healthful."

"It may be that, in part," said Mr. O'Brien, "but the problem is greatly compounded by the lack of good physicians."

Beatrice found these remarks very interesting as they concerned London, and she was all ears.

"Is there a shortage of physicians, sir?" asked Mrs. Forsythe.

Mr. O'Brien answered before Mr. Barton could. "There is no shortage, ma'am, there is merely a lack of men who are brave enough to enter the lanes and tenements where the illness is rampant."

"Bad show, O'Brien!" exclaimed Mr. Barton. "Many a doctor has ventured into those noxious areas and ended up dead for his trouble, that's what. We can't have every last physician in London giving themselves up for the sake of the poor."

"And what if they were rich, sir?" he asked. "Could you spare your physicians for the sake of the rich if they were the ones affected?"

Mr. Barton stopped and smiled a little, as if he realized he'd said the wrong thing, but then he rallied. "I daresay, there would be far less fear surrounding the issue, and many more doctors willing to treat people if they were; for the rich do not suffer themselves to be surrounded by the very sources of putrid and noxious vapors that make them ill, as the poor do."

"As the poor *must,* you mean, sir," the curate said. "They have nowhere else to go, nor do they have the means to clean up these filthy tenements that harbour illness." He paused and added, "In addition to which, physicians can catch sickness from attending the rich as well as the poor; and if the lower classes had the means for better quarters, they would take them; if they had the education to know their mistakes, they could live healthier lives."

"Education," said Mr. Barton, "for those who begin their day with gin and end it likewise?"

"There are some who drown their life in gin, to be sure," agreed the cleric, "but you cannot think they represent the greatest mass of poor people who dwell in London!"

"I daresay, I do think so," said Mr. Barton, who was warming to his subject. "I have seen an innumerable number of them — men, women, and children, alike — who not only drink gin, but beg for it, steal for it, and would die for it, I've no doubt. Women and children, sir!"

Beatrice was watching and listening with a concerned expression. Her liking of Mr. Barton made her partial to his arguments, but she could not deny the sense of, nor the ring of truth to, everything Mr. O'Brien countered with. It troubled her.

"Mr. Barton," said Mrs. Royleforst, who had been near dozing, but wakened to his loud tone, "your subject is not fitting for the drawing room, sir!" She looked to her nephew as if he, too, was to blame.

"I merely mentioned a news item," Mornay said innocently, though he had to grin.

"Well, read us some more, then!" she demanded.

He eyed her with a sanguine expression, and then turned to the paper, which he had allowed to drop to his lap while listening to the gentlemen debate. "I quote," he said, looking to his aunt as though she might challenge him. "From *The London Medical Repository.* 'Fevers are still prevalent . . . Relapses have been noticed as of frequent occurrence in the instances of the late epidemic.' "

"Epidemic?" asked Mr. O'Brien. "It must have spread very rapidly. I heard nothing of an epidemic before I left my parish, though I did call upon a few families with the fever, and heard of others."

"But you did not fall ill yourself, sir?" asked Beatrice.

"I never did, no. I have called upon the

sick numerous times; it is one of my chief occupations, I'm afraid." His eyes flicked upon Miss Barton, who still listened with interest. "But I gave no thought to opening myself to harm, and I never did succumb to an illness, even in cases where the sufferer later passed on." He paused; Mrs. Royleforst leveled a reproving glare at him for continuing what, to her mind, was conversation best fit for the tavern.

"I suppose it was God's grace," he said. "It is part and parcel of my calling to visit the sick and counsel the distraught." He looked at Anne, and she froze, seeing his look. She had to turn her head away, but his attention at that particular moment was very distressing to her. *What did he know? And how could he have known it?* His eyes were gentle and not reproving, but she felt suddenly exposed, and was distressed, indeed.

Mr. O'Brien looked at Mr. Mornay. "What are the symptoms of the fever in this case?" he asked. "Does it say?"

Mr. Mornay instantly read, "Besides febrile symptoms, there are pains in the legs and back, aching of the bones, and soreness of the flesh, as if the patients had been beaten." He paused and continued, "During the most formidable symptoms, the patient falls into a state of stupor, delirium, or coma, and, in the absence of an extreme perspiration, does not recover."

"Such a morbid discussion!" said Mrs. Royleforst.

"Indeed!" cried Miss Bluford.

"But it must be wise to stay abreast of these things, ma'am," offered Beatrice. She was not enjoying the topic, but she did feel it was a precaution to be aware of such things.

"Overstated nonsense," said Mr. Barton. "I tell you, we've just come from London, and we neither saw nor heard a thing of this! Were you to go there today, you would see or hear nothing of it, I assure you."

"Is that not a shame?" asked Miss Barton quietly, who had applied herself to behaving as normally as possible. She picked up her embroidery canvas and calmly made a stitch. But then she paused. "Is it not a shame that there should be an epidemic in the poorer sections of the city, and yet others should know nothing of it?"

"The rich are always insulated from the poor," said Mrs. Royleforst.

Miss Bluford added, "Indeed!" nodding her head vigorously.

"Insulate them too well," murmured Mr. Mornay, "and you get a revolution. Witness the French."

Mr. Barton crossed his arms, and his countenance was armed, though he said nothing.

"There has been discussion before the House," said Mr. O'Brien. "The doctors are hitting heads on how to treat the fevers, whether by bleeding, as in the previous century, or by cordial and similar supports. It's been a *hot* topic," he added, cracking a rare joke.

"And what has been determined?" asked Mrs. Royleforst. "Concerning the treatment? Which is most effective?"

"Well," he said, "half the physicians treat their patients by trying to force the crisis, keeping them blanketed and in airless rooms; while others swear they see the most recoveries where they have done quite the opposite: opening windows, even moving the sick person out of doors if necessary, for brief periods of airing."

"Sounds like an old rug being cleaned," Mrs. Forsythe remarked, offhandedly.

"That's all very well in the warmer months, I should think," said Beatrice, "but you cannot mean that exposing the ill to cold wind and weather can help them?"

Mr. O'Brien shrugged. "Many of the worst epidemics occur in the places that are most closed up, which, unfortunately, tends to be the houses of the poor," he said.

At that moment Ariana came back into the room, and she immediately felt there was something afoot. "Well!" she said airily. "What have I missed? Are we to see the vicarage?" She paused to smile at her husband, and then went toward him, giving him a kiss on the cheek. She had not yet had a chance to thank him for Mr. O'Brien's new situation. "You were so right, my love," she whispered to him, leaning down to speak into his ear. "Our curate is delighted with his lot. I thank you for that."

Beatrice could have blushed, and looked around apprehensively to see if anyone was scandalized by the public display of affection between the pair, but the others in the room seemed to accept it as being just the sort of thing one must expect from the Mornays.

TEN

Mr. Hargrove received the letter from Aspindon House with great joy. He motioned for the servant to wait, and hurried into his study to pen a reply.

"Mrs. Persimmon!" he called excitedly. A lady quickly appeared from the kitchen, still removing her apron. She was both housekeeper and cook for the establishment, a thing which would strike any Londoner as an odd coexistence; but for country cottages, doubling up on duties was not at all unusual. There was also a single manservant, dressed in worn ivory-colored breeches and a waistcoat and jacket, who accepted the apron with a nod, and went to return it to its place.

Mrs. Persimmon wore a white cap, from which some thick graying curls peeked out. She was of a matronly age, perhaps fifty, and had been pretty in her youth, one could tell. She had large, light eyes and an expression that seemed to be always just upon the point of saying something, or expecting a request. She was eager to please.

"Mrs. Persimmon!" the man exclaimed again upon her appearance. "Can you conceive of it? Mr. Mornay has a curate to send to me directly!" (He rolled the "r" in the word as if to emphasize the astonishing immediacy of the fact.)

"Directly, sir?" she asked, amazed, but with a dawning worry upon her heart. "How directly?"

"He comes to see the vicarage this very day!" The man was practically whistling with excitement, but Mrs. Persimmon cried, "Mercy me! This very day! And the house in such a disorder!"

The vicar's expression sobered. "Mrs. Persimmon," he said more sternly. "It is only to be expected that I must be about my packing. It will not signify, I assure you."

"Yes, sir," she said at once, turning to go. "Shall I prepare some refreshments for you and your guest, sir?"

"Yes, do, refreshments, of course. Very good, Mrs. Persimmon."

Mr. Hargrove wrote out his response for the owner of Aspindon House, and gave it to the messenger, who took off with it apace. The vicar then continued pulling pieces of paper from his drawer. He had more writing to do, and he had best get it done. He had letters to pen for the leading families of the area, as a courtesy. One for the magistrate, even though Mr. Mornay had mentioned notifying him as well. One for the bishop; a copy for the warden; one for his relations in the north. He hoped that after meeting the new man today he might even be able to supply them with a possible date for his installation as their new vicar.

His blood seemed to surge in his veins while he wrote; ah, there was nothing like good fortune to make a man feel young. He had long anticipated this event, and now that it was upon him, it felt too good to be true. He hoped that this Peter O'Brien would be willing to step into his shoes as quickly as possible. Sunday next would not be too soon for him! (His congregation, he knew, would be unhappy that he was leaving during Lent; but what could he do? His new congregation expressly wished to have him for the Day of Resurrection, and here the Lord seemed to have provided his way of escape from Warwickdon. It was out of his hands.)

Anne Barton excused herself and went in search of a place of privacy — unfortunately the only room that came to mind was the privy, but she knew that even in a great house like Aspindon, the slightest unsavoury odor would empty her stomach of its contents at once.

She really had not felt up to being in society today, and she was angry that she had allowed Tristan to bully her into it. Thing was, she had not been feeling well for three weeks now. She hid her condition from Tristan as much as possible. He did not know, for instance, that following every meal, Anne had to give it up into a chamber pot.

She tried to hide her growing thinness with a good deal of shawls, and wore her robe over her morning gowns at home every day now. Her brother was like a thorn in her side; his disgust of her was sufficiently daunting that she had to make sure she gave him no further reasons to disregard her even more. He would be repelled if he knew how sick she really was.

A footman in the corridor caught her eye, and so she stopped and asked, "What room is this, if you please?" She nodded toward a door which he seemed to be standing guard before.

"The library, mum."

"Oh, excellent," she said, a little weakly.

She was not going to make it much farther. He opened the door for her, and she went into a beautiful, cozy room, warmly wainscoted and with an abundance of wall shelves. There was no fire, and it was cold in the room, but she looked around hurriedly for a vessel; anything that could suffice. Spying a small coal scuttle, she picked it up like treasure. It would have to do.

Six minutes later, her composure regained, Miss Barton exited the library and headed back toward the drawing room. A maid had been about to enter, evidently prepared to start a fire for her.

"Oh, that won't be necessary," she said.

She hoped the girl would not notice that someone had been sick and then dumped the evidence in the grate. She had seen no other place to discard it. She sniffed, and went her way.

Mr. O'Brien waited only long enough for the slight young woman to go some distance from the library before turning the handle quietly and slipping into the room. What had she been doing? He had a suspicion, and needed to know. He looked around for a likely object and spied the very same vessel Miss Barton had seen. In less than a minute he had deduced what he needed to know, and left the library with a thoughtful look upon his face.

The guests were excited to see Warwickdon. Despite a deep winter chill in the air, the sky was blue and inviting; the sun high in the sky. Since Mr. Hargrove was happy to open his home upon so short a notice, they would all get to take a tour of the vicarage.

Phillip opted to use an open barouche; it was rarely used during the winter, but the bright clear sky and sun, the lack of snow or ice on the roads, together with the fact that Ariana usually preferred it to a closed carriage, made him willing to do so. He was always happy to please her, and she considered that the tenants delighted so much in spying the couple if they rode in it, that it was worth a little discomfort of cold to lift their spirits. Finally, the occupants of the barouche were able to see a great deal more of the country as opposed to those in closed carriages, so the vehicle was quickly wiped down and brought forth.

Ariana wore a walking-out dress of striped yellow cambric; her sleeves were gathered above the elbow, and again at the forearm, and there were pretty, laced cuffs. There was also lace at the bodice, a matching striped silk ribbon belt, a contrasting ribbon train, and over this she wore a velvety brown spencer, and then a redingote. She had a fine woolen shawl and a yellow silk bonnet adorned with flowers to complete her outfit, along with half-boots, a muff, and a lorgnette. (A little magnification could be handy when surveying the countryside.)

Ariana, her husband, and Beatrice sat across from Miss Barton, Mr. Barton, and Mr. O'Brien. Mrs. Forsythe, Aunt Royleforst, and Miss Bluford had opted for the closed carriage.

"Beatrice, I meant to tell you," Ariana said, looking across her husband, "that gown is lovely on you!" Beatrice thanked her, but blushed faintly; she hoped no one else of the company knew, as did she and Ariana, that it had been given her by Ariana the day before. Phillip eyed her now, and of course he knew, and his eyes revealed that he knew, but he said nothing. The walking-out gown was of printed cambric, in lilac and yellow, but Beatrice's pelisse was lined and sturdy, with a raised neck that offered further protection from wintry winds. Her bonnet included a bow-tied cap, an extra layer that did much to keep one warm. Like her sister, she also sported half-boots and a muff, as did Miss Barton.

Ariana's arm was entwined with her husband's, and she snuggled into him as the carriage picked up speed. She was already enjoying this outing with Phillip beside her. Besides keeping busy with the estate, he served as magistrate for the parish and sometimes sat for hours on end, though he always tried to make quick work of any matter brought to him. He was surprised to discover that he enjoyed seeing justice served too. Every now and then he had to sentence a criminal to Newgate, or worse, recommend hanging. But he avoided doing so whenever possible.

Ariana's gaze wandered to the occupants sitting across from her. If only she could ascertain whether there was an interest on the part of Mr. O'Brien for her sister, or vice versa, she might have reason to ask one last time about granting the living to the cleric. She had seen him leave the drawing room shortly upon the heels of Miss Barton, however, and reflected that he might prefer the pretty, quiet young woman of a serious nature, to the outspoken, pleasure loving sister of hers. She sighed.

And now he had Warwickdon and would be in mind of starting a family, no doubt. She had seen the place once before, when Phillip had brought her to meet Mr. Hargrove. It was an ample and respectable house. Of course, less superior than Glendover, the parsonage of their parish; for, unlike many she had seen, Glendover was designed to hold a large family. The people who had planned and erected the building had evidently understood that clergymen liked to raise families as much as anyone, which ought to have been standard for parsonages, but wasn't. It stood three stories tall, in the dignified Georgian manner; windows aplenty, and was kept up well by the warden, in the absence of an occupant.

Ariana could envision her sister happily living there. Her mother, father, and Lucy could take a nearby house, and the whole family saving the Norledges (her sister Alberta and Johnathan Norledge, who owned a large property in Chesterton) would be closely situated again! How comfortable it would be!

As Mr. O'Brien and Mr. Barton kept up a small conversation, Ariana reflected on having the curate back in her circle of acquaintance. How surprising life was! She had not thought to have laid eyes on Mr. O'Brien for many a year. She felt certain already, despite how short an acquaintance they had had thus far, that he had improved in his character — he was no longer the impetuous boy who had taken advantage of Ariana to steal a kiss. He was a man now. And his polite aloofness was just the way he had ought to treat a married lady, she thought.

He was not bad looking, either. She studied him from her spot across the barouche; his hair, which was no longer light blond, was still wavy, for little wisps around his ears could be seen below the hat; his style of cravat seemed to have improved, which she could see above the deep cut of his coat. Mr. O'Brien had thick, light brows and a face that seemed to be perpetually sporting the stubble of a day's growth. It actually added to his allure, whereas even Phillip could look rather sinister without a fresh shave every morning. She wondered if the man simply lacked the right shaving tool. Even his short stubble, however, was golden brown, and could not hide a strong, wide chin. He had a decisive forehead, it seemed to her now too.

Suddenly Ariana felt her husband's eyes upon her and his voice whispering in her ear. "Enjoying the scenery, or is it just our curate that fascinates you so?" He didn't sound irked, merely amused.

She turned to him, bright-eyed. With care not to speak loudly, she said, "I am just imagining."

He gave his little smile. "Regarding . . . ?"

"The match," she whispered. "How convenient if we should not have to search for a husband for Beatrice when we are in London! And then they would be our neighbours!"

"You are still setting your hopes upon it."

Still keeping her voice carefully low, Ariana said, "Perhaps I am inclined to, due to my own happiness. My experience of having a husband is so pleasant I can do naught but wish that women everywhere were married as I am. Husbands are a wonderful breed," she added, smiling at him. His eyes sparkled at her, but before he could say anything, Mr. Barton, who had been watching the pair with an unreadable expression, said, "I think we should have given the barouche to the Mornays alone; they are determined to speak only to each other."

"Actually," returned Mr. Mornay, "we were speaking of marriage. Is that a subject you take an interest in, sir?"

Mr. Barton smiled, as though he were up for a game. "I daresay every gentleman must take an interest in it sooner or later —"

Mr. Mornay did not let him off that easily. "And is your interest sooner, or later?"

Barton smiled again, while the others listened, Beatrice feeling her toes begin to curl. He finally said, "I can have no serious interest in marriage, sir, until I have a seri-

191

ous interest in a young lady with whom I may hope to share that estate, do you not agree?" He kept his eyes steadily upon his host, did not so much as glance at Beatrice, but she was already blushing lightly. Ariana saw his careful avoidance of her sister, and felt a small alarm. That kind of care was not without purpose; he did, then, entertain hopes of her!

Ariana did not dislike the man, but she felt a caution regarding him in her spirit, and would need to know more of him before willingly allowing him an interest in Beatrice.

Mr. O'Brien said (mercifully, in Beatrice's opinion, for somehow his remarks were more general), "Without a young woman in particular, you may still have an interest in your future marriage; you must know whether or not you intend to marry, and whether it will be for pleasure, er, rather, love, let us say, or duty."

"Is not marriage something to enter chiefly for duty?" asked Beatrice, who did not consider herself to be of a romantic nature at all. But she smiled, adding, "That is what my mama says."

"My mother could never say such a thing," returned Ariana, sitting forward to look curiously at her younger sister, "for I am sure she would be the first woman to protest that one must marry for love, not duty alone."

Barton volunteered, "Chiefly for duty, indeed; do we not see it done all the time? More young women and first sons are sacrificed to 'duty' than should be allowable in any society."

"So you do think some sacrifices should be allowable?" Mr. Mornay could not help it, and had to plague the man. "But not so many."

"There are times when the preservation of one's house or estate or even one's title, depends upon the sacrifice of a son or daughter's preferences in marriage. Would you not agree?"

"Royals must marry for duty," murmured Ariana. "It is a price they pay for that station. And I pity them for it."

"And those who have large properties and must have an heir," added her husband.

Mr. Barton immediately said, "You have a large property, to be sure, sir. Did you marry for duty?"

Coming as this question did in the presence of his wife, it was felt as no less than a challenge. It might have been that Mr. Barton was trying to understand the family fortunes of the Forsythes. It might have been a deliberate attempt simply to have Mr. Mornay admit that he had not; whatever the motive, Mr. Mornay did not take kindly to the question. He was framing a cutting reply when Mr. O'Brien, surprisingly, beat him to the quick.

"Have you no eyes, sir? The Mornays share a love that every aspirant of marriage might study to their benefit. If you cannot honestly think you will adore your spouse in the manner of their example, then in my opinion, marriage should not be sought except for the most urgent of reasons."

"You mean, such as when a title might go defunct? Or there is no heir to a large estate."

"Precisely. But for the average man, his challenge is to find a good wife, to love her well, and trust his fortunes to God."

Mr. Barton attempted to chuckle. "I believe we are hearing one of your Sunday sermons, sir!"

"If so, I like it a great deal!" exclaimed Ariana.

"This is all neither here nor there," put in Beatrice, in a tone that was rather irked. "The thing of it is, it is all well and good for a man to say he shall marry for love. But for a woman, it is entirely a different matter! She could love herself out of an advantageous situation, and straight into poverty or ruin —"

Here Miss Barton, who had been inconspicuously silent heretofore, was overcome by a sudden coughing fit, and everyone paused to ascertain her condition. When she had sufficiently recovered herself Beatrice continued, "As I daresay many a woman has, and shall continue to do; for a woman is subject to her emotions, to a much greater degree, I might add, than men seem to be."

"I cannot abide with that," said Ariana. "Men have feelings every bit as strong as a woman's!"

"But they temper their actions and behavior based upon their *reason,* more than their feelings; whereas we women, though we know it might be our ruin, will love a man whether he be right for us, or not." Beatrice added quickly, "*Most* women, that is. I fancy myself too levelheaded to make that mistake."

Miss Barton raised an agonized pair of eyes to Beatrice's, which only her brother — and Mr. O'Brien's sharp eyes — seemed cognizant of. Miss Barton felt as though Beatrice was pouring vinegar into her every wound. She began to feel ill.

Mr. Barton tried to move the discussion forward. "A man may temper his actions

195

based on reason, as you say, but he may still be subject to being snared by the wrong woman, just as a woman is subject to placing her heart on the wrong man."

"Snared by his heart, or his actions, sir?"

"Does it matter?" he returned. "A man must be as cautious in love as a woman, which is my point."

"On the other hand," added Mr. O'Brien, "women must sometimes marry for duty, as much as a man. They are quite often charged with saving the family from ruin or starvation by making a good match. Is this not so?"

Miss Barton wrapped her arms about her middle; Ariana did not know whether she suffered from the cold, or had some other ailment. She would ask her about it afterward.

"In either case," the cleric continued, "whether for duty or love or honour, any two people, I am convinced, can learn to love one another; or failing a spontaneous, deep love, may grow into a steady and mature sort of love. The kind that is required of us as Christians, at least. It is my firm belief that no marriage is doomed to fail without the consent of the parties in it."

"Those are strong words," said Mr. Barton, wonderingly. He was of the mind that saw marriage primarily as a union of convenience, to have children, perhaps; but certainly not as a thing to devote oneself to.

"Think of it," said Mr. O'Brien, very much warmed to the subject, "at the very heart of marriage is the means of survival, the continuance of our race. Regardless of our emotions upon entering into that estate, the end result is that families are born, and mankind continues."

"Which is precisely why both men and women must at times marry for duty," said Mr. Barton.

"And disregard love," added Miss Barton, surprisingly.

"Miss Barton," said Mr. Mornay. "Are you unwell?" For his keen eyes had not missed her growing discomfort and unease.

"My sister is fine," put in her brother quickly — a little too quickly, so that everyone else could not miss his excessive interest in Anne's state. "The outdoor air is always difficult for her." To Anne he added, "I daresay, you should have worn one of your veils. It might have afforded you sufficient protection."

"Oh, veils are nothing!" said Ariana. But she removed her shawl and passed it to Miss Barton. "Here. The air is cold. Cover your face to the eyes; and when we return, take the closed carriage with my mother and aunt." Miss Barton tried to smile; Mrs. Mornay was indeed very kind. "I thank you," she said, doing as she was bade. She eyed her brother with resentment, however, as she did so.

They had arrived at Warwickdon. The scenery had been little noticed or remarked upon, as the topic of marriage had taken everyone's attention. Ariana was sure that Mr. Barton's ideas could only be injurious to any woman he might take as his wife; but how to say so to her sister without raising her ire? She might inadvertently push the girl into his arms by outright opposition to him. She would speak to Phillip about it; he always knew how to proceed in tricky matters.

ELEVEN

When they alighted from the carriage and stood admiring the vicarage from the road, Miss Barton said, "A capital dwelling, sir," in her quiet voice. She was making an attempt to come out of her brown study, as Mr. Mornay's inquiry had alarmed her. She had to be discreet!

Mr. O'Brien thanked her kindly.

"It is a charming little house," said Beatrice.

"Little!" laughed Ariana. Warwickdon was not as large as the parsonage at Glendover but it was not little. The house was a picturesque dwelling of two stories, not counting the basement and garret. "How can you say so?"

"It is fine, I grant, for a vicarage, for a parson's family," returned Beatrice, as though Mr. O'Brien was not in hearing range, "but after staying at Aspindon House, you can hardly expect me to find it commodious."

"One does not compare a vicarage with an estate!" Ariana said.

Beatrice shrugged. "I just have," and she smiled mischievously at her sister. But Ariana's face creased with worry. That girl! Why were her sights set so high?

To make matters worse, Beatrice turned around to face her, still walking forward (which in this case, meant backward, now), "I daresay I know your thoughts. Where does a country girl develop such thoughts? But I warrant you," she announced, with an earnest gaze, "that where there is sufficient character, and manners, and good connexions, a personal lack of wealth is not at all the obstacle to an advantageous match that many think."

Beatrice actually hoped that she had made herself known to Mr. O'Brien with those words. Now he would never think to raise the issue of her old absurd promise. Further, she would not have to concern herself with any worries about misleading him.

Ariana was shocked that Beatrice had shown her hand so completely and openly. She had as much as declared that she was hoping to wed a rich man, based upon her charms or "connexions." Despite any amount of talk to the ideals of marrying for love, every person in the party knew that this young woman, for one, was no idealist. Not in that sense, at any rate.

Mr. Barton looked appreciatively at Beatrice. His mouth was formed in a small smile while he considered her words. She was bold indeed, but now he understood perfectly her situation. He'd been right in thinking that she had little in the way of money, but much in the way of connexions. And Beatrice herself was aware that marriages might be based upon those things. She even approved it! He was beginning to think that he and Miss Forsythe would actually make more than a match of convenience, as he at first thought. They might even be suited to one another in temperaments. They seemed to think along similar lines. They both looked at life and marriage as matters of supreme practicality, not with overly romantic notions of "love."

Mr. O'Brien had bent his head in thought and now offered a response, aimed only at Beatrice, though the others could hear. "I am sure you are right in some cases; only do keep in mind that a strong character is necessary to enjoy the privileges and advantages that such a marriage may provide. Unless we wish to become dull of heart, or close our eyes to those less fortunate, we must maintain a good conscience before God in all that we do, whether it be choosing our friends . . ." and he hesitated here, "or our spouse."

Beatrice was listening without looking at him. "Spoken just like a good curate, sir," she said, in a tone that was mildly dismissive.

Ariana glanced at her husband, half expecting him to offer some reproving remark to the girl, but he said nothing. *Oh, dear.* These few minutes of talk had certainly not supported Ariana's hopes of matchmaking in the least.

Suddenly Mr. Hargrove was hurrying out to greet them. He was a large-bellied man, which was evident despite the greatcoat, knee breeches, and shoes. His hat was brown, and in the style of a country parson. If he had sported a white wig and curls, Ariana would not have been surprised, but she could see, as he approached, grinning and gesturing, that his hair was gray. After a few minutes during which he bustled them into the hall of the dwelling, introductions were made and niceties said. A footman ran up from the Mornays' other carriage, with Mrs. Forsythe coming up the path to the door.

"Mrs. Royleforst wishes to inform, sir, that she is returning to the house; she is satisfied with having seen the vicarage from the coach." Mr. Mornay understood that she had not liked what had appeared to her as a property requiring a great deal of walking. He nodded. "Fine. See that the coach is returned to us; we'll need it when we leave here."

Mr. Hargrove had waited politely, smiling and nodding at the others, and now burst into a multitude of comments and questions, directing his first remark to Mr. Mornay. "I cannot say how overjoyed I was to get your correspondence, sir."

Turning to Mr. O'Brien, he peppered him with a series of utterances, not bothering to wait for a response from the gentleman.

"You will be happy here, my boy; very happy, I daresay."

"I have a thousand little things I must remember to tell you!"

"How soon, sir, can you see your way to occupying the house?"

"Can you preside for services Sunday next?"

"I will show you every foot of the place, but I think we must start on the grounds."

Mr. Mornay said, "Is that necessary? It is cold for the ladies, you understand."

He seemed struck by that thought. "Oh, yes, sir, oh, yes, indeed, we must think of the ladies, of course!" They were shown into a good sized, somewhat elegant parlour. "I will tell you about the grounds, since it is too cold," he said, while checking the grate and then hollering, "Sykes!"

A manservant appeared, to whom he said, "It is a sniveling fire, my dear man!" Sykes hurriedly attended to the fireplace, not quietly, but no one cared. Warmth was their concern. Afterward, Sykes began to collect the hats, coats, and scarves of the guests, while Mr. Hargrove pulled up a sturdy stool from near the fireplace so that he could face everyone in the room at once.

"Yes, well, let me begin, then. I am ecstatic to meet you, sir" (again, to Mr. O'Brien).

"You were going to tell us about the grounds of the property," said Mr. Mornay.

"Oh yes! The grounds, of course. You won't be disappointed, my boy; you won't be disappointed!" He spoke very fast, and no one could look away for a moment lest they miss something.

"Let me see — the grounds; we have a moderate glebe of a hundred and fifty acres, which I have planted these past ten years, sir. I have already ordered this year's seed, which I have the honour of offering to you at cost. I have no use for it in Yorkshire, as very few crops grow successfully there! (He laughed at this.) If these terms are suitable for you, sir, I will take the liberty of deducting the cost of the seed from your salary, and I daresay you should have it covered quite soon, quite soon, my boy, etcetera and company and so on."

"Sell it to him at half-price," said Mr. Mornay. "He is coming to your aid, taking over your parish with all possible speed. I think an allowance can be made for him under the circumstances."

Mr. O'Brien would usually have blanched at negotiating of any kind, but this was Mr. Mornay doing it for him. He looked to Mr. Hargrove. The vicar's face had dropped for a moment, but this *was* Mr. Mornay — he said, "If you say so, sir, he shall have it at half-price."

He went on, talking speedily: There was a dovecote, replete with doves. "You will always have the softest of mattresses and pillows, my boy, as well as meat on your table, from it. Mrs. Persimmon (she is your housekeeper and cook) is expert at dressing pigeon and doves and very skilled in the art of cleaning and using feathers, etcetera and company and so on." Everyone looked at Mr. O'Brien to see his reaction to this interesting bit of information. He was embarrassed, but saw that a reply was expected, so he said, "Very good, sir," which was sufficient so that Mr. Hargrove continued:

"You have a chicken coop with some very excellent layers, sir, the very best layers, I daresay, in this countryside; you have a dairy, sir, and a buttery; a sty (though I confess I have no pig in it at present, but you may get yourself one); you have a front garden (which is perhaps not ideally situated, I allow, since a small park would be more fetching to the eye); but I assure you there will soon be an abundance of violets and spring bulbs aplenty to colour the garden, so that your landscape will be a profusion of cheerful hues, etcetera and company and so on." (A smile.)

Mr. O'Brien was already smiling, listening to the delightful catalogue of his future property. "Sykes and Mrs. Persimmon, as both have family here, sir, and were born and raised in Warwickdon, etcetera and company, are staying with the house, and so on. And they are loyal and faithful and will serve you well; and Mrs. Persimmon, I must say, is an excellent cook, sir." He paused to collect his breath before steaming on. (A second of respite!) "You will pay their salaries for now on, o' course, but it won't break you, sir! It won't break you." He thought for a moment. "I am leaving a good deal of records of all the running of this household in my study. I won't need a bit of it where I'm going; and Mrs. Persimmon will help you find what you need, etcetera; the names of who to call in the village when your fields are ready, or your fence needs mending, and so on."

Beatrice whispered to Mr. Barton, "He forgot to say 'and company,'" to which he grinned, and she let out a giggle. Mr. Hargrove ceased talking abruptly and stared at her as if he were quite in shock.

"Was something funny?" he asked in earnest. "What was funny?" He looked around as though someone in the room must surely be able to help him at his present loss. But no one did.

Ariana and Mrs. Forsythe were both sending frowning looks at Beatrice, who felt mortified by all the eyes upon her. "What was funny?" Mr. Hargrove continued to ask, until Mrs. Forsythe said, in her kindest tone, "Please continue, sir. We are all enthralled by your vicarage."

He looked gratified, finally forgot about something being funny, and finished his speech with his eyes large in his head, staring at Mr. O'Brien. "I do believe that is all I have to tell you," he said, as though he himself were surprised. "Mrs. Persimmon will show the whole of the house to you and your guests now, sir, etcetera, and Sykes and I will have everything ready for tea at your return, company and so on."

Ariana herself had to suppress an urge to laugh, while Beatrice merely exchanged comical looks with Mr. Barton. Somehow they all managed to stifle their mirth and filed from the room, following Mrs. Persimmon, with Mr. O'Brien right behind her.

"Wait!" called Mr. Hargrove, before they had so much as got five feet from the room. He appeared in the doorway, and he looked alarmed. "Did you see the church?" he asked the group, with widened eyes.

"Only from the road, sir," said Mr. O'Brien.

"Well, well, you must needs see it, you know; very fine church; very fine." He thought for a moment. "After seeing the house, we should go there, directly. Show you where things are, etcetera." His countenance brightened as a new thought entered his head. "And then we'll all be comfortable together and take our tea, eh? Does that suit?"

Beatrice had been hoping that tea might

be served before the tour, but she said nothing. Mr. Barton caught her eye, however, and he shook his head in the negative, as if Mr. Hargrove was a dimwit. She stifled a giggle.

Mrs. Persimmon waited in the hall. *"As you can see,"* she said in a tone that was calculated to be of sufficient volume to reach the entire group in her charge, "we have a very fine old wainscoting. This house was built in 1701," she said, "and has enjoyed only four occupants." Her gaze fell upon Mr. O'Brien. "Prior to Mr. O'Brien, that is. He will be the fifth." She spoke loudly and carefully, pronouncing her words as though she was addressing a group of children.

When later they had reached the bedchambers, Mrs. Persimmon turned to them and with eyes sparkling, assured Mr. O'Brien that he would "find it is quite a large abode, indeed. Quite fit for a sizeable family." She smiled broadly. "Mr. O'Brien will be the second parson to raise a family in this house!"

Mr. O'Brien said, "I hope I may, ma'am." Ariana and her mother were smiling, while the others said nothing.

Later, Beatrice had to admit that it was a good-sized house; much roomier than their home in Chesterton. In addition to the hall and parlour, there was a hall chamber, parlour chamber, drawing room, and library; and upstairs, four separate bedchambers, as well as a maid's chamber and a room that looked to be a nursery at one time, or schoolroom; and off the kitchen, a cheese chamber. The library held four leather chairs and a great quantity of books, which Mrs. Persimmon said belonged to the house.

She pointed out every object that was staying; this settee, that set of wing chairs, a modest chandelier, and other furnishings. Even the drapery was mentioned, with the added information that Mrs. Persimmon prided herself on keeping it "spankingly clean."

"Etcetera and company and so on," murmured Mr. Barton behind Beatrice's ear. She dared not laugh aloud, but smiled and gave him a mock look of reproval.

While they all filed back downstairs, the housekeeper stopped on the staircase to say to Mr. O'Brien, "Sir, I do not wonder at your finding yourself a wife directly, and setting up housekeeping. It is all ready for you; your future wife will consider herself fortunate, indeed, I assure you."

Her eye fell upon Beatrice. "Is this young lady so fortunate as to be in way of becoming Mrs. O'Brien, may I ask?"

To Beatrice's mortification, she blushed furiously. "We are mere acquaintances, ma'am!"

Mrs. Persimmon smiled without the least bit of repentance for having been so direct. Her gaze roamed to Miss Barton, and as soon as her brow went up, Miss Barton smiled but exclaimed, "No, ma'am! We have only just met."

Looking back to the young cleric, she said, "No matter; a handsome young sprig as you are should have plenty offspring about you soon enough, I warrant!"

Ariana and Mr. Mornay exchanged amused, surprised glances. Mr. Barton muttered something about the "bald pluck" of the servant, but Miss Barton said, "She means kindly. Do hush, Tristan!"

Mr. O'Brien was amused more than embarrassed. He was in too much rapture at his good fortune to allow anything to spoil the day. He would still be a perpetual curate, but he could be called a parson, and there was a circulating church warden who saw to the care of the building. There was a part-time clerk, and now his own little house with two servants! He had to force himself not to let his heart swell.

By the time the little party had seen every

211

room, and admired it sufficiently, they were happy to sit in the drawing room to enjoy refreshments. (Mr. Mornay suggested that some warming beverages would fortify the women before returning to the cold out of doors to see the church. As ever, Mr. Hargrove was pleased to defer.) Mrs. Persimmon helped Sykes serve the guests, while Mr. Hargrove sat close by Mr. O'Brien and shared notes upon the clerical life, "etcetera and company and so on." It was a pleasant hour, except that Ariana and Mrs. Forsythe were still somewhat mortified by the behavior of Beatrice and Mr. Barton. They sat rather too close to one another, and only joined the general conversation when obliged to.

Mr. Barton, in fact, seemed intent upon one thing only: making Beatrice laugh. She was in a mood to be amused, and found whatever he did, funny. He mimicked Mr. Hargrove — she giggled. He pointed to a strange little portrait — she snickered. He feigned boredom and a long-suffering attitude — she chuckled and nodded in agreement. Beatrice was not trying to encourage him to misbehavior, but she was oppressed by the length of time they had been listening to Mr. Hargrove and Mrs. Persimmon. She was also happy to be distracted from a host of disturbing, intrusive thoughts that she disliked.

For instance, when seeing the nursery, she had thought, *What a perfect little room for a child's bed!* The vision of children upon the floor, playing with toys, came to mind. She did not welcome it. Children in that room would not be her children! The mother of the household would not be she!

Beatrice was irked that she had the feeling she ought to be paying close attention to it all, as though it must matter to her. *It doesn't matter to me!* she kept telling herself. Her antics with Mr. Barton were largely in defiance of these feelings — she would *not* be serious! She would *not* marry Mr. O'Brien!

And then, the realization that she had thought such a thought seemed so absurd to her that she had laughed out loud. *Mr. O'Brien had not offered for her* — why was she thinking such nonsense? Even Mr. Barton gazed at her in surprise, though he slowly smiled at her. No one else did, though.

Mrs. Forsythe endeavoured to catch her daughter's attention to discourage her outbursts. *Beatrice is behaving like a lackwit!* she thought. Mr. O'Brien was doing an admirable job of completely ignoring her; which was the only comfort Mrs. Forsythe could take during the whole affair.

When they had all bundled up into their outer garments, including Mr. Hargrove, who was happily directing them outdoors, they moved as a group toward the church. From this distance, they could see the spire above the horizon, rising among the trees and calling to mind the best picturesque scenes of the country that anyone could desire. Their path led them up a gentle hill, and then back down, before widening into a lane that led around to the back of the building. There was a separate path from the road, but this one was how the vicar always went to church.

He and Mr. Mornay were now in the lead, and the others came up behind, first Ariana and Mrs. Forsythe; followed by Beatrice and Mr. Barton; and then Mr. O'Brien and Miss Barton.

"This must be a lovely sight in spring," breathed Ariana, looking all around. The others concurred. Even the little cemetery coming into view was picturesque, with its odd assemblage of old stones, some at angles, which spoke of their antiquity. Beatrice saw the little winter scene and could not call it displeasing; she said nothing, however, and merely stopped when the others did, admiring the little hamlet where the church sat, and was surprised to find that she felt refreshed by the view.

They entered the actual churchyard through a lych-gate, and followed a little stone path through the lawn, which held the cemetery. Behind the cemetery was a tall privet hedge, almost as high as her head, and Beatrice hurried toward it, leaving the others, calling, "Oh, what do you think is on the other side?" Mr. Barton watched her for a moment, and then he, too, started toward the hedge. He caught up with her as she reached the wall of greenery.

"Come, Beatrice," Ariana called. "We're going inside!"

Mr. Barton said, "Shall we look for a hole in the privet?"

Beatrice wavered. He was a handsome young man, and looking deeply into her eyes. She had a near smile upon her mouth, but did not answer directly. He turned and looked back to see the progress of the others, and saw they had all gone inside the building. He started to lean his head down toward Beatrice's — to her amazement, for she hadn't a thought of being kissed — when Mrs. Forsythe, who had lingered at the door was suddenly there, calling,

"Beatrice! Come at once!"

Mr. Barton froze, and then came to his full height again, and offered her his arm, all the while looking intently into her eyes. "Shall we?" he asked.

She took his arm, but all the way to the door her heart beat with the thought that this man had very nearly kissed her! Beatrice had never been kissed by a gentleman, and it was a rather shocking thought.

Further, she had no idea if she ought not to allow a man to kiss her once; was it a sin? When they were not betrothed? She suddenly felt young, and not altogether sure of herself. Perhaps she had been flirting with Mr. Barton too much. When they reached her mother, who was giving her a look of large-eyed alarm, she moved her arm off of Mr. Barton's and entered the building. "Thank you, Mama! We were just looking to see the prospect beyond the hedge! But I do wish to see this place."

" 'Tis only a simple country church," said Mr. Barton behind her.

"I suppose you would have preferred the privet hedge?" asked Mrs. Forsythe in a rare, dry tone, seldom heard from her.

Inside the structure, they stood, blinking a minute to let their eyes adjust to the dim light.

"Look," said Mrs. Forsythe, and she pointed up at the eaves. Two small stone cherubs stared out, unseeing, at the entrance.

"Oh! What made you look up?" asked Beatrice.

Mrs. Forsythe smiled. "Even the smallest churches are often laden with little astonishing architectural details," she said. "Your papa and I have gone through many a country church looking for just such things." Ahead they could hear the vicar speaking, pointing out things he was particularly proud of, but Beatrice was content to let her own mother be her guide. Mr. O'Brien was suddenly there as well.

"Did you see the little cherubs?" he asked, his tall head only inches from the lowest one.

"We did! My mother pointed it out." He reached up and touched the foot of one of them.

"Not very smooth," he said, with a smile. Beatrice thought, *How very tall he is.* "Come, we can peer up into the tower," he said then, and she followed him. Mrs. Forsythe and Mr. Barton trailed behind them. At the bottom of the tower, he pointed up to where the bells were, way on top. "I'm glad this church has a spire, and not a 'witch hat,'" he said, flashing another smile.

Beatrice breathed a laugh. "A witch hat! Why would they call it that?"

"In the absence of an actual spire, some churches do have tops that look like witch hats," he said, "though you can't tell from inside."

She gazed upward. The heavy ropes for the ringing of the bells disappeared into the darkness of the cavernous large bells above.

"I should like to hear the bells," she said, looking up at the large, silent forms.

"I hope you may." Their eyes met. His were earnest and quite blue, even in the dim light. He pointed out the steps which would twist and turn all the way to the top of the tower.

"I shan't be climbing those today," she said, in case he was considering it, but he only said, "No, in warmer weather, perhaps."

They turned back to the direction of the nave where the rest of the party, save Mrs. Forsythe and Mr. Barton, had gone. The others looked up at the bells, and continued to follow behind Beatrice and Mr. O'Brien.

While they were still in the porch, Beatrice asked, "What is this?" She was looking at an old plaque of tarnished brass or some such metal that was engraved, but she could not quite make out the inscription. Mr. O'Brien produced some tinder and a box, and he soon had lit a wall sconce which helped.

"It's a list," she said. "But who are they?"

Mr. O'Brien came and peered at it. "They are the past vicars or rectors, I believe."

"Shall your name be added to this list?" she asked, excitedly.

He smiled. "I don't know."

They looked again with the same thought at the same time: to see if the name of Mr. Hargrove was on it. Their heads were practically touching, and Beatrice said, "I do not see it. He isn't here."

"I'm afraid not" he agreed.

She turned and his face was right beside hers. Startled, she nevertheless noted afresh that Mr. O'Brien had undeniably beautiful eyes. There was something so benevolent in them; unreproachful, though she knew she deserved to feel his reproach, for she had done nothing but undercut the pride he must have felt at his new house. All of her big talk about making a rich match — why had she felt the need to put him in his place?

Once again their eyes met, and Beatrice turned away.

TWELVE

Now Mrs. Forsythe had come up behind them, and saw their proximity to one another, and she did a remarkable thing. She put her hand firmly upon Mr. Barton's arm (he too saw the pair standing tantalizingly close to one another) and said, "Sir, I desire you take me to the rest of the party."

He hesitated; he looked at the couple; he looked at Mrs. Forsythe; she was staring at him, waiting. He looked at the couple again.

"Sir, if you *please!*" she said, in an urgent whisper. It was a strident tone coming from this gentle lady. With a breath of resignation, Mr. Barton led her forth, out of the porch, and into the long nave.

"What is this?" asked Beatrice. She had seen such things before, a large stone in the floor with a design of some sort, or writing worn beyond recognition, and never thought to ask about them. This one was hexagonal and stood out in stark contrast to the brick shaped stones around it.

"It's called a memorial stone," Mr. O'Brien said. "Someone of wealth or high standing pays to have it here, usually to remember a loved one." He searched around the floor. "Look, here are more of them." When he looked up again, his eyes were alight. "I say, this building is a delight!"

Beatrice came and admired the other memorial stones, noting how they were each different, and what their similarities were.

"The others seem to have moved on quickly," he said. "But we should look at the baptismal font, for it might be an ancient one; and the stained glass windows often have little areas telling who made them or paid for them."

"Upon my word!" said Beatrice. "I feel as though I am in a museum!"

He stopped and met her eyes. "But you are, Miss Forsythe. Every ancient structure is history come to life. Especially a church."

The silence in the large nave (for the others had moved on ahead) was peaceful. She stood, looking about at the pews, the high rafters, and spacious depths of the ceiling; the soft, filtered light that made its way in from the stained glass was just enough to make it all out, but almost as though it was a halo substance; cloudlike, ethereal. They stood side by side for a full minute or more, just gazing around them, taking in the peculiarly intimate atmosphere of a place that could hold a hundred or more people, but was empty except for themselves.

They moved forward, past many rows of pews, while he pointed out everything of interest that he discovered, and all in his lovely, soft voice. Memorial plaques on the walls, or the indentation where a stone had been, but was no longer intact. After they had peered into the choir loft and admired the high platform from which Mr. O'Brien would give his sermons, he bade her examine the altar-screen. It was an elaborate carved piece of artistry, and Beatrice said, in an awed voice, "Do you know? I have never really looked at one before. I have been raised in the church, and yet I have missed so much of its beauty! Why is that?"

Mr. O'Brien was silent a moment, and looked away with an unreadable expression. When he looked back at her, he said, with the smallest hint of a smile, "Perhaps it is because you never looked at one with me, before." There was a question mark at the end of his statement, and it hung there in the air between them.

From somewhere else in the building, far away, they could hear the muted tones of the others; still his question remained, until she said, "I think you are exactly right! I must tell my mother what a good church guide you are; a historical guide." He stepped closer, saying, "Allow me to show you the leading pews, which I have a suspicion will be carved quite spectacularly, since the altar-screen is so elaborate." He moved her forward, putting one arm lightly about her waist, and then they both heard someone clear his throat rather loudly.

Mr. Barton stepped forward out of the enchanting foglike darkness. "May I join you?" he asked, in a loud voice that contrasted with the low tones Beatrice and Mr. O'Brien had been using. It was such a sharp, jarring note to her ears that it sounded like an impurity within a holy vale. He had ruined a magic moment, and the worst part of it was that Beatrice hadn't known it was magic until it was over. She felt the loss of it, and wondered briefly why being alone with Mr. O'Brien — whom she had thought too sober-minded to be any fun — had been comfortable and warm and lovely; while the entrance of Mr. Barton — whom she always found so amusing and agreeable — should be felt as an intrusion.

"I hope you find your new church agreeable?" he said, coming toward them.

Mr. O'Brien said, "Utterly. I thank you."

"Excellent," he replied. His eyes did not match the smile upon his face. "I also hope you have seen enough of it for your satisfaction. The rest of the party waits outside for you." This last was finished in a more serious tone, and Mr. Barton made sure, even though Beatrice had taken Mr. O'Brien's offer of his arm, to put her other hand upon his own, so that she came out in the middle of the two men.

Over her head, while she smiled at her sister and mother, the gentlemen exchanged looks. The eyes of Mr. O'Brien were curious, and at most, cautious; Mr. Barton, however, gave the curate a look calculated to chill; it was by turns challenging and defiant. He had no intention of letting Miss Forsythe slip through his fingers.

When they reached the waiting party, Beatrice slipped away from both men. She fell into step with the other ladies, and they shared their impressions of the old building and its surprising beauty and history, as they returned to the carriage. Ariana and her mother exchanged wondering, happy looks: To find Beatrice so enthralled over the old building was a singular surprise. And encouraging.

The sun was near setting. The day had

gone by swiftly!

Ariana went on to praise the vicarage, which Beatrice thought was rather too rapturous, until her mother added her admiration of it, which made it sound like the finest house in all England.

She understood their object; they wanted her to admire it, to agree that it would make a perfectly respectable and comfortable dwelling. She understood that Mr. O'Brien certainly found it so, and that she, too, ought to have. But she thought of Aspindon House, and her heart hardened.

She could not be happy, she was sure, in a common house like the vicarage. Mrs. Forsythe had lost patience with her silence, however, and asked, "Beatrice? Do you not admire the house?"

"How can I?" she returned. "When you are doing it far too brown already?"

Ariana had to smile.

Soon they were sitting in the barouche, except for Mrs. Forsythe and the Bartons. Miss Barton was quick to take the coach as she thought it would agree with her more. Somehow Mrs. Forsythe managed to get Mr. Barton into that equipage as well, though Beatrice could not guess how. She knew Mr. Barton would have preferred to keep an eye on her and Mr. O'Brien — she sensed it.

But it was done. And so, for the twenty or so minutes of the slow drive back (Beatrice did not know why the barouche proceeded so slowly), she sat with Mr. O'Brien directly across from her and conversed with him. Ariana had put her husband to the far left side of the seat, and herself in the middle, next to Beatrice. She proceeded to snuggle against her husband, and whisper to him with such small talk and little chuckles that husbands and wives enjoy at times, as though the rest of the world ceases to exist, that the other two in the carriage were virtually alone.

Soon Mr. Mornay threw a lazy arm around the shoulders of his wife, and Beatrice felt as though she really was alone with Mr. O'Brien again. She wondered if that strange sense of intimacy would return, but he began to talk, for some reason, of why he entered the church for a vocation, and soon she was lost in the conversation and forgot all about her own feelings. She only knew that Mr. O'Brien had every reason in the world to be a churchman, and that he was supremely fit for it.

She also realized that, in contrast to his, her devotional life (which she had thought to be sufficient for any Christian) was actually rather devoid of life, of excitement, of genuine communication with the Lord. The way Mr. O'Brien spoke of his devotions, of his time spent in Bible readings and prayer — oh! How had she missed so much instruction when she sat in the family pew every Sunday of her life? She almost felt as though she knew nothing of God — but that could not be true!

When the barouche pulled up to the estate, Mr. Barton was there waiting in front of his own carriage, for he and Miss Barton were returning to the Manor. His arms were crossed, as though he'd been waiting for an age, though it could only have been a few minutes.

He went directly to Mr. Mornay as soon as he'd jumped down from the equipage. Mr. O'Brien handed Beatrice down, and offered his arm for the short walk to the house.

Before going, Beatrice heard Mr. Barton say, "Sir! May I have just a word with you? It is quite important." And then they had moved on. She wondered what he would have to say that was "quite important," but had no clue.

They had only been gone for one afternoon, but as the dusk closed in, just as they went inside the house, Beatrice had the feeling that she'd been on a much longer outing. A journey of some kind.

A change of heart.

Mrs. Royleforst desired to hear every detail of the vicarage and Mr. O'Brien's situation that she could wring out of the others, during a quiet dinner in the dining room that was strangely subdued. Ariana spoke warmly of the house, as did Mrs. Forsythe, and it was easy to see that Mr. O'Brien felt a great deal of pride in his new situation, but he was inclined to fall quickly back into silence. Beatrice, keeping her eyes carefully away from the curate's, had to admit some admiration for the house and property. It was a place that a family could be comfortable in she said, thinking to herself that it was nevertheless not *her* kind of dwelling.

"I believe we are all fatigued," said Mrs. Forsythe, by way of explanation to Mrs. Royleforst, who was complaining at the lack of spirit about the table. When the meal had ended, the ladies rose to leave the gentlemen to a customary glass of port and male conversation, which for the very first time felt comfortable to Mr. O'Brien. Contrary to anything he had expected — Mr. Mornay was fast becoming agreeable. *Astonishing.*

In the drawing room, the ladies took up

their needlework, but Beatrice could hardly focus on her canvas. She was about halfway done with a Bible verse that she had chosen to embroider as a present for Papa. The verse was, *Seek ye first the kingdom of God, and his righteousness; and all these things shall be added unto you. Mt. 6:33.* It was a favourite scripture of her father's, and she stared at it. She had chosen it for Papa, not for her own use, not so that she could meditate on its meaning or significance, but she found herself doing just that.

Seek ye first the kingdom of God: that much was finished, in a lovely purple thread that she had saved up, tuppence by tuppence, to purchase. She felt as though the words were being emblazoned, not on her canvas, but on her conscience. Was she seeking God's kingdom in desiring to make a rich match? *Yes! She would use her wealth in good causes; for the sake of the poor!* Wouldn't she?

She sighed.

She could not lie to herself. Her desire for a rich husband had nothing to do with God's kingdom, and she knew it. She felt entitled to wealth simply because Ariana had got herself a rich husband, with a beautiful house, and servants and luxuries. She swallowed the lump forming in her throat and looked at the room she was in. The elegant furnishings, the warm draperies, the Chinese wallpaper, and rosewood-bottomed sofas, topped with plump upholstery. A tear or two came into her eyes. *It was not fair! Why could her sister enjoy such beauty in her home and be perfectly acceptable to God, while she was required to forgo it?*

"Beatrice? Are you unwell?" Ariana was looking at her, and Beatrice blinked the tears away.

"I believe I shall retire early tonight," she said, folding up her work and putting it neatly into her work basket. When she had said her good-nights, and was leaving, the men were just coming into the room, and she met them at the door.

"Good-night," she said. She tried to smile, but it was a poor attempt for a girl who usually did not lack smiles.

"Good-night and God bless you," Mr. O'Brien said. She barely heard Mr. Mornay's "Good-night," and then strode swiftly down the corridor.

She suddenly wanted a good cry, and was going to have it.

The next day at breakfast Beatrice ate little, did not attempt to play with Nigel or show the least interest in the baby, and answered only if spoken to. Mr. O'Brien studied her quietly, but she would not return a single look. Her habitual cheerfulness seemed to have deserted her.

Finally she asked Ariana, "Have you decided upon a date for going to London? When I may come too?"

Mrs. Forsythe raised her brows at her daughter, but said nothing.

Ariana, surprised, said, "Mr. Mornay and I have not had a chance to speak upon it, actually." After a pause she added, "The Season won't begin until near May; there is plenty of time." She exchanged a look with her husband. His brief meeting with Mr. Barton the previous evening had raised the subject of a trip to London — or Brighton. Mr. Barton had said, "I beg your pardon, sir, for I meant to speak of this to you already, but the time never seemed quite right."

"Yes?" Mr. Mornay answered.

"I have had a note from His Royal Highness," Mr. Barton lied. He had settled upon the creation of an imaginary note from the prince as the most innocent way to broach the subject so that it did not appear premeditated. He waited to see if that would sufficiently impress his host, who merely nodded, however, to his disappointment. He went on, "The prince has asked me to get you to him; he desires to move forward with the viscountcy."

Mr. Mornay merely said, "Hmmm."

"Have you corresponded with the College of Heralds to settle upon a name for the title, sir?"

Without answering the question, Mr. Mornay merely said, "So he asks you to be his emissary? Why did he not write directly to me?"

Mr. Barton cleared his throat. "I believe he has gone down that path, sir, and found it to be blocked at both ends."

Mr. Mornay nodded, amused.

"Very good, Barton. Obliged. I will write to the Regent later this week." As he started to walk off, he turned back to say, with a knowing look, "You may inform him of such."

"Thank you, sir." But his tone was not enthusiastic. His eyes narrowed as he watched the man offer his arm to his wife, who had waited at a polite distance, and then turn toward the house. Dashed if Mornay wasn't as slippery as a net full of eels! He had made a small step of progress, but it was not the sort of letter he was eager to send the prince. He had to find out *when* the man meant to accept the title.

As he climbed into the carriage beside Anne, who still had Ariana's shawl (for she would not take it back), he saw her pull its ends closer about her as she shivered with the cold. She did not ask about Tristan's words with Mr. Mornay. But suddenly Mr. Barton had a brain child. He'd been speaking to the wrong person. Surely Mrs. Mornay understood her husband's intentions in the matter.

They would return the next day, and he would ply that lady with his questions. He was bound to fall upon the truth, and then he could write the prince and know some success in the matter! Then, he could turn his thoughts to Miss Forsythe entirely. He had plans for her.

When they were back in the Manor House, Mr. Barton said to his sister, "I was pleased to see you engaging in conversation today for a change. You are much more fetching when you are in a good humour, I must say."

"I begin to feel better," Miss Barton said, taking a breath. She removed her bonnet and gloves and gave them to their manservant, and then her redingote.

Mr. Barton said, "Huzzah for that. Do you think it will last? This feeling better?"

"I have no idea, to be honest!" she eyed him brightly. "But I intend to make the most of it." But she sighed. "Mrs. Mornay and her mother are the kindest women!"

"What about Miss Forsythe?" he asked, following his sister into their parlour.

"Oh, she is agreeable, to be sure, but she is young, that's all."

Mr. Barton positioned himself lazily upon the sofa, one leg upon the brow comfortably, taking it down only to allow their manservant to remove his shoes, replacing them with slippers.

"Stoke up the fire, will you, Dilworth?" he said. "It's dashed chilly in here!" Anne had already wrapped herself in a heavy shawl so that only her arms were free and peeking out, for she had taken up her needlework. Barton wasn't paying attention, and she wanted to complete the little booties she was working on. Her next project would require white yarn, for she wished to knit a little dress and cap for Miranda. From where she sat, she heard Barton sigh loudly. She looked over at him, her lips compressed in disapproval at his lackadaisical posture upon the couch.

"Of what are you thinking?" she asked.

"I am thinking of how to accomplish my mission. Mornay is as sly as a weasel; every time I try to learn his thoughts on a matter, he ends up making quick work of me. Dashed if I know how he does it! He is somehow eluding me, and I cannot say whether he is up to tricks, or if it is simply his way."

"Why should he be up to tricks?" She raised her eyes again to him, a small alarm upon her features. "Do you think he suspects your motives?"

"Why should he? I told him outright what I was about for the Regent. But I do think he has reservations about me. Don't know what for, that's all." He had a thought. "I hope it isn't you!"

"That's impossible!" she said. She thought of her dealings with the man up to now. Whenever his eyes happened to fall upon her, or if he spoke to her, she saw a softening as though he understood, instinctually perhaps, that Miss Barton was a gentle creature, and required gentle treatment. She said, "He has been nothing but politeness and consideration to me, in fact."

"Very well; so it is me he is concerned about."

"*I* know what it is!" said the sister, with a sudden realization.

"Well?" he waited.

"You have been flirting shamefully with

Miss Forsythe, and he cannot like it. If you would wish to win the man, you must steer clear of his sister."

"His wife's sister."

"Same thing."

He frowned. "Hmmph! I suppose you have hit it. I will have to proceed carefully, henceforward."

"What do you mean? Only cease your attentions to her, your little jokes — and you will have an easier path."

"Well, the thing is, I happen to enjoy giving my attentions to Miss Forsythe, and our little jokes, as you put it. In fact, if she returns my feelings, it may just as likely put him off his guard, as on it. Could he not hold me in favour simply for her sake?"

"You are naive, sir!" Miss Barton was smiling, almost finding it funny that her brother could be so muddleheaded. "Men do not favour other men who show affection for females within their households! *You* know this to be true."

He sat up abruptly.

"Not necessarily! They might become chums, you know."

Miss Barton knitted on. "Are you forming an attachment for Miss Forsythe, Tristan?" Her quiet words held more than their usual gravity, and she stopped working to survey him with wide eyes.

He put his hands behind his head and blew out a breath, thinking. "I do not know, if truth be told. But I do not consider it impossible. She is young, which I like, and above pretty, and sweet, and she is in Mornay's family. If I were to get hitched to her —"

"Must you be so vulgar?" Her expression was pained.

"Very well," he said smiling. "If I were to marry her, I would be in Mornay's family. He would then of necessity favour me, would you not say?"

She said nothing for a moment, concentrating on what was in her hands, but her face wore a deep frown. "Do you see this as your way to convince Mornay to accept the title?"

"To the devil with the title! I'll be in his family if I win Miss Forsythe! That's far to my advantage, and if he becomes Lord Mornay, or whatever his title, all the better!"

Miss Barton sat back herself, but she was worried. "I pray you don't give him a disgust of you, Tristan. I do like them, you know." She paused, thinking of the new acquaintances. "Each of them — they are all exceedingly kind." She looked at her brother, and her eyes held a plea. "Be careful in how you present yourself."

"I cannot fathom your concern. I am intent upon cementing myself to the family through marriage, and you speak as if I were about to create a chasm."

"If you truly are to form an attachment to Miss Forsythe," she said, "I hope it will be for herself, not for her family connexion. Be thoughtful of her, Tristan. Do not take advantage of her youth."

He scowled. "Miss Forsythe stands to benefit from our alliance as much as I do! She is seeking a wealthy match, Anne, and I have the fortune to support her in style."

"You mean, you *did* have the fortune; but you have gamed away a good portion of it. Is that not why you sold our family home?"

He shrugged. "You speak as though I am ruined; nothing like it, I assure you!"

Miss Barton was not assured. She had long suspected that her brother was gaming away his entire subsistence. However, she only said, "But is there also admiration for herself?" She paused, looking plaintively over at him. "Do you love her, Tristan Barton?"

He looked in surprise at her. "My dear Anne! How can I tell if I love a girl apart from her bringing some advantage to me?

The thing is impossible, I tell you! I like her well enough, I've said so. May we leave it at that?" He looked pained at having to even consider the matter.

Anne returned to her work. "I sometimes think you are incapable of loving a woman," she said quietly.

He heard her, and tried to make sense of her statement, but in the end gave up, and lay back down upon the sofa, replacing his one leg upon the brow comfortably. *What was she talking about? He'd loved women before. Almost took on a mistress, dash it! What did Anne know of love, in fact? She was certainly not one to talk, by Jove.* He closed his eyes, hoping for a few minutes' nap.

THIRTEEN

Beatrice was too restless to remain at the table a moment longer, and she came to her feet. Mrs. Forsythe knew something was niggling at her daughter, and asked, "Where are you off to, my dear?"

"I am in need of some fresh air," she said. "Some exercise, I think. I'll just take a turn about the property, if I may."

Ariana said, "It's very cold. Stay close to the house. We can't have you getting lost on us."

Mrs. Forsythe said, with a careful look at Mr. O'Brien, "I do not think you ought to go off alone at all."

Mr. O'Brien's response warmed her heart when he immediately wiped his mouth with his napkin and said, rising from his chair, "If Miss Forsythe will grant me the honour, I'd be delighted to escort her."

"Why, thank you, sir!" exclaimed Mrs. Forsythe.

Beatrice had been about to decline the offer, but now she could say nothing.

"You are very kind," her mother added, and she sent Beatrice a look of warning. Beatrice wished she could say aloud, *I know exactly what you are about, Mama, and it shan't work, I promise you. Nothing will come of it. You think that by throwing me together with Mr. O'Brien, a romance may happen — but nothing could be further from my mind. My heart is set on London, for I am determined to have a proper coming-out, and I expect to meet many marriageable gentlemen there.*

Instead, she merely compressed her lips and went toward the front entrance hall. Mr. O'Brien came fast on her heels, and said, to her relief, nothing.

Mr. Horton's face was set in a stern look.

Frederick had informed the master, as soon as he'd done with his morning meal, that his steward waited upon him in the business office on the ground floor.

"Have him come to my study," Mr. Mornay said, and started at once for the room. He felt a twinge of concern when the steward entered, and he saw the man's face.

"What's the trouble?" he said as he motioned for him to take a seat. Mr. Horton shook his head; he would stand. He took a breath.

"Sir, I am sorry to have to inform you — there's sickness in the cottages."

"What sort of sickness?" Mornay asked.

"That's just it, sir; I can't be sure, yet. It's supposed to be the London fever."

"*Supposed* to be?"

"There's talk among the men, sir. It always starts out this way; one man don't want to lose his wages, so he keeps quiet if someone in his house falls sick. But the women get whiff of it, somehow, and it starts to get out, see."

"But the one who lets it out must know the truth."

"No one'll take credit for that, to be sure! That's like treason, sir, among the working class, for it ends with a man losin' his work."

"Of course," he murmured, mostly to himself. "We'll have to do a sweep."

"Right, sir! That's precisely why I come to you. I'm ready to go knockin' on doors, but I wanted your permission afore I did. I'll send word as soon as I know what's what."

Mr. Mornay was nodding his head, but he said, "Be very thorough, but do not be harsh or alarming. No one is to know what you're searching for, saving yourself and the man you take with you. And if you find a hint of the fever, we'll get Mr. Speckman here at once to diagnose and treat it."

"Even if I find sickness, they won't let me call a doctor, sir, it's far too dear —"

"Unless the illness is everywhere rampant, it will be at my expense. I'm hoping we're in time to contain it."

"Very good, sir. Thank you, Mr. Mornay."

"Thank you, Mr. Horton."

Mr. Mornay sat at his desk a few moments longer. This could be very bad news indeed; on the other hand, it might be nothing. Rumours did have a way of getting magnified as they spread. Nevertheless, he took out a sheet of paper and dipped his quill. He would write to Mr. Speckman, the family physician, to put him on the alert of what might be brewing. He told him to study the latest remedies for the fever which was sprouting up in London of late — in case.

When done, he used the bellpull to summon a servant to deliver the message immediately to the village. Then, his gaze fell upon the Bible, and he placed his hand upon the leather cover, feeling the grain of the leather. God. God was the Great Physician. He put his hands together, rested his head upon them, and prayed.

Afterward, before returning upstairs, he decided to say nothing as yet to any of his guests, nor even his wife. There was no reason to cause anyone to fret when he had no real facts to go on. Once he heard back from Mr. Horton, and once the doctor had seen those who were affected, he would make any necessary announcement. He hoped that it would not be necessary.

Beatrice maintained her silence all the way around the turn of the house and past the stables, to the maze. It surprised her that Mr. O'Brien followed her lead, and did not talk. She was glad of it, however. She was glad of the silent stillness of winter. There wasn't another human being in sight save themselves. The workers, which might have been about the grounds in spring or summer, tending plants or crops, or repairing fences, were nowhere to be seen; and the servants who might have journeyed along that very route to the great house each morning to appear for their duties had long ago arrived and begun their tasks.

She looked about them, and saw that off to one side of the grounds, a wood began. There looked as though a path was in it, but it wended out of sight and she could not tell how far it went.

"May we take the woodland path?" she asked him, pointing over at it.

He looked over, but said, "Are you not cold, yet?"

"No, I'm fine," she said. "And I enjoy a brisk walk. If we move quickly, we can stay warm and still see where it leads." She could not help but feel more optimistic now that she was out of doors. The day was bracingly cold, but only her face was really exposed. Beatrice had on as wintry a costume as a lady could procure. She had chosen a hooded cloak to wear over her jaconet muslin gown and velvet spencer; a bonnet beneath the hood, and a cap beneath the bonnet; an extravagantly oversized rabbit muff enclosed one of her gloved hands, such as was in style for ladies; so only her feet and cheeks reminded her of the weather, or, during a sudden breeze, her legs, which were protected only by the dress, the open cloak, and stockings. Her half-boots of kid leather were sturdy enough, but not precisely warm.

"Very well then," he said. "Why not?" A brief smile lit his face and was rewarded with a look of thanks from Beatrice. Mr. O'Brien had his overcoat and a scarf wrapped around his neck and lower face, and a hat, and gloves, and still wore the hunting boots he had appeared in the day before.

About a quarter mile from the house, following the well-worn path, Beatrice said, "It seems less cold here."

"There is no wind," he said. "The trees are bare, but they are so thick that they break it before it reaches us."

"This must be a lovely trail in summer."

"I am sure." They walked on, moving briskly. His long strides now and then were shortened to keep equal pace with her smaller ones. "Let me know at once, Miss Forsythe, if you are tiring, or wish to turn back."

"I *am* tiring," she said with a little smile (and he was very glad of that smile too), "but I am above all things curious. I must know where this comes out!"

He said, "Mr. Mornay has a great property here; we will probably come out to a field, taking its winter rest from growing some crop or other. Do you know what he plants?"

"I have no idea," she admitted. "But it may not be a field, and you see, sir, I have to know!" She hurried on, with the feeling that they were surely near the end of this path; the tree trunks around them were gradually thinning. She could see an opening to one side, which added to her hope of reaching a clearing. They walked on, and even Mr. O'Brien's long steps were not equal to her haste.

But the path went on. Beatrice was getting cold, and her feet hurt exceedingly from it, and she was feeling cross that the end of the path was still not visible. Still she refused to turn back.

"I daresay we are going too far in this cold," the curate finally said, slowing to a halt.

"I see something," she cried, and quickened her pace even further. "I think it's a house!" Her nose and cheeks and chin were all red with cold, but she hurried on, crying, "Oh, look, it *is* a house!"

The path veered to the right, and there was the end of the woods, abruptly and suddenly, and after that, about a hundred feet before them, the building she had glimpsed through the trees.

She stopped to catch her breath, panting from the excitement and exercise. Mr. O'Brien took hold of her scarf, saying, "Cover your mouth and nose when you breathe that hard in this weather."

She nodded, doing as he said, but she kept looking at the little dwelling before them.

"What do you think this place is?" she asked.

They both surveyed the house, and Beatrice started walking toward it again. There was a gated fence with a stone path that led to the door of the modest-sized cottage, and it made a cozy picture. As they drew nearer, they could see there was a small stable behind the house; only large enough for one or two horses.

"What a quaint, cheerful place, is it not?" Beatrice asked. "Right out of the pages of a storybook!" Then she looked at him as if struck. "This must be Glendover! The parsonage!"

He was looking ahead too, and slowly nodded. "It may be; it is small, however. I seem to recall Mrs. Mornay speaking of it as being larger than Warwickdon's parsonage." They had reached the gate, and he stopped; but Beatrice reached down and undid the latch. "May we see if the house is open? My feet are rather numb." She was stamping them trying to warm them. His brows came together in concern.

"Are they?"

"I cannot feel them at all, I think!"

"Miss Forsythe!" He was now very concerned. "Why did you not say something to me sooner?" With one arm he hurried her through the gate. He was looking around urgently, and he said, "We won't find anyone here, I can tell you that, for there's no fire inside. Anyone would have a fire in this weather."

She looked up at him, and his face was now creased in worry. "I should not have allowed us to come this far!" He looked ahead to the house — should he try and carry her? The girl was not large, and he knew he could easily lift her, but something told him it was better for her condition if she kept putting some weight on her feet. She had to keep using them.

When they finally came up to the front of the cottage, there was little to shelter them except for a foot or so of thatched roof, overhanging the eaves. Mr. O'Brien said, "I'm quite sure it isn't occupied, but I'd best knock first." He did, firmly, a number of hard raps to the door that anyone within would have heard. No response. He put his hand to the door handle and pressed his lips together: "Here goes." He tried the long brass handle, and with a little, miraculous "click," he felt it open, and then pushed with his shoulder to make the door move. He helped Beatrice over the threshold, and then firmly shut the door behind them.

"Now I cannot see!" she cried.

"Your eyes will adjust," he murmured, squinting himself to get their bearings. He began feeling with his hands over and around the doorjambs. He came across a candle in a sconce, and then found some flint and a piece of char-cloth. "I believe I can get this lit," he said, "if you will hold the candle." She came toward his voice and put out her hand and felt — his overcoat. "Here it is," he said, taking her hand in one of his and putting it to the candle.

She held it up. After a few failed attempts, suddenly there was a spark, and a quick application of the char-cloth, and then a small flame.

"Well done," Beatrice breathed.

The candle was lit, and he held it out so they could see a little more of their surroundings. The cottage showed no evidence of recent occupation; there were no personal effects or small things such as would be about if someone lived there. But there was furniture and a candle lamp, and he went and lit that also. The fireplace was swept clean and empty, but Mr. O'Brien said, "Thanks be to God!" and he knelt down and began shoveling coal from a bin beside the fireplace, and began forming a pile in the grate. "Unfortunately, it will take some time to get good and hot," he said, as he came to his full height and started looking for something to help get the coals to accept a flame.

"Here," said Beatrice. She had seen a vase that was empty on a window sill, and, chancing to peer down it, discovered that it was full of small twigs and cloth scraps, and lint.

"Perfect!" he exclaimed. In a few more minutes she could smell that the coals were beginning to burn, and she drew a wooden chair closer to the fireplace and sat down upon it.

Mr. O'Brien pulled up a wing chair, cushioned, and placed it beside hers. "Sit here," he said.

"Is there one for you?" she asked. She was embarrassed, for some reason, by his kindness.

"How are your feet?" he merely asked, in response.

"They are hurting," she admitted, feeling as foolish as a child.

"How are they hurting? Describe what you are feeling."

"They're quite heavy! I do not think that walking briskly was sufficient to keep them warm, after all!"

"Is there pain?" He was trying to calculate how far they had walked, and guessed about a mile.

"Yes," she said. "It's as though I am being

stabbed by many pins." Her voice was calm, but she was beginning to feel a dread that she might have injured herself.

"Pain is a good sign," he breathed, but he pulled the other chair up close enough so that when he sat in it, he could pick up her foot. Which she tried, at first, to resist.

"Mr. O'Brien!"

"Miss Forsythe," he said, his eyes large and innocent, "you must allow me to help you. And every minute right now is important to your welfare."

That shut her up abruptly. She lifted her left foot and gave it to him. He received it gently and began removing her half-boot.

"It's getting hot," she said.

He halted, and looked at her. "Do you mean just your foot?"

"Yes; both my feet. They still hurt and now they're burning!" She felt frightened. "Why are they burning, Mr. O'Brien, do you know?"

"Yes," he said, but his head was bent over her boot, which he now pulled off her foot. He quickly took her limb between his two hands and started rubbing hard and fast, as though trying to warm it up. Beatrice gasped from the barrage of pain and heat, and she automatically tried to draw her foot away from his reach, but Mr. O'Brien was strong, and retained his hold on her.

"Do not," he said. "I'm afraid this is necessary." He continued rubbing and kneading her foot with his hands. The feeling of being a pin cushion grew stronger than ever. "Does my foot feel hot to you?" she asked.

"No."

"Oh, it is burning to me!"

He put her foot down softly, and then took her right leg, and began removing the boot. Despite working quickly, he was actually very gentle. It was only the rubbing and kneading that caused her pain, and that, she knew, could not be helped. She watched him; he stopped to throw off his overcoat and went right back to the work; and she felt helpless and unworthy. Here he was, rubbing her feet back to life, while she had been filled with the worst sort of thoughts regarding him, earlier.

She had told herself she would not speak to him at all on the walk; he was too "holy" for her, too much a sermonizer, boring, no fun at all, and more such things. She knew that the biggest resentment she felt was based really upon the fact that she found him — underneath it all — utterly likeable, thoughtful, interesting, and handsome — but poor! He was now less poor than he had been, having Warwickdon, but she did not aspire to be a parson's wife! She did not want to live upon the lesser tithes and a glebe! Even if he were a rector, it would mean the greater tithes, but that varied by church in its amount, and promised no re-assurance of being substantial.

He dropped her second foot and returned his efforts to the first. "How do you do, Miss Left Foot?" he asked, with an attempt at humour.

"I think the burning is going away!" she said, as surprised as she was relieved.

"Excellent," he said, and he began to ease up on his administrations to her foot, now using his thumbs to gently keep the blood flowing.

"What makes them burn?" she asked. She knew the answer but needed something to say. The silence only magnified her unease.

"Frostbite," he said, simply. "It does that." He went back to her right foot, and using his thumbs, pressed firmly but gently, and with much less urgency than before. He did her toes, and then the sole and top of her foot. Now and then he added a little more vigour; now her right foot, now her left. Meanwhile, the radiating little fingers of needlelike pricks had slowly been abating, and now ceased altogether. Instead, his hands felt warm and soothing, causing a new sort of burning — in her cheeks!

She had allowed a gentleman to remove her boots; she was alone with him in an unknown cottage, with no one aware of their whereabouts. It should have been frightening, or at least shocking. But she wasn't frightened, and she wasn't shocked; she was rather mortified, but it was more a sense of humility for what he had needed to do for her, than mortification for his handling of her stockinged feet.

How well did she know this gentleman, really? And that is what he was — a gentle man. Their past acquaintance was so long ago to her now; she had only been a child, then. And yet, she trusted him at this moment as fully as if he had been a brother.

Finally, he fell back upon his knees, but he took his coat and, lifting her feet, wrapped them both up in it. It was not soft enough to really swath her limbs, however, so he removed it and asked for her muff, which answered the purpose much better. He laid his coat over the muff where her feet were nestled inside, and rested her legs upon the wooden chair. He then turned to stir the fire. Beatrice watched him and felt a sadness rise up within her, as well as gratitude.

She did not know how to thank him. "How is it that you are so skilled in treating frozen feet?"

He kept facing the grate while carefully turning the coals to nurse them into a real source of heat, but he said, "That's what comes of serving in St. Pancras." He turned to face her. "You can't pass a single winter without some poor, frozen souls casting themselves upon your doorstep." He picked up her muffled feet, and sat himself down before placing them back, gently, upon his lap, as though it were the most natural thing in the world. Beatrice stared at her legs for a moment, trying to comprehend that she was resting her feet on this man's lap. She searched his face for a sign that he, too, found it strange, but there was none. He was talking on as though he were likely to place a young lady's feet upon his lap at any given moment.

"I had a neighbour by name of Mrs. Clotham who taught me how to help in these cases." There was a pause while he sat, remembering. "We had a man who ended up losing both legs."

Beatrice gasped. "Losing his legs! On account of their freezing? Like my feet?"

"No, he was much worse! I never discovered him until the morning, and it was too late for him by then. I spent the whole time waiting for the doctor in rubbing his legs, and a parishioner joined me, but it was no good. He never felt a thing, and his legs were grey as death. Your feet were already turning rosy, so you'll be perfectly fine, I assure you."

She quieted down, but after a moment, asked, "Did the man live?"

He turned thoughtful eyes upon hers. She could not see their colour by this light, but she could see that they were sympathetic. Gentle. "You do not truly wish to know the answer to that question, do you?"

She averted her gaze. *Goodness! She had been fortunate never to have suffered having her feet freeze during her winter walks at home! And now, how providential to have Mr. O'Brien with her when such a thing should occur!*

"Mr. O'Brien," she ventured. "My feet are growing hot. May I remove them from the muff?" He took off the covering of his coat, and smiled, but he put one hand protectively upon the muff, inside of which were her beleaguered limbs.

"Not yet."

FOURTEEN

"I think we must go after them," Ariana said.

"I agree." Her husband rose and spoke to the footmen who were standing against the walls in the dining room, as footmen usually did when not needed at the moment. "Tell Freddy and Fotch to join me, as well as two or three of you who can ride."

"I can ride, sir!" His tone was eager as footmen did not often get to ride.

"As can I, sir," said the other, firmly.

"Send a man to the stables quickly so that the horses can be readied. And let's to it, gentlemen!" He paused, and then added, "Dress warmly."

"Yes, sir!"

In minutes a group of men were following their master to the stable yard, where a groom and a stable hand were leading out horses for them, all harnessed and ready for a rider.

Mr. Mornay stopped to pat the head of his own horse, named Tornado. It was a sixteen-hand black stallion, bred in his own stables, and never ridden by anyone but him. He spoke softly to it while the others began mounting, and then in another minute he was astride as well. He turned his horse to face the men, and quickly gave orders. Fotch would ride with him; the others were to go off in various different directions on the grounds, all in search of the missing couple. Each man was given a weapon and was to fire off a shot in the air if he found them, alerting the others.

When they trotted off, Fotch said, "It's hard to believe that yesterday was so fair, sir! This weather has taken a nasty turn!"

"Indeed. I'm afraid it may have caught them by surprise. Let us hope we do not find them stuck somewhere."

"How might they be stuck, sir, if I might ask?" asked Fotch, who had no imagination for such things.

"Supposing Miss Forsythe was to get hurt; I can easily imagine her keeping Mr. O'Brien with her, for fear of being alone. And he might just be pigeon-headed enough to think it the right thing to do."

"Aye, sir, I see what you mean," the valet nodded. He started looking around more carefully, as they entered the path that wound through the woods going southeast.

Mr. Mornay kept his pace at a steady trot, slowing down when the woods grew dense, stopping now and again to listen.

"Give a yell," he said, now and again. Fotch would take one hand from the reins, cup his mouth, and shout, with all his might: "Mis-ter O-Briiiiiien!" Not a sound. "Miss For-syyyyythe!" Nothing.

They continued on.

Ariana was impatiently looking out the south windows of the grounds, but continued to see nothing of her sister or Mr. O'Brien.

"I cannot account for so long an absence in this cold," she said. "Our property is not dangerous; there is a ravine, but that is on the far side of the land, and I do not think they could have possibly walked that distance!"

"A ravine!" exclaimed Mrs. Forsythe. She was obligingly playing at wooden soldiers with Nigel but looked up in alarm.

"No, Mama, I should not have mentioned it; they could not have reached it with less than a day's walk."

"Oh." The lady returned to the game, now picking up all the fallen soldiers that Nigel had mercilessly murdered with his toy black cannon. "You win again!" she exclaimed, to his delight.

"I beat the Frenchmen, Mama!" he cried happily. He had actually turned his cannon upon the men in the Regent's colours, but Mrs. Forsythe wasn't about to ruin his joy with the facts.

Ariana paused to congratulate her son, opening her arms and giving him, when he arrived at her legs breathlessly, an earnest kiss upon the head. "Well done, sir!" she cried. "Your father will be proud."

"Yes, Mama!" But he stopped and yawned, and Ariana looked at Mrs. Perler.

"Yes, ma'am," she said, instantly getting up and coming toward the child. "It is high time for Master Nigel's nap, to be sure."

"Not my nap!" he cried. "Please, Mama, make Mrs. Perler leave me be! I do not wish for a nap!"

Ariana bent to one knee to speak to the boy at eye level. "When you get to the nursery," she said, in a conspiratorial whisper, "you may pretend to nap. Take a toy with you into your bed and play. Mrs. Perler will never know." This was a little game Ariana used to get her son to sleep. He would take the toy with him, ostensibly to avoid his nap, but inevitably fall asleep.

"Lately, ma'am, Master Nigel refuses to get into his bed for his nap."

"He will fall asleep at playing, and you can put him to bed, then." She went and bent over her sleeping baby, as Miranda had already been fed and changed, and she said, after planting a soft kiss on the infant's head, "Call for me when she awakes and will not go back to sleep. Not until then."

"Yes, ma'am." The lady curtsied, and, after picking up Miranda, took a sad looking Nigel by the hand, and made her way from the room.

Ariana was instantly all briskness. "Mama, I am too restless to sit here and wait. I wish to go walking myself; I should have had Mr. Mornay take me with him."

"Well, there is no sense in my staying put, then."

"Mrs. Royleforst will be happy of your company, I am certain."

"I have seen neither hide nor hair of that lady today, nor her little Miss Bluford! I daresay Mrs. Royleforst is having one of her topsy-turvy days."

Ariana nodded; she was familiar with her aunt's "tospy-turvy" days. It meant that when Mrs. Royleforst tried to get out of bed in the morning, she was struck with a heavy feeling in her head (top-heavy, she called it); if she persisted, she got light-headed. Hence, it was a topsy-turvy day. Miss Bluford came in very handy for such days, as the regular servants would have been put out to do so much for a guest. Knowing Phillip's relation was being tended to, Ariana therefore said, "Let us go!" and the two ladies left the room in quick succession.

Beatrice sighed and sat back, enjoying the warmth that was emanating from the grate. Mr. O'Brien, right from his chair, was tending the fire now and again as though Beatrice's legs weren't still resting upon him, ending with a giant muff that he had to duck around as he aimed his poker at the coals.

"Mr. O'Brien," she said, drawing her feet away from him, "my feet are better. They are not hot nor cold, nor prickling with a thousand pins." She held the muff and extracted her stockinged feet, trying not to feel silly. "You have been excellent, and I am much obliged to you. But surely my sister and my mother must be growing perplexed at our absence."

"I have had much the same thought," he said, nodding, and rising from his seat, "but I did not wish to distress you with it."

"Thank you," she said, looking at him appreciatively.

"I must put out the fire," he said. "I don't like to leave an empty house with something burning in it. Wait a minute, if you please. Warm your muff and boots close to it before we must leave."

In truth he was concerned about the return journey. One mile on a nice day would have been nothing, but in the cold, and for feet that had already suffered a frost, he knew they would easily succumb to the same problem again. He was near the front door, thinking of finding some source of water outside such as a running brook, when he had a new thought.

"Miss Forsythe — I think it best if I leave you here with the fire, while I return to the house and get you a mount."

She looked up at him, her eyes large as she considered his words. "Oh, I do not think it necessary," she answered, standing up. She had been warming her boots obediently, and now went to put them on. She sat back down and inserted one foot, saying, "Oh! I have warmed it too well!"

"It will cool soon enough," he murmured, watching. "In fact, I do think our best course is to avoid your having to walk any distance in this weather. I promise you, I will make haste. You can lock the door behind me." He started preparing to leave, putting on his greatcoat.

"No!" she cried, and then was embarrassed by her own fear. In a lower voice, she said, "We do not even know for certain that this is the parsonage. What if we are . . . trespassing?"

"This is certainly Mr. Mornay's land, and you are a member of the family; I do not think you can be accused of anything; particularly when your reason for coming in was so dire."

She looked around and although the cottage had lost none of its rustic charm, she did not want to be left alone there. She looked to him and said, "It's no good; I cannot stay alone."

His face softened, but he said, "There is a bar for the door which you may close once I leave. You'll be safe here, I'm certain."

"I'll be miserable and worrying the whole time."

"That's better than to be frostbitten again." He wrapped himself in his scarf and put on his gloves. She tied her boots and stood, and hurried over before he could leave. She got right in front of him. "I'm afraid that, *where you go, I go.*" Belatedly she realized that the allusion of that statement came from the book of Ruth, implying a "til death do us part" sort of commitment, and she blushed faintly. *Oh, fie, he couldn't think I meant anything by that!*

And, though his clear blue eyes were fastened on hers, and may even have twinkled, being the good and sensible man that Mr. O'Brien was, he made absolutely no remark or joke, or anything to make her suspect that he did. *How kind!* Mr. O'Brien was a gentleman — he cared about her sensibilities.

"Miss Forsythe; I insist that you stay. Your sister will never forgive me were I to allow any harm to come to you; I was already remiss in letting us walk so far as we did. I cannot make that mistake again."

Beatrice listened, her large eyes revealing alarm, but she knew she could not allow him to have his way. Her feeling changed to amusement. He was sweet to try to protect her feet, but it was the rest of her that Beatrice was worried about. "I am sorry for it, sir," she said, with a smile, removing his hand from her arm where he was holding her back. "My sister will understand when you tell her how adamant I was in accompanying you back to the house. She knows that I am . . ."

"Willful?" he supplied, with a sideways smile.

266

"I was going to say, 'strong-minded,' " she replied, but she was still smiling. Pulling on her gloves she said, brightly, "Well! Shall we go?"

He looked at her wryly a moment. "Miss Beatrice," he said, softly, getting her full attention. When they were acquainted in the past, she had been "Miss Beatrice," and suddenly days gone by were coming back at her. He put out his hand. "May I see your gloves?" She had just put them on, and she held out her hands. He peered at them a moment, and then suddenly took both of her hands and swiftly pulled the gloves off!

"What are you doing?" she asked, and then immediately knew. He was not going to let her accompany him!

"I still have a muff!" she cried, and grabbing it, made a dash for the door. He was too much the gentleman to stop her she thought.

He pulled her back by the waist with a surprising strength, and with a sigh, said, into the back of her head, "Must you make me take hold of you to keep you safe? You are being . . . naughty!"

She said, "No, sir! *You* are! You ought not to have touched me!" She pushed away and turned to face him, but in a few seconds they both smiled, and then started to laugh.

He had already massaged her feet at length! He looked at her appraisingly.

"If I allow you to leave this cottage, do you think Mr. Mornay will ever hold me in the least respect?"

"He already does," she said, knowing nothing about it.

His brows went up. "No. Your feet, once having frozen, are more prone to it, again." He looked outside. "It only gets later and colder. You must listen to me, and stay put. I will run the entire distance, or at least until I drop from exhaustion."

Her eyes widened with alarm, but he grinned.

"I'm jesting; I won't drop from exhaustion, I assure you. I will *run,* Miss Forsythe. You have only to stay by the fire like a good girl for a short while. Now, do I have your word?"

She looked around at the place. It might have been cozy, with more candlelight and cheery furnishings, but it had an empty look about it. She knew, the moment he left, she was going to feel a vague fright. It would be nameless and unreasonable, perhaps, but she would feel it, just the same.

She looked at him plaintively. "I cannot. I am sorry for it. Please let me accompany you."

He was puzzled. "Why cannot you?"

She sighed heavily. "I will be frightened here alone." She hated the sound of her own words; despised herself for being such a coward, but she had to tell him. She could see he was not going to let her leave with him, otherwise.

He walked over to her, and once again reached for her hands. She thought he would give her the gloves, but he had already stuffed them into a pocket. Instead he held her hands within his own larger ones, and said, "Allow me to pray for you." His eyes were so kind and compassionate, that she did.

He prayed simply, and to the point. He thanked God for their safety and the use of the cottage, and for the restoration of Beatrice's feet with no lasting injury. And he prayed for the mighty hand of God to rest over her and this little house, for angels to minister at its doors and windows, standing guard, and to keep her, now and eternally, safe.

Beatrice was struck by his words. His earnest, wonderful, gentle words. He was so caring! She had a terrible urge to reach up and kiss his cheek. But instead she turned away and went and sat by the fireplace. "Lock the door, please," she said, in a quiet voice.

"I'll be back for you as quickly as possible!"

What on earth was wrong with her? One minute she was angry and resentful that she might not have a rich husband like Ariana; the next she wanted nothing more than to fall into Mr. O'Brien's arms!

It was madness. It was irritating. She wanted two things, and could not have them both. If she were to open her heart to the curate, she was kissing her dreams of grandeur good-bye. If she did not, she would never forget his kind ways and earnestness, and large blue eyes, and handsome demeanour . . . Oh, it was too vexing to think upon!

She caught movement from the corner of her eye and looked out a window just in time to see the last of Mr. O'Brien disappearing into the wood. He was running.

Mr. O'Brien figured that he had run about half the distance, and had to stop and catch his breath for a moment. He used his woolen scarf to protect his lungs from the cold, and was about to resume his trek when he heard the sound of a horse approaching, and let out a cry of, "Ho, there!"

He saw the animal first, and then its rider,

but did not recognize the man immediately. The rider said, "Whoa," and pulled on the reins, and then clip-clopped up to the cleric. The horse whinnied to a stop.

"Here you are!" the man said. "I see I'm still in time to be of service."

Mr. Barton pressed his heels lightly into the horse's side and circled Mr. O'Brien, making it very difficult for the curate to speak to him, but he cried, "You can be of service, sir, by lending me your horse!"

Mr. Barton eyed him and then asked, "Where is Miss Forsythe, sir?"

Mr. O'Brien fell silent. He did not wish to send Barton to a woman alone. Finally, he said, "Make room for me; I'll take you to her."

He climbed atop the horse, and directed them back to the cottage. Beatrice, watching from a window, was ecstatic at the speed at which she was being rescued. She burst out the front door before the men had a chance to reach it. As they rode up, she saw Mr. Barton first, and smiled in surprise. His face was drawn. She realized Mr. O'Brien was behind him as he got off the animal. He held out a hand to her, and she came forward.

"Come," Mr. Barton said, "extending his own hand toward Beatrice. I shall return

271

you to the house at once. Help her up, will you, O'Brien?"

Mr. O'Brien lifted Beatrice as high as he could, looking deeply into her eyes when they chanced to be close to his. Mr. Barton did his part to bring up her up securely in front of him. She sat with his arms holding the reins on either side of her, her legs on one side. Mr. Barton put one arm protectively about her middle, while tightening up his hold on the reins.

With a nod, he dug in his heels, and Beatrice felt a stab of regret as they turned around to be off. "Thank you!" she cried to Mr. O'Brien, looking tall and dignified in front of the cottage. "Thank you!"

He acknowledged her words with a simple nod, but there was a grim look on his face. It was not an expression she had seen on him ever before.

Mr. O'Brien found a bucket in the house, but no water. If there had been water, it would have been frozen in any case. He had to scoop out the hot coals and tote them outside in a black pot that was made for such things. He carefully scraped every last bit of ash just to be safe, and then finally blew out the candle lamp, and the smaller candle. In the dark, he found the door, and then closed it behind him. He was mildly worried that Mr. Barton would not return Beatrice directly to the house, but there was nothing he could do at the moment. He wrapped his scarf again more securely about his neck, and adjusted his hat. Bending his head against the cold, he started the long walk back.

Beatrice didn't usually ride a tall horse, and never with a man. She was uncomfortable and a little bit frightened at how far the ground was, not to mention the jerking of the animal. Mr. Barton could tell she was scared, and he tightened his grip about her.

"Do not worry," he said, "I've got you!" And he did; but she did not care to have him holding her about the middle.

"Perhaps you would do better to slow down," she yelled. He seemed not to have heard her, but Beatrice would not turn her face toward his — not when she was practically in the man's lap. He was able to speak right into her ear, however, and he yelled, "I am delighted to be of service to you, Miss Forsythe!"

She winced. He did not need to yell for her to hear! She merely nodded her head. Suddenly a man was there ahead, upon a great black horse, blocking the path with his large mount. Barton slowed down, and they came abreast of each other. Without a word, the man lifted a rifle from somewhere, and Beatrice's heart jumped into her throat! What was happening? But she caught a glimpse of a handsome face beneath the hat, behind the high collar — it was Mr. Mornay! Thank God!

Mr. Mornay held the gun in one hand, and balancing it against his leg, cocked it, and sent a shot into the air. Beatrice jumped despite herself, making Mr. Barton tighten his grasp all the more. If Mr. Mornay had been surprised to find Mr. Barton on his property, with one of his own horses, and his sister-in-law almost in his arms, he did not show it. Mr. Fotch appeared on his animal.

"Where's O'Brien?" Mr. Mornay asked.

"We left him about half a mile back, I should think," said Mr. Barton.

Mr. Mornay leveled his gaze at Beatrice, who felt suddenly like a naughty child caught doing something mischievous. "Is all well?" he asked her.

"Yes."

"No one hurt or anything?"

She paused. "No. Nothing of moment." He caught a note of hesitation in her voice, and eyed her for a moment, but looking back to Barton, said, "Obliged, Barton. Take her to the house. I'll check on O'Brien."

He nudged his horse forward, already rehearsing in his mind a few choice words for that young man. Was he *always* trouble? Everywhere he went? Or was it only to plague Mr. Mornay that his appearance always seemed to coincide with some sort of ill happenstance? At any case, he wanted to give him a good combing for it. A gentleman should have known better than to worry half the household, not to mention going off alone for hours with a young woman of quality.

He moved on, ready to deliver himself of such thoughts to the man.

FIFTEEN

Mrs. Forsythe and Ariana came apart from praying together for Beatrice and Mr. O'Brien — which they did just in case there was some danger afoot, though Ariana could not imagine what it could be, other than exposure to the cold.

"They may have got lost," the older woman mused, as they went on. "You have such a large property, and there are paths and woods, are there not?"

"Yes; I suppose they might have lost their way." Then Ariana had a thought. "Mama, do you think they would have attempted the maze?"

Mrs. Forsythe's response was assured. "No. Your sister has a dread of mazes! She said so just the other day."

They walked on, and Ariana said, "Let us go toward the cottages. Perhaps they wanted to see them. They may have been invited inside by someone. We have the loveliest tenants, Mama! Not a one of them is trouble to us."

"My dear," Mrs. Forsythe did not like to think badly of anyone, but doubts were assailing her, as they tended to do whenever circumstances lacked an explanation, temporarily. "You know Mr. O'Brien best, I daresay. Is he an honourable man?"

Ariana said, breezily, "But of course! Very honourable, indeed!" And as soon as the words left her lips she remembered the matter of his persistence and refusal to accept Ariana's rejection of his suit, years ago. And what about the time when he had lost his head completely, and plucked her into his arms for an unexpected — and unwelcome — kiss?

Her mother was well sastisfied with her response, however, so she said nothing more, but now Ariana had her own worries and doubts. Finally, she said, "There is no doubt that he would never harm Beatrice; or abuse her. He has, in the past, been persistent in his addresses to me, is all."

Her mother eyed her with fresh worry: "I did consider him a polite, gentlemanlike man; and of a strong religious sensibility. Am I to regret giving them leave to go out walking unchaperoned?"

Ariana fell into thought, but said, "I cannot believe that he would do anything at all amiss! We must trust his character! He is . . . a good man."

Mrs. Forsythe nodded. Then she added, "Beatrice is young, but she is exceedingly sensible." She sounded more wishful than certain.

"Yes, I am sure you are right." Ariana stopped walking, and touched her mother's arm.

"We have prayed for them, have we not? We have put them into God's hands! Let us not waste another thought fretting about them!"

"You are right, indeed, my dear!"

"Yes, I'm certain I am," she said, moving on. Her cheeks and the tip of her nose were rosy from the cold, and she blinked from the wind bringing tears to her eyes. They had reached a small rise in the landscape, and a neat row of cottages could be seen, still far in the distance, but in sight.

"There," said Ariana. "These are the first of our cottages. They are all newly roofed or thatched!"

From inside her cottage, Mrs. Taller was staring mindlessly out of the single window facing west; she saw the figures of the women — yes, it had to be women, for they looked to be wearing gowns — and suddenly a forlorn hope rose quickly in her breast.

That had to be the mistress! Mrs. Mornay was kind and good. Everyone knew it. People put their names on a waiting list to rent a house on the Mornay property. Not only did the Master do his utmost to see that all of his tenants remained gainfully employed, but Mrs. Mornay was more than generous, and sent things to her tenants numerous times throughout the year.

One year she had spearheaded an effort to make sure all the children had coats and shoe. Another time, the Mornays paid for a new young pig for each and every family. What good eating that winter! There was only one weakness in their goodness, which had arisen since the arrival of the two children in the household, which was that, if anyone fell ill, they were supposed to notify Mr. Horton at once. The measure was implemented after a terrible incident in a nearby house of the gentry where the heir, a little boy only six years old, had been playing with a tenant's child, who no one knew was sick. Symptoms didn't arise until the next day, when it became obvious the lad was ill. The son of the household also fell sick a day or two later. Only, when the first recovered, the little heir had not.

This sent a wave of fright around the countryside, so that many families began to treat their tenants like outcasts; others, like the Mornays (whose children were still too young to play much with other children, anyway) implemented precautions. This was why Giles had not wanted MaryAnn's sickness known. The other side of the precaution was that if a man had any sickness in his house, he should not report to work on the property; he could take a situation elsewhere if he could find one; but until all question of contagious illness was past, he was to stay clear of the other hands on the property, and, of course, the family in the big house.

Mr. Horton himself had adopted such rules, having learned from another steward of a nearby property that they had done so. Mr. Mornay thought it reasonable, and let it remain in effect.

Ariana knew nothing about it, simply because her husband had never thought to inform her. He saw no reason to, as, to his knowledge, only once had a man needed to lay off work for reason of sickness. There were actually numerous incidents of such occurring, but only Mr. Horton needed to be aware of them, and he did not bother his employer for every little development.

In any case, when Mrs. Taller saw the two women, she suddenly knew she must act. The apothecary's medicine had done naught for the girl. MaryAnn, she felt, was near the end of her suffering. She hadn't been conscious for two days now, and her skin was still hot to the touch. She needed to beg Mrs. Mornay to send their family physician — the Tallers could not afford a physician, and usually relied upon the apothecary. But it hadn't done; his herbs hadn't worked. His poultices were of no effect. Mrs. Taller was at her wit's end.

She had no way of knowing that Mr. Horton, the steward, was making a sweep of the cottages at that very moment; or that, knowing of her daughter's condition, he would send a physician. But it suddenly seemed absurdly obvious that Mrs. Mornay should be applied to for help. Of course! Why had she not thought of it sooner?

Giles was on his way home. He had got word of the sweep going on by Mr. Horton and knew that his game was up. He had been preparing to come clean in any case, as he belatedly accepted that his daughter might die. She was the sickest of the lot. He couldn't very well have just showed up for work one day and announced her passing.

Mr. Horton would look into the matter. No, Giles had to admit the situation now, while he could. He was going to stop at the cottage and then go look for the steward; either that or he'd just wait for the man to come to them. It was only a matter of time.

Mistress Taller saw her opportunity. Surely that was Mrs. Mornay up there on that hill! This could be her only chance. Once again, she had to leave the children alone while she went out. But she hoped that this time, her mission would result in the visit of a real physician.

Just then, she heard a strange noise coming from the vicinity of her daughter's sickbed. She rushed over, felt the wet cloth she had left on the girl's brow, and dipped it in fresh water. After wringing it out sufficiently, she replaced it across the hot brow. Another sound came from the girl's throat, though she appeared to still be sleeping. Mrs. Taller bent her head to try and hear.

"MaryAnn! Are you speaking, child?" When there was no answer, she put her face right up to her child's face, willing her to talk, willing her to regain consciousness. But only the same shallow, labored breathing was to be heard. She hurried back to peer out the window and saw that the two ladies were moving in her direction. *Mercy!*

She quickly pulled a shawl from a peg and hurried out the door. She was going to break a rule by speaking directly to Mrs. Mornay when her daughter was ill, but what could she do? She had to risk it.

Mr. O'Brien was running and never heard the sound of the hooves approaching. All he knew was that suddenly there was a monstrous horse rearing up in his face, and he shielded his head with his arms, expecting the worst. But nothing happened. The horse was whinnying and Mr. Mornay shouted to regain control over the beast, but no great heavy legs came down upon him. Soon, he stood and watched while the animal circled, as Mr. Mornay slowly quieted his animal, and then clopped over to Mr. O'Brien. The curate had thought it was Barton again, but instead found his host looking at him quizzically from atop the huge mount. His look was not benign.

"Do you need assistance?" he asked.

"No, sir. I am making my way back."

"What happened?"

"We walked too far, I am afraid. Miss Forsythe began to suffer frostbite on her feet; we had just come out at the parsonage —"

At this, Mr. Mornay scowled. "You mean

to say, the two of you walked as far as that? All the way to Glendover?"

Mr. O'Brien hesitated. "Well, yes; it did not seem so very far."

Mr. Mornay took an exasperated breath. "It hardly seems possible!" He looked back at the cleric. "Well?"

"We found the door unlocked, and went in to start a fire —"

"To the house? It was indeed open?"

"Yes!" He paused, watching the other man with some surprise. "I made a fire, and did what I could to safeguard Miss Forsythe from incurring permanent damage. I have had experience with such things, in St. Pancras, you know."

Mr. Mornay had been reining in his horse, while the animal stamped impatiently. He suddenly barked, "Get on behind me, O'Brien."

Mr. O'Brien hesitated. "I do not ride very often . . ."

"Yes? So? Up with you." He held out one arm to help him. Mr. O'Brien, being tall and slim was able to climb atop Tornado better than most men would have. He was obliged to hang on to Mr. Mornay, which felt ludicrous to him, but what could he do? He'd fall right off the animal if he didn't. He hoped no one would be about save the groom or stable hands when they returned.

After his recent discussions with Mornay, he had felt — at long last — they were approaching more of a friendly footing with one another. Was this day going to ruin all?

"Is it not a pretty day?" Ariana asked.

"It is a cold one," Mrs. Forsythe returned, for she was beginning to feel the effects of it about her feet; and without a muff, and no pockets on her redingote, even her gloved hands were starting to grow stiff with cold.

Ariana stopped in her tracks. "Are you cold?" She sounded surprised.

"My dear, it must be near freezing; yes, I am cold. I think we should go back."

"Mama — we can call upon a tenant and escape the cold. Mr. Mornay has had every cottage whitewashed on the inside. I should like you to see one. And, would you not like to meet some of our cottagers? They are the dearest people!"

Mrs. Forsythe surveyed her daughter. Ariana had a cap on beneath her bonnet, a lined heavy redingote, and half-boots. She did not, in fact, appear to notice the cold.

"How is it you are not chilled half to death as I am?"

Ariana's mouth dropped open just a little. "Oh, my! I do not seem to feel the cold as

285

much as other people. I think since my mishap falling from the boat that time, I seem to have developed a resistance to cold air! But I will return with you, since you are so uncomfortable. We'll see a cottage another day."

They turned back toward the house, but in seconds, they both heard a woman's voice calling out to them. No; it was to Ariana. *"Mrs. Mornay! Mum! Mrs. Mornay! If you please, mum!"*

"My word!" she breathed.

"Who is that woman?" asked her mother.

"I cannot tell . . . though I believe it may be Mrs. Taller. She seems to be in some distress! Wait here, Mama!"

Ariana began walking quickly back toward the woman, who was now running toward her. Mrs. Forsythe waited only a few seconds before deciding that she must know what was happening, and so she hurried after her daughter.

Mr. Barton was elated that he had been able to rescue Miss Forsythe.

At the house he waited impatiently after their arrival for a man to come and help her down; he thought it was safer if he stayed astride the horse until she had been helped off it. When a hearty shout of "Ho, there!"

still failed to produce a boy or footman, he gave a sigh, and said, "We'll go to the stables for help; and then I'll get you to the house in a trice."

"I can climb down right here," Beatrice said.

"No, ma'am! You're liable to break an ankle!" He had taken the horse he was offered, after coming to call at the house and finding there was a search going on for Miss Forsythe and the curate, but it was a good-sized mare; fifteen hands, at least. That the clergyman was gone off with Miss Forsythe angered him. Was that pesky cleric trying to make an inroad to Miss Forsythe's heart? That was not allowable. Having conceived of marrying her himself, he was fast growing overfond of the idea. He liked it very well. He relished the thought of finding himself a relation of the Mornays. And if he was to buy the Manor House, they would be neighbours as well. He and Mornay ought to be fast friends in no time.

It made such a cozy picture in his mind that he was determined to be as pleasing to the young lady as possible, and so to win her. With a protective tightening of his hold about her now, he smiled to himself and turned the horse toward the stables.

After Beatrice and he were leaving the

stables, she turned to her companion. "Mr. Barton — may I ask for your confidence, sir?"

He was thrilled to be asked for such a thing from her. "You have it, my dearest Miss Forsythe — with all my heart!"

"Thank you, sir. You see," and she hesitated. "I comprehend that you may have a mistaken notion since it appears that I was alone with Mr. O'Brien —"

"If it is a mistaken notion," he said, carefully, "you need only say so; and I shall believe you, utterly."

"Shall you! Oh, I thank you, sir! For there was nothing at all improper about it! My feet were frozen, and Mr. O'Brien was good enough to build a fire for me."

He had no doubt that she was speaking the truth, so it was easy for him to assure her of that.

"But what I most need from you, Mr. Barton, is your assurance that you shall tell no one about the cottage." She had stopped walking, and they gazed at one another. He was wishing he could declare his intentions right then and there, but was momentarily lacking the courage.

"I am sorry to ask you to participate in what seems to amount to a lie," she said awkwardly, and she turned away and resumed walking, for she was very agitated. "But I fear that if Mr. Mornay learns what happened, he will insist upon believing other lies — that we were improper or some such thing! And that would mean a marriage!"

Now Mr. Barton became utterly soothing. His worst fear at that moment was precisely that which she dreaded might happen. Mornay was the type, it seemed to him, to sit upon points. "Miss Forsythe, I would sooner die than reveal your secret," he told her with entire honesty. "I came upon you in the wood, let us say. And brought you back from there."

"Thank you, Mr. Barton! Then we are agreed upon it!"

"Does Mr. O'Brien know of your concern?" Mr. Barton asked. "Will he keep your secret?" How could Beatrice not have thought of that! For a moment, she floundered in uncertainty. "Oh, dear!" But then her look cleared and she exclaimed, "Mr. O'Brien is a new curate! He shan't want a hint of scandal about his name! I daresay he will be happy to go along with us!"

Mr. Barton nodded, his eyes narrowing shrewdly. "I think you have the right of it. Excellent."

■ ■ ■ ■

"Oh, Mrs. Mornay!" Mrs. Taller had now reached Ariana and started to sob. Ariana's large eyes, filled with compassion, had broken a growing dam of tears inside the lady, and suddenly she was crying uncontrollably. Ariana put out her arms, and the woman fell into them, sobbing. In fact, she was not feeling well herself. All of the strain of worry, and tending her sick children, had resulted in an alarming measure of faintness. Mrs. Taller blinked, and tried to remember her mission, and that this was the mistress, and she stepped back.

"How can I help you, Mrs. Taller?"

Mrs. Forsythe, standing back a few feet out of politeness, was wondering the same thing.

"Oh, my lady!" she cried, forgetting that Ariana was not a "real" lady, " 'tis my daughter! MaryAnn!" She had to suppress more sobs at this point.

"What has happened to MaryAnn?" Ariana asked, to prompt more of the story from her.

"I fear she's dyin'! I give 'er the 'pothecary's cure, but it ain't done nothin'! She's worse'n ever!"

"Tell me what happened to MaryAnn," Ariana instructed.

"She's got the fever! Three or four days, now! I've tried to nurse 'er through it, but she's only got worse! Ah fear — ah fear she's dyin'! Please say you'll 'elp us, Mrs. Mornay! You're me last 'ope!"

Mrs. Forsythe felt terrible, but she had to speak: "What can Mrs. Mornay do, madam? She is not God."

"Come and look at 'er!" she cried. "Pray for my child, mistress, ah beg you!"

Ariana hesitated, not sure of what to do. Finally, she turned to her mother. "Mama, I pray you, go back to the house and see that Mr. Speckman is sent for at once. See that he comes directly to the Taller's cottage!"

"Oh, bless you, mum!" the lady cried. "Bless y'er good 'eart!"

Mrs. Forsythe turned to do as she was bade, but there was something she did not like about the situation — only she could not think what it was. The doctor was needed and she must hurry back. But then it struck her, and she whirled back around. Her daughter had already gone a few yards, hurrying along beside Mrs. Taller.

"Ariana!" she called, loudly as she could. "Do not go to that gel! You may get sick!"

"I am not afraid of that, Mama!" She turned away.

"Ariana! The *children!* Your infant!"

This stopped Ariana in her tracks. She turned back around. When her gaze met her mother's, the older woman nodded her head. *Yes, you must think of your children!* her eyes seemed to say. But Mrs. Taller pulled on her redingote. "Ahm beggin' you, Mrs. Mornay! Ah jus' know if *you* pray over 'er, she'll get better! Ahm sure of it!"

Ariana turned to the woman, and her face creased in regret. "Mrs. Taller, I will pray for MaryAnn, I promise you! But I cannot go with you to see her. I am sorry, ma'am, truly!"

Mrs. Taller fell silent and stared at Ariana for a long moment. Then, she lost her wits. She fell upon Ariana, crying and sobbing. "We'er goin' to lose 'er! Ah know it!" She couldn't stop; she began to pull at Ariana's gown, and fell to her knees, still sobbing. Ariana just stood there helplessly, not knowing what to do. She began to gently extricate herself, only the lady was not ready to let her go.

Mrs. Taller wasn't thinking straight. In fact, she suddenly couldn't even *see* straight! What was she doing outside in this freezing air? She was shaking, and held on with an iron grip to this white vision in front of her. Was this an angel from heaven she had caught? *Please!* she begged. *Heal my daughter! Heal her! Have mercy on her!*

Ariana saw men approaching and waved wildly to them. She could not get Mrs. Taller's strong hands off of her legs, and she was beginning to have difficulty staying on her feet. Mrs. Taller was becoming incoherent; she never heard the shouts of the man coming up swiftly behind her. Ariana recognized him; it was the woman's husband. Thank goodness! He said, "Betsey!" in a strong voice, but when she heard it, Mrs. Taller froze for a second, and then wrapped her arms around Ariana's legs as though she would hold on for dear life. *"Heal my daughter!"* She still sobbed.

"A physician is on his way, Mrs. Taller! He will help you, I promise!" But Ariana's voice was weak, and the tears in her eyes were no longer from the biting cold.

Giles Taller took hold of his wife's hands and pried them loose from Ariana. His face was set in a mean frown, and his eyes were troubled. "What're you doin'?" he asked his wife, in weak tones of dismay. He was bewildered, or horrified, Ariana could not tell.

"What're you doin'? Ye're goin' ta make

everythin' worse!" He had turned her around to face him, and the lady had stared up at him with glazed eyes. Suddenly, she went unconscious, just like that. He pulled her to her feet, slumping against him, and then he hefted her up into his arms and turned and tromped back to the cottage carrying her.

Mr. Horton had been approaching from some distance but reached her now, astride his horse. "Did she touch you?" he asked Ariana.

Ariana was so surprised by that question, and still in a bit of shock over what had just occurred, that all she could do for a moment was look at him silently. She wanted her husband's arms to collapse into, but he wasn't there. "Mrs. Mornay, did Mrs. Taller touch you? Please, I need to know!"

"Yes. Yes, she did. Why?"

"The fever. Her daughter's sick with it, and she may 'ave it too."

As soon as he said that, Ariana realized that Mrs. Taller's hands had been hot. Here they were, out in the cold, and her hands were *hot*. Mrs. Taller had the fever, like her daughter. That explained her odd behavior, her begging Ariana to heal her child.

Mr. Horton was looking back at the couple, smaller now as they approached the distant cottage, and was shaking his head. He'd give them the boot, for sure. After all his precautions, how had this happened? What was Mrs. Mornay doing out here, anyway?

"Mrs. Mornay," he said, jumping down from the animal. "Take my horse and get you back to the house. I would advise you, ma'am, to send for Mr. Speckman, and not to see the children until you see him."

Ariana looked at him wonderingly. The situation was still sinking in on her. While she hesitated, he grew more exasperated. "Madam, please!" He lifted her upon the horse, and handed her the reins.

"Mrs. Mornay." He finally got her attention fully. "Go to the house and call the doctor." She nodded, but her mind was still on the sad plight of her tenants, of Mrs. Taller's desperation and fear; she turned the horse around, however, and soon saw Mr. Mornay, still astride his own mount, coming over the hill. Ariana gave her horse a slap of the reins, and went to meet him.

Mr. Horton turned in their direction, but his steps were heavy. His heart was even heavier. He'd only found out about the sick children minutes earlier, from the cottagers who lived right behind the Tallers. Now what would happen? And what would happen to *her?* The beautiful wife of Mr. Mornay?

What if she had already caught the illness? How would he forgive himself? And what would his master do about it? All these questions flooded his mind, and he made an instant decision to ask in town for the latest news of the malady. Where was it spreading? How many were dying from it? Most importantly, *could anything be done?*

The husband and wife, meanwhile, conferred together, their horses side by side, while he watched, approaching. Mr. Mornay reached across from where he sat, and took his wife bracingly by the arms. He kissed her face. She was now in tears, it appeared. Finally, after he had spoken something more to her, she gently pressed her heels into the horse's side, and soon disappeared over the hill.

When Mr. Mornay had come about and was facing him, he could tell, even at the distance he was, that his employer was not happy. Nor should he be. He plodded on to face him.

Sixteen

"Mr. Barton, you are more jovial than even your usual jovial self," observed Mrs. Royleforst, in the drawing room. She had finally made her public entrance feeling much restored after taking breakfast in her room.

Miss Forsythe was rosy-cheeked and glowing, but seemed downcast; Mr. Barton, also red from the outdoors, was full of witticisms and good manners; and Miss Barton seemed to be at peace on this day, as though she had resolved some nagging, pressing issue. Mr. O'Brien entered the room just then, and he, too, looked as though he had just come in from the cold.

"Ah, you are observant, ma'am," Mr. Barton replied, with a bow of acknowledgement. "I am merely pleased that I was able to be of service to our Miss Forsythe just now."

Beatrice said nothing, especially since she

was watching Mr. O'Brien cautiously. She had to let him know how important it was to keep to the story she and Mr. Barton had agreed upon!

"And how were you of service?" Mrs. Royleforst wished to know.

"I rescued a damsel in distress!" he said, with his usual well-spoken aplomb; he made sure to make eye contact with O'Brien. *Good. He was listening.*

"*Rescued?*" Her little black eyes grew wide, as wide as they were capable of getting. "Tell me everything!" she cried. "What happened? Is that why the house was deserted? When Miss Bluford and I came down this morning, we could not so much as locate a footman! No butler! Nary a housemaid! I said to my companion, 'Miss Bluford, it appears that this house has gone deserted! We are abandoned!' "

Miss Bluford was already nodding her head in earnest agreement. "Indeed!"

"We could hardly get a cup of bohea, much less a bite of refreshment," she added. "And at Aspindon!"

Mr. O'Brien said, meeting Beatrice's eyes (which were unaccountably alarmed, he thought), "I can tell you what happened. Nothing exciting, I'm afraid." She was still staring at him apprehensively. He studied

298

her, and knew something was distressing her.

"Yes?" said Mrs. Royleforst.

Mr. O'Brien continued, very slowly. "Miss Forsythe was getting her exercise, and I offered to escort her."

"What sort of exercise?" asked Mrs. Royleforst curiously.

"Just walking, ma'am. On the property."

"Miss Forsythe was walking and so you joined her."

"Exactly."

"Not alone?"

"She would have been alone, but I walked with her."

"Just the two of you?"

"Yes, just the two of us," he said, very deliberately, as if anyone who dared to challenge the propriety of it must needs answer for it. Beatrice's heart was pounding. It was all going to come out, she knew it! She looked with a panicked expression to Mr. Barton, who was waiting for his moment to take over the story, watching with as much interest as Beatrice.

Mrs. Royleforst started to take a sip of tea, but stopped in midair. "Where did you walk to, alone, just the two of you?"

"We *saw* Glendover, ma'am," Beatrice put in. She could not stand to be silent a moment longer, for fear that Mr. O'Brien would spill the whole business.

"What? Impossible! Not on foot, in this cold!" Her teacup was hastily returned to its saucer, causing a small amount of liquid to splosh on her gown. Miss Bluford instantly produced a handkerchief and came to her mistress's aid, while the lady, ignoring her companion, said, "I am all astonishment!" and cast a sly look at first Beatrice, and then the cleric, who had taken on a look of concern. *It was odd,* he thought, *that both Mr. Mornay and Mrs. Royleforst had found it hard to believe they'd been to Glendover. Could he and Beatrice have found a shortcut to the place? But no, it was a well-worn path. Why was it hard for them to believe they might have walked the mile or so to the cottage? And what was Beatrice about, anyway?*

Before anything more could be said, Mrs. Forsythe came into the drawing room and just stood, looking at everyone for a moment. She had already been apprised of her daughter's safe return, and she would certainly discover every last detail regarding the event — later. For the moment, she surmised from Beatrice's calm visage and manner, that the gentleman had indeed acted a gentleman throughout the ordeal.

Then, looking at Mrs. Royleforst, she said,

"I gave my express leave for Mr. O'Brien to accompany my daughter, ma'am. He is an old family friend, and we trust him implicitly."

Mr. Barton's eyes narrowed; he did not like to hear praise of his competition. Mr. O'Brien, meanwhile, could almost have stood a little taller. He was grateful for those kind words. And Beatrice breathed a sigh of relief.

Mrs. Forsythe turned to the whole room. "There is a sick child on the estate; her mother was quite distraught. I beg each of you to think of her when you say your prayers this night." Mrs. Forsythe had already located a flustered Frederick, who had just returned from searching for the missing couple, as he had heard the shot. He now had to send for the doctor apace, and see that he went directly to the Taller cottage. (Mr. Frederick was not used to such excitement. A multitude of guests always did upset the apple cart, he reflected . . .)

Mrs. Forsythe came into the room and sat down. She took a breath, then stood and pulled the bellpull. "A cup of China tea," she said, when a maid appeared.

Mrs. Royleforst thought she had given this interruption enough time. "Well, I can allow that you had permission, but now you must relate your adventure in full," she said, putting her eyes upon Beatrice.

Oh, no! But Mr. Barton now came to the rescue. With a pointed look at Mr. O'Brien, he said, "Allow me, ma'am. We were all concerned for the safety of our friends because of the cold, and when the other gentlemen rode out to search for Miss Forsythe (he did not mention the curate), my sister and I arrived just after. I knew immediately that I must do my part, of course. I found a horse, and went searching for them, and I was fortunate enough to be the man to find the wayward couple," he finished playfully. "Mr. O'Brien was good enough to give Miss Forsythe a hand up, and I was able to take her back to safety."

While Mrs. Royleforst nodded, listening, he added, again with a look at O'Brien: "There was no question of impropriety, you see, unless you wish to think that two people, dressed to the nines in coats and gloves and scarves can be very much improper with each other."

"Oh, sir!" Mrs. Forsythe said, for she knew nothing of the cottage. "Of course there is no question of impropriety! Upon my word!"

Mr. O'Brien was understanding enough

to comprehend that Beatrice wished to keep the full extent of the event under wraps; and, since he saw no harm in doing so at present, said nothing to contradict Mr. Barton's account. But he was curious to know exactly what was afoot with Beatrice and Barton. Besides which, if he was questioned by Mr. Mornay, he would tell the entire truth.

Beatrice said, "Exactly so. We merely walked to the parsonage. We followed a pathway that was so well worn we simply had to know what lay at its end!" Beatrice smiled at the memory.

Mrs. Royleforst, who knew the estate, raised her eyebrows above both of her little black eyes. "You're certain it was the parsonage! Glendover!" Her tone was infused with disbelief.

"Yes, ma'am, and we were charmed, you must know, by its quaint air and lovely prospect."

"*Quaint* air?" She seemed more surprised than ever.

Mr. O'Brien decided to do his part in the telling. "The worst of it was that Miss Forsythe's feet began to suffer the cold. I would think you should keep close by the fire," he said even now, turning to her. She gazed at him apprehensively. He appeared to be keeping their secret. But all eyes were upon her, so she looked around in surprise and exclaimed, "I am fully recovered, I assure you!"

Mr. O'Brien cleared his throat and Beatrice watched him cautiously. He was going to require an explanation, that much she could tell. So be it. As she thought what to say to him, the door to the room burst open again, only this time it was Mr. Mornay. The look upon his face had the effect of silencing even the thoughts of each member inside it.

Mr. Mornay stood for a moment, surveying them all. He still wore his full outdoor costume except for his hat. But the fact that he had on his overcoat and gloves, and his face, ruddy from the cold, made them all aware, even before he spoke, that he had something of moment to impart.

"The sickness upon the estate is the fever," he said.

There was a collective gasp. Miss Barton's hands circled her middle. Beatrice just stared, blinking. Mr. Mornay wore an odd, disquieting look. In a low voice, Mrs. Forsythe asked, "What is it, Phillip?" She knew there was more, something more that kept him standing in the doorway, with that odd, eerie look about him. She dreaded to

304

hear him say that the girl had died. When he hesitated, she said, "I had your butler send for Mr. Speckman, who is to go to the cottage directly."

"He must stop here first and see Ariana."

Now the whole room went deathly quiet. Mrs. Royleforst found her voice first. "Why should he see Ariana?" It was a statement of dread more than a question. He looked at his aunt.

"The child's mother also has the fever, and she had contact with my wife. We will have to wait and see if she has contracted the illness. In the meantime, pray for her. And for all our tenants." He bowed slightly, and said, "I beg your pardon; I must see to Ariana."

"I don't understand, sir," Mr. Barton said hurriedly, stopping him before he could go. "How did your wife become exposed?" Mr. Mornay thought for a moment, and his eyes fell on Ariana's mother. "Mrs. Forsythe will explain," he said. She nodded her head in obedience, and he left the room.

The adventure of Beatrice and Mr. O'Brien was now wholly forgotten, as each occupant of the room digested this disturbing announcement.

"I daresay we should all avoid any contact with the villagers, and certainly the tenants of this property," said Mrs. Royleforst. The others were mute, but no one disagreed.

Mrs. Forsythe said, in a quiet, grave tone, "We were out walking, hoping to come upon Beatrice and Mr. O'Brien." (Beatrice covered her mouth with her hand. Could it be that her sister was exposed to a disease on her account? What a dreadful thought!) "We saw Mrs. Taller hurrying toward us, and as she got nearer, we could hear that she was calling for Ariana, for Mrs. Mornay." She stopped to glance at her listeners, and saw that she had the attention of everyone in the room. Staring ahead then, as if at nothing, she said, "When Ariana reached her, the lady threw herself upon her, sobbing so that you'd think someone must have —" but the next word was not uttered.

Exclamations of concern were made by Miss Barton and Mrs. Royleforst; Beatrice's face was wrinkled in concern, and she stared down at her lap, ready to cry.

The story continued to unfold. "Neither of us thought of any illness; and she was so distraught, poor woman, that it took some time to make her errand known! She told us of her daughter's condition, and begged for Ariana — Mrs. Mornay, that is — to come home with her and pray for the child.

I believe her name is MaryAnn."

Mr. O'Brien could not help himself. "She did not *accompany her?*"

Mrs. Forsythe met his eyes. "No, sir. She started to, but I reminded her of the children. Little Miranda is most at risk, as I'm sure you'll all agree."

"Oh, yes!" Miss Barton spoke most feelingly, and her face had registered the horror of the idea of the little infant contracting the illness.

"My word!" Mrs. Royleforst said, taking a heavy breath and expelling it in a deep sigh.

Miss Bluford crossed herself. Although she was a Protestant, it seemed like the moment for such a thing.

Mrs. Forsythe picked up her story: "I left for the house, to send for Mr. Speckman, but I looked back once and saw that lady throwing herself upon Ariana's mercy; and I mean, clinging to her legs and dress!"

Again there were sighs and murmurs from the room.

Mr. O'Brien said, "Where is Mrs. Mornay now?"

Mrs. Royleforst replied, "I am sure she has gone to change her clothing; it must be washed or discarded, directly!"

Mrs. Forsythe came to her feet. "I must

confess —" she paused and seemed at a loss for a moment. "I have lost my appetite for company." She looked regretfully at the Bartons, and then Mr. O'Brien. "I beg your pardon; I pray you will excuse me," she said, and with an air of suppressed grief, strode from the room. The men jumped to their feet in order to bow her off, both with eyes of concern. Her leaving in such a state, even more than her story, served to inform the others of the level of distress she felt.

"Poor woman," murmured Mrs. Royle-forst. "We must all hope for the best."

"Dear, me," said Beatrice, now sitting at the edge of her seat. She looked at Mr. O'Brien. "What do you think? Is this all my fault? Ariana was out walking on my account!" She looked so pretty and yet so distressed at the same time, he thought. But his heart swelled because she had looked to him for succor, not Mr. Barton. He quickly got up and went over by her.

"Mrs. Mornay knew that others were already in search of us. And, even if our absence was the reason for her excursion," he said, gently, "you cannot take the blame upon yourself. I am the gentleman, and older than you, and certainly more at fault for allowing us to remain at large for so long a period. I should have anticipated the anxiety which would be felt at your absence."

"You, Miss Forsythe, are certainly *not* to blame!" Mr. Barton was determined to offer her comfort as well. "The only person at fault is that deuced woman, Mrs. Taller!"

"Tristan!" said his sister. "You are not at one of your gentlemen's clubs, to say such things. You are in the presence of ladies, sir!"

"I beg your pardon," he allowed, with an impatient air. "But she had the gall to approach her mistress while being sick! To throw herself upon her betters! 'Tis unconscionable!" These words went unchallenged, as no doubt the others in the room felt similarly. But when he quietly added, "She ought to be brought to the magistrate — if she doesn't die, first!" Beatrice gasped.

"Barton!" His sister looked at him, appalled. "How *can* you be so unfeeling! When Miss Forsythe is already quite upset at the whole business?" No one bothered to mention that Mr. Mornay *was* the acting magistrate in the district — it was neither here nor there.

Mr. O'Brien sent a quelling glance at Mr. Barton, and looked back to Miss Forsythe with concern. Beatrice had a suddenly dry throat. She came to her feet abruptly, and with a mere, "I beg your pardon!" rushed from the room too quickly for either man to even stand up. Mr. Barton was not happy with the result of his speech, and after a moment's hesitation, while he knew himself at fault, but did not know what to do about it, he finally said, "Excuse me!" and went in pursuit of her.

Mr. O'Brien considered whether to dash after him. Was Mr. Barton trustworthy? He was thoughtless, that much he knew. Would he make Beatrice feel worse? As if reading his mind, Miss Barton said, "He means no harm, you know. Tristan just doesn't seem to . . . anticipate the effect of his words upon others."

"Well, that is a deep failing, I daresay," said Mrs. Royleforst. "If a man cannot speak but what is injurious to others, he shall all his lifetime be rushing after people to apologize! He must learn to control his tongue!"

Mr. O'Brien glanced at the empty seat, and then at the doorway. He was itching to follow after Barton. That man would no doubt catch Miss Forsythe off alone somewhere. That did it — with that thought he was on his feet. He met the eyes of Mrs. Royleforst, who nodded at him, as though she knew precisely what he had on his mind.

It gave wings to the thought, and he was instantly heading after them.

"Miss Forsythe! Please wait! I beg you." Barton's voice stopped her in the corridor, where she was hurrying toward her bed-chamber, but she halted, trying to compose herself. She was already tear-streaked, but she raised her skirt to wipe her eyes, and waited for him to reach her, though she did not relish the meeting.

"I am an oaf, a cad, and an addlepate!" he said when he came up to her. "I am here to allow you the opportunity to tell me so, yourself, my dear Miss Forsythe. I am at your service and your command. Tell me to go and drown myself, and I will; I avow it; I will do it!"

At that, she had to glance at him through her wet lashes, and smile just a little.

"You do not deserve to drown," she had to admit.

"What then? Only say what my punish-ment shall be, and it is done! I am at your mercy, Miss Forsythe." When she said noth-ing, he added, watching her closely, "And I must say, there is not another living creature whose mercy I should prefer to cast myself upon."

She looked away quickly, as this sort of

flirtatious statement was not something she was accustomed to hearing. A blush crept into her cheeks, but she was intrigued and delighted by the pretty words.

Mr. Barton saw his chance. If he was to marry into this family, then Beatrice must become his wife; so he added, "I should, in fact, be quite curious to know if I may cast my *future* upon your mercy, as well."

This was just cryptic enough to make her eye him curiously. His future? What could he mean? It couldn't be — but no, that was absurd. They'd only met days earlier.

"I wish very much to pay my addresses to you, Miss Forsythe . . . Beatrice. If I might be so bold?" He had inched closer, and his voice went down a tone. He wanted to make sure she understood his intentions.

Beatrice was utterly amazed — did men usually declare their intentions so quickly after forming a new acquaintance? She was not displeased. Yet, she felt suddenly cautious. Mr. Barton was an entertaining fellow, dashing in appearance, amusing and agreeable. He had to be in possession of a good fortune, for he was keeping company with the Mornays, he dressed fashionably, and he could buy the Manor House if he pleased. He also lived in London. She thought of all these things in swift succession, and then slowly said, "Yes?"

With a surge of elation — she was not averse to him! — he instantly bent his head and landed an unexpected kiss upon her lips. It lasted only a second; and he seemed quite as surprised as did Beatrice by it. But she said, rather wide-eyed, "You must speak to Mr. Mornay! Or my mother!"

And then she saw that Mr. O'Brien was only a foot or so away, and she gasped in surprise. He had not meant to sneak up on them, but the corridor was lined with carpets, keeping his footsteps quiet. Her eyes opened wide in surprise, and she turned on her heel, mortified, and now blushing furiously. She fled quickly away, making Mr. Barton call after her, "I beg your pardon, Miss Forsythe!"

She was so flustered she almost forgot about Ariana. Knowing that Mr. O'Brien, who had been so pleasant and gentle that morning and rescued her freezing feet, had seen that kiss — oh! Her heart filled with frustration. It was too unfair! She hadn't meant to allow Mr. Barton to kiss her! This day was indeed a day of disaster! When she reached her bedchamber (after opening the doors of two others, which were not hers), she fell upon her bed and shed a few tears.

Had Mr. Barton really meant that he

wished to marry her? How could he? They barely knew each other! And yet, what Mr. O'Brien had seen! Could she ever forget it? Only, when she remembered it very carefully, she had to confess that it had not been unpleasant. (She'd been kissed!) But she ought not to be happy about that! It was not proper to allow a gentleman to kiss her.

To think that Mr. Barton had been forming serious thoughts of courting her! How astonishing!

She remembered suddenly her words to Ariana that she was determined not to even consider a man until she had gone to London for a Season. And now here she was with thoughts of not one, but two gentlemen — both turning her head. Was not Mr. Barton just the sort of man she had envisioned meeting in London? And then she thought about Mr. O'Brien. He was not at all the sort of man she dreamed of meeting or marrying. But the thought of his feelings being injured by her was oppressive.

The first order of business, she decided, would be to inform Mr. O'Brien of Mr. Barton's honourable intentions. When he understood that, she was sure he would judge her less harshly. He was possibly the most understanding gentleman of her acquaintance. She found her prayer book, and opened it, but ended up with dark musings for some minutes while she lay there upon her bed in her walking-out dress.

Her thoughts fell upon her sister, and her sense of misgiving returned forcefully. But Ariana was not actually sick. They had no reason to believe that she would definitely get the fever. Only time would tell. She looked over the leaves of her book, and settled down to turn her thoughts toward God. *I will concentrate on this collect! And I will pray for Ariana and her tenants. And for Mr. O'Brien and Mr. Barton!*

Seventeen

Mr. Mornay saw to it that Mr. Speckman examined his wife before going to the Taller cottage. His news was not encouraging. He ordered a hot bath, instructed her husband to see that the clothing she'd worn was discarded or, better yet, burned (he wouldn't normally go to such lengths, but he knew Mornay could afford it, and better safe than sorry). The London fever, he said, did not seem to spare its newest victims a long wait; if they were exposed and had caught it, it needed only two to five days to reveal itself. In the meantime, Mrs. Mornay's children must be sent from the house; in fact, he recommended complete separation for her from all members of the family.

"*Two to five days!* Not to see the children? It's not possible, sir! That won't answer, I assure you!" Ariana was trying not to collapse into tears in front of the man.

The doctor took a heavy breath, and

looked to the husband. "It is necessary, I am afraid, if you would ensure the safety of your offspring."

She started crying then, and Mr. Mornay went to put his hands upon her shoulders, for she was sitting upon a sofa in their bedchamber, while the men were standing. But the doctor said, "Sir, you, too, must stay wide of your wife. For the time being. It won't be for long."

Mr. Mornay looked at Mr. Speckman, and then slowly, deliberately, put his arms about his wife, even dropping to sit at her side. She turned to him at once and fell against him, sobbing softly. Mr. Speckman's mouth pressed into a frown, and he sighed again. "As you wish, sir. But be sure your house is in order." He turned to leave, closing up his leather satchel. He hesitated, and turned around once, and Mr. Mornay looked at him expectantly.

"You will have to stay apart from your children, now, as well, sir." Mr. Mornay took a deep breath, which he seemed to need of a sudden, and nodded. Ariana, hearing that, popped her head up.

"Leave me, then, but do not abandon the children! They have already lost their mother! You cannot be gone from them as well!" The doctor was looking on, unhappily. But he said, "Ma'am; if I may? Children are resilient and they will soon forget this episode. I daresay it will be harder for yourselves than for them. I pray you think only of what is best for them — in the long term — and keep both of you apart from them until I have examined you in six days' time —"

"Six days? Did you not say five days, earlier?"

"I am in mind of your youngest child, ma'am. At such a young age, babies are subject to very violent illness if exposed; I daresay we must take every precaution." He turned again to leave. "If in that expanse of days you are still well, the ban is lifted; you are free to smother your children with affection."

She fell once more against her husband's shoulder, and he circled her with his arms, and kissed the top of her head. "It will go quickly; all will be well, I expect."

Ariana pushed him away and sat up. "The baby! I am Miranda's nourishment! We must send to the village at once for a wet nurse!" She tried not to even think of the discomfort she would have to endure at the sudden cessation of suckling her child. It was said that an application of ice, a few times a day, for a few days, would teach her body to stop producing mother's milk. She despaired that she was going to need to test the theory. More tears began to spill from her eyes on that account, until her husband said, "Stay here and rest; I'll see that we find a wet nurse; and I think I must send our guests on their way."

"Do you have guests, sir?" the doctor asked. "In that case, they must all be sent away too! I am sorry to say it, but we can never be too careful in these cases."

Mr. Speckman followed Mr. Mornay to the drawing room, where still the guests were congregating save Beatrice and Mrs. Forsythe. Servants were sent to fetch them, while Mr. Mornay entered the room and introduced the physician.

"How does Mrs. Mornay?"

"Is she ill, sir?"

"Is it the fever, sir?"

To this onslaught of questions made in chorus, Mr. Mornay held up one hand. "If you please." With the ensuing silence he looked about and said, "Mr. Speckman has something to speak of, and I will return to you shortly; I pray you, hear him out."

Mr. Speckman cleared his throat, and his eyes settled on Mrs. Royleforst. "May I inquire as to the nature of your business at Aspindon? Are you staying long?"

"I am a relation of the family. We have been here these past two weeks, and mean to stay for another month or more." Mr. Speckman nodded and then looked to Mr. Barton.

"My sister and I are neighbours," he supplied.

"Are you the man who has let the Manor House?"

"The very one, sir." He nodded his head at the man in acknowledgment.

Mr. Speckman then turned to Mr. O'Brien, who, guessing his intent, instantly offered, "I am the new curate for Warwickdon, sir."

"The new curate, eh?" He looked interested. "I am happy to make your acquaintance, sir." But he frowned, looking around. Mrs. Forsythe appeared in the doorway, behind him. She had been listening and now waited to see what else would happen.

"It is my medical opinion," said the doctor, "that each of you must fly from this house at your soonest convenience! There is no saying how much distance is required from one who is ill; we simply do not know. However, if you remove from the house, I think I may safely say that you will not contract an illness from under its roof, if it is to appear."

"Does Mrs. Mornay have an illness, then, sir?"

Mr. Speckman turned in surprise since the question had come from the concerned mother, who was still standing in the doorway, behind him.

"And who might you be, madam?"

"I am Mrs. Mornay's mother."

He blanched, but said, "Well, there is no way of telling, until the time for the sickness to appear has passed. But in the meantime, if she is harboring the illness, you are all at risk, every moment you spend here."

"Upon my word!" Mrs. Royleforst cried.

"What of the children and Mr. Mornay?" Mrs. Forsythe's face was clearly distressed.

"The children must leave this abode as well. Mr. Mornay chooses to stay with his wife."

"I should rather stay with her!" cried the mother.

"It is too late for that," said another voice, and Mr. Mornay appeared. He kept back, and added, "Please go into the room, and give me a clear path so that I may speak to you all at some distance."

Mrs. Forsythe eyed him sadly, but did as he bade. Mr. O'Brien quickly moved from his chair and crossed the room, as did Miss

Bluford after seeing his example, so that now all the guests were assembled on one side of the room. Mr. Mornay delicately stepped inside, and quickly went to the opposite end of the room, where he turned to face them.

"I regret to say that Mr. Speckman's advice must be followed. I will put up every one of you who needs a room at the nearest inn, or any place of your choosing. I put my children into your care," he said to Mrs. Forsythe, "only I ask that you keep them here in Middlesex if at all possible. I have already sent servants to seek out a wet nurse for the baby." He paused, thinking. Everyone's face was grave, indeed.

He said, "Where is Miss Forsythe?"

"I believe she retired to her chamber," said Mr. Barton softly.

Mr. Mornay fell silent a minute longer, but then added, "I apologize for your inconvenience," but everyone stopped him with great objections, saying how sorry they all were for this threat of sickness.

"If, in five or six days Ariana has not taken ill, you are safe to return, and I must say, very welcome to do so. In fact, it would bring my wife great pleasure if you did."

"Of course!" Mrs. Forsythe said bracingly, hoping she was speaking for everyone in the room. They were all quick to agree.

"Phillip," she added, "she is my daughter; I have tended to her illnesses in the past, and I daresay it is I should stay with her, not you."

"I have already had a deal of contact with her," he said, shaking his head. "There is no reason to put you, or anyone else, at risk."

"But think of the children, sir! They will need their father!"

Mr. Speckman said, "Mr. Mornay is right, ma'am; he must keep clear of them."

"Sir," she said to the physician, "will you check on them daily? And give us your findings?"

He hesitated, but said, "Certainly, ma'am. Just tell me where you are stopping, and I will send word."

"Where are we stopping, indeed?" she asked to the room in general. Miss Barton looked questioningly to her brother, as if to ask, "Shall we invite them to the Manor?" But he shook his head in the negative, almost imperceptibly; she saw it and remained silent. Her face was troubled, however. She felt ashamed to have a house with empty bedchambers, but not to offer them now.

Mrs. Forsythe had not seen the exchange, and she said, timidly, "Mr. Barton, would it be too great an imposition, sir, to ask if you might have room for us for the few days we must wait? Is it possible, sir, if you will forgive my boldness in asking? I am desperate to remain in the neighbourhood, you see."

Mr. Barton opened his mouth to reply, but for a moment he knew not what to say. Finally, he said, "We lack the servants for so many."

"I can send you servants aplenty," said Mr. Mornay.

"But we lack the room for so many," he added, looking around.

"I do not need a room," said Mr. O'Brien. "I must to London to gather my belongings, and then I shall be settling in at Warwickdon."

"I can return to London as well," put in Mrs. Royleforst, reluctantly. She really had no wish to leave the little ones in the sole care of their grandmama, as she delighted in being part of the family. What an advantage it would give Mrs. Forsythe now! The children would learn to adore their grandmama, and forget all about their Auntie Royleforst!

Mr. Barton saw that he was quickly being backed into a corner — but he had a sudden thought. "Sir — if I may speak to you privately?" He had addressed Mr. Mornay, who nodded, then said to the others, "Begin to pack what you'll need; best to take all, I suppose. We'll iron out where you shall go, in the meantime. Except you, Mrs. Forsythe, if I may have a word with you?"

"Certainly, sir!"

"Mr. Barton, I need a moment with my relation, if you please, and I'll speak to you directly."

"Of course," he said, with a slight bow, and left the room with the others.

Mrs. Forsythe turned to her son-in-law expectantly.

"Have you ascertained yet, what kept your daughter and Mr. O'Brien so long from the house earlier?"

"I have most of the story, I believe." When he waited, she began, "They appear to have walked to your Glendover."

"I cannot credit that; it is nigh two miles."

"Beatrice's feet suffered frostbite, so I think we can safely believe it, sir."

The door opened suddenly just then, and Beatrice rushed into the room. Her face was evidence that she had already been given the news that they would have to abandon the house.

Mrs. Forsythe held an arm open to her, so that Beatrice rushed to her side. "Oh,

Mama! I am to blame for this! If Ariana had not gone looking for me!"

"What happened between you and Mr. O'Brien?" Mr. Mornay asked directly.

Beatrice stared at her brother-in-law. "Between — ?" Her face was all astonishment. "Nothing, sir!"

"No? Mr. O'Brien tells me you entered the parsonage, and that it was empty of anyone save yourselves." Her heart sank. So he already knew about it.

"Yes, that is true. He made a fire so that I could warm myself," she said, "He knew exactly how to help me. And that is *all* he did." She met his eyes with her own. She was subdued and felt defeated, but she knew there had been no impropriety. Every touch of his had been like that of a physician. (Saving for when he had to pull her back from leaving; but that was nothing!) In fact, the thought of what happened, now that her feet no longer hurt, was rather pleasant. He'd been brisk and yet gentle, and so natural and calm that Beatrice had never even thought of feeling embarrassed until afterward, though the idea that he had taken her feet in his hands did, at this moment, seem rather scandalous.

"I trusted him like an older brother, sir, and he behaved no differently than one."

Mr. Mornay looked at her evenly. "You have no older brother to judge by."

"Yes, sir, I have you."

Did she see a sparkle of humour in his eye? "I assure you, there was no question of impropriety. I daresay, I thought nothing of it, perhaps on account of the pain in my feet! He only did what was necessary." Her eyes were wide with sincerity. "Why do you question it, sir?"

"The two of you were gone for more than two hours. Alone. Unchaperoned. It is my duty to question it."

She breathed a sigh of relief. "Well, if that is all, now you know nothing occurred —"

"I would hardly call that nothing," he replied.

Mrs. Forsythe was frowning. "I encouraged them to go," she said.

"Not to Glendover," he replied. "Certainly not to be inside a dwelling alone."

"I understand how it looks," Beatrice's face was growing worried, "but you have my word on it, that nothing improper occurred." She looked at her mother. "You believe me, do you not, Mama?"

"I do, but it does not signify. What matters is what others must think. What the Bartons will think —" Actually, a small flame of hope burst forth in Mrs. Forsythe's breast. Might this not be the very thing she desired? A matter to ensure that her Beatrice must wed the curate? Ought she to say something regarding the settling of Glendover? But not at this time, no.

"No one but Mr. Barton knows we were in the dwelling," Beatrice said, with passion, "and he is the last person who will wish to make it known —" She stopped abruptly.

"Why is that?" Mornay asked.

She blushed, but spoke quickly. "Mr. Barton wishes to pay his addresses to me. He told me last night; I assured him he must speak to you, or to you, Mama."

"He wishes to pay his addresses?" This was a surprise. Here he had been ready to put his family into the care of the Bartons at their estate, but now this changed his mind. He said, "Let me speak to your mother."

She curtsied. "Yes, sir." But she hesitated. "You are not disposed *against* Mr. Barton for any reason in particular, are you, sir?"

"I am disposed to doing the thing that is proper, whether it involves a Mr. Barton or not."

Her mother said, "You are not disposed against Mr. O'Brien for any reason in particular, are you, Beatrice?"

She was silent a moment, and she frowned. "I like him very well. Only I do not wish to marry him."

Mr. Mornay could not help it and replied, "Do not take long walks with a gentleman you do not wish to marry!"

She frowned again, bobbed a curtsey, and left.

Mornay turned to Mrs. Forsythe. "Beatrice should be sent home until I have had a chance to sort through this muddle. I was hoping all my guests might stay at the Manor, but under the circumstances, I think it best to keep more space between your daughter and Mr. Barton. Unfortunately, the same thing holds true concerning Mr. O'Brien."

Mrs. Forsythe cleared her throat, making him eye her curiously. "I am not averse to having more of an acquaintance develop between my daughter and the curate, sir."

He raised his brows. "Indeed!" After an ensuing moment of silence he said, "Well, she is your daughter; I will leave her in your hands. Only, pray be careful. Another hint of scandal between them and they must get a license! Is that agreed?"

"Agreed." She met his eyes sadly. "I will be thinking of Ariana every moment of every day. And yourself."

"Take good care of my children, and I am content."

"We shall! Oh, you know we shall!"

Brighton Pavilion

"Your Royal Highness?"

"Yes, take a letter for me, quickly, man." The Prince Regent winced, while his physician continued to poke and prod, but at least the bloodletting was done. For today.

"Busy today, Your Royal Highness," said the physician, Mr. Watson. "Dictating a letter while your physician examines you!"

"Nothing of national importance, Watson," he replied dryly. "Have a care there, sir!"

"I need to know if the swelling in your ankles is grown worse, Your Royal Highness."

The secretary waited patiently, and suddenly the Regent spotted him. "And stop distracting me from my purpose! I want this dashed business over with, directly!" He looked at his secretary. "Yes, well, 'To Mr. Tristan Barton' (you'll find his direction in your records; he's in Middlesex, near Aspindon House). Where was I? Oh, yes; 'What's the news, Barton? When can I tell the Lord Chancellor to summon Mornay for the presentation of the title, eh? If there's to be another dashed postponement of the business, I want the reason for it!' " When the man still waited, the Regent added, sounding annoyed, "That's all, man! Get it sent!"

He was never in good spirits if he needed his physicians, and he had needed them this day for numerous complaints. Since the unhappy passing of his only child, Princess Charlotte, the year earlier, the Regent's health was rarely stable. Despite a great deal of bad press regarding him as a father, her passing had been like an arrow piercing his heart. It was lodged there, still, and forever would be, he thought. Some of the pain of the arrow was indeed the hollow ache of regrets, memories of disputes he had had with her; scenes of keeping her from her mother, Princess Caroline, for fear of that lady's ill-advised influence upon his daughter. But had it been his wish really to protect the girl from her mother? Or just the power of spleen, revenging himself upon his estranged wife by separating her from her only child? It all seemed quite, quite empty of reason, now; all it had served to do was cause unhappiness for Charlotte; and now she was gone, and he could never make it up to her.

With this sorrow upon him, every annoyance of state, every governmental duty was more tiresome than the last. At least if he got Mornay in the House of Lords, it would put another vote in his favour; he had no energy to influence the Lords, no energy for most things, in fact. Except when he was at table; yet his epicurean delights on that head were catching up with him more than ever. Hence the deuced need for frequent blood-letting, and attacks of the gout, and his accursed digestive difficulties, not to mention the ever-widening girth which the press loved to attack him for!

He no longer cared what the other Lords would make of it; he wanted Phillip Mornay's vote in the House, by Jove, and he wanted the business done with. He was willing to create a new title — the College of Heralds had already sent Mornay a list of possible usages, and he had only to approve one. They'd studied the Mornay family tree as far back as they could go to create their list of names.

Meanwhile, the Regent's letter was written up properly, transposed for palace records, and stamped with the prince's seal. It went by special messenger to Middlesex.

Tristan Barton was granted a reprieve, which he met with secret rejoicing. When

Mr. Mornay had emerged from his discussion with Mrs. Forsythe, he quelled the possibility of their housing any of his guests at the Manor, using as his reason a desire to keep his relations beneath one roof, if possible. The Manor was not large enough for all of them. Barton breathed a sigh of relief. Then, when he finally had Mr. Mornay to himself, he saw the opportunity as one in which to ply the man further on the business for the prince.

"Mr. Mornay, as you know, my sister and I descended upon this neighbourhood rather suddenly, would you not agree?"

"I'll grant that."

"I wanted to come clean to you, sir."

Mr. Mornay raised his eyebrows.

"Yes?" He little wanted a long conversation at the present time, but this was an offer too intriguing not to pursue. What did Mr. Barton have to come clean for?

"I came to this neighbourhood solely on your account; to speak to you on behalf of the prince." When Mr. Mornay only made the slightest response, pressing his lips together with a look of mild disgust, he added, "Does that not astonish you?"

"You are not his first emissary, Barton, and shall likely not be the last. I suspected you might have been, actually. What does he want this time?"

Mr. Barton felt his trump card had just been snatched from his hand, but continued, "Well, sir, I shan't beat around the bush; he wants you to accept the honour of the title, and to take your seat in the Lords, with all haste."

Mr. Mornay waved his hand dismissively. "I know that; I have no time for that, now. You may tell him I'll speak with him when next I'm in town."

Mr. Barton eyed him regretfully. "I do hope, Mr. Mornay, that you will give me leave to speak of this again to you when your wife is recovered."

"My wife is not ill," he returned, softly. *Was he trying to remind Mr. Barton, or himself, of that fact?*

"There is one other matter, if I may be so bold."

Mr. Mornay looked at him knowingly. "My sister-in-law."

Mr. Barton's brows drew together in surprise. "You knew?" He was astonished, because it seemed impossible to him that Mr. Mornay could have construed his feelings regarding Beatrice when he had only so recently determined them himself! How on earth did Mornay surmise them?

"I do, now," he said.

Mr. Barton did not know what to think. Was Mr. Mornay telling him he had known before, or that he had suspected such, and that he, Mr. Barton, had only now affirmed it? Dashed if this man wasn't some sort of mystic! No wonder the prince wanted him in his party.

"Your acquaintance with her is too short for us to discuss anything on this point," Mornay said. "And, I must tell you, her future may already be settled."

Mr. Barton blinked at him. "Are you telling me, sir, that she is betrothed?"

"Not exactly; no."

Mr. Barton was still perplexed, but his brows cleared at this response. He had a new thought. "Is there a reason for which I would not wish to align my name with Miss Forsythe's? Is that what you allude to?"

Mr. Mornay took a breath. "How could that be the case, sir, when my name is linked to her family's?" Before Mr. Barton could respond, he added, "However, if a small dowry is reason enough for you to avoid an alliance, then you should reconsider. Otherwise, I merely think you are too hasty in your thoughts, and I have reason to believe there may be a prior complication."

"A prior complication?" He stared at the man.

As if reading his thoughts, Mornay added, "Nothing to cast doubt upon her character, I assure you."

His brows cleared. "You are referring to the incident this morning with O'Brien. I am prepared to accept the word of Miss Forsythe upon that matter." But that had indeed been his first thought; if Miss Forsythe was in any way connected to a scandal, it would make her less of a prize; yet that in itself might not affect his hopes. In fact, it might seal his standing with Mornay, who could be grateful to the man who would take her, despite this past "complication." He gazed evenly at his neighbour.

"May I take it then, sir, that you have no objection to me as a suitor, if this . . . *complication* can be resolved to your satisfaction?" This was the least he needed to know, but it was something.

"I have made no declaration to the contrary." Mornay's voice was mild, as well as his eyes. "I am not averse to you, if that's what you mean; and it does well for you that you volunteered the information regarding your purposes here. I shan't forget that."

Dash it, but the gentleman was wary. No outright denial, nor an outright endorsement. Slippery as an eel. "May I speak to

Miss Forsythe, then, regarding my hopes?"

"I understood you had already done so," he replied dryly.

Ah! Now he knew what was what. Beatrice had told him — he liked that; it meant she would no doubt welcome him as a suitor. "But do keep in mind, sir," (and his words were spoken deliberately and slowly) "that I *have* spoken to you, and have hopes of her. And that if there is any concern regarding her morning's adventure with the clergyman, I am fully prepared to ignore it entirely." He smiled wryly, and Mr. Mornay met his eyes with an appraising, thoughtful look.

"I shall."

Barton considered his position. He'd have to work on Beatrice, to be sure. She had seemed pleasantly surprised at his interest in her. Now, he only needed to strengthen it, so that the thing would be done. He also needed to ascertain that the "complication" was nothing other than the matter of their being unchaperoned in the cottage. That was enough of a problem to be sure. If it got out, his hopes could be dashed. He'd have to think upon the situation, devise some scheme to protect his interests. But first, he needed to get himself and his sister out of Aspindon House. It was devilish contaminated!

EIGHTEEN

Mr. Frederick knocked hesitantly upon Mr. Mornay's study door. He then entered and shut it behind him.

"*The Black Boar* has been consulted, sir; they have one room available, only. The innkeeper expects that he may have two rooms on the morrow, and wishes to know if you will be laying a desposit on them."

"Two rooms! Hardly enough for four women and two children, plus servants and nurse." He stood up from behind his desk, saying, "Perhaps I'll have to take Ariana to another property, and let the others have this house." He was thinking aloud, which meant that if Frederick desired to say something of the matter, he might properly do so.

"What about Glendover, sir? Without a vicar in it, there's no reason why the women could not stay there. Plenty of room."

"I'll have to see if that's permissible,"

Mornay said, rubbing his chin. The house of worship was on his land, and he held the advowson, but it properly belonged to the bishop of the Anglican Church. He looked appreciatively at his butler. "Well done, Freddy! You may have saved the day. Get a boy to run me a message to the Ordinary. He ought to know."

"Yes, sir." Freddy was elated to have been of help, and, despite the worrisome events causing this mass exodus of the guests, he was ready to go off to accomplish his master's bidding with a spring in his step — almost. "There is one thing more, sir."

When he saw the dark brow go up in expectation, he said, "I wish to be certain you understand that Fotch and I will remain in the house with you and Mrs. Mornay. In addition, one housemaid, and Cook (so long as she is required only to stay in the kitchens), will remain. I'm afraid Monsieur René is packing his things as we speak; but he will inquire next week to ascertain if it is safe for him to return.

Monsieur René was an expensive French chef whom Mr. Mornay kept on because he had a discriminating and fussy palate. The Frenchman, in turn, was discriminating and fussy regarding the use of ingredients, and was often requiring trips to London to restock his pantry. But since his culinary creations were precisely of the caliber that Mr. Mornay most enjoyed, his eccentricities were appreciated rather than found chafing.

"That seems in keeping with René, to be sure. Tell the other servants who choose to stay that I'll pay double wages, but I want only those who aren't afraid; and if anyone is prone to illness, see that they do not stay." He had another thought. "What of Mrs. Hamilton?"

"Oh, staying sir, I beg your pardon! She is devoted to the mistress, as you know."

"Of course; and I suppose Molly . . . ?"

"She is the housemaid I referred to earlier, sir. Staying like an oak in the ground."

Mornay only nodded. It was beginning to feel as though the country had been invaded at last, and they were about to face battle — no matter that the war with the French had ended.

"The footmen have informed me, all save Harry, that they will stay until it is known whether . . . whether . . ." He did not want to say the words: Whether *Mrs. Mornay has contracted the fever.* But Mr. Mornay spared him the need.

"Very good, thank you, Frederick."

"We must say good-bye to Ariana," Mrs.

Forsythe said, as soon as Mr. Mornay appeared from his study. The servants had been dashing from guest bedchamber to guest bedchamber, helping with packing. Miss Bluford alone took care of her mistress, but still there was a great scurrying about going on. Mrs. Forsythe had not yet packed. She had been on her way to do so when it occurred to her that if her daughter did in fact have the seeds of illness within her, that she might not see her again! Banish the thought! But she could not. Once conceived, it continued to be felt, making its presence known like a little dog at one's heels, forever nipping . . . So she had returned to the corridor to find her host and let him know her intentions. It felt so odd, to be always speaking to him across a wide chasm, as he continued to keep his distance on account of his exposure.

"I do not think it advisable," he said, but the usual authority in his tone was not present. He had to admit that it might be important to his wife — or would it upset her more? Who knew? Who could tell such things! So he said, "Allow me to speak with her, first. Are you packed?"

"Not yet; I did not wish to risk missing you."

"Please see to that, and I will see what my

wife says."

"Thank you! Do tell her I desire most urgently to see her before I go."

"But you will be in charge of the children," he suddenly remembered. "If Ariana must endure the separation from them, and you were to get the illness from her anyway —"

"Oh," she moaned. "I see your point. I will not see her. Perhaps Beatrice may —" But she looked up and saw his face and realized that Beatrice would be helping with the children too; the same separation must be kept regarding her as her mother, between them and Ariana.

Mrs. Forsythe cleared her throat. She had to try, once more. "Phillip," she said softly. "I can stay with you. Allow me to stay with my daughter — I am her mother, after all. The two of us can support one another if she falls ill; split the burden of her care. I cannot see you carrying this alone."

He eyed her a moment, remembered instantly his earlier prayer and replied, with a feeling of hope more than conviction, "I shan't be."

Mrs. Forsythe lowered her eyes for a second or two. "You are a father as well as a husband," she added, in that same soft tone. "If you wear yourself out, you are more likely to fall ill; only think how much worse it will be for the children if —"

"No, ma'am," he said. He was eyeing his mother-in-law with as grave a face as he had ever been known to wear. But then, in a soft tone, a very soft, sad voice, he whispered, "Do not even think it."

Just then Mr. Speckman appeared in the corridor, hurrying toward them. The physician's face was grave, and he merely shook his head sadly to the husband's inquiring gaze. "Have the children been removed from the premises yet?"

"They're going now," Phillip's voice sounded hollow.

"Good." Mr. Speckman licked his lips nervously. "And the ladies as well, I presume?"

"We're just on our way, sir." Mrs. Forsythe's voice was also low and inanimate.

"Very good," he murmured. "Leave the direction of your destination with a servant so I may reach you." His grave countenance only heightened the sense of dread and fear that Mrs. Forsythe felt in her heart at that moment. "Thank you, sir."

She went to oversee the packing of her things, while Mr. Mornay checked on his wife. He'd only gone a few steps, however, when he heard, "Mr. Mornay!" It was the voice of Mr. O'Brien, and so he stopped and waited. He could almost welcome the hour when everyone had gone! It was one bother after another.

"I have had a notice from Mr. Hargrove," he said, excitedly, when he'd come up to him, still holding the missive in one hand. "He is abandoning the house as we speak and wishes me joy of it! The housekeeper and servants are wondering if they should close up the place until I return — or keep it open and ready for my use.

"He asks me to let them know at once, and he even desires me to consider taking up residence as quickly as possible, as he does not like to leave his parishioners without a man to perform the duties of service!"

O'Brien's shining eyes did little to enlighten the other man's, for Mornay felt he had much more serious matters to think about than whether or not this cleric was able to begin housekeeping. But he forced himself to be polite.

"I wish you every happiness," he said, hoping to hide his annoyance. He made to turn around to join his wife; he knew she'd still be upset.

"Do you not see, sir?" O'Brien asked, almost with a grin. "I am able to offer rooms for each of your guests, and they may join me at Warwickdon directly! This very day."

Mr. Mornay's eyes lost their annoyance. Since Mr. O'Brien had been formally approved for the curacy, he was in legal possession of the parsonage (or soon would be), and he could invite others to the house. There was no need to bother any local officials over the matter, and his family and children would be safely removed from Aspindon with speed. Additionally — and this mattered in his decision — Mrs. Forsythe actually wished to encourage more contact between Beatrice and the clergyman. It was enough.

"Well done! I am obliged to you."

"Not at all, sir! I am happy and grateful that I am for once in a position to offer you some help." As indeed he was. It was truly the first time for such a thing, and the fact that his circumstance was possible only because Mr. Mornay himself had recommended Mr. O'Brien for the curacy was like poetic justice.

The serious nature of the need for lodgings was not lost on Mr. O'Brien, either. He considered Ariana a friend, and he was stricken with concern for her as much as anyone. To his delight, he'd discovered that Ariana Mornay was still the sweet and earnest young woman he remembered. She had acquired no airs, but nevertheless invited admiration by her presence and kindness. Mr. O'Brien held her in a deep admiration himself, but he had no improper thoughts to plague him regarding her; no old hopes springing up in his breast. He had accepted the marriage, and the ensuing years had served him well in conquering his old feelings for her. It felt deeply satisfying to his manly self that he was finally, in some way, able to be of service, and that it was an important service.

In addition to which, the younger Miss Forsythe was beginning to fill his mind. Bothersomely so. She was very pretty, but he was not yet allowing himself to admire her openly — he must not! Had he not determined never to even think of Beatrice Forsythe as a prospect for marriage? Yes, his past dealings with Ariana were sufficiently quelling to his sensibilities for him to ever aspire to a match with another Forsythe girl. Pity, though.

But he had to live up to his situation: He now saw himself as the friend and neighbour to the Mornays, and the very last thing he should be considering was falling in love with their sister. While the Glendover curacy remained unoccupied, he would encourage them to attend his church, and would endeavour to exercise a clerical attitude toward them, as he would toward anyone in his parish.

It was the least he could do after Mornay had helped him get his new living. That he could be in it so quickly as to be of service during this dire happenstance was a double boon.

An hour or two later, he was handing up the ladies into Mornay's carriage; Mrs. Royleforst, who harrumphed her way in; then Miss Bluford, accepting his help with a big, wobbly smile (which surprised him a great deal, since she usually sat quietly and rather expressionlessly while the others spoke); then Mrs. Forsythe, with a polite word of thanks and ladylike ascent; and pretty Miss Forsythe, with a sad nod and word of thanks. Finally, the two children were brought out. Nigel was all aflutter, for he loved to ride in the carriage, and he scrambled up, hardly allowing Mr. O'Brien to so much as guard his back; and Mrs. Perler came holding the baby. Servants were following with all manner of luggage and blankets and toys in their hands, to be transported in a second coach which sat behind the first.

When both the large coaches were stuffed with passengers, supplies, and luggage, they started off. Mr. O'Brien had given the family the first vehicle, and sat across from a wet nurse from the village who appeared to be a young mother in good health, who had her own child in tow, a sleeping infant in her arms. She had only a single valise with belongings in it, and a large cloth sack of other things. A few other servants were along, a chambermaid and parlour maid, and Harrietta. The lady's maid was red-faced from crying, and sat forlornly, often wiping the tears which kept falling down her face with a sodden handkerchief.

She raised the volume of her crying most remarkably as the trip commenced, though the wet nurse scolded her for it, saying she was like to raise the dead, and what was the new curate to think of such a display?

Harrietta sobbed, "I can' 'elp it! My poor mistress! My poor Mrs. Mornay! They say MaryAnn's dyin'!" She blew her nose loudly into a handkerchief, while Mr. O'Brien said, "There, there, she isn't even sick yet. She may be spared entirely, you know."

"I know it, sir." But her eyes once more welled with tears. "It's 'avin' to leave the 'ouse an' all, I suppose! It's just like she's got the plague!"

"Now, look here," said Mr. O'Brien, who was becoming slightly incensed. "There'll be none of such talk, do you hear? If you spread your pessimism to the other servants, I'll speak to your master about it."

At this Harrietta's head came up and she studied Mr. O'Brien. She did not want to cause trouble, but she had to think him a most unfeeling man. They all ought to be worried about Mrs. Mornay as much as she was. But perhaps they did not love her like her lady's maid did. Harrietta was a devoted servant since the day that Miss Forsythe's coming had raised her from the position of housemaid to that of lady's maid. Mrs. Bentley (now Mrs. Pellham), her former employer, had provided the necessary instruction for her to learn how to style hair, and to care for the expensive fabrics used for ladies' clothing. She had, in one short week, gone from a life of drudgery to that of, comparatively speaking, luxury. And Mrs. Mornay was so pleasant and kind! Why, if anything were to happen to her — and here Harrietta began to shed fresh tears, only she turned away from the parson so he wouldn't see them.

He did, of course. But he looked to the other maids. "Understand this regarding your mistress. She has only been exposed to one sick person. Physicians come into contact with the sick every day of their lives,

349

and yet most of them live to a ripe old age. Mr. Speckman is merely being cautious on account of the children." The maids listened, wide-eyed, interested in knowing every detail they could get hold of. He nodded toward Harrietta.

"This lady has exerted herself far beyond what is merited by the situation. See that no one of you goes off on fanciful notions like hers; we have left Mrs. Mornay in good health and in good hands, and we will add to that our sincere and earnest prayers. If any of you should wish to join us in the drawing room for prayer, we will hold them, say, about nine o'clock of an evening. Does that suit?"

"Yes, sir, thank you, sir."

"Yes, thank you, sir," added Harrietta, almost apologetically.

When the carriages with their luggage and supplies and servants and guests reached Warwickdon, Mrs. Persimmon came out to greet the new master of the house. She had received word barely an hour since that such a numerous company was to come! Her heart was lifted up at the thought; and to have children beneath the roof! What a blessing! Of course, she had quite a load of new concerns, and meant to ask the new master if help might be available, but as she saw the servants exiting the carriage, she took a sigh of relief.

She knew nothing of the reason why all of these people were descending upon the rectory — which she would have to remember to begin referring to as the vicarage — at once, and with her previous master's departure only that morning, it was all a bit unsettling; but she knew that a square was a square and a circle a circle; in other words, all would settle down in its place in time. She had shed a few tears at the loss of Mr. Hargrove, but Mrs. Persimmon was a woman of high energy, and she bounced back from setbacks quickly. Further, she lived upon being needed; and she was elated at the change in the vicarage that was happening.

By the time Mr. O'Brien made his way to the front door, she could almost have kissed his face. "Sir!" she exclaimed. "Might I be allowed to say how very welcome you are to this establishment? How wonderful it is, to have you here directly!" She made a small motion, so that he looked past her to the butler and the maid, the other servants of the place. The butler bowed, holding back a smile; and the maid curtseyed, though the incoming parade she could see on the walkway, and behind her new master, set her heart beating in a flurry. What a great deal of work she was in for!

Mrs. Perler came in directly after the new curate; Mrs. Persimmon almost melted at sight of the infant. But she had a sudden thought: "Mr. O'Brien, sir! You did say you were an unmarried gentleman, did you not?" She was eyeing the infant with wide eyes.

Mrs. Perler blushed, and he answered, "I *am* an unmarried gentleman." He motioned to the baby and the woman. "This is Mr. Mornay's child, and the children's nurse. I will explain all to you shortly, Mrs. Persimmon. The order of the day right now is to find rooms for all of our guests. In the meantime, send a servant to the village — and there are a number of them come with us, who will help you in everything — to put together a dinner for us."

From behind him, a maid spoke up. She was a kitchen maid, helper to Cook, and she said, with an earnest countenance, "Oh, sir, Cook says she'll be sending over the meal, for she 'as enough for a regiment, sir, and no bodies to eat it at all!" Mrs. Persimmon was already counting the little crew of servants from Aspindon, with excitement. "Very good, very good!" she repeated.

To the servants, she added, "Go with Bessie, here, then, and she'll show you to your quarters where you can leave your things. Then hurry down to help our guests!" She paused. "Mr. Sykes, see that our guests are shown to the drawing room and given our finest bohea! I will settle them in their guest chambers soon enough, if you please."

"Yes, ma'am," the butler replied, with a deep and proper nod of the head. It was easy to ascertain that Mrs. Persimmon was the head of the staff in this household.

Mr. O'Brien was welcoming the Forsythe ladies, and then Mrs. Royleforst and Miss Bluford into his abode. Ah! How good it felt, to be master of the house! His own establishment! The papers hadn't all been filed, yet, but here he was! It was a miracle.

Mr. Barton plopped down upon a sofa in his house, and exclaimed to his sister. "Thank goodness we got through that business without having to entertain the lot of them! Quite a production that would have been. Would have sent me to Bedlam, I'm sure!"

"Tristan." Her quiet rebuke made him look up, innocently.

"Did you actually wish to have that whole

lot here? With us? Farewell to peace and quiet, then!"

"Since when have you ever sought or required peace and quiet?" she asked. "And what do you intend to do with yourself now that Mr. Mornay is in quarantine with his wife?"

Barton was silent for a minute, eyeing her while he considered the matter. He had kept his hat and was absently tossing it into the air and catching it while he lay back, his feet upon a table.

"May I remove your boots, sir?" It was his manservant, who served as butler, footman, and valet, all in one.

"Goodness, no! I shan't stay home for long!" To his sister, he continued, "I'm going to the vicarage to see if I may offer my services. With all the moving in and other business going on, this ought to be a diversion." He yawned.

"Offer your services?" she asked doubtfully. "Get in the way, is more like. You ought to give them time to be settled properly, before adding to the commotion."

At that moment the manservant was back, and he held a letter upon a salver, which he offered to his master, saying, "For you, sir. Just arrived — by special messenger."

Barton took the missive, spied the seal,

and sat up quickly. "Did you pay the man? Does he await a reply?"

"I directed him to the kitchens for refreshment, sir. He will carry a reply."

He paused while Barton tore open the seal, exclaiming, "It's from the Regent, Anne! What did I tell you? He writes to me! *Me!*"

"If I may, sir," the servant said. "Since you have only carriage horses, the man will need to rest his horse for some time before he returns to London."

Barton was already reading, and his face crumpled at the brevity of the note. He made no answer to his servant.

"What does he say?" asked Anne.

"He wants an answer from Mornay." Barton's face was frowning. "Dash it, but I've made precious little progress on that head."

Anne was silent a moment. "Tristan, no man in his right mind will turn down a peerage — or any title. Mr. Mornay is a peculiar sort of person, to be sure, but he is imminently practical. I cannot expect that your mission can do anything but succeed."

Barton surveyed his sister, meeting her eyes. "Are you suggesting I give the prince a reason to hope?"

"Yes!" She looked very decided. "Would he deny his chance for his wife to be 'Lady

Mornay'? Or 'Lady Something-or-other'? He has a son and heir! Would he deny his son the chance to inherit a title? To sit in Parliament? Nay. I think not."

Tristan slowly smiled. "You know, Anne, you are proving your worth to me."

She did not smile in return.

"Does that not please you?" he asked, perplexed.

She looked up. "I should never *have* to prove my worth to you, Tristan. I am your sister. Your flesh and blood." She returned her eyes to her knitting, which she had instinctively picked up after sitting down. "I do worry about you! About who you are as a man, in your secret heart of hearts! You do not respect me, for you did not respect mother. And how can you think to make any woman happy as your wife?"

He almost laughed, blanching. "Upon my word, Anne! You do draw the most confounding conclusions!" When she just continued to knit in silence, he added, with a mildly troubled look upon his face, "I daresay, men do not marry to make a wife happy; they marry to be made happy themselves! The woman was made for the man, not man for the woman! Where do you form your preposterous opinions?"

She met his gaze evenly. "I am glad, by

God, that I should never be your wife. I pity the creature who is."

This angered him. He got up and shook out his shoulders, smoothing down his apparel. "I did nothing to deserve that! And I pity you, for you shall never be any man's wife! No one marries a soiled woman." He turned and looked at her intently. "Mind you how you speak to your brother, Miss Barton! Your welfare is in my hands, I remind you!"

He paused, nettled to see that she had heard him without making the least gesture of sorrow or regret for her behavior. To his frustration, she was not even done with him, and said, "If you do not care for your family, you are worse than an infidel or a heathen!"

He let out a breath of derision. "I will not abide this." And with that, he strode from the room. He went first to his bedchamber, where he had stowed some foolscap and a quill and ink. He wrote, after thinking for a moment, "To His Royal Highness, the Prince Regent. I am highly gratified, sir, to have the best of news to impart to you . . ."

NINETEEN

Ariana was red-eyed and crying when Mr. Mornay found her. She had been unable to stay in the bedchamber but had been drawn, inexorably, as a moth is drawn to a candle's flame, toward the large Venetian window which overlooked the frontage of the estate. It was going to hit her very hard to watch the others leaving, but she could not stay away.

So she stood there, standing off to one side so that Nigel would not spy her, and saw the departure of her relations. Her servants. Her son and daughter. She felt well in mind and body, and it was too, too unfair, this terrible result of a morning's walk on the property! She was being treated like an outcast, a leper!

When Phillip came up to her, his eyes were filled with compassion, and she turned to him with a sob in her throat and fell into his arms. "I am not ill!" she cried. "T'isn't fair! To be separated from my babies! And now, to keep you apart from them too!"

He held her up against him in a tight embrace. She sobbed into his shoulder, "No one even said good-bye! I feel like an outcast!"

He gently broke apart from her enough to see her face. "I forbade them. They are with the children! What use is there in this separation if they have contact with you, first?"

After a moment, in which her face appeared as forlorn as before, she frowned saying, "You're right! I know it! But I still feel like an out . . . outcast!" She could not help but to keep crying.

And just when everything had been going delightfully! Her mother and sister and Aunt Royleforst, all exulting in the children; now Mr. O'Brien was taking the curacy of their neighbouring parish; and even the appearance of the Bartons (though she had her doubts about Mr. Barton) was still a positive happenstance. They had been able to hold their own little ball without the worries of having to entertain a crowd of London personages! Dancing at Aspindon House most often occurred only at Harvest Home, or Christmas Hall and Twelfth Night festivities. This had been an elegant little affair without all the noise of the villagers. She adored it.

But now all was ruined. She was being quarantined, and for what purpose? Because of a chance encounter with Mrs. Taller! She still felt terribly sorry for the woman, but she was unable to shake the thought that if she had only not ventured outdoors, none of this would be happening. And there had been every reason to stay inside. For one, it was extremely cold outdoors. She might have called for the children and spent that time happily playing with Nigel and watching his blossoming relationship with his Aunt Royleforst and his grandmother.

But no, it was too late.

A feeling of impending tragedy fell upon her. She was like Queen Gertrude, who had just sipped from the cup of poison, though the king tried to stop her in time. She was at death's door. No, she was like those poor people of Siloam, who were out walking, just like any other day, when the tower of Siloam suddenly fell, crushing them all in a moment! Mrs. Taller had been her tower of Siloam. It was not a comforting thought. Perhaps she was (not for the first time) like Jepthah's daughter! Sweet innocence, so wrongly repaid! Why, oh why, had she stepped out of the house? Why had she not turned back when her mother spoke of the cold?

She was a headstrong, foolish girl! And she clung to her husband in her grief.

All she had was Phillip. He was still holding her, but he gently began to caress her neck with small, soft kisses. She stopped crying. It felt suddenly different, being almost alone with him in the large house.

She pushed slightly away, and surveyed him with her large eyes, still red-rimmed from crying. Her nose was pink, and her cheeks, and he had to smile a little, for he always found her adorable when she'd been upset. He said, "Do not forget that we are only quarantined for a matter of a few days. You are crying as though we'd lost our children forever."

She sniffed. "It feels that way."

"We must endeavour to pass the time in some useful employment, or we shall both go mad."

"I agree. I am already Jepthah's daughter!"

"What, again?" His look of concern was genuine. "Anyone else?"

"Queen Gertrude."

"Ah. The poisoned cup."

"Yes."

He waited. "That cannot be all."

"No, I was at Siloam when the tower fell."

"Of course." He smiled.

She sighed. "Mrs. Taller was my tower of Siloam, I'm afraid!"

He kissed her neck again, and then her face, and was chuckling lightly. She suddenly felt somewhat lighter of heart too. It was so wonderful to have him to share her dark imaginings. He understood these moments, when dark fears assailed her, and there seemed to be a cloud of gloom hanging over her. No, it was more than that — a cloud of *doom*. And it felt inevitable. But Phillip knew how to put his finger on her fears, and his amusement somehow reduced their power over her. It was vastly comforting.

She took his cravat in her hands and played with it, or seemed to, only when she gave it a final light tug, it fell apart. "I love undoing your cravats," she murmured. "You have a marvelous neck, Mr. Mornay, and though I admire your skill at the cloth, I admire your neck even more."

He was smiling, and he suddenly swung her into his strong arms, and carried her, moving toward their grand bedchamber. "Yes?" he said, making her grin back at him, for she could never resist that full, handsome smile, "Is there more you admire that I may know?"

She giggled. "You should ask if there is something I do not admire about you, and then perhaps I could settle upon an answer."

For response, he kissed her, lifting her head up with his arm to reach his head.

"I should rather you let me tell you what I admire in you, then." Ariana had heard this before, of course, many times, but the words he used when appreciating her traits aloud were like nectar to her heart.

"By all means!"

He was walking while he carried her. He said, "Where shall I begin? I have it! I admire you ardently, passionately, and," he paused, and eyed her with love, "with my whole heart." Already she was melting at his tone.

"You feed my heart when you say such things."

"Then allow me to offer you a banquet." He paused, eyeing her in between watching their progress through the house. "Your eyes, your nose, your mouth, your ears, your neck — you are like an exquisite sculpture, only far better, being wholly of flesh, and entirely — mine."

"Yes, utterly yours."

He now stopped at the chamber door, managing to open it with his hands though he would not put her down. Still smiling as they entered the room, he kissed her again. And then closed the bedchamber door behind them.

Back at Warwickdon, the guests were trying to make the best of the situation. After they had all had time to visit their assigned bedchambers and change out of their morning or afternoon dress, they were assembled in the drawing room. True to her word, the cook at Aspindon had sent over a feast. It was the meal she would have served had the guests remained at the estate.

Beatrice's gowns were feeling tight so she arrived for the meal determined not to make a spectacle of herself by eating too much. The food was so good at Aspindon! Each new course with dishes more delectable than the last. She had seen such artful and imaginative ways of dressing a turbot or goose, or pheasant, since her arrival to the house than she would ever have believed existed. One of her goals, in fact, was to go down to the kitchens and secretly observe the chef as he prepared his exquisite culinary creations. How interesting and unusual it would be!

Mr. Barton had called just before the meal, and so he joined the table with the rest. Unruffled, Mr. O'Brien recalled that they were almost neighbours, though residing in different parishes. It struck him forcefully that in the eyes of the world, he seemed to have accomplished an amazing feat these past few days: Namely, securing a generous living while at the same time increasing his acquaintance and standing among the gentry. The Mornays in fact were *good ton,* friends of the Regent, welcome in the highest circles of society! He had never been on an equal footing, and here he was with their relations lining his table.

Somehow it was not the triumph he might have considered it years earlier. He ran his gaze over each of his guests, wondering over the state of their souls. This was his real business in the world; the reason he had taken Holy Orders, and that which he meant to carry out. The business of tending to eternal souls. To many people, it was a business that ought to be reserved for the Church or chapel. Religion was too controversial to be acceptable for polite conversation. But here was an opportunity like no other; Mr. O'Brien had these people in his house, at his disposal, so to speak. A captive audience.

He must find a way to influence their religious sensibilities. He had no desire to offend, but if offense came from such a duty, so be it. However, in the interest of treading lightly for the sake of the nonreligious, he had begun the meal with a short prayer: "Heavenly Father, for this food we Thee thank; for this day, we Thee bless; for our lives, we Thee entreat; and for our usefulness to Thy kingdom, we Thee pray. Amen."

In no time, Mr. Barton regaled Miss Forsythe with London *on-dits* while her mother and Mrs. Royleforst listened. He seemed to have endless stories of London, which amused Miss Forsythe enough so that she was laughing merrily from time to time. In between her laughter, however, she reverted shortly to a look of discomfort. No one could quite forget that they were here at Warwickdon on account of the terrible possibility of Mrs. Mornay falling ill.

"I beg your pardon," Mr. O'Brien said, getting everyone's attention. "I will be conducting prayers for the Mornay family, and the Tallers (their tenants, with the fever). I hope I may expect all my guests to join me. In the drawing room, at around nine. Does that suit?" He looked around.

"Capital, sir!" cried Mrs. Forsythe. "I am obliged to you."

"Yes," echoed Beatrice. "How thoughtful of you."

"I will gladly be there, sir," said Mrs. Royleforst, and Miss Bluford's head bobbed in quick agreement: "Indeed! Indeed!"

Mr. Barton merely smiled and nodded his head. *Rather peculiar,* he thought, *but Mr. O'Brien was a clergyman. Only to be expected; however, what a dull dog the man was!*

Miss Barton was sitting quietly by the fire, knitting as usual. The dress, cap, and little pair of booties already finished and in her basket were for little Miranda; however, she had another cache of little garments, and she was now at work upon a blanket. She hoped to add to the pile continually with little garments and another blanket, for *the child.* So far she had kept her activities in such endeavours away from the eyes of her brother. He was so cross and vexatious, he would no doubt give her a combing for making them. But what else could she do for her own flesh and blood?

In her heart, Miss Barton was dreading the inevitable outcome that she would have to give up the baby to some unknown country woman. How she longed to tell his lordship of the child! He would be affected by it, she knew. His heart was not coarse, and he was not as her brother thought.

Yes, they had been wrong to come together. But was it not also wrong for society
to keep them apart? Why could not the
world see its way to rewarding true love —
from wherever it sprang up — with marriage for the lovers? Would not society be a
happier place? It only added to the general
misery to force people apart when they
loved each other, when both were unmarried, available to be wed. *Why not to each
other? Why not!*

When his parents had ruined all their
hopes in their "final judgment" (or so they
termed it), she and his lordship had met
secretly — merely to say good-bye. Neither
had any thoughts of disobeying the parental
strictures, or the rules of society, or of mor-
als. But their farewell meeting had wrenched
the hearts of them both — so much so that
his lordship had kissed her for the first time.

And then — oh, rue the day! He lost his
head, and, knowing full well that it could
mean her ruin, her banishment from polite
society, Anne had not the will to fight his.
Thus, her fate had been sealed. She ought
never have agreed to the assignation with
him. It was wicked and wrong, but she was
desperately in love! How could she have
refused to say goodbye to him?

She blinked back tears. She laid a hand

upon her belly. She had gained some weight, she was sure of it. The child was growing. And in her heart, she could not wish it otherwise. What's done was done, and in a *just* world she would marry his lordship. He wanted it, and she wanted it. Why could his parents not deem his happiness on an equal footing with their social pretensions? Why were not the Bartons considered good enough for a second son?

She heard a clock chime the hour from the dining room, and glanced at the one upon the mantel. Ten o'clock. No doubt Tristan would stay out as late as his presence would be tolerated at the parsonage. With a sudden surge of hope rising in her breast, she lit the candle in a sconce that could be carried with her, got up, and left the room, heading to her bedchamber. Why had she not remembered to do this sooner? It had been in her thoughts since their arrival!

In the corridor she saw Peggy, their maid of all work, who said, "Pardon, miss, but would you be wantin' your tea, now?"

"Yes, very good, Peggy. Thank you. Leave it in the drawing room."

"Aye, miss." She curtsied and was off.

Miss Barton arrived at her room, and, making her way to her little escritoire, set down her candle, opened a drawer, and pulled out a sheet of crisp foolscap, a quill, and ink. She sat down and took a deep breath. Where to start? She wrote, *My Lord —;* but her pen froze in her hand. She could not do it. She could not bring herself to write to Lord Horatio.

What if he wanted nothing to do with her? What if he was glad she had left London and wished never to hear from her? She felt an urge to crumple up the paper, to abandon her scheme. It was doomed in any case, was it not? Perhaps Tristan was correct, and now that his lordship had got what he wanted of her, he would turn his back on her. He had to, no matter what he felt or thought, did he not? That was the problem to begin with!

She had just thrown the page into the fireplace when suddenly the maid was back. "There be a gentleman here to see you, ma'am!"

"A gentleman?" *Could it be? Had his lordship found her?* With a gasp of joy, Miss Barton quickly came to her feet. "Did he give his name?" she asked, while smoothing down her hair, and taking up a small looking glass to observe herself in.

"Aye, mum; It be Mr. O'Brien." The maid watched her with large eyes. Miss Barton's face fell, and she swallowed and slowly replaced the looking glass. "Show him into the parlour, Peggy. I'll be right there." *Why was Mr. O'Brien calling upon her,* she wondered?

When Miss Barton entered the parlour, she paused in surprise when she saw that Mrs. Forsythe was there too. Her face was kindly, however, and so Anne smiled. Holding her stomach, which was quickly becoming a habit, she walked over to the settee and sat, facing the other two.

Mr. O'Brien spoke first. "My dear Miss Barton," he said. "I am here in my official capacity as a curate; you will forgive me if we are here without cause, I hope."

"Of course, sir." But she had a suspicion they had not come without cause.

He looked at Mrs. Forsythe. "Anne," she said, very gently. "We must know if there is anything we can do to be of help to you."

Anne averted her gaze. *Did they know? How? Had Barton told them? But why would he?*

"I pray you, do not be alarmed, Miss Barton. Your secret is entirely safe with us."

She took a deep breath of relief. "Is it?"

Mr. O'Brien said, "We desire to know if anything can be done to help you. That would mean you must confide in us. But it is entirely up to you."

She fell silent a moment. "Where is Barton?" she asked.

"Still at the vicarage," Mrs. Forsythe said. "Mrs. Persimmon is playing the pianoforte and practicing hymn-singing for them."

She looked amused. "And my brother endures it?"

"He has Miss Forsythe to make it endurable for him. And Mrs. Royleforst to make sure it is *only* just endurable." They shared a smile. But hers did not last, and soon she had resumed a look of abject sorrow. "I am afraid you can do nothing for me," she said. Her gaze went up to meet the curate's. "Unless you can teach me how to happily give up a child when it must be done."

"Is the father unmarried?"

"He is."

This answer made Mr. O'Brien's hopes rise in his chest. It might turn out that there was really a way to help this young woman! That is what he had prayed for.

Mrs. Forsythe came and sat down beside the girl. "Now," she said, "start at the beginning . . ."

About half an hour later, the two visitors left, and Anne returned to her room. Only this time she went more confidently to her writing equipment and began a new letter. *My Lord Horatio —.* No, she had to scratch that out and take yet another new sheet of paper. She would not use his name, in case it fell into the wrong hands. This thought brought fresh tears, but she remembered her conversation just now with the curate and Mrs. Forsythe, and she was able to stop crying quickly. That was a change. She got up for a handkerchief from a different drawer. Just in case.

She almost lost her courage a second time, but with the encouragement and the promise from the curate, she found it again. She moved the little flame closer to the sheet before her, and dipped her quill in the ink pot. She would have her say.

"If you do not allow me to get some water into her throat, I tell you, you will lose your daughter to dehydration." Mr. Speckman's assistant had returned to the cottage reluctantly, but Giles Taller had been beside himself. He was a large ox of a man, and not one to be dismissed lightly, so here the doctor's helper, Mr. Hannon, was, back in the stuffy cottage, and giving his professional advice. Mr. Speckman had made him go; if Mr. Mornay heard his help had been asked for, but refused, he'd be in deep trouble with the man. And what explanation could he offer? That he fully expected the girl to die? That it was hopeless? How could he say that to the landowner, when his own wife might have just contracted the very same illness?

Giles Taller was indeed feeling desperate. Not only his daughter, but his wife was now gravely ill; what if he lost the both of them? His other children were whimpering from their beds, because their mama was ignoring them. They had inexplicably overcome the same illness that was threatening the lives of their mother and sister. They would have been wailing inconsolably had the fierceness in their father's tone and eyes not cowered them into mere whimpering. He was generally a good papa, and affectionate. But something in his attitude, a thing which the children could intuit, as children did at times, caused them to lower their cries, and make do with clinging to one another, and watching the proceedings with large, frightened eyes. With any luck, they would fall asleep.

Meanwhile, Mr. Hannon had taken a vial of water and was forcing open the child's senseless mouth, directing the flow to the side of her throat where it would be swallowed into the stomach. He was taking quite a long time at this, and Giles himself was propping up MaryAnn's head to help the operation.

Mr. Hannon was only too aware that were he to accidentally allow the liquid to slosh to the centre of her throat, she could inhale it, which would be a disaster. Drops of sweat fell from his face, but still he held the vial up to the girl's mouth. When this was done, he would have to do the same thing to the mother. In his experience, if they did not die from the complications of the fever, sufferers died from the accompanying dehydration. He must not allow that to happen.

TWENTY

Beatrice's eyes blinked open. Where was she?

Oh, yes, the vicarage. Her bedchamber was a cozy room, and she shared it with her mother, who slept on a bed against the opposite wall. Of course there was nothing near as fancy as what Aspindon offered, but Beatrice found she was enjoying the informality, surprisingly enough. She supposed it was on account of this house being closer to what she was accustomed to at home.

She wanted to reach for the prayer book and do her reading — and pray for Ariana — but she was hungrier than usual this day, and so got up. She woke her mother to help her dress. The ladies could have asked a maid, even Harrietta, but they felt awkward about it, and so helped each other instead. Mrs. Forsythe accompanied Beatrice to the morning room, where Mr. O'Brien sat, reading a newspaper (a subscription belonging to the previous owner, but which had not run out), and lingering over a cup of coffee.

"Good morning, ladies," he said, in his sober but not unfriendly manner, rising to give a polite bow. "Please, help yourselves." The sideboard drew the women with its covered dishes, from which emanated an array of welcoming odours. Once again, servants had scurried to bring supplies from the big house: eggs, sausages, kidneys, ham, scones, and toast; the usual fare. The women each accepted a plate from the manservant, Mr. Sykes, and began to select their choice of the repast. Beatrice brought her plate to the table, and then returned for a cup of hot tea. Her mother did likewise.

Mr. O'Brien tried to concentrate on his paper, but felt his eyes drawn to watch his guests; in particular, the younger lady. Beatrice had chosen a morning dress with an open bodice, but lined with muslin lace, a muslin frill at the neck, and frilled cuffs. Only because of the cold did she also wear a laced cap that tied beneath her chin; and over her shoulders was draped a warm shawl in a dark pattern that contrasted prettily with the light-coloured gown. The cap made her appear older, for young girls did not often wear a cap any longer; Mrs.

Forsythe's cap was a heavier and lacier affair, but Mr. O'Brien's eyes most often glanced up to watch the young lady's progress. Her cheeks held a rosy morning glow that he could not dislike.

Nevertheless, when she turned to put her plate down, he felt her face was drawn, as though her thoughts were of a melancholy nature. He, too, was not in the best of spirits, and the reason was chiefly from the news article before him. There was more notice of the fever in London, notably the poorer sections, including St. Pancras, which was called "a hub" of sickness. He had considered removing to London to gather his things, give his last sermon, and say his good-byes; but there was a second, part-time curate. He would write the man, instructing him to pick up the services at once. He felt a pang of concern for the parish, but read yet more.

The Chronicle strongly advised its readers of the metropolis to remain home as much as was convenient; and, if they must go abroad, to venture only into those parts of the city that were respectable. The practice of taking shortcuts through dubious alleys or byways was cautioned against, saying that, aside from the danger of foot pads, these alleys were often the worst culprits in spreading the sickness. They held filthy hovels, where toxic and noxious vapours might be inhaled, making innocent travelers ill, and passing the disease onto other, cleaner areas of the city.

As Mrs. Forsythe sat down with her tea, she eyed her host, and glanced at the newspaper in his hand. With that one glance, Mr. O'Brien developed a terrible feeling of foreboding — she was going to ask to read the paper after he'd done. He could not have explained, were someone to ask him, how he knew what that glance had held; but he did. And he also knew, simultaneously, that he must not allow her to read it — not today.

Mr. O'Brien had no objection to ladies reading newspapers; truly he did not. But he could not distress his guests by allowing them to see the bad write-up about the fever. In a split second, before Mrs. Forsythe could even voice whether or not she did wish to read the paper, all of these thoughts fled through his mind like a coach and four run amok; and in a blink, he flipped the paper shut, folded it again and yet again, and in another second had tossed it directly upon the fire in the grate. It had taken only a few quick movements, and both women at the table froze from surprise while he did it. Mrs. Forsythe almost gasped. It was such a speedy and unexpected thing her host had done!

Both of the women stared into the fireplace, and there, the newspaper could be seen, plain as day, burning up.

"My word!" said Beatrice, with consternation. "Do you burn your newspaper every day?"

He cleared his throat, and answered slowly. "I beg your pardon. I did not mean to startle you."

Mrs. Forsythe found his behavior rather odd, but said nothing, choosing instead to begin eating. It was a shame, really; she had hoped to read it herself.

Beatrice smiled a little, and took a tentative bite of her egg and sausage.

Mr. O'Brien was satisfied. He had saved them from the newspaper, and he had escaped having to answer Miss Forsythe's question.

When Mr. Speckman called the next day at Aspindon, he had only the faintest dread of finding Mrs. Mornay in ill health. He doubted there had been any transmission of the illness during the lady's brief encounter with Mrs. Taller, choosing to believe it took a lengthy exposure for the mechanism of sickness to spread. Nevertheless, he would call upon her daily, just to be diligent. With his apprentice, Mr. Hannon (highly recommended from Guy's Hospital), looking in on the Tallers, Mr. Speckman had less contact with the sick himself and no qualms about seeing the lady every day, therefore.

Ariana submitted to his ministrations, giving her hand for the pulse to be felt; allowing the stethoscope to touch her chest; and staying quiet as a mouse even when he laid his broad hand upon her forehead and the back of her neck. Mr. Mornay leaned against a wall, and watched.

"She's as right as rain, sir," the doctor finally pronounced, bringing out a much gratified look upon the features of the landowner.

"May we call back the children?" asked Ariana. Although she knew he was bound to deny her the request, she could not help but to ask anyway.

Mr. Speckman frowned. "Nay, ma'am, you know you must wait; another three to four days, at a minimum."

"Yes, Mr. Speckman." With a regretful glance at her husband, she glided from the room.

To Mr. Mornay, the physician said, "Keep an eye on her, sir. At the first hint of a fever, call for me."

"I'll do that; I thank you." He ushered the doctor out, wishing it might be the end of their trial.

"Mama, may I take a little air? I am in need of the exercise."

Mrs. Forsythe surveyed Beatrice, and frowned. "I should think your adventure the other morning to have been sufficient to keep you indoors during this cold weather."

"Mama, I shan't be out for long; I promise you."

"Are you wearing the woolen stockings I made you?"

Mr. O'Brien was reading a book in the corner of the room, and Beatrice blushed. How could her mother mention such a thing in front of a gentleman? "Of course."

Mr. O'Brien kept his gaze glued to his book, hoping it would not be incumbent upon him to accompany the young lady. Oh, Miss Forsythe was looking lovely this morning, as she always did; but he was newly determined to remain aloof, and to steer clear of any situations in which they might be alone together. Every reflection, every meditation upon his life and situation told him he must resist the pleasant girl. He would not think of her in a romantic way;

he would not think of her in a practical way, as a girl who might make a fine wife; in short, he must not think of her at all.

"Keep your exercise to a quarter hour, then, and I have no objection," said the mother just then, as she handed an infantryman to Nigel, who was at her skirts upon the floor, hiding his little soldiers among the folds of her dress. "I shan't have you damaging your feet; when you return you will sit by the fire and warm them."

This seemed embarrassingly juvenile to Beatrice, who raised her gaze to the ceiling as soon as she had turned her back on her mother, but she said, "Yes, Mama." And with that, she left the room, gathered her coat and scarf and bonnet and muff and her warmest gloves, and ventured outside. It was a bright clear wintry day. She could see the old stone church of Warwickdon, and automatically turned her feet in its direction. She would walk to the church and back. Surely that was no great distance, as she could see the church clearly already.

How pleasant it had been to have Mr. O'Brien as her guide on her last visit here! As she approached the cemetery — was there not always a cemetery? — she appreciated the ancient stones, set at odd angles, with slanted heads protruding from the ground like the poor teeth of an ogre. She was following the walkway, but today decided to read some of the stones, if she could make them out.

Simon Sewell, 1700–1742; Charlotte Sewell, 1685–1730. Gunther Sewell, 1680–1732. A family. Suddenly Beatrice remembered the portrait gallery at Aspindon, showing generations of Mr. Mornay's family. A cold breeze made her shiver, and she moved on. The gallery portraits ranged in quality and the people within them were sometimes not well recalled (she thought); but each one of them had lived and walked the earth, just as she was doing now.

With a heavy sigh, Beatrice kept moving toward the church. Life was so brief! And yet her own journey seemed already so long as to be tiresome. Until recently, anyway. At Aspindon, everything had been getting more and more delightful; suddenly her life seemed filled with possibilities. Especially since the arrival of Mr. Tristan Barton. She envisioned his dark curls and strong green eyes. His expensive twin-tailed coat and snowy cravats. His coming to Aspindon had quickened her pulse, to be sure. She remembered that one impulsive kiss and almost blushed right there out in the cold. Did he really have serious intentions? It was true that he had called at the vicarage the day before, but he had been all politeness and aloof amiability, nothing more.

And yet Beatrice had been somehow relieved that there was nothing more. When she was not looking into his strong green eyes, she was often engaged in conversation with the man of clear blue ones: Mr. O'Brien. And his conversation was somehow more important, more significant, than Mr. Barton's. She could not think of the curate's soft-spoken gentle words with any disregard whatsoever, whereas she sometimes found Mr. Barton's loud and jovial tones excessive. Even his conversation was loud.

But Mr. Barton loved wit and laughter — was there really anything so wrong in that? Mr. O'Brien was not sporting at all! He was intelligent, but sober. She suddenly recalled how they had laughed together in the cottage when she scolded him for taking hold of her. Even the walk through the wood had been fun; but he was often reading a book of some sort, not asking to play cards or seeking a diversion as Mr. Barton did. Oh! Which one suited her better? She could not be sure.

When she returned to the house, Mr. O'Brien was upon the floor, playing with Nigel. He did have the most agreeable manner with children. She had to admit that Mr. Barton did not call on the days when Mrs. Perler was gone (and thus the children were with the adults almost all day), nor did he ever show the slightest regard for the youngsters. It was as though, in his opinion, they were not quite people yet. But she supposed it would be different for him if they were his own children. Men were often like that, were they not?

She took turns trying to envision herself as the lady of the Manor; then the parson's wife. Why was it that she could only picture a happy family at Warwickdon? Mr. Barton *was* the sort of man Beatrice wanted! Wealthy, fashionable, urbane, and witty. If he bought the Manor, she would be neighbour to her sister in the country, and able to attend as many Seasons as she liked, when in London! In all, Mr. Barton, it seemed to Beatrice, was exactly the man she wanted: handsome, wealthy, with social standing, and able to offer her the life she envisioned for herself.

She would not have the luxury of Aspindon as Mrs. Barton, but she would be well enough to do, and able to live quite comfortably, and with plenty of diversions. What more could she want?

Watching Nigel laughing with the curate,

Beatrice's thoughts fell upon her sister, and dark fears began to intrude upon her mind. But she shook them off. Ariana was young and healthy and strong, and she had not spent a great deal of time with Mrs. Taller. What danger could there be?

When Mr. Mornay blinked awake on the fourth day after his wife's exposure to Mrs. Taller, he was beginning to feel less anxious about his wife. He and Ariana had been making the most of the time alone, in fact; he'd taken her through the maze (he never got lost, himself, as he had committed it to memory years earlier), and enjoyed her bafflement at ever coming out again. They'd reminisced at the day far past when she had been running on the estate and ran smack into him — to his great displeasure. How he apologized for treating her so shabbily, then! For his instant combing!

Ariana was delighted at the memory, however, for it served to highlight how much she had since won his heart. The change in him, she said, was magnificent.

They had gone riding together, which was not uncommon, but somehow felt more special at this time, and they'd been in each other's company more than ever, as Mr. Mornay was not making his rounds with the steward, or meeting with solicitors, or hearing disputes from the townspeople, or doing any of the innumerable activities which often pulled him away from his wife's side.

Ariana was now in the worst of the discomfort from having to abruptly cease nursing a baby, and Freddie had been fetching ice from the icehouse himself, in order to supply it for Mrs. Hamilton, who made cold compresses with cloths to ease the swelling. As Mr. Mornay put one arm over the sleeping figure of his wife, and snuggled against her, he luxuriated in the fact that once again they had no responsibilities for the day except to entertain one another. It felt like a guilty holiday; this having none of the usual work of the place upon his shoulders.

He felt the wetness of the compresses through her nightdress and considered whether to ring for new ones. But then he noticed that the damp cloth was rather warm. In fact, it felt hot. He quickly placed a hand upon Ariana's neck and forehead, and then shot up from the bed. He rang the bellpull with vigour. Fotch appeared in a moment —

"Sir! Awake, I see! Let me —"

"Send for Mr. Speckman! On the double, Fotch!"

"Yes, sir!" And with widened eyes, the servant turned and hurried off to find the butler. Mr. Mornay was already in stockings, and pulled on a pair of pantaloons, followed quickly (as soon as he had found them) by hunting boots. Ariana was still asleep, and he feared to wake her, but he rang again, and again, until Fotch was back, panting.

"Mr. Frederick has gone for the doctor, sir!"

"What, Freddy had to go?"

"We are down to precious few servants, sir."

"Right. Have Mrs. Hamilton get a new cold compress up here, and tell her to be smart about it!"

"Yes, sir." Fotch's face might have been amusing at any other time; for he was itching to get to work on his master's neck cloth, and watching Mr. Mornay hurriedly tying it himself was almost painful. Mr. Mornay, meanwhile, running into his first difficulty with his cravat, realized how idiotic it was for him to bother with the thing at all, and pulled it off hastily. Ariana was ill! She had the fever! Nothing else mattered. He sat beside her on the bed and touched her skin now and then, gently, grimacing at how hot it felt. He was careful not to wake his wife, knowing that she would have to stir soon enough, when the new compresses were brought.

He thought he would go mad with impatience, when he suddenly remembered that he ought to pray. He took one of Ariana's hot hands into his own while he sat there on the bed beside her, and closed his eyes . . .

The Bartons returned to the vicarage the next day, giving Mr. O'Brien the thought that Mr. Barton was either bored to tears, or more interested in Miss Forsythe than he had given him credit for. Since Miss Forsythe was decidedly "wife material," he knew that the latter must be the case. But this worried him. Not because he had any claims upon Beatrice Forsythe himself; indeed, no. But Barton was evidently a man of the town, and surely must be ignorant of the fact that the Forsythes were not in the way of wealth such as the Mornays.

What if he had the mistaken notion that Miss Forsythe was an heiress? He no doubt assumed, as many had in London, that if Mr. Mornay, the Paragon, had married a Forsythe girl, the family must be well lined in the pocket. He worried that once Mr. Barton was disabused of his mistake, he might drop Miss Forsythe abruptly and break her young heart. What could he do?

They were sitting in the drawing room, engaged in a rubber of whist. Miss Forsythe had just returned from yet another outdoor venture quite unharmed, and her cheeks were rosy. Mr. and Miss Barton were in fine form, and had proposed the game. Miss Barton had nodded at Mr. O'Brien pointedly, letting him know that a certain letter had been dispatched. *Good.* The children were upstairs in the nursery with Mrs. Perler, and so even Mrs. Forsythe had agreed to play. Mrs. Royleforst had opted to remain sitting upon a settee, with Miss Bluford beside her, as she lacked the energy, she said, for cards, at the moment. Instead she was paging through a ladies' magazine which she had brought with her from home, and talking of the latest fashions as they appeared in the illustrations.

"My, but the hems are all embroidered or bejeweled this year!"

"Turbans, turbans everywhere! Look at this gold-coloured gauze! I should get some of that, directly!"

"My word! Is not that waistline lower than what we are accustomed to seeing? My dears, the waist on these gowns is dropping, I say! Quite a change for the empire style!

What a nuisance! I will have to bespeak a new wardrobe if I dare set foot in the capital this Season!"

Beatrice eyed her hopefully. The idea of a new wardrobe sounded wonderful to her ears.

"Do you expect to be in London for the Season, Mrs. Forsythe? And your daughter?" asked Mr. Barton.

Beatrice glanced up at him from behind her hand of cards, while her mother said, "As for myself, no; I am intent upon returning to the countryside in Chesterton. My husband and another of my children are there, you see, as well as my married eldest daughter."

They spoke more of the family for a minute, then, without seeming eager, Mr. Barton inquired, "And what of you, Miss Forsythe? Will you be gracing the ballrooms with your presence this year?"

Beatrice had to smile at his words, but said, trying not to grimace, "I cannot say for certain, sir. My sister is still considering whether to take me. My hopes rest upon her entirely, I'm afraid."

"Oh, but the Mornays do return to Town for the Season, do they not? It would be most peculiar of them not to!"

Mrs. Forsythe interjected gently, "I believe

they are happy in domestic life, sir. They go to Town less and less. Perhaps when the children are older —"

"The children!" he exclaimed. "I fail to see what they've got to do with it! Children are no trouble at all so long as you have servants and nursemaids enough!"

Beatrice almost blushed at this remark. His sentiment might have been a common attitude, but it was not one that the Forsythes — or the Mornays, for that matter — shared. Or Mr. O'Brien.

Their host cleared his throat. Laying down a trump card, he said mildly, "We cannot all be of such a mind as to ignore our own offspring," with the hope of shaming the man into a retraction.

But only the women understood his intent, as Mr. Barton blithely continued, "Well, sir, my advice to those who are not, would be to become of such a mind. If they wish to continue to enjoy life — the opera, the theatre, the ballet, music, and dancing — what place is there for children at such events? None whatsoever. I tell you, there is no drawing room in London that will welcome the little creatures, and what would become of polite society if they did?" He took a breath, topped Mr. O'Brien's card with one of his own, and took the trick, saying, "Proper servants is all one needs. A nurse, a governess, a tutor, perhaps; and any couple may rove the Town to their heart's content."

Mrs. Forsythe laughed. "To rove the Town, sir?" Her eyebrows were raised, exceedingly. "I hardly think a person of good character would wish to rove the Town!"

"I only mean to participate in society, ma'am," he said, with a look at Beatrice to see if his remark had met with equal reproof in her mind. He thought it had. She was staring at him in surprise, but she quickly lowered her eyes when he glanced her way. Beatrice decided to change the subject.

"Mr. O'Brien, do you intend upon continuing prayers this evening?" They had been meeting around the fireplace of an evening and joining the curate in a short but heartfelt time of prayer. "Mr. Speckman has brought us only good news, these three days."

"We must continue in prayer," said her mother. "Until the quarantine is ended. There is still a danger, my dear."

"Upon my word! I adore this bonnet! Look you, Mrs. Forsythe, and tell me if you do not agree!" Mrs. Royleforst had given her magazine to Miss Bluford who obediently rose and came to show the page to the ladies at the table. "Would you not snatch it up directly?" she said, beaming from her little eyes at Beatrice's mother.

Mrs. Forsythe was not given to high fashion at any time, but she politely looked over the bonnet in question, and nodded, saying, "Very pretty, to be sure!" She directed a kind smile at Mrs. Royleforst, who said to her companion, "Now show Miss Forsythe! And Miss Barton!"

The two ladies each surveyed the bonnet in question, making appropriately admiring remarks, and even the gentlemen were curious and had to look. Mr. O'Brien said, "There is endless variation to women's hats, it seems to me! And all so fetching!"

Mr. Barton said, "All fetching? I say, not! A lady must choose her headwear so that it fits the shape of her face, the style of her gown, and her standing in society."

"Oh, Mr. Barton!" said his sister, with an embarrassed glance at him. She and Beatrice exchanged a look as if to say, "How absurd he is!" Beatrice was happy for that exchange. Mr. Barton might not have been the sharpest wit at the table, but neither was she, Beatrice, quick of tongue. Besides, she felt surely she could have a good influence upon the man — if Mr. Mornay gave his consent to the courtship.

Mr. Speckman's face was blank. He was endeavouring to awaken Ariana gently, but her only response was to moan softly. Mr. Mornay looked on, trying to contain his agitation.

Mr. Speckman removed the cold cloths that Mr. Mornay had placed upon his wife's forehead, saying, "Cold of all kinds must be avoided to bring the fever to a crisis. Once it has passed, she will recover. But we need heat, not cold, to do that."

Ariana weakly opened her eyes. What was happening? Everything was swimming around her. She couldn't move. She could hardly keep her lids apart. She could make out her husband's face and whispered, "Phillip." She had not meant to whisper, but to speak, but a small whisper was all she could produce.

He flew to her side, and took her hands in his. "I'm here!"

"What is it?" she asked. "Am I sick?"

"Just a little," he replied, hoping his lie would calm her. Or was it the pounding of his own heart he sought to relieve?

"Mrs. Mornay," said Mr. Speckman. "Are you in pain?"

She had to close her eyes for a moment.

Think. *Think.* Was she in pain? She was hot. Her throat ached. Actually, her legs and arms were aching too. And she was thirsty, very, very thirsty. She nodded.

"Where is your pain?" he asked.

"My head," she said, in a whisper. After a pause, the doctor said, "Only her head?" He was surprised. "That is good."

But she whispered again. "My throat. Legs . . . my arms."

Mr. Mornay studied the man's face, and took him by the arm to move away from the bed. "Is this the same fever the Tallers have?"

Mr. Speckman sighed. "It appears so, sir. I am sorry to say."

"In that case, what is your best treatment?"

Mr. Speckman studied the woman upon the bed, and his face was creased in thought. "There is only so much we can do, sir."

"I do not want to hear what you cannot do," he replied. "Tell me what you can do."

Mr. Speckman took a deep breath while he quickly searched his mind. "We can keep her warm and meanwhile bleed some of the noxious elements out of her, I daresay."

"Then do so." Mr. Mornay's face was such that Mr. Speckman was glad to have something he could do. He prepared the instruments and then stood up to face Mr. Mornay. "I think it best if you leave the room. My assistant will help me." Another man who had come with the doctor nodded his head. "Do what is necessary," Mr. Mornay said, "but I'll stay."

Frederick stopped Fotch in his tracks. "We must inform the family. You must ride to the vicarage and tell them."

"I, sir?" Fotch looked bewildered. "I am no horseman, Mr. Frederick!" He had ridden perfectly well with his master when searching for Beatrice and Mr. O'Brien the other day, but he said nothing of that.

"Nor am I!" he replied.

"Send a groom," said the valet.

"Where are they? I think they've flown the nest! As soon as they heard, the dashed coves!"

"The stables!" said Fotch. "There's always an extra hand to be had there."

"Go and send one, then." Mr. Frederick had the undoubted authority to have Fotch do so, but the valet hesitated, grimacing. "I need to help the master, Mr. Frederick."

"This is the best help you can give him right now, Fotch." They eyed each other for a moment, and then Fotch slowly nodded his agreement. He went to find a groom.

"My lord." The butler held out a letter upon a salver, and Lord Horatio took it, murmuring, "Thank you, Prescott." The servant bowed his head and left. Horatio glanced at the note, his heart suddenly set aflutter by the seal upon the dark wax. It was from Anne! Instead of reading it, he shoved it into a pocket of his waistcoat, and tried to look utterly carefree.

"Aren't you going to read it, sir?" his father, the Marquess of Stratham, asked. They were sitting at table eating breakfast, and all the occupants turned and looked at him curiously. "Just a note from an acquaintance, sir," he replied, "which I've no doubt will entreat me to some club or other today."

"Well, you've had enough of clubs, sir!" responded the father in a gruff tone. He had paid a considerable sum in gambling debts for his son recently. He was prepared to allow the boy a good measure of diversion at cards, particularly as he had been forced to dash his hopes of that abominable Miss Barton — but enough was enough. No second son had ought to cost him so dearly as that which he had been forced to part with of late.

Horatio patted his mouth with a napkin, and then laid it aside his dish. "Indeed, sir. No fears on that account. I have given it out that I am all laid up, and no one who wishes to be paid his winnings should hazard my company for any game of chance."

"Very good, sir," his father said approvingly. He exchanged a look with his wife. They'd been concerned for this son of theirs since the ruined love affair with that deuced woman, but all seemed to be ending just as they wished. He had not mentioned her name, not sat about pining and sighing as he had done a month ago; and he seemed to be going forth in society with less cares upon him than he had done since meeting Miss Barton, near three months earlier.

It was no more than to be expected, of course. Second sons knew that they had to marry a woman of sufficient means; Five hundred pounds a year was not going to keep Horatio in style, that was certain. He simply had to do better for a wife, there was no way around it.

Lord Horatio, taking a last sip of coffee, put down his cup, and then stood, excusing himself. "I think I'll go now, Mother; sir." He nodded at each, in turn.

"Go and find yourself a wife," muttered

his father. "It's high time, sir."

Her ladyship's brows went up exceedingly, for she was amazed that her husband would say such a thing to Horatio — so recently dashed in his hopes of one.

"I recall asking your permission on just that head only lately," he replied, trying not to grimace.

The marquess studied his son with cool, suspicious eyes, while he chewed his toast and kippers. "Find one I can approve of, sir, and then it is done. I'd best not hear of that . . . er . . . Barton woman again," he added, glancing at the pocket where the letter had been hurriedly stashed.

"I have no clue where Miss Barton has gone to, if you must know, sir, and I daresay you have no need to worry on that account!" His tone was woodenly bitter.

"Good!" He kept staring, coldly now. "Let it remain so."

As soon as he was safely in his own chamber and alone, Lord Horatio pulled out the letter and tore it open. He starting reading, and his face grew creased with worry; he ran a distracted hand through his hair, his eyes filled with tumbled thoughts. Anne, with child! No wonder Barton had taken her off so abruptly! But — a child — *his* child! This changed everything.

He'd done his best to put her out of his mind, but he'd known all along it was a hopeless business. He did not *want* to forget Anne. She was so good, sensible, and full of kindnesses and wise advice. She wasn't like the flighty girls he met daily in drawing rooms and ballrooms. Girls who cared chiefly about their attire, their status, and the number of admiring beaux they had. Anne was so much older in her mind; she would make some man a wonderful wife; she would be a doting, caring mother. Dash it, he wanted her to be his wife!

He finished reading the letter. *By Jove* — she had a parson who would marry them if he got a special license — capital! This settled it. No amount of his parents' disapproval could erase the fact that she was carrying his child. No amount of anger on their part would now suffice to keep him from his object: he would marry Anne Barton. Directly. He could hardly wait to be off.

He cursed his own impatience and melancholy, which had sent him on a spree of late-night gaming, and in the process emptied his pockets of all ready cash. He'd overspent his stipend as it was. But he must get a special license.

His heart was beating strongly with such

thoughts — he'd be going against his father's express will in the matter. But did not duty and honour require that he take responsibility for this child? How could it be right that one's duty at home did not mirror doing what was most honourable? His father would see his next actions as tantamount to treason to the family, whereas he would be making his past sins right. Perhaps the parson helping Anne would speak to him, too, and help him find peace with himself. Life was certainly getting complicated! But he knew what his next move had to be, and he must force himself to focus only on that.

He began to rummage through all of his belongings, every pocket in every piece of clothing in the room, every drawer and box and space where he might gather some coins or banknotes carelessly forgotten from some other day. He would need every shilling, every last tuppence. He'd get the license. Get to Middlesex. And then, God willing, marry Anne. The thought filled his breast with a wild hope.

Twenty-One

Just as Lord Horatio was making his way, with long determined strides, toward the door of the house, his father appeared in front of him in the hall. "You're in a dashed hurry, sir!" he barked. The look on his face was formidable, and Horatio stopped in surprise. His recent determination of marrying Miss Barton was all in his thoughts, and his face took on a guilty look. Did his father know his plans? How could he? But the marquess astonished him by breaking out into a grin, slapping him on the back, and saying, while handing him yet another note, "The prince wants to see ye, m'boy! Now that's the kind of company I like you among! Can't get any higher than His Royal Highness, eh?"

The marquess had become all amiability, having read the note intended for his son out of curiosity. "Get ye off to 'im, m'boy! And send His Royal Highness my deepest compliments, eh?"

"Yes, sir," Horatio replied, valiantly trying to smile. He was not a stranger to summonses from Carlton House, but they had become scarce of late. Ever since the princess's death, the Regent had done less entertaining, less carousing, less socializing altogether. Horatio hadn't seen him in person in quite some time, in fact. He wondered what on earth was behind the summons — and today of all days! Just when he'd found his purpose and was chafing at the bit to get it done.

When he was finally seated in a lavish drawing room in the palace, ornate even by aristocratic standards, he felt a mild anxiety. Dash it, why did the prince want to see him? Why was he anxious about it? It wasn't as though anyone else knew about Miss Barton's condition — or did they? But his thoughts fled as he heard the approach of his host, and in moments he rose to his feet to bow before His Highness.

"Take a seat, take a seat," the prince said, coming and sitting across from the young man. His attendants took their places against the wall and assumed the stoic faces of statues, while the Regent asked about Horatio's family. The prince did not look well; his size had continued to burgeon, and his clothing looked too tight. His face had folds of heavy skin upon it, and it seemed that the loss of his daughter the year before had aged him grossly.

He leaned in toward his guest. "I daresay you are aflutter with curiosity as to why I've summoned you."

Horatio tried not to swallow, but felt himself on edge. "Indeed, sir." He forced a smile.

"Here it 'tis," he said. "I must ask a favour of you. I have sent some young ninny as my ambassador to Phillip Mornay, and all to no purpose. He sends me a letter about 'hopes.' " He paused and looked at Lord Horatio as if that young man should certainly comprehend the meaninglessness of mere hopes. "I wish to present Mornay with a viscountcy; I want him in the House before the next vote on my income, if you must know."

Horatio nodded, a quick relief flooding his veins that the topic was nothing to do with him or Anne Barton. "Still putting you off, is he?"

"I do not know if he is putting me off; I don't know what he's up to, dash it! I haven't had a word from him these past six months! My ministers have all the paperwork ready and I need only for him to come and accept the title. Won't take long to decide on the actual title, much less his coat of arms. Deuced unfriendly of him to keep me waiting, to say the least! Does not the man recognize an honour when it is presented to him?"

"I suspect, sir, that Mr. Mornay is occupied in his domestic responsibilities."

"If he is, then he is far too occupied at them! No man should be a slave to his own house! Least of all the Paragon!" He paused, allowing Lord Horatio to nod sympathetically.

A manservant entered and placed a tray of some cordial beside the Regent. There were two glasses, which he proceeded to pour. The prince took his impatiently, while the servant held one out to Horatio, who gladly received it as his throat was dry from nerves. The Regent put back his head and emptied his glass, smacking his lips afterward. Horatio took a good sip, thinking of emptying the glass as his host had done, but the prince said, "Here's the thing: The man I sent is — a Mr. Tristan Barton."

Lord Horatio, still holding up the glass, opened his eyes in shock, and practically choked on his drink. He began to spit and cough in response, while the prince, looking on sharply, asked, "Do you know him?"

Horatio, recovering, put down his glass and said, "Er, Mr. Tristan Barton? Not friendly with him, but I know who he is." Did he know him, indeed! Anne's brother!

"Well, I sent him above a month ago, and he sends me 'every hope' that Mornay will oblige me in this, but —" here he turned and studied Horatio as before — "I smell a rat in it. I have had no correspondence from Mornay, the Lord Chancellor waits upon his reply — and I want the thing done. I want you, sir, to call upon your old friend and see what's what. I should have used you to begin with for this, now I think on it." He looked squarely at the young lord. "What say you?"

Horatio was meanwhile trying to suppress his surprise and amazement at such a request. Here he had been planning to throw his luck to the wind, buck his father's wishes, and go to Middlesex and marry his bride. He had intended on seeing Phillip anyway! He, too, needed the man's help. Now he would be on a royal mission, and have his father's approval for the trip! It was propitious.

He controlled every urge to show his true feelings, and asked, "Why'd you send such an innocuous puppy as Barton? He'd never carry the day." "I sent him for lack of a better man who would agree to hide in the country for me and groom Mornay to his duty — Barton was eager to please; even let a house there; I'd no doubt of his willingness to do his best." The prince sounded a bit dubious, however.

"Ah, so that's how it is. I'll find my way to Aspindon directly, Your Royal Highness. I'm sure I can sound the depths of our friend's thoughts upon this subject, and to your satisfaction. I daresay I can possibly convince him to return with me to London. He is overdue for a stop here, in any case. I can't remember the last time I was at Grosvenor Square!"

"Exactly!" agreed the prince. "I knew you should help me! You have my sincerest thanks, Horatio," and his eyes were fixed steadily upon the young man in a look that said he would remember the favour. "If you succeed in this, I will consider myself indebted to you, sir." This statement was paramount to saying that he would have the right to ask a favour of the prince at some future time. But Horatio realized there would never be a more needful time for him than right now. He hadn't done his part to help the prince, yet, but he *would* do it. Did he have the courage to ask the ruling prince for help in his cause, today?

He stared at the royal figure sitting across from him, a man who had certainly had his share of petticoat problems, and thought that he could. He must try, at least. He cleared his throat and gathered his wits about him. "Your Royal Highness," he began. "There is a young woman, who happens to be the sister of this Mr. Barton . . ."

The Regent's eyes filled with surprise — and understanding. "Indeed?" and he slowly smiled. "Pretty, is she?"

Lord Horatio's face became pensive. "She's lovely, sir."

The Regent was silent a moment.

"Now I understand why you almost had an apoplexy!" He eyed the younger man affectionately. "Your father won't appreciate my interfering in his family," he said, catching on at once that if a second son was asking for his help, how things stood. "And little good it would do me, if I gain Mornay's vote only to lose the marquess's." His expression was not promising. "I'm not sure there is anything I can do for you in this."

Horatio's face fell. "I see your difficulty, sir." He fell into silent contemplation of the matter for a moment. There had to be a way . . . "Your Royal Highness!" He had a sudden idea. "If one of Lady Hertford's most respectable friends were to put Miss

Barton forth as a prize, at some event with my mother the Countess in attendance, it would certainly lessen the blow to the marquess when I marry her."

"So you're determined upon it, are you?"

"I am. Her family is respectable, just not ancient or rich enough to suit the marquess. The right word from the right hostess would smooth things over for us, sir."

The Prince rubbed his chin thoughtfully with one hand. "You mean, to pretend that your Miss Barton has a fortune or some such thing? And we need not supply that fortune, only allude to it."

"Even if she was spoken of as being *good ton,* sir! It would do the trick, I think!"

The Regent made his decision. "Done! Now be off with you to Middlesex, and get me Mornay! He must learn the ropes of the House before anything important to *me* arises."

"Yes, thank you, Your Royal Highness!"

When Fotch entered the stables, he found the groom brushing down the master's favourite horse, Tornado. Mr. Mornay broke the black stallion himself, two years earlier, and thus it obeyed him beautifully, but he was testy for anyone else. He neighed at the intruder, and lifted his front legs about a foot off the floor, in protest.

"There now, easy boy," said the groom, looking at Fotch in surprise.

The mission was explained, with all due sorrow and exclamations of concern over the mistress being said by both men; but Fotch made it clear that the news had to be delivered speedily, on the double. After he left, the groom, a man by name of Rudson, was preparing to close the stall door on Tornado when it occurred to him that there was no faster horse in the master's stable than this one. Why not take him? He'd always wanted to ride the animal; and Tornado knew him. He'd been the groom at Aspindon and at Grosvenor Square for years. And what better reason for him to presume upon riding the master's horse than to alert others regarding the condition of the mistress? This was important. Finally, and this was the strongest reason yet for him to use the master's mount: *Mr. Mornay would never know.* He wasn't about to leave his wife's side — not at a dire moment like this.

Indeed, at any other time, there would have been a number of stable hands about, but Mr. Rudson was the only one left. Most of the young men had fled to their homes as soon as the first exodus of guests had occurred. So only Mr. Rudson, the head groom, remained.

That settled it. In a moment the man was saddling up the horse, taking special care to talk soothingly to the creature. Tornado grew restless; he was eager to start. With a momentary plea to heaven, Mr. Rudson got himself up in the saddle, and lightly kicked the horse's side. He rode him right out of the stall.

Perhaps that was why Tornado was immediately on to the fact that he had a new rider. Or maybe it was simply that the animal knew his master too well; knew that this rider was not the man he was accustomed to; and as soon as they cleared the stables and were heading down the drive, Tornado snorted and rose up on his rear legs. Mr. Rudson yelled out at the horse in alarm, and pulled firmly upon the reins. Tornado returned to all fours and went into a trot. All seemed well, but then he hastened into a gallop, and Mr. Rudson could only hold on for dear life. He huddled down like a jockey at Newmarket and just clung to the animal with all his strength. Tornado went on a circuit, turning from the drive and heading out toward the fields, beyond which lay the first row of cottages.

"Lord, have mercy!" yelped Mr. Rudson,

peeking up at their progress. He only hoped he would live to get the animal back in its stall and then complete his mission to the vicarage, before the master found out what was up. If he did find out, it would cost him his situation. Right now he felt he could live without his job. He just prayed the episode wouldn't cost him his life.

The drawing room of the vicarage was growing noisier and more bustling by the minute. Mrs. Perler had brought the children downstairs, as both Mrs. Royleforst and Mrs. Forsythe had instructed her to do, every day, for an hour or more. Beatrice had immediately begged to be excused from the game of cards she had been engaged in with Mr. Barton and Mr. O'Brien, as did the other ladies, except Miss Bluford. Nigel was a bundle of energy and did not know whom to give his attention to first. Mrs. Royleforst held out a biscuit and called him, so he veered in her direction. Mrs. Forsythe received the baby into her arms, smiling, while Miss Barton sat beside her. Miss Barton seemed as though she could never have too much of admiring the child.

Mr. O'Brien put the cards away, looking on and enjoying the picture of domesticity in his house. *His house!* It was still too fresh

and new a thought for him to be oblivious
to it. He watched while Miss Forsythe chose
a toy from Mrs. Perler's little basket of toys,
and then attempted to get Nigel to play with
her. *Someday,* he was thinking, *it will be my
children in this room.* As he watched Miss
Forsythe he suddenly felt a pang that it
would not be she who was their mother.
How could she be? She was "Miss Forsythe," the sister of Mrs. Mornay, and out
of his league.

He could just imagine the reception he
would get were he to express an interest in
Beatrice. Mr. Mornay would no doubt cast
a withering glare at him, and vow to have
him removed from the living at Warwickdon. Not that he had the means to do it,
but one never knew what means he had, or
could acquire. And, if Mr. Mornay were to
become his enemy, his life would be more
difficult in countless small ways. He had no
wish for that to occur.

Beatrice giggled at Nigel's feeble attempts
to aim the ball with accuracy, but she
encouraged him on nevertheless. The last
throw of the boy had nearly resulted in a
direct blow to Miss Bluford's head, but the
lady had shown remarkable fortitude by
instantly catching the wayward object

(though her face was all amazement) and hastily returning it to the child. Nigel, thinking she was joining the game, proceeded to lob it back to her, making her cry, "Oh, my! Oh, oh, my!" But she laughed for the first time that Beatrice had ever heard, and it was a warm laugh, and she looked almost normal while it lasted, instead of her usual nervous, beady-eyed self.

"Here, Nigel! Throw it to me," Miss Forsythe said, and almost immediately got a ball coming at her, which she caught, and then gently tossed back. She happened to glance up at the men. Mr. O'Brien was looking on with a serene half-smile, but Mr. Barton was sitting back with a resigned air, his eyes on the ceiling, his features set into a frown. Beatrice wondered what was bothering him. It could not be the children, could it? Miranda was smiling and gurgling for her two female admirers, and Nigel was merely playing catch with her and Miss Bluford. She found the scene nothing but charming. Did not Mr. Barton enjoy family life?

Mrs. Royleforst was also enjoying the atmosphere and making affectionate comments at intervals: "See how well he throws for one so young! I daresay he'll be athletic like his papa!"

This was a poor choice of words, for Nigel, dropping his ball on the instant ran to her and pulled on her gown, crying, "Papa! I want my Papa! And Mama! I want my Papa and Mama!" And just like that, the boy crumpled into tears. Mrs. Perler stood up and picked him up, but he fought her saying, "I want Mama!" Even little Miranda's head had turned to listen to him, and her little face began to wrinkle as her expression turned to one readying to wail.

"Oh, oh, oh!" cried Mrs. Forsythe, who immediately stepped up bouncing the child upon her knee. Miranda's face slowly lost its threatening appearance, and once again she gave her attention to her grandmama; but her large eyes were still wary, and the perfect little mouth remained in a pout.

Mr. Barton, meanwhile, had jumped to his feet. Speaking loudly to be heard above the child's cries, he said, "Anne, I think it high time we made for our own abode; do you not agree?" Anne turned her head toward him in surprise, and, with a last, longing look at the baby, said, "Yes, of course, Tristan. Whatever you say." Her face went blank, but she stood up, and then started her good-byes. Meanwhile, Mrs. Perler was fighting to keep Nigel in her arms, making her way slowly from the room. She said to Mrs. Forsythe, "I'll send . . . a nursemaid . . . for Miranda!"

"There's no hurry," she returned, watching the young boy fight his nurse. "See to poor Nigel."

Beatrice came to her feet and hurried to the pair. She offered her arms to the boy. His mouth shut as though she was something that he indeed needed to pay close attention to. He looked up at Mrs. Perler, then back at Beatrice, and then turned to her, arms open. She smilingly took him from the nurse, and went and sat down, speaking soothingly to him. She only nodded as her good-bye to Mr. Barton. She did not like to see him leave; but her nephew needed her attention; and she would give it. Their eyes caught for a moment: his were not sorry.

Directly following that, Beatrice chanced to see that Mr. O'Brien was gazing at her and Nigel. She saw quite a different look in his eyes, though he hurriedly turned away. She frowned, while stroking Nigel's dark black locks, thick and curly like his papa's. How was Ariana, she wondered? Nigel whimpered a little bit, but he quieted and put his head upon her breast, and snuggled against her. She did not look exceedingly like Ariana, but the child recognized some likeness in her that soothed him. He sat up once or twice to study her face, and then lay down upon her again, satisfied in some manner.

"Has there been a recent word from Mr. Speckman?" Beatrice asked.

"I was wondering that very thing," said her mother.

Mr. O'Brien came to attention as all eyes turned to him. "Come to think of it, no; I haven't had word. Let me check with Mrs. Persimmon," and he left the room.

As soon as he'd gone, Mrs. Royleforst said, "Mr. Barton is too good for the children, I see."

"What do you mean, Aunt Royleforst?" (Beatrice called her "aunt," although she was not technically Beatrice's relation.)

"Did you not see his face when the little ones arrived? It fell like an anchor at bay! And he could not have escaped any quicker when Nigel, poor thing, started crying. Did you not note it?"

"I did," agreed Miss Bluford, not surprising anyone. She always agreed with her mistress.

"I believe you have hit upon something," said Mrs. Forsythe. "But not all young men can appreciate children. Not even all men who are fathers can!" She gave a little laugh.

"Men hardly consider young children to

419

be people," offered Beatrice, who desperately wanted to defend Mr. Barton.

"Well, I must say," continued the large woman, "when we had to leave Aspindon, it was, in my opinion, the time for Mr. Barton to be gallant, and offer us the use of the Manor. He ought to at least have offered some small number of us a room. I daresay that house is big enough for a regiment!"

"A young man feels awkward being host to female guests, ma'am!" was Beatrice's reply.

"Fustian," she replied comfortably. "Mr. O'Brien has handled us beautifully, without a doubt, and he is certainly a young man; and Miss Barton is with her brother and would act as hostess, depend upon it. It gives one the thought that they have something to hide. A secret."

"Really, ma'am!" cried Beatrice, shocked. "I think you make too much of it. Mr. Barton had no need to offer the Manor, when Mr. O'Brien was already so obliging to open his house to us."

"Yes, my dear, a house that is all fine and good, but the Manor is finer, still. He must have far more resources at his disposal than our curate, and yet not half so much generosity! A man who is not compelled to be generous, to my mind, is a man who is *not* generous."

"Indeed!" said Miss Bluford.

"She's asleep," said Mrs. Forsythe just then, hardly above a whisper, but ironically, it was this very air of silence that made the others stop and pay attention. Only one side of Miranda's small round head could be seen, for she was nestled against Mrs. Forsythe's shoulder, head turned to one side. The blondish wisps of hair about her face were angelically sweet.

"I believe I'll take her to the nursery," said Beatrice's mother, rising carefully. "I should like to put her to bed myself, and sit and watch her sleep, afterward." She looked pointedly at Beatrice. "Do send me word at once if anything is heard regarding your sister!"

"Of course, Mama!"

No sooner had Mrs. Forsythe left the room with the baby than Mr. O'Brien returned, leaving no opportunity for further conversation about Mr. Barton. It was exceedingly irksome to Beatrice that Mrs. Royleforst had called his character into doubt. Perhaps it was true he did not care for children — were not many gentlemen like that? Particularly young gentlemen? And if Nigel had not been her own relation, would Beatrice have felt any less plagued by his crying than Mr. Barton had? Probably not. Oh, dear; it was all very befuddling. Beatrice adored children, and how could she seriously consider a man who seemed to have only disregard for them? Of course, they were not betrothed, yet. No agreement had been made, no promises exchanged. He had not yet spoken for her to either her mother or Mr. Mornay.

Mr. O'Brien pulled her from her thoughts. "There has been no word as yet from Aspindon. If you like, I can call and inquire of a servant."

"I should think you would be safer inquiring from the doctor himself," said Mrs. Royleforst. "Do you know his residence?"

Mr. O'Brien shook his head. He was as new to the area as anyone else in the room. "I'll call for the carriage," he said. Mr. Mornay's carriage was at their disposal, since the man had three of them, and had thoughtfully instructed his servants to stay at the vicarage for the sake of the women, who might need transportation for any number of reasons.

Suddenly Beatrice said, "Wait. I'll go with you, sir. With a chaperone, of course!" she added, quickly. Beatrice was growing increasingly restless and disturbed in her thoughts. Was it because Ariana might be ill? Because her Season in London might be in jeopardy? Was it because of Mr. Barton's increased attentiveness to her? Or, it might even have been the steady and thoughtful gaze of the intelligent curate that was grating on her nerves. Everything about his looks told Beatrice that he felt no *dis*like of her — but he said nothing of affection, either; and she did not know what to think. Beatrice felt that she *must* accompany the man — like a moth driven to a flame, she wished to simply be in his comforting presence.

"Whatever for?" asked Mrs. Royleforst. "And with Nigel asleep upon your lap!"

But Beatrice had the perfect way to obtain her wish. "Please?" she asked, looking to Mr. O'Brien, and motioning so that he came and lifted the sleeping child. "Give him to Mrs. Royleforst," she said, which he did. The child blinked sleepily, but did not fully awaken, and he snuggled into his new "pillow" and settled down. Mrs. Royleforst was delighted, and took her shawl from around her shoulders (with the help of Miss Bluford) and lay it over the boy, tucking it in around his little chubby legs.

"I daresay, we'll take a nap together!" she chuckled.

And when Beatrice got up to leave with the curate she said not another word.

TWENTY-TWO

Mr. O'Brien said, as he led the way to the front door, "I would feel more secure if you sought your mother's leave before accompanying me, Miss Forsythe."

Beatrice stared at him. "Do I make you uneasy, sir?" Her eyes twinkled and she turned away smiling, but he said, "Not at all. As I suspect you well know." His countenance was serious, but she detected a slight gleam in his eyes.

"Then have no fear!" she returned. "I promise not to get frostbit."

He smiled gently, and helped her with her coat. Mr. O'Brien had on a double-breasted coat of black cloth, dark pantaloons, and hunting boots. The linen frill of his white shirt showed over his waistcoat, and his neatly tied cravat was nevertheless voluminous, as though it held up his head. He put on a black fawn hat and gloves, and allowed Sykes to help him wrap his face in a warm scarf.

Beatrice, meanwhile, was watching as she tied her bonnet, and put on her own gloves. She grabbed her large fur muff — it certainly had come in handy the other day! Mr. O'Brien motioned to one of the servants who had come from Aspindon, and the man fell into step behind them.

"If I hear a word of reproach about this," he said to her as they went toward the coach, "I will turn it right back around to you."

"My mother will never reproach you, sir," she said mysteriously.

The servant hopped onto the back of the carriage, and they entered and took seats facing each other. Mr. O'Brien looked at her quizzically. "And why will your mother never reproach me?"

Beatrice considered how best to answer him. Perhaps she should not have teased him with that statement. But it was true.

"Because I have opened the parsonage to you?" He was guessing.

"Because she finds you so agreeable," she said, finally. "She utterly approves of you." He smiled. "And is your mother the only Forsythe who finds me agreeable?" he asked, looking at her directly.

Beatrice smiled. "Why, no, not at all!"

When he smiled at her response, she said, "My sister has always found you so!" They laughed quietly.

"Little Beatrice," he said, shaking his head. And she was instantly reminded of the promise she had made at twelve years old, only she did not want to be reminded of it. And why *did* Mr. O'Brien call her "Little Beatrice"? It made her feel like a child. It put her at a disadvantage. And what was next? Was he going to raise the memory of her rash words? Or the way she had undoubtedly embarrassed him before his family by speaking about it?

"I will marry him," she had said right to the man's mother. *"As soon as my papa gives his leave!"* Why did it haunt her so? She had decided that if he was going to reproach her with it, he would surely have done so by now. Beatrice fell silent just thinking about it. Meanwhile, she noticed he looked quite as elegant as Mr. Barton, but with a less studied air. His choice of attire was eminently suitable for a clergyman, and may have been less dear than Mr. Barton's, but Mr. O'Brien was taller and more manly in his bearing.

Mr. Barton chose his garments, she thought, to make a dash, to cut a wave. Mr. O'Brien on the other hand, wore what was

427

necessary and practical. He was not averse to being in fashion, but he did not depend upon being so. Mr. Barton would likely stay home, however, rather than appear in anything less than perfect attire. Mr. O'Brien would not.

Ariana had spoken of the young Mr. O'Brien once — or was it Aunt Bentley? As a tall, young sprig, slim as a whip. He was no longer so slim as that; he had taken on a manlier look, perhaps he fenced often, as did Mr. Mornay. *And why was she thinking of such a thing?* She turned to look out the window.

"When we arrive at the house," he said, "you must stay in the carriage; I will discover the news, if there is any." She said nothing, only took in his earnest blue gaze, and felt a great annoyance that she kept noticing those eyes. How irksome, to see nothing in him but a beautiful, sincere man. He caught her gaze, and for a moment it looked to Beatrice that his look was full of something — was it *longing?*

Oh, she felt too dishonest to bear! How could she admire him so, and yet be sure that he would ruin all her hopes if she were to marry him? Was it wrong to have admiration for him without telling him of it? But she must not tell him of it, for she meant to marry Mr. Barton. She just knew she would be happier in the course of her life with a secure and comfortable income to depend upon.

She would have to make Mr. O'Brien understand her so that he would not become bold, or entertain romantic notions of her and end up with ruined hopes.

"Sir, may I speak plainly with you?" she said, looking around a little furtively.

He was intrigued. Her lovely green eyes contrasted prettily with the russet curls framing her face. She was truly a lovely sight . . . *Oh, dear! Why must he always think thus?*

"I am at your service, Miss Forsythe." He added, with a smile, "I am a curate, after all. Many people desire to speak with me in that office, and I am happy to oblige."

"Precisely! And that is why I must speak to you!"

This little bit of information got him curious. "I see!"

Beatrice blushed lightly. Her rosy cheeks contrasted well with her gray redingote and black half boots. Her face was framed in a bonnet that accented her green eyes, and altogether it struck Mr. O'Brien forcefully that Miss Forsythe was as pretty and desirable a young woman as any man should be happy and proud to own the affections of. More, she was excellent with children; not overly impetuous or silly (as many young women of his acquaintance were); and *wishing to speak to him.*

She cleared her throat.

"May I ask —" he began, while at the very same moment, she said, "Here is the thing —" They both stopped and exchanged a smile. "Here is the thing," she said again, wondering why on earth she had wanted this conversation. She felt far too embarrassed now that she had demanded his attention. But she had no alternative but to plunge ahead, and so continued, "I have been given — to understand —" and she peeked at his eyes.

"Yes?" He was curious to understand her dilemma.

"By Mr. Barton . . . that he desires to court me." (*Goodness, that not was not what she had meant to say!*) Mr. O'Brien drew back. His face went blank, but he said, "And this is troubling to you?" He was trying desperately to ignore the pang of disappointment in his breast. "Has he sought the permission of your parents? Or of Mr. Mornay?"

"He means to, but on account of my sister's exposure to the fever, I believe he lacked an opportunity to speak with Mr. Mornay."

He nodded, his eyes very intent, listening. Beatrice wished she were talking to him of something else! Of her very real admiration for him — but it was impossible. *How had she thought she could speak of such a thing?*

"How may I be of service to you?"

She took a deep breath. "Your acquaintance with Mr. Barton is new, I grant, but I need to ask for your honest assessment of his character. I am having some difficulty making it out . . ." She trailed off.

A look of concern flitted across his face, and in an apologetic tone, he said, "I fear I am not in a position to judge his character." He fell silent a minute. Indeed there were a few things that he had noticed about the man, but it did not seem fair that he should warn her against another man; not when he knew how much he wished he could be in that man's position. He was doing it again, was he not! Making a cake of himself over a Forsythe girl!

"As a churchman, sir, I ask you. As a curate, do you not form opinions of people?"

He gave a little smile. She had no idea of his feelings, he could see. That was actually a good thing. "I form opinions as a human

431

being, but I do not think it is fair to Mr. Barton if I say anything of him based upon so short an acquaintance." He swallowed, and said, "He is evidently a man of some standing, and seems to have a good enough fortune to deserve you."

It was true that she thought so herself. Nodding in agreement, she said, "Yes, I do expect that he could purchase the Manor, and it is a fine, large house. Not so fine as Aspindon, of course, but still a proud dwelling."

"Yes." He thought of his pride at being the occupant of the vicarage, and could only imagine how much larger and finer the Manor House must be. He felt his own pride deflating, such as an air balloon when it has lost the gas inside it. But Beatrice deserved such a house.

"And he goes to London for the Season every year, I understand."

"Does that suit you?" he asked.

"Yes! Exceedingly." But as she said this, her own words felt hollow for some reason. She did not understand why they did. She desired to go to London, did she not? The thought of a Season every year — why it was thrilling; it must be so!

"I think I should say," he offered, making her look hopefully at him, "that it speaks well of Mr. Barton that he would offer for you (and I hope you won't take this badly, for I mean nothing against you by it), but his circumstances are above yours, do you not agree?"

"Oh, yes, that is true! I have family, with Mrs. Mornay as my sister; but he has fortune, I grant him that."

He looked at her assuringly, if not enthusiastically. "He will keep you in good style."

"Yes."

"In short, I can only say that there appears to be no reason against him, unless you know of something in him that I do not."

Her pretty eyes widened. "But I am asking what *you* know of him! As my friend! Gentlemen are often knowledgeable of other gentlemen in ways that we females are wholly ignorant of. We have no manner of knowing or judging a man in his true character when we only see him in company, at his best behaviour. I am asking you, sir, if you know of anything undesirable in him. Something I would not see in him in a drawing room!"

Her manner was so earnest, that he searched his brain for anything that might answer. He cleared his throat. "Well, I do not take him for a man of deep religion, if that is what you seek to know."

She nodded eagerly. "Yes?"

"I have not seen evidence that he and his sister share a great love between them, as some siblings do."

"I have noted that too!"

"But I must tell you —"

"Yes? Yes!"

"Mr. Mornay is the man whose opinion you must seek. He will know whether Mr. Barton is suitable for you better than I."

A strange sort of disappointment filled her breast. Mr. O'Brien did not want to discourage her regarding Mr. Barton's suit. Why was that the least bit deflating? She should have welcomed it as a good sign. As evidence that Mr. Barton had no grievous failings that should rightly warn her away. But instead, she felt disappointed. Another matter occurred to her. One that she had no idea she would raise, but suddenly she did:

"Mr. O'Brien, I must discuss one thing more with you, if I may?"

"By all means."

"I wanted to mention how good of you it is that you have not once even alluded to my childish promise to marry you!" She tried to laugh while she spoke, to show him that she knew it was merely a joke, now. He nodded, but said nothing for a moment.

"Of course."

"You knew, then, that it was my youth and inexperience speaking?"

"Of course!" But he looked very uncomfortable.

"It does not pain you, that I mention it?" she asked him gently, and he met her gaze, noting her large pretty eyes, and surprised her by answering, fully as gently as she had asked the question, "Little Beatrice, no man of honour would hold a child to such a thing."

"No," she agreed, her eyes suddenly seeming to shine. She turned her head away, looking out the window. "I was only a child!"

"Of course. A very fetching, affectionate one," he said, smiling at the memory.

"I daresay I embarrassed you a great deal!" She met his gaze again, and the watery look had vanished. The carriage slowed to a stop, and he came to attention.

"Remain here. I'll be right back." He spoke with decision, almost abruptly.

"Yes, sir." He did not look at her but climbed out of the coach and was at the door of the house in a minute.

Mr. O'Brien was troubled. As he waited for the door to be answered, he wondered: What did Beatrice want of him, really? What did his opinion of Mr. Barton matter? It would normally be precisely the thing a young lady should not wish to know, if she cherished hopes of marriage to a man. Why look for trouble? Why seek to know what might alter the course? Did she truly want Barton or not, that was his question.

After waiting at the door for a few moments, the housekeeper finally answered. She looked frazzled. Her eyes widened at sight of him, and she stepped back. "Come no further, sir! The mistress has fallen ill! She's got the fever! God have mercy on us!"

Somehow Beatrice had convinced herself that her sister would not take sick. The atmosphere in the carriage had swiftly changed to a dark foreboding feeling when Mr. O'Brien returned almost at once with the dreaded announcement. He ordered the carriage to return to the vicarage before rejoining Beatrice.

"A fever is not always severe," Mr. O'Brien said, in an effort to comfort Beatrice.

"Yes," she agreed, in a low voice. But her eyes were filled with worry.

"We will continue to hold Mrs. and Mr. Mornay in prayer. You must trust God's faithfulness."

She looked up to meet his gaze. "God's faithfulness, sir, did not prevent a score of deaths in London from this illness!"

"Yes, but many of those people were undernourished, not attended to in their illness, and already in a weakened state before they got the fever. Your sister is young and strong; and in the best hands. We have every reason to hope!" She nodded, but nevertheless a tear slipped from one eye. He rummaged in his clothing to produce a wrinkled handkerchief from an inside pocket of his waistcoat.

"Thank you," she said, receiving it and dabbing her eyes. The next few minutes were passed in complete silence except for the noise of the carriage wheels and the horses upon the road.

"Truly, I did not believe — that she would get ill."

He nodded. "I know."

"I may yet be at fault for her death!" More tears came.

"Miss Forsythe — Miss *Beatrice*." (He could not help but to use her name after remembering her from when she was younger). "You are leaping to conclusions that are not warranted by the circumstances! Please, let us take each day as it comes, and attend only to the trouble it brings. Do not borrow troubles that have yet to occur."

"But I cannot help thinking she may die! Other people have died from this! And her exposure was all — *my* — fault!"

His voice was suddenly firm and strong. "Beatrice! That is enough of such nonsense!"

She looked up at him in surprise. "Is it nonsense?"

"Utterly."

She sniffed, but stopped crying, and hereafter had to eye him with a surprised regard. Mr. O'Brien was not one to tolerate nonsense, and she appreciated him for it. Indeed, she even felt better now that she had stopped crying. Perhaps Ariana would not have a severe case of the sickness. She might even be recovered by the following day! Why ought she to worry? Mr. O'Brien was right! They would pray for her and keep a chin up until they heard reason to warrant greater concern.

"As to our former discussion," he said suddenly, leaning in toward her a little, "if I may be of any further help, please do call upon me. But I advise you to voice your concerns to Mr. Mornay as soon as he is able to hear them."

"I shall; I thank you."

Mr. O'Brien paused, but had to ask: "Are

you to be considered betrothed, then? To Mr. Barton?"

"No promises have been made. He has not spoken for me, yet."

"It is what you wish, however?"

She hesitated. His earnest blue eyes were actually quite beautiful for a man. There was a hint of fine blond stubble about his chin, but it was not unbecoming. He was in no way fastidious, and yet his appearance was neat and clean. Moreover, he had been nothing if not exceedingly kind and helpful.

She had to answer him, so she said the only thing she could say.

"It is, yes." As she said it, however, she felt it was *not* what she wished. How irksome! It had to be, for only Mr. Barton could provide everything she based her hopes upon. Yet there was something in the curate that drew her to him, and it had nothing at all to do with his situation, or his fortune, or his lack of one. It had nothing to do with the size of his house, or with whether or not he would go to London for the Season. It had nothing to do with reason, for goodness' sake! It was utterly unreasonable, and went against everything she thought she had wanted in a man. But Beatrice was suddenly feeling as though she were in love.

With Mr. O'Brien.

Oh, dear.

TWENTY-THREE

Some of the colour had drained from Mr. Mornay's face, but he nevertheless stood watching while the physician finished up the messy business of bleeding his wife. Ariana had showed little response except to moan softly now and then, at which her husband had taken one of her hands. *So hot. So abominably hot!*

When the doctor's assistant went to empty the basin with that precious dark fluid from Ariana's body, Freddie came in holding a letter salver.

"I want no correspondence now," Mornay said sourly.

"It is from Carlton House, sir." He held out the silver tray with a single, thickly folded note. Mr. Mornay sighed and took it, saying, "Hold off." The butler waited. Phillip opened the blob of sealing wax and began to read. There wasn't much; it was merely an invitation. A thinly disguised command, more like, for the Mornays to stop at Brighton to see the Regent. He'd be entertaining at his palace for a few weeks, and wished them to come as soon as possible.

Mr. Mornay's look was grave. He crumpled the paper into a ball and tossed it into the fireplace. "Freddie, have my secretary send a response. Tell the prince that Mrs. Mornay is ill, and that we can go nowhere at present."

"Er, sir, I beg your pardon, but there is no secretary in the house. Shall I send for one?"

"Can you not write?" the master asked, making Freddie's eyes open in surprise.

"I, sir? To the prince?"

"Yes, yes, it does not matter. So long as you can write legibly!"

"Yes, sir." He stood up straighter, resigned to what was coming.

"Do as I say." He paused, and Freddie, from long acquaintance with the man, waited again. "And tell him to pray."

"Yes, sir." He bowed and went down to the business office. He felt very inadequate to the task at hand — a butler writing to the Prince Regent! But he also felt a new sense of importance; he was so inured to his position at Aspindon that he seldom felt his own importance as the butler of the establishment, but today it was borne in upon him in a new way. He hurried his step to get the missive done, and sent back with the man who had delivered the royal message.

At the secretary's desk, Frederick found a piece of the best foolscap and a plume pen, and opened the little inkwell upon the polished wooden surface. "To His Royal Highness, the Prince Regent," he began. When the letter was finished, he opened a jar of blotting sand and sprinkled it liberally over the single paragraph of writing. After shaking off the excess, he folded it twice, lit a wafer of sealing wax with a tinder box, and dropped a good blob of the wax — he used black, to stress the point of the reply — and pressed the master's seal, a tiny imprint of the initials "P" and "M" in a miniature ornate style onto the wax. He had signed the letter, "Your Humble and Obedient Servant, Mr. W. Frederick, Butler."

When Mr. Frederick had found the prince's messenger in the kitchens, having a bite — a place that was deemed safe from the illness — he gave the note to Cook, who was told to wipe it clean of Freddie's breath or touch. (Who knew how the sickness might be passed?) And it was sent on its way, with one of Mr. Mornay's horses. The bother was that the groom was not in the stables, and neither, Freddie noticed, was Tornado! Could the man still be away to deliver his message to the vicarage? Surely he should have been back by now. And to take Tornado! Dashed presumptuous of him!

He himself had to choose a mount for the messenger, and to the man's complaint that no one had come to see to his horse and he had been forced to take the animal to the stables with his own hand, Freddie replied, "We have only a skeleton crew, here, sir, as our mistress has the fever."

The man's eyes widened, and from that moment on he could not exit the place fast enough.

But where was Mr. Rudson, the head groom? And what had he done with Tornado?

Mr. Rudson opened his eyes and blinked. A pain in his head assailed him. When he tried to move, more aches shouted their presence, but he saw that he was beneath a tall tree, and it all came flooding back. While he slowly managed to get to his feet, and was brushing himself off, he reviewed the events which had landed him there — literally.

Tornado, after getting into a frenzied and

wild gallop, had began to buck at odd moments, trying to rid himself of his rider — he, Mr. Rudson. He'd grasped the pommel, the animal's mane, the seat of the saddle, anything and everything to keep his seat. Up hills and down, he'd hung on grimly, knowing that he was likely a ruined man. Mr. Mornay would not, could not forgive him for this, he was certain. Nor would Tornado, who reminded him often of his resentment by bucking. The horse was a sly devil, too, for he began to close in on tree trunks, trying to graze the man's legs, doing anything to make him lose his hold on the reins or the saddle.

Finally, with a surprising and desperate buck that went into a spin, Mr. Rudson had gone flying off the seat as smooth as a stone being flung upon the water. And then all had gone black. And now here he was. Freezing from cold, far from help, and sore as a blind carpenter's thumb. He supposed he was lucky to be alive. That was something, anyway.

Tornado made his way back to the stables slowly and at his leisure. He found his hay bin and helped himself. His stall was not open and he whinnied in annoyance, but eventually settled upon standing just outside it, munching hay as though nothing at all had occurred.

Mr. Rudson, two miles from the house and stables, had come to his feet, sighed heavily, and began walking. He was going to be sore for days. With any luck, that devil of a horse would be back at the stables when he got there, and he was sure, very sure, that he would never mount that demon again.

Ariana was growing worse. She was sweating a great deal, and hair clung to her face and neck, despite Mr. Mornay's attempts to wash it back periodically with a damp cloth. When she wasn't tossing and turning restlessly, she either moaned or spoke out in delirium — a thing which Mr. Mornay discovered, to his shame, that he could barely stand. Was he so weak, he asked himself? Since when had a little suffering reduced him to speechless dismay? He remained by her bedside, however; and when she chanced to call his name during her moments of unconscious speech, it was heartrending to see him leaning over her and trying to reach her, to let her know that he was there. It was useless.

In response to her worsening condition, Mr. Speckman insisted that his treatment was having its effect. "Mrs. Mornay will soon reach a crisis, sir; and when it has passed, she will begin to recover." The husband wanted to ask, *And if it does not pass? If it is too much for her?* But he could not bring himself to do it. He was beginning to doubt the wisdom of the medical man's judgment, however. "How many people have you given this treatment to, and did most of them recover?"

"Oh, sir, I've treated dozens of fevers in my day! I daresay most people do recover. It's the weak ones, the aged and the infirm, who succumb, and infants don't do so well, either."

"But is this a regular fever of the sort you often see?"

The man looked down thoughtfully at his patient. "Well, it may be more severe; it does seem to have grown worse rather rapidly —"

"And so in fact you are not certain that my wife will recover."

"Certain, sir? Only God is certain." The doctor drew back at the fierce stare from Mr. Mornay.

Mr. Mornay was already exhausted, and now he was bordering on terrified. He had barely taken anything to eat or drink, and the doctor was hard-pressed to get him to leave the room for any reason whatsoever.

"You can be of no use here," Mr. Speckman said, finally. "If you do not strengthen yourself, and your wife recovers, you may then fall ill — and not recover. Do not treat her so shabbily. Go and eat something, man!"

Mr. Mornay reluctantly agreed, and slowly made his way to his study. Although he knew the house to be empty of guests, he could not face a public room. The housekeeper was very relieved to be able to fetch him some nourishment, and delivered it herself. The Mornays had given her a second chance at life — when they might have had her arrested for theft! — and she would never forget their kindness. They were family to her now. Mr. Mornay was her master, her employer, but also like her own flesh and blood.

When she entered the room with the tray, Mr. Mornay was at his desk, staring ahead of him, unseeing. The family Bible lay open before him, but he was lost in thought. He looked dreadfully weary.

"Here you go, sir," she said in a gentle voice. She placed her tray down and moved aside the Bible to put it before him. "I've made you a good stiff drink, sir," she said, "which will help you bear your sorrows, I daresay."

He looked down at the glass stupidly for a moment. Then he raised his head to look at her and said, "Take it back. Pour it out. Pour it out, or down your own throat, if you like, but I shan't drink it."

"But sir, Cook assures me it is a favourite of yours." She stared at him in wonder.

"That has nothing to do with it, Mrs. Hamilton. I have a cup to drink, apparently, that has already been given me. And it is the only one I shall sip from until it is emptied, I'm afraid."

Mrs. Hamilton searched his desk with her eyes. She saw no other beverage. Tears came into her eyes. "My dear sir," she said, leaning against the desk weakly, for she was that overcome by seeing him in such a sorry state. "Allow me to have Mr. Speckman prescribe some laudanum for you!"

He realized that she did not get his meaning. "Mrs. Hamilton — I am not out of my senses. I am in the midst of a trial, and I shall see it through. I shall see it through with the strength God gives me. I want nothing other than the weakest port, do you understand?"

"Oh!" She came to her full height again, rejuvenated by his little explanation.

He looked at her, as if he was surprised

that she still stood there. "Well, fetch it!"

"Right away, sir!" She left with a sniffle, but it was a happy sniffle. The mistress was still poorly, but at least the master was holding up . . . well . . . *masterfully!*

Lord Horatio had been given the family coach to get himself to Middlesex, and he climbed out of it now even as his footman was already at the door of Aspindon, waiting to announce his arrival. It was long into the evening, but it seemed oddly quiet, and he hoped the Mornays were not away. But the door opened at last, and a little wisp of a maid peered out at them. As he approached, his footman stood aside.

"Is Mr. Mornay at home?" he asked, moving as if to enter the house, only the little maid moved to block his path. He stopped in surprise.

"He is, sir."

"You are speaking to Lord Horatio," the footman said, without a blink.

"Beggin' yer pardon, yer lordship," Molly said.

"Well . . . may I come in? I am here to see your master."

"Beggin' yer pardon, yer lordship," she said again, "but mistress is ill, and no one's to come into the house, sir — yer lordship."

"Ill? What sort of sickness, do you know?"

"She's got the fever, sir — yer lord —"

"That's quite all right," he interjected quickly. "But I'll take my chances. Let him know I'm here, will you?"

"Yes, yer lordship, sir." Molly's wide eyes almost made him laugh except that they were alarmed. She moved aside and let him enter the house, where he stood for a moment, looking around at the great hall. Mr. Frederick came briskly through a doorway and saw Lord Horatio.

"Why it's Lord Horatio! How do you, my lord?" he said, bowing.

"Very good, Freddie. How's yourself?" He was holding out his hat and cane, but Freddie made no move to take it. "Oh, I know, I know, Mrs. Mornay is ill. Well, I'm not leaving, so tell your cantankerous master that I'm here. Sent by the prince, in fact." He was still holding out his effects, and Freddie reluctantly took them.

"He'll bark at us for giving you leave to enter."

"Sorry, old fellow, but I need to see him."

"Very good, m'lord," he replied, but his voice was doubtful. He led the man to a drawing room and left him with a bow. "If you need anything, my lord . . ."

"No, no, thank you, old man. Just bring

me your master."

About eight minutes went by, and then Freddie returned to the room. His face was drawn.

"Well? Did he bite your head off?"

"My lord," and Freddie's sober face finally caused a worry to come upon his. "Mr. Mornay cannot be disturbed. Mrs. Mornay has reached a crisis in her sickness, sir." The butler's eyes were red, and he was blinking quite a bit.

Lord Horatio looked really surprised. "Upon my word! It is as bad as all that?"

"We may lose her, your lordship."

"My soul! This is terrible! What can I do?"

When Lord Horatio showed up at the vicarage, it caused a stir. For one thing, prayers had ended and Mr. and Miss Barton had returned to spend the evening with the assembled company. Mr. Barton had become adept at knowing just what time it was safe for him to return without having to endure the religious zeal of the curate.

The cook from Aspindon was still sending large amounts of victuals to the household (master's orders), and just then the guests were taking tea with biscuits and cake which she had supplied. It was all very nice, indeed. But then his lordship was announced by Sykes, in a voice that said he understood the importance of this guest (a *lord!*).

The room fell silent, except that Miss Barton gasped and actually dropped her cake onto the carpet. Lord Horatio looked at her, then, and his mouth gaped open for a second, and then shut again in fast succession. The letter had directed him to the vicarage, not the Manor House where he supposed Anne and her brother to be. Mr. O'Brien rang for the housekeeper, and then went to welcome the newest guest to his household. Lord Horatio stared at him for a moment, and then said, "O'Brien! That is you, is it?"

"Yes, your lordship." He smiled gently. "Please come in and join us." When the housekeeper arrived, she had another tea cup, though already there was china from two different sets in use, in order to accommodate everyone. Horatio had to endure endless introductions, but when it was Miss Barton's turn, he bowed lower than he had for anyone else, stepped up, and took her hand and kissed it. "I believe I am acquainted with Miss Barton."

Mr. Barton was watching him with an eagle eye, and Beatrice noted that his usual friendliness of manner seemed to have

453

deserted him.

"What brings you to Middlesex, my lord?" Mr. O'Brien asked. "At this hour too?"

Lord Horatio forced his eyes away from Miss Barton's face and said, "Well, that's just it. I have some terrible news." Beatrice gasped, and the room fell silent. He looked around. "Mrs. Mornay has reached a crisis in her illness. Mr. Mornay asks you to pray, to pray very hard." He felt rather strange delivering such a message. Lord Horatio had never asked anyone in his life to pray for anything. Also, despite the gravity of the situation, and despite all of his past friendship with Mrs. Mornay, he was preoccupied with another errand, and he could not rest until he had seen to it.

"Mr. O'Brien," he said, right out loud and in front of everyone. "I have come here with a special license, signed by the archbishop. I would like you to marry me to Miss Barton, and at your soonest convenience!"

"Oh!" Miss Barton stood up, with one hand against her waist, and was staring at his lordship as though she was not aware of other people in the room. Mr. Barton was exceedingly surprised, but did not seem displeased. He looked at his sister and nodded at her, when she finally turned her eyes to him for a second. He said, "Well done,

Horatio!"

Mrs. Royleforst's little eyes were as wide as they could get. Miss Bluford's eyes were even wider. She asked, without realizing perhaps, that she was speaking aloud, "Do you mean you approve of this match?" Her voice had come out in a high, reedy tone, and not a person in the room could believe they had actually heard from Miss Bluford; or that she had truly questioned the match. After recovering her astonishment at her companion's audacity, Mrs. Royleforst said, "Here, here! I second that question!" Miss Bluford gave a look of sheer adoration to her mistress. Instead of the companion agreeing with her employer, for this once, for this one occasion, Mrs. Royleforst had agreed with her companion.

Mr. Barton said, "To both your questions, I can answer, yes, I do; with all my heart."

But Mrs. Royleforst had more to say. "Surely Miss Barton does not wish to accept a man who does not propose but in a roundabout way; who barges in on genteel company at night, with a license in hand, indeed!" Everyone looked to Miss Barton. Lord Horatio's face grew shadowed.

"I do accept him!" she cried, as a tear slid down her face. To Horatio she said, "You received my note, then?"

He nodded. "It gave me the courage to come after you."

"Courage?" she asked. "When I always hoped you would!"

Beatrice was smiling despite her embarrassment at this show of affection, between two virtual strangers, for she had still not reached that level of friendship with Miss Barton where one becomes comfortable with another. But this was too sweet not to smile at, despite being so irregular.

"And you will marry us?" Lord Horatio turned to the curate.

"After I examine that paper, yes. Shall we say, tomorrow? In the church?"

Miss Barton could contain herself no longer, and at this she flew to the side of her betrothed. He received her with one arm about her, and their eyes met and held fast. Miss Barton was smiling and crying at the same time.

"I am greatly obliged to you, Mr. O'Brien," she said, through her happy tears. "Greatly obliged!" Mr. O'Brien merely nodded kindly in acknowledgment. She turned to Mrs. Forsythe and added, "And to you!" But Ariana's mother could scarcely pay heed.

"My *daugh-ter!*" she cried. Her voice was so loud that everyone's attention flew to her.

"We must pray for Ariana! She has reached a crisis! Time is of the essence!"

"Of course!" said Mr. O'Brien. Mrs. Forsythe stood up, and then, with a look around as if she were daring anyone to cavil, she dropped to her knees by the table and began to pray silently. Beatrice quickly stood and went and joined her. Miss Barton, tugging lightly onto Horatio's sleeve, motioned for him to come, and they, too, slowly took places around the table. It was exceedingly unusual, his lordship thought, but somehow it did not feel improper.

Mr. O'Brien had opened his Bible, and now he came and got to his knees near the others. There was room for one more, and he looked at Mr. Barton expectantly. Mr. Barton grudgingly moved toward him, but at the last minute he stopped, and without another word, turned and left the room. In a minute, they heard the noise of the front door. He had left the house. In another minute, Mrs. Persimmon, who had cleaned up the cake that Miss Barton had dropped, returned, and she came and fell to her knees, making the little circle of people around the table complete.

Mr. O'Brien found a page in his Bible, and then said, "We will agree in prayer tonight for the safety and recovery of Mrs.

Mornay." Beatrice had tears in her eyes, and she clung to his words as great reassurance. He saw the look on her face, a look of deep distress, and he said, looking directly at her, *"If two of you shall agree on earth as touching any thing that they shall ask, it shall be done for them of my Father which is in heaven.* This *is* the Word of our Lord."

"Amen." The others spoke in unison.

He nodded at her very earnestly. It was as though she could hear his voice again, saying, "You must trust God's faithfulness!" And, "Do not borrow trouble." Ariana might have reached a crisis, but she had not died, yet. There was still hope. And here she was in a prayer circle, agreeing on the Word of God about her sister's recovery. *"It shall be done for them of my Father which is in heaven."* She would dare to believe it.

Mr. O'Brien said, "And now, each of us must pray from the bottom of our hearts for Mrs. Mornay. From the bottom of your hearts!" He looked about at the circle of faces. "Who will agree with me?"

"I will," said Beatrice. He nodded.

"I shall also," said Mrs. Forsythe. Mrs. Royleforst, who was still upon a sofa (for she was a large woman and lame in one leg) said, "I do agree, sir."

"And I!" put in little Miss Bluford.

Miss Barton and Lord Horatio looked at each other askance. Miss Barton shrugged. This night had been an answer to every prayer that she had uttered of late, and so she said, "We also, sir."

"We are all in agreement, then!" said a satisfied Mrs. Persimmon.

Mr. O'Brien said, "Please, let us take hands with one another." Obediently, with teary smiles on some — this was so peculiar! — they did so. Horatio was happy to have a reason to take Miss Barton's hand, most affectionately; and then the curate led the little gathering in a prayer for Ariana that was at once both heartfelt and encouraging. He prayed for healing and health; for a speedy recovery; for the continued health and prosperity of the Mornay household and all of its tenants. And finally, for each one in the room there tonight. "We are gathered in Your name, Lord, and in Your name we pray. Amen." When Beatrice looked up, his tall head was still bowed in a reverential attitude, and she felt the most ardent admiration for him. How wonderful that he had appeared when he did!

What would they have done if Mr. O'Brien had not generously opened his new house to them? What if they had been scattered, without news of Ariana? And what if he had not been there to lead them in prayer? To be the beacon of strength in this time of sorrow? How foolish she had been, to speak to him in the carriage, yesterday! Why had she told him of Mr. Barton? Beatrice was now certain that Mr. Barton, despite his wealth, or amiability, or social connexions, could never make her happy. Nor could she please him. How could her grasp of both men have changed so substantially in one day? But it had!

His head came up and he glanced at her. Quickly she averted her eyes. How embarrassing!

Mrs. Forsythe began thanking him; Beatrice quietly asked the housekeeper for a night candle to find her way to her bed-chamber. There was much in her heart to consider.

Twenty-Four

Mr. Barton left the vicarage in disgust. That Lord Horatio had showed up to claim his sister's hand should have thrown him into the best of spirits; it was the very thing he had never for a moment believed was possible, but had happened. Lord Horatio had honourable intentions and meant to marry Anne! It was indeed one weight lifted from his shoulders. He no longer had to worry about social disgrace for his sister, or that his name would be tainted as a result. Of course, some people were bound to whisper when the child came early . . . but that was nothing at the moment.

The thing that sent him from the house in disgust was the "prayer meeting." He knew O'Brien was an Anglican curate, but dashed if he wasn't acting like a Methodist! Or worse, a Dissenter! And the others had gone right along with him as if it wasn't the least unusual thing in the world. Why, for all he knew, it might have been heresy! Weren't people supposed to pray in church? He knew it did not look well in Beatrice's eyes, but he could not bring himself to kneel at the table. It was impossible.

Worst of all, the reason behind the impromptu prayer gathering was also highly irksome. If Mrs. Mornay was at a crisis, then Mrs. Mornay might be deathly ill. She could die. And if she died, there was no longer anything to tie Miss Forsythe to the Paragon. Knowing Mornay, he'd have nothing to do with the family; he'd no doubt retreat into his old, miserable, caustic nature and become a recluse — or a terror. Either way, there would be no advantage for him in marrying Beatrice Forsythe.

He felt sorry about it. He liked Miss Forsythe. She was a good-natured girl, prone to enjoy a laugh, and pretty to boot. But when she'd been family to the Paragon, he liked her better. Or if she'd had her own fortune, say, ten thousand pounds or so, he'd have found her irresistible. Without either one, he was afraid he could not afford her — not unless he was prepared to give up his nights at the clubs, which he was not.

When he reached the Manor, he was still deliberating on what his next move would be. Mornay was still in quarantine and there wasn't a deuced thing for him to do in Middlesex. He was itching to return to London. Dash it, but this country life was deadly dull! He was sorely tempted to drive himself back to the city that very night. But highwaymen would be a threat; and he didn't relish going it alone.

In the end, he had a drink and just lost himself in thought before the fire. When Anne came home much later, escorted by his lordship, she was hoping to question her brother, to understand what had caused his earlier disappearance, but not much information was to be had from Mr. Barton by that time.

He was asleep, spread-eagled, on the floor in front of the fire, an empty wine bottle beside him. He was oblivious to the most ardent shaking and to all efforts to make him stir.

When Agatha and Randolph Pellham, or "Aunt and Uncle Pellham," received a letter from Mrs. Forsythe telling them about Ariana taking ill, there was only one thing to do. They must leave their nest and get Mrs. Pellham to her niece directly. Mrs. Pellham detested leaving her house. She detested travel of any sort. But she had a special fondness for Ariana. It was so strong a fondness that it was stronger than her dislike of travel or leaving home; and so fly to her niece she must.

Her decision, once made, had to be executed with the utmost haste. She therefore had her servants in such a flurry of activity and tasks as would make the most seasoned housekeeper quake. And she liked to check on it all: She oversaw the packing of their trunks, the closing up of the house, the readying of their coach and four, and the preparation of a basket of victuals to take for the journey. Bricks were heated, woolen stockings donned, hats and coats and waistcoats and jewellery (Mrs. Pellham never went anywhere without her jewellery), all packed up and stowed in the boot of the coach. Carriage blankets were ready, and even a small vial of brandy — in case the cold became too ruinous to Mr. Pellham's constitution.

When all was stowed and ready to go, the coachman sat hunched atop the vehicle, clad in a heavy, many-caped coat and ponderous hat, so that his face could not be seen. He knew his orders: He was to go with all possible speed and haste to Aspindon of Middlesex. Beside him sat Haines, equally prepared for the cold — and for hoodlums.

He had learned to use a weapon since the unfortunate events of the past when Lord Wingate had abducted his mistress at point of pistol; he now prided himself on his accuracy, and Mrs. Pellham considered him indispensable to her comfort when travelling.

In addition to her dislike of travel, Mrs. Pellham had an aversion to sickbeds. Thus her journey, and her object, were rather extraordinary. In the back of her mind, however, was her hope not only to be of assistance to her beautiful (though very particular) niece, but to see the children again. She adored her great-nephew Nigel, and had not yet met Miranda. There was no question, therefore, that she would have to go to them. And where she went, of course, Randolph went also.

She brought her little leather-bound *Book of Common Prayer* for the journey, and she held it within her gloved hands for most of the ride. Even if she didn't open it, the sight of the worn black leather tome in her possession was enough to reassure her.

To this day, the memory of the Season five years earlier when Mrs. Pellham (she'd been Mrs. Bentley then) had sponsored Miss Ariana Forsythe in London was one of the highlights of her life; an *annus mirabilis,* a miraculous year, when Mrs. Pellham had been welcome in the finest drawing rooms of the aristocracy; when Ariana had done the impossible and snagged the famous Mr. Mornay for a husband! And she, Mrs. Bentley, a widow for well-nigh ten years, had finally agreed to marry Mr. Randolph Pellham, her dearest and most loyal companion. They had been happily together since.

This was why she moved with such haste, and ordered her coachman to make good time. The mercy of it was that the Pellhams were at their London townhouse when they heard the news, instead of their country estate. Mrs. Pellham always left the country for town before March, well before the Season started, to ensure the best seamstresses were at her disposal. Thank goodness, for that reason only, they could reach Aspindon in less than three hours; had they been home in the Cotswolds, it would have been an overnight drive, at the least.

"My dear Mr. Pellham," said the lady, when they were both comfortably seated among a canopy of blankets and pillows and had heated bricks beneath their feet.

"Yes, my dear Mrs. P?"

"I feel that we ought to pray for Ariana. I must confess, Randolph, to having a most unnerving and unnatural feeling of dread concerning her."

"Mrs. P, you must not distress yourself so; allow me to read from the prayer book, and you, rest your head upon me, here, with this pillow —" and he moved a small travelling pillow so that she could lean her head comfortably upon it, which in turn, rested upon his left arm — "and I shall begin. I was about to read the Collect, myself, you know."

"May we pray together, first, Randolph? I despise this terrible suspicion! I must vanquish it — or rather, ask the Saviour to."

"Oh, it is like that, is it? Yes, we must pray, then." He took her hand warmly within his own, and bowed his head to lead his wife in a "prayer of agreement" over the safety of their journey; and the health of Ariana. Mr. Pellham's faith had grown along with his wife's over time, so that to turn to the prayer book or Bible was second nature to them now. And to pray together was not just a duty but a privilege. They had seen the effectual power of prayer too many times to doubt its use.

"Oh, you are such a comfort to me, Randolph!"

"As you are to me, Mrs. P."

After praying, they travelled on while he read to her. He chose selections from the prayer book, the Bible, and then from a book of sermons. Next to travel books, sermons were Mr. Pellham's favourite reading material.

Mr. Mornay was losing all sense of hope. His wife's delirium had ended, but was replaced with an ominous silence. Her previously restless limbs were still; her face, as though asleep; and yet it was much worse than a normal sleep, as nothing could rouse her. His eye fell upon a framed bit of verse on the bedside table, something Ariana herself had written out with painstaking neatness and had framed and placed where it sat. He picked it up on a whim, and then returned to her side. Taking his seat, he began to read it aloud to her: Who knew if she could hear him? She had loved this enough to take the trouble to write it out; he would read it to her now.

When on her Maker's bosom
The new-born earth was laid,
And nature's opening blossom
Its fairest bloom display'd;
When all with fruits and flowers
The laughing soil was drest,
And Eden's fragrant bowers
Receiv'd their human guest;

No sin his face defiling,
The heir of Nature stood,
And God, benignly smiling,
Beheld that all was good!
Yet in that hour of blessing
A single want was known;
A wish the heart distressing;
For Adam was alone!

O God of pure affection!
By men and saints adored,
Who gavest thy protection
To Cana's nuptial board,
May such thy bounties ever
To wedded love be shown,
And no rude hand dissever
Whom thou has linked as one!
— *Reginald Heber*

He finished reading; Ariana did not stir or show a sign of change. With a deep sigh, he fell to his knees. "O God! Where is Your protection, indeed! Do not dissever what You have linked in one!" Mr. Mornay had not felt as helpless, hopeless, or desperate at any time in his memory. In fact, he felt a slow panic beginning to rise within his breast. How often had he said that a man needed only God to get by in life? How often had he spouted such nonsense? He needed more than God — he needed Ariana! He couldn't face his life again without her!

He looked up once more to see her face, very white and pale, despite the heat that still emanated from her skin. He was losing her, he knew it. Losing Ariana! He had to do something; it was impossible, suddenly, for him to remain helplessly by her side a moment longer.

He rushed from the room, falling, bumping into his own furniture, into the columns at the top of the stairs. He moved like a blind man, like one drunk; he could not see for his eyes were filled with tears. He did not cry — but he needed something to put his hand to or he'd go mad! He felt so helpless! He made a fist with his hand and moved it as though he would slam it against the wall, against a bust, but he stopped himself, looked at his fist in despair, and dropped it.

He rounded the bottom of the stairs. Where was he going? He didn't know. He'd been thinking of the Taller family. If only Mr. Taller would show up at his doorstep this very minute! He could kill the man! It was his fault! Why had he not come forward with the truth earlier? Why had he not let them know in time, before Ariana went near them! It *was* his fault, by God! If he lost Ariana, it was Mr. Taller to blame for it!

He was slowing down, becoming spent. He was going only on the energy of rage and despair. *Where was God now, when he needed Him? Where?*

Losing energy quickly now, he stumbled to the front hall. Mr. Frederick came to an interior doorway, apparently having been there for some time. He stayed back and watched with a sad, grim expression. Mr. Mornay picked up a small statue — something resting upon a tall urn. He looked at it, and then threw it to the ground. The butler's lips compressed even more. He'd never seen his master like this in the twenty years of his service; not even when the old Mr. Mornay had died, or Mrs. Mornay, his mother. Not even when his brother Nigel died.

Just at that moment, the knocker sounded on the door. Mr. Mornay looked up, as if struck. Mr. Frederick hurried out, but his master saw him and said, "No. I'll get it." Mr. Frederick stopped where he was, and watched with an expression of sad regret.

When he reached the front door and flung it open, there, to his utter astonishment, stood Mr. Taller! The very man he was feeling positively murderous toward!

"You!" he said.

"I 'ad to come," the man muttered. "I 'av to know. How is she?"

Mr. Mornay threw himself out the door, leaning upon a wide column, which flanked either side. He stared with a terrible look at the cottager. "You've killed her, if you must know! You've killed her!"

Mr. Taller's face broke up into tears. He shook his head. "No, no, *I* didn'! Don't say I did!"

"You and your cowardly lies!" His face was in the other man's face, but Mr. Mornay slowly regained control of himself. He wanted to strike the man, but when it came down to it, he knew too well that it was wrong.

"She's dead, then? Truly?" He looked almost as distraught as Mr. Mornay.

"Not yet. Not yet." He seemed to think about that for a moment, as if newly realizing it.

"An' what're you doin' down 'ere, then, eh?" Mr. Taller was angry, now. "She's got life in 'er, and you're missin' it! Ma Mary is gettin' better. Ma MaryAnn's better! Your wife may get better. But you should be wi' 'er, that's what!"

Mr. Mornay stood up straight, staring at the other man's face. He was right. And his

472

wife was improving? His daughter had improved! That meant there was hope for Ariana. When he came back in the house and dashed up the stairs, Frederick just stared, surprised. But it had to be good. Mr. Mornay had energy again.

He didn't stop until he had returned to his wife's bedside.

She was still unconscious. He bent over her and felt for a pulse, then, gratefully, with some small relief, he knelt down at the bedside and prayed. One hand slowly groped until he found hers, and he clutched it, though she could make no response.

"Forgive me!" he prayed. "And have mercy!" His eyes were still wet, and he suddenly gave in to the first real sob he had ever succumbed to in his memory. He tried again to pray, but was overcome by another racking sob. Then, he lifted his head and studied his wife's face, and suddenly was seeing her as she had been, always with a ready smile, with love in her eyes for him and for the children. He dropped his head again. "Do not take her, my Lord," he prayed, "but I give her to You. I give her to You."

Mr. Speckman came into the sickroom. He had taken a brief absence, to eat something in the kitchen. He frowned, seeing Mr.

Mornay on his knees by the bed, with his head in his hands. He, too, was feeling utterly helpless. He pulled out his watch fob and read the face of the timepiece, but his frown only deepened.

Ariana lay on the pillow, in the exact position Phillip had left her in, near an hour since. The physician sat by the counterpane, sadly looking out over the wintry countryside view. He turned when Phillip woke up in a chair by the bed, however, and rose from his seat.

"Has there been a change?"

"None, sir."

Phillip looked down at his wife, and put forth one hand to her brow. She was still burning with fever and the touch of his hand made her turn her head, eyes closed, and moan in a low tone, though no words could be discerned. He felt his heart tug at him in such a strong manner that he wanted for a moment to take her up in his arms. But what good would it do? He could not help himself, and he sat down beside her.

Mr. Speckman looked at him sadly, and turned away, directing his gaze back outside the window to give the man a degree of privacy. But he almost shook his head. He'd seen such cases before, and seldom did the sufferer recover. And such a young woman! It made his own heart ache, but there was nothing he could do to help her. She was entirely in God's hands.

It was early in the morning when the Pellhams' coach pulled up to the house in Middlesex. Haines had a time trying to get someone awake, though his master and mistress were still comfortably snuggled together in the vehicle. Finally, when no amount of banging the knocker produced a response, he was getting ready to inform the Pellhams that they would simply have to wait for the house to stir, when the door opened.

It was Mr. Mornay, but Haines stared at him stupidly for a moment. Such a change in a man he had never witnessed! Mr. Mornay looked to be the one fallen ill. His hair was disheveled, his face had some days' growth of stubble, he wore no neckcloth, and his white cambric shirt looked as though he'd slept in it, and it hung sloppily outside his pantaloons; in short, Mr. Mornay was a mess. It was rather a shock, even for someone who had not seen him in many months.

Noise behind them revealed that Mrs. Pellham had seen him and left the carriage, followed by her husband. Mr. Mornay was blinking at them tiredly, but he held the door open and allowed them to enter the house. Mrs. Pellham stopped beside her nephew-in-law and gave him a sharp, appraising look. He half expected a set-down, but all she said, finally, was, "How is she?"

His ghastly appearance was a fright, to be sure; but even Mrs. Pellham knew that what it signified must be far more frightening, indeed. *Ariana was in worse condition than she feared!*

Mr. Mornay was unable to speak, and could only shake his head in the negative. Mrs. Pellham was already removing her bonnet and shawl, but he found his voice to say, "You mustn't stay here; it is contagious. I apologize for the lack of hospitality . . ."

But Mrs. Pellham ignored him. "I have come to see my niece, and I will see her."

Mr. Mornay eyed her uncertainly for a moment. Freddie came out, still buttoning his waistcoat, and joined the small group in the hall.

Mr. Pellham said, "Show me to a guest bedchamber, sir, with room enough for my wife and me; we are staying." His firm tone conveyed that the decision had been made. Freddie looked to his master who said nothing, so he bowed and said, "This way, if you please, sir." It actually encouraged him that new people had come; fresh blood, which was not already discouraged or exhausted, like the rest of them.

Before they left, the butler found the courage to face his master, saying, "Perhaps you can take some rest now, sir. With Mrs. Pellham here —"

Mr. Mornay turned an acid eye upon his servant, who wisely dropped the matter and turned away to take Mr. Pellham to his quarters. Meanwhile, a footman had appeared, who hurried to get the luggage for the guests brought into the house. Everyone was cold, and tired, and should have been miserable, but even Mr. Mornay felt a twinge of hope. For what reason? There was none. Only more people to share the misery with. But even sharing misery was better than not, it seemed.

"Take me to her!" Mrs. Pellham's authoritative voice stirred some energy within the man, and he said, "This way." The morning light had grown enough to make his taper of no use, and he blew it out as they climbed the stairs.

Inside the bedchamber, Mrs. Pellham's shrewd eyes took in the situation at once; the face of the doctor, worried; the gel on the bed, smothered in blankets and sweat;

the heat in the room. She opened her eyes rather wide and said to Mr. Mornay, "I want you to remove this man from the room, if you would, sir." Mr. Mornay eyed her with some surprise, but he looked at the physician, whose face was registering shock at such a thing, and said, "Do as she says, sir."

"You desire that I leave the patient, sir?" Both he and his assistant were deeply disapproving of the request, their faces clearly showed.

"Go to the kitchens and have some refreshment," Mr. Mornay said. "Leave us for now."

Mr. Speckman took a look at Ariana. Then, still looking bewildered and none too happy, strode from the room, trying to keep his dignity intact.

The moment the door closed upon them, Mrs. Pellham, said, "Get some buckets of water up here at once!" Mr. Mornay had been growing in his distrust of the doctor's methods, and he did not so much as question her intentions. He pulled on the bell-pull, strongly, and more than once. He went immediately to the windows and threw them open as far as they would go.

"My thought exactly!" said Mrs. Pellham approvingly. She was already pulling off the heavy blankets that were upon Ariana, and she was so disgusted that she merely threw them to the floor. She saw the basin of water beside the bed, and the cloth, and wrung it out, and placed it across Ariana's forehead.

"Is ice available?" she asked, just as a bewildered Haines appeared at the door, followed quickly by Fotch. "Gentlemen, we need water; douse the fire; we need ice; on the double!" Both men seemed energized by the requests — finally, there was something they could do! They turned and hurried off to get the supplies. Meanwhile, Mrs. Pellham said, "Help me open this nightdress! It is far too heavy."

But Mr. Mornay said, "We'll soon have ice on her, surely it makes no difference."

"Mmm, well, I suppose you're right." She studied her much-loved niece for a moment, then demanded, "How long has it been since Ariana has taken any liquid?"

He thought for a moment. "Many hours."

"Hold her head up for me," she ordered. There was a decanter of water and a glass, and Mrs. Pellham poured a little out, and sat down upon the edge of the mattress. Mr. Mornay had come and sat down himself, raising his wife so that she now rested against him, and he held her head up with his hands. He automatically helped to hold her mouth open so that Ariana's aunt could

479

pour little drops of water to the side of her throat, knowing that a reflexive action would force her to swallow them.

But Mrs. Pellham had to shake her head sadly while doing it. Ariana's beautiful little lips were dry and cracked; no longer did they hold a healthy red appearance, but were colorless; and her face quite, quite pale. She also saw the marks from the *bleeding instrument,* and she almost shivered with distaste. "That man *bled* her? For shame!"

She laid accusing eyes on the husband. "How could you allow it?"

That was not the thing to say to Mornay in his current state of mind. His look darkened. "How could I not, when a man of medicine assures me it is the thing to do? I would gladly let him cover her with leeches if I thought it might save her life!"

Mrs. Pellham's brows drew together in a frown, but she said, "I daresay, you're right; I beg your pardon, Phillip."

The ice arrived, slivers and chunks in buckets from the icehouse.

Mr. Mornay told his butler and Fotch: "Do not allow the doctor upstairs until I tell you."

"Yes, sir!"

Mrs. Pellham and Mr. Mornay set to wrapping pieces of ice in cloths and laying

480

them upon poor Ariana's hot body. Mrs. Pellham put a little pillow on the floor, got on her knees on it, and stayed at a vigil there, changing the ice, wringing out cloths, and looking for change in her niece.

It would be a long and very chilly day.

Twenty-Five

When Beatrice awoke, she felt an unhappiness that she could not, at first, account for. Oh, it was Ariana! Last night they had prayed for her recovery; but was she safe? Had the crisis passed? Beatrice felt she had to do something; she must act, use the time in a productive manner. But what to do?

When Harrietta came and helped her into her daydress, and did her hair up (for the lady had nothing else to do, she protested, and wanted no recompense for her trouble other than the recovery of her mistress), Beatrice thought and thought and finally settled upon a course of action.

To her relief, Mr. O'Brien was in the breakfast room as usual. He was quite regular in his habits, which included rising early, having his private devotions and prayers, and then his breakfast. Without a response in kind to his, "Good morning, Miss Forsythe," she stopped inside the doorway and cried, "Mr. O'Brien! I need you to take me to Aspindon! Directly, sir!"

He was chewing some food, but stopped abruptly. He had to think for only a second. He stood up, wiping his mouth, and said, "Of course. At once."

With Sykes atop the board as coachman, Beatrice hesitated outside the vehicle, as Mr. O'Brien held her hand to assist her in climbing up. She had not meant to prolong the touch of his hand, but she was very much aware of it right through her gloves, while she said, "There is no need for you to accompany me. You should limit your exposure by all means."

"Oh, nonsense!" he replied. "Of course I'll come." His gentle tone filled her with gratitude, and for some reason — it must have been her concern for her sister — she was suddenly blinking back tears.

She tried to hide the state of her watery eyes, but Mr. O'Brien seemed to miss nothing concerning her. Beatrice was trying to understand how her life had changed so quickly. One moment she had been enjoying being a guest at Aspindon and having the attention of two gentlemen. Both men were mere diversions, nothing more. At least, that is what they ought to have been.

Mr. Barton changed that when he spoke to her of his wish to court her. She had to consider him differently from then on, and she had not been averse to doing so. He was just the sort of man she had always envisioned marrying. And now, Mr. O'Brien was refusing to remain a mere diversion too! He was supposed to be a fond acquaintance only, brotherly, held in affection. But what she was feeling for him was more than a sisterly love. It was not what she wished to feel for him, and his being near her now was comforting and vexing all at the same time.

If only she could believe that Ariana would be well again, and they would go for a Season in London. She could escape this curate's impact over her, and she would not have to feel the unmistakable loathing she now had for Mr. Barton, the cowardly cove! He disappeared like a wisp of smoke when they gathered to pray for her sister, so little regard had he for her or Ariana.

Her life would go back to the way it was. She could meet a fine gentleman of good standing and family (and wealth) in London, and be married and done with it, without a single further thought of Mr. Peter O'Brien to plague her. It would certainly be best for both of them, for he deserved a good young woman who was content to live in a country parsonage. A young woman who did not fill her head with thoughts of wealth or large estates or grandeur. *How could she even be thinking these things,* she scolded herself, *when she might even this minute be losing her sister?*

She glanced up to find Mr. O'Brien studying her with a look of concern and compassion. He immediately spoke up. "Miss Forsythe, may I assure you of my constant prayers for your sister, and, indeed, your entire family?" He pulled a little well-worn book out of his coat pocket and handed it across to her. "These are some of the most comforting verses in English literature that I know of."

Beatrice put out her gloved hand and accepted it, looking at it in surprise. "I did not know you read poetry." She was pleased to discover this, for Beatrice loved poetry.

"Oh, yes. I am very fond of Cowper and Coleridge, and Heber and Mrs. Hemans. Mrs. More is nearly too didactic even for me," he said, smiling gently, "but I believe I have one of hers in these pages."

"Is this your collection of personal favourites?" This was even more surprising to her, as it cost money to have one's own writing bound up properly.

"I have a good friend who is a printer," he explained, while she leafed through the pages of his handwriting, which was fine and neat.

"Do you like Burns?" she asked curiously. "I have always found his verse to be wonderful, once one deciphers it enough to follow the meaning."

"The Scottish accents are a bit of a challenge at times, yes," he agreed. "But I do like his work."

They shared a little smile. Here her sister lay dying, possibly, and first she was thinking of her marriage prospects, and now, poetry! Her face grew more sober with the thought.

"I gave you the book," he said, "for you to read if you happen to fall into any darker moments. There are times when our minds are so confused that we cannot quiet ourselves enough to hear the whispers of the Holy Spirit through Scripture — do you not find it so?"

Beatrice had only lived long enough to experience small disappointments heretofore, but to the young, small disappointments are felt as falling so severely upon them as war or famine is felt among older individuals. So she looked at him gratefully and nodded in all due earnestness.

"When I have such moments, I often turn to poetry," he said. "Until I am restored enough to turn to God from my heart."

Beatrice nodded, feeling as though she was his pupil, and liking it very much.

As they drew near to Aspindon, he said, "You realize that on account of the children you will not be able to return to the vicarage today."

She had not thought that far, but said, "Yes, of course! I hope you can send your servant to deliver my clothing and effects to me."

"I'll return at once and see to it myself," he replied, with his clear blue eyes fastened upon her intensely.

"You are too kind," she answered.

"For you, Miss." The manservant at the Manor House held out a salver upon which a letter lay, and Miss Barton took it, wonderingly. Who, if not Lord Horatio, would be writing to her?

"My word!" she exclaimed, after opening it. "It's from the Countess of Weverly! I wonder that she even knows who I am!" Anne's black hair was curled up around her ears, and she had on a gilt headband that further emphasized the blackness of her locks.

Lord Horatio, who had slept in a guest bedchamber, gave her a pointed look, and she knew at once that something was afoot. "What do you know of this?" she asked, beginning to smile.

"I know only that you shall be invited to one of her parties, and that her ladyship will let it out that you are some sort of heiress."

Miss Barton frowned. "An heiress! But that is a falsehood! Explain this to me, my lord!"

"Call me Horatio, darling."

"Yes, I shall. Only please explain your meaning in this, first, sir!"

He thought for a moment. "Anne — I'm going to marry you, no matter what. You know that."

She now grew alarmed. "Yes?"

"But if my mother hears her ladyship speak well of you, my parents will cease to frown upon our union. With their blessing, things will go far better for us, for the rest of our lives. Is it not worth acquiring?"

"Not in this way! *Horatio!*"

He had to smile simply because she had used his name. "There is no other way to accomplish the thing speedily; and since we must wed without further delay, it must answer." He merely glanced down at the region of her belly for her to understand him.

"When the child comes, your parents will know."

"They will be eager to hide the fact, and they will adore having a grandchild! God knows when my brother and his wife will supply one. Katherine seems to be barren."

"I am sorry for her."

He smiled at her. "Do not be. If they have no son, and we do, he will be next in line for the title."

She feigned astonishment. "You are avaricious, sir!"

He laughed. "No! Only practical! It's the law, but I didn't write it!"

In the next room, the sound of their voices woke Mr. Barton. He felt at odds, and remembered the news about Mrs. Mornay being in a crisis, and this only worsened his mood. He wanted to marry into the family, but if that lady died, his hopes were dashed. He decided his safest course was to distance himself from Miss Forsythe for the time being. She was no use to him at all if her sister was to die. He'd make a trip to London; he'd been stuck in the country for too long as it was. Anne was getting properly married now, and he no longer needed to hide her from anyone. And Mornay — that man was devilish tricky about his plans. The sad demise of Ariana Mornay loomed before him like a spectre, and even the allure of Miss Beatrice Forsythe could not hold him in Middlesex a day longer.

He would compose a short message to explain his absence at the vicarage. He would say that he'd been called away on "business." He laughed to himself. Business — it was convenient to fall upon, if nothing else! With a slow gait caused by drinking too much the prior evening, and waking up in an uncomfortable spot — on the floor — he made his way toward the others in the morning room.

"Speaking of our being wed," Anne was saying when he entered, "when shall we? Have you settled it with Mr. O'Brien?"

"No. Why do we not go to the vicarage right now and do so? I cannot bear waiting a day longer to call you 'Lady Horatio'!"

At that moment a sound in the doorway made them both look up in surprise. Mr. Barton was standing there, rather disheveled, rubbing his head. "Did I hear you mention going to the vicarage?"

"Yes, Tristan! His lordship wants us to be married directly!" While he ingested that thought, she added, "I am surprised to see you up and about." When he was in his cups, he did not usually awake before noon or later.

"I heard your laughing from the parlour," he grumbled. "If a man would sleep, he must have silence."

"If a man would have silence, he must sleep in his bedchamber," returned Lord Horatio. He and Anne exchanged little smiles while Tristan merely scowled. "We'll need a witness," he said, "so do come along."

Mr. Barton stopped and thought about this for a moment. He nodded. "Very well, then," and left to get dressed.

Lord Horatio looked at Anne. "Do you need to change?" he asked, noticing she was in a morning dress.

Anne held out one arm, and showed him that, cleverly hidden beneath a lace frill which served as a hem for the puffed shoulders of her gown, was a placket where the sleeves were attached. They could be unattached. Smiling, he did the unbuttoning, first for one sleeve, then the other.

"Voila!" she said, folding the fabric carefully. "I have a day dress."

"Astonishing," he said.

"And economical too," she added.

Now they had only to wait for Tristan.

■ ■ ■ ■

Before Beatrice exited the carriage when it pulled up outside her sister's estate, she turned to Mr. O'Brien, hoping that she was not about to dig herself in deeper in misunderstanding than what already existed, in her mind, between them.

"Did you take note of Mr. Barton's hasty exit last night?" She knew he had; but desired to know his thoughts about it. Besides, she wanted to somehow raise the subject of Mr. Barton so that she could let Mr. O'Brien know of a certainty that Beatrice no longer wished to be courted by him.

He looked at her in surprise a moment. "I did, of course."

Beatrice was studying the upholstery of the Mornays' fine coach. "May I ask, what you made of it, sir?"

Mr. O'Brien cleared his throat. Here he was again, in a dashed uncomfortable spot. But his honest opinion, he felt, was true enough to be shared. To withhold it from any young woman seeking counsel could not be right. "I think we must assume that he is lacking in his religion, Miss Forsythe." He tried to say it as gently as possible; he knew she had hopes of the man.

Her eyes flew to his.

"That has been my suspicion, exactly!" She looked up at him earnestly, searching his eyes for a sign that Mr. O'Brien just might, *might* have some feelings upon the subject; some feelings for her. She saw nothing to give her that assurance. In response, she had to try to dig deeper.

"Do you consider Mr. Barton to be a man of good character?"

He stared at her. He was perplexed that she should be asking his opinion. When he had no right, no authority over her, no reason to involve himself in her decisions . . . Finally, he said, "Miss Forsythe, if you have doubts regarding the man, again I can only advise you to speak of them to Mr. Mornay. Allow him to decide if the man is worthy or not."

Her eyes widened. "Do you think Mr. Mornay is a good judge of character?"

He let out a breath of amusement. "I should say so! I think he is an excellent judge."

When she made no answer, he added, "Does he know anything of Mr. Barton's intentions toward you? Or of your . . . er . . . hopes regarding him?"

This made her turn her head sharply and

look up at him again. "My hopes? At this moment I do not know what to think or feel regarding the man! He fled from me the moment he understood that my sister was seriously ill! He failed to offer rooms in his house for anyone, though he had available space. He fails to show the concern that any friend should offer in such a situation. I do not know if I have any hopes of him at all."

His brow furrowed. "I took it to understand that you desired his courtship."

She met his gaze. "I — I did. I *thought* I did." She took in a deep breath. "I found him agreeable and amusing; I thought he was an honourable gentleman; but I have since seen things in his character and nature that give me pause."

"I see." He was studying her with a very perplexed look, as if he did not see, not at all. "I think you are wise to think through such a step. You are young and have plenty of life ahead of you. Do not settle yourself upon a man who does not deserve you."

"May I ask you?" she was emboldened to say, "if, in your opinion, Mr. Barton deserves me?" It was an awkward question, and only Beatrice's desire to ascertain whether or not Mr. O'Brien had any feelings at all for her, made her ask it.

Mr. O'Brien laid his head back against

the cushion. What could he say? Mr. Barton was a social superior. "I know that he has the means to support you in style, which I have understood as being of importance to you. He appears to be a gentleman; and I can say nothing against his actions until I have understood them." He was taking care to be absolutely fair to the man, and he felt unable to seize the opportunity to put himself forward. It would be wrong of him to do so. "I do not take him for a man of religion, and that *is* cause for concern; but only you can decide how great a concern that will be, Miss Forsythe."

This was plainly not the answer she had hoped for, and she set her mouth into a small frown.

The carriage stopped, and with a quick "Good day!" she began to step out without giving him or any servant time to put down the steps. She opened the door, and would have immediately fallen to the ground had not Mr. O'Brien grasped her around the waist.

"You will injure yourself!" he said, surprised.

Beatrice stood back and turned to look at him. She saw nothing of reproof in his eyes; nothing of reproach; only honest concern.

"Do you *never* run out of patience?" she

asked, as though it was a vexing thing. The steps had been let down by the butler/ coachman, and now Beatrice stomped off, leaving him blinking at her for a second, but he hurried to catch up.

"Were you not going to return to the vicarage and retrieve my things?" she asked, turning to him in impatience. "If you come in with me, you may not be able to return to your home."

"I will need to bring a report back to your mother. If I return without learning of your sister's condition, she'll want to throw me in the stocks, I imagine."

It was meant as a small joke, but Beatrice was too piqued to respond at all. Mr. O'Brien had the distinct impression that he had somehow transgressed, but he hadn't a clue as to how. He was doing his honest best to be a friend to Beatrice, to give her his counsel, and without burdening her with a jot or tittle of his own admiration for her. He was being as generous with himself as he possibly could be; her reaction did not make sense to him.

The last thing she had asked was if Mr. Barton deserved her. He wished he could have shouted! He would have said, "Of course Mr. Barton does not deserve you! You deserve a man of God, who will honour you as a co-heir of salvation! You deserve a man who is thrilled by the look of your green, beautiful eyes, and the shine of your hair in the sun. You deserve someone who finds your temper exhilarating, and your strong emotions energizing! Like me. Like *me!*" But of course he could not so speak.

"Was my opinion of Mr. Barton not good enough to please you? Is that what vexes you?" he asked. She was about to turn the door handle when the door opened from the inside. Frederick stood, looking out at them with the peculiarly dour gaze of a butler. Ignoring him, Beatrice turned back to the curate.

"Not good enough? It was far *too* good, if you must know! You are the most uncaring man in the world!" And with that, she started crying, and entered the house. Frederick waited for Mr. O'Brien to decide whether he would enter too. The Curate stood there for a moment feeling utterly perplexed, looking after Miss Forsythe with near shock on his face. Remembering himself, he asked, "Is there news of Mrs. Mornay?"

"Mrs. Mornay continues as she was, sir." The servant's eyes revealed that he knew somewhat more. "Mrs. Pellham has come to tend to her, however. It gives us all hope."

The clergyman nodded. "Pray for her, Frederick. Pray very hard!"

"I have, sir. I will again." Before he shut the door, as Mr. O'Brien turned to go, he added, "Thank you, sir."

Back at the vicarage, Mrs. Persimmon brought the Bartons and Lord Horatio into the drawing room, where only Mrs. Forsythe was nervously working on a piece of needlework.

No one seemed to know where Mr. O'Brien had got to, and when it was discovered that Beatrice was also gone, and the carriage, Mrs. Forsythe guessed aloud that they were inquiring about Ariana's health. She was poking her needle into the canvas rather feelingly; Miss Barton felt too shy to mention their errand — that they were come to be married. She felt badly about Mrs. Mornay herself.

Mr. Barton was standing looking out the window. He had come to witness the marriage for his sister, but he had nothing to say to either Mrs. Forsythe, or Beatrice, really, until he knew where things stood with Mrs. Mornay. If she recovered, he would pursue the alliance with Beatrice as before; if she did not, he was prepared to wash his hands of the whole business; admit his failure to the prince; give up the Manor House, and get back to his life in London. He had hoped to find himself in the prince's debt, to be celebrated at Carlton House or Brighton; but so be it. His life was not so bad just as it had been. This country living was what he could not abide!

He suddenly had a thought intrude upon his brain, however. If Mrs. Mornay did recover, and he wished to pursue Beatrice, would the curate be an obstacle? Both were gone from the house. That put them together somewhere. Dash it, he did not like it!

He turned to Mrs. Forsythe. "I understand that your family has long known our Mr. O'Brien, is that correct, ma'am?"

"Some of our family has long known him, sir. Particularly Mrs. Mornay."

"Does he often take one of your daughters abroad with no chaperone?"

She eyed him with surprise. A sense of unease sniffed at her heels, and she replied, cautiously, "He is a trusted acquaintance, sir, if that is your question."

"Tristan, mind your manners!" put in his sister.

He turned to her. "Does it not strike you as odd? They're being out together? Did they not once get lost upon the Aspindon grounds? Let us hope they have not agreed on another adventure of some sort today!"

"I am certain they have done no such thing, sir," said Mrs. Forsythe, wondering at this sudden censure from the gentleman. She suddenly realized that Mr. Barton was speaking like a disappointed young man. Like a man who thought himself thwarted in love perhaps? She was not averse to the curate in any way, and if this time with her daughter might be conducive to a romance, fine. But she needed to tread carefully. It must not seem scandalous in any fashion. So she added, "My daughter knows that I will rest easier when I have heard of Mrs. Mornay's condition this morning. You can be assured that this was their object."

"Of course," he replied politely; except that his tone lacked an ounce of sincerity. "I beg your pardon."

"All we can do now, is to wait," said Mrs. Pellham. Phillip sat upon the bed beside his wife, holding her hand. He and Mrs. Pellham had already taken turns applying cold cloths to her head and body. A poultice of ice was upon her brow. Additionally, he had taken a wet cloth, wrapped it over some ice, and smoothed it over her face and neck and arms, even her chest. If the fever made it dry, he passed the cloth again. Nevertheless, through it all, Ariana was still, quiet, and limp.

Mr. Mornay released her hand, and went and stood before the casement. It was a typical winter day, not too sunny, but the silent landscape was now an unfeeling reminder of happier days. The bedchambers looked over the rear of the estate, and he could see the maze, and he thought suddenly of the day a young blond-headed woman had run into him at top speed; she was exceedingly pretty, but that he ignored; he always ignored women. Instead he proceeded to give her a set-down, and she had thoroughly surprised him by returning him one.

Her spirit, that was the first thing that attracted him to her. Looking over at her now, so pale and silent, and still hot with fever, was totally disheartening. If only this would pass, if the blasted fever would just leave her! A light knock at the door revealed Mr. Speckman, who was greeted with a blast of wintry cold air. The windows were now only open an inch or so; but the fire was out; his patient was exposed to the air, and the room was cold. His eyes opened in shock. "What the devil are you doing? Do you want to kill her?" He rushed over toward the window, but Mr. Mornay sprang to his feet and put himself in his path.

"You'll kill her, sir!" the doctor maintained. "I tell you, she'll not survive!"

"If you cannot give your approval, Mr. Speckman, I suggest you take yourself off."

With a look of gravity, almost fear, the man eyed Mornay for a moment; recognized the air of assurance. His advice would no longer be followed. He went and collected his bag. His assistant, behind him, gathered more things, and the two of them left, giving only the slightest bows. At the doorway, the man stopped and turned around. "Her death will not be upon my shoulders."

"True; not any longer!" cried Mrs. Pellham. He looked injured at that, but turned and was gone. In another moment, Beatrice came into the room. She had seen the doctor and his assistant in the corridor and thought the worst; that they were leaving due to failure! Her sister was lost! She burst into the room, stopped to glance at the scene, and then, with a great sob, threw herself at her sister's limp body.

"You'll hurt her," cried Mrs. Pellham, sharply, trying to pull her off.

"What?" Beatrice blinked at her. "She isn't — ? I saw the doctor leaving."

"Oh, no, my dear! Your sister is alive!"

"Oh! Thank God!" She sat up, brushed a bit of ice from her gown, and turned and studied the form upon the bed. She met the gaze of Mr. Mornay, who nodded a greeting. She had nothing helpful to say to him, and so she turned her attention back to Ariana. She reached out her hand to smooth away a stray bit of hair, and felt Ariana's pale face. Curious, she touched the back of her neck, then her arms, and hands. Mr. Mornay saw her doing this, and he started over, an intense look upon his countenance.

"She isn't hot!" cried Beatrice.

Mrs. Pellham and Mr. Mornay at once both began to feel her skin in various places, and in a rapture of joy, Mrs. Pellham threw herself against him, into his arms, and they actually hugged. The two of them both loved Ariana, and if Mrs. Pellham had never expected to find herself embraced by the Paragon, she did not show it now. Beatrice was also overcome, and she put her arms about the two of them as best she could.

Mr. Pellham, meanwhile, had been warned by his wife to stay clear of the sickroom, but he, too, was quite fond of Ariana. Unable to help himself, he timidly opened the door, expecting to find a sad scene before him. When he saw the three in a circle of closeness, he thought the worst had occurred. He crept silently into the room, and, not wanting to disturb the mourners, took a glance at the lovely lady upon the bed. His eyes filled with tears. And then, suddenly, Ariana was looking up at him.

He blinked, thinking he was imagining it. But then she blinked.

"Upon my soul!' he cried, causing the others, who did not know of his presence, to jump apart in surprise.

"Randolph! You frightened me!" cried his wife.

"She's awake!" he said, in delighted response.

Mr. Mornay had just discovered this, and he fell to her side on his knees and took her into his arms. He was cradling her head against him, and he kissed the side of her face, and whispered, "Thank God! Thank God!"

The others looked at each other, and by silent motions agreed to leave the pair alone. In a few seconds they had gone, while Mr. Mornay held his wife, who was still too weak to talk or return his sentiments. He shut his eyes, knowing what was coming, but it was too late; a tear slid down his face. He had almost lost her, but she was back! She would recover! Thank God!

■ ■ ■ ■

Mr. O'Brien, unfortunately, had the unhappy honour of delivering only bad news. The fever hadn't broken, yet, to his knowledge, and Ariana's danger had not passed. To say the atmosphere in the house was dampened would be an understatement.

Lord Horatio got the curate alone and said, "Look here; would it be improper, under the circumstances, to ask you to perform the ceremony for us?"

Mr. O'Brien said, "I think it is acceptable; one sad event does not mean there cannot be a happy one." He pulled out his watch fob. "Is your bride ready?"

"Yes." Lord Horatio smiled. "I am much obliged." He shoved some banknotes into Mr. O'Brien's hand. "Please. Let me take care of this, now."

"Thank you!" Mr. O'Brien, so used to officiating at ceremonies for the poorest of London, was not used to accepting paper notes, as those beneath his care could usually part with only a few shillings. There was no set amount for his services, and he had always been grateful for whatever came his way, but Lord Horatio had managed to eke some money out of the marquess as well as the family coach. And he was a generous man.

The pair were married in the parlour, and Mrs. Forsythe wished that Beatrice could have seen their curate in his surplice, his official robe and collar, Bible in hand, delivering the ceremony without hindrance.

She felt so proud of him, herself! Almost as though he was a son, which was strange because she had never been closely acquainted with Mr. O'Brien before. When they were pronounced man and wife, she managed to smile and give the new couple her sincerest best wishes — along with a few shillings for a new bonnet, she said — and tried to keep up her spirits while Mrs. Persimmon provided some refreshments afterward. It plagued that lady that she had not known in advance of the wedding, for she would have had a finer table, she said. But Miss Barton certainly did not care. She was all smiles, and had never looked lovelier.

The moment the couple left, the children came down for their daily time to be with the adults, and so Mrs. Forsythe wore only smiles for their sake, and made sure to stay in the parlour while their visit lasted. She would not let Mrs. Royleforst have them all to herself!

"Dash it all, I've just remembered something!" said Lord Horatio.

"Well?" asked Tristan. They were just turning in to the drive of the Manor. "I'm supposed to get Mornay to London for Prinny."

"Are you? That's deuced interesting because I am supposed to do that very thing, also!"

"Tristan has had no opportunity," explained Anne. "Mrs. Mornay's illness makes it impossible."

"Did you tell the prince?" Lord Horatio asked.

"I told him of the threat to Mrs. Mornay; and that the Paragon would no doubt accept the viscountcy."

"He has agreed then?"

"No, not in so many words. But would you turn down a title? He's an Englishman, is he not?"

Horatio whistled. "One never knows with our dignified friend."

"The place is a sickbed, in any case," snapped Mr. Barton. "We'd take our life in our hands if we try and see him now."

"Let us call there in a few days," said

507

Anne. "By then, the outcome with poor Mrs. Mornay will be determined, and we will know whether to try the man or not."

"Well, and since you are newly wed, I think I'll just take myself off to London, and leave the Manor House for your pleasure."

"And abandon Miss Forsythe to the curate?" asked Anne, half joking.

"She is stuck at Aspindon now until her sister either recovers, or dies. I should not likely see her, in any case."

"See here," said Lord Horatio. "Mrs. Mornay is a dear friend; do not speak so unfeelingly of her, I pray you."

"I beg your pardon," he said, surprised to discover this. "I only mean that my interest in Miss Forsythe must cease if Mrs. Mornay does not rally through this."

"Is that so?" asked his lordship, still feeling protective of Ariana.

"She brings me no advantage without her sister, you addlepate! I can't afford to marry beneath me," he answered.

"You dare to say that to me? When I have just married your sister with a dowry so small as to be unacceptable to my parents!"

Mr. Barton eyed him with an unreadable expression. "You are a better man than I," he said. "But a poorer one."

"On the contrary," said his lordship with an easy smile, as he put one arm around his new wife, "I have riches ye know not of."

TWENTY-SIX

By the time word had spread that Mrs. Mornay had survived the crisis, Mr. Barton was back in London. He threw himself into his clubs and gaming at tables, and congratulated himself on finding an escape from the tedium of the countryside. During quieter moments, he saw the pretty face of Miss Forsythe, or heard her delightful laughter, or detected a sparkle of mischief in her bright eyes. It was a pity, that's all. But he decided he must soon make the drive and find out what was what before giving her up entirely.

He did not have the latest report — that Ariana had survived the crisis — so that instead the news went around swiftly that she was in grave danger. The Regent himself heard this, and sent a gift for the children. He did not know what else to do.

Then, exactly three days after Ariana had awoken from her sickness, word trickled in of her recovery. Mr. Barton had still been dragging his steps and hadn't returned to Middlesex, but at this news he made haste and was on the road speedily. Now that he knew his course, he wanted to see to it with all due haste, before that deuced parson had a chance to usurp his place.

Ariana was growing stronger by the day, but her husband made it clear to Beatrice that his wife would not be setting foot in London until she was absolutely fully recovered. When she accepted this information without a qualm, he assumed it was on account of her good sense in the matter. She understood that her sister could not be rushing about from ballroom to dinner party after having suffered such a devastating illness. Little did he think her meek acquiescence had far less to do with Ariana than with Beatrice's changing hopes.

What had she wanted so badly in London, she now wondered. It was true that Mr. O'Brien had nothing so fine as an Aspindon; he was not a man about town; he was not a glib, amusing Mr. Barton. And yet, somehow she had become thankful that he was not! In fact, she suspected that she loved him all the more for it! A finer house might have been a boon, but in her heart she had developed this odd feeling that *where* she lived was not nearly as important as *who* she lived with. In fact, it was worse than that: She was feeling that she belonged in the vicarage, with Mr. O'Brien. Indeed, could it be that it was her place to be at his side no matter where he lived? Yet, for all she knew, Mr. O'Brien thought her a foolish girl, not worth his time. He had not given her any indication of his thinking otherwise.

She had not seen the man since the day he brought her to the estate, the same day that Ariana had overcome the worst of her danger. But she thought of him often. If only she had not expressed an interest in a fine house! In a Season in London! In Mr. Barton! How foolish her words sounded to her own ears now! Oh, she assuredly had been most foolish!

"Miss Beatrice," said Mrs. Pellham, for she had been at table when Mr. Mornay let fall the news regarding a London Season. "You might consider returning to the metropolis with Mr. Pellham and myself. I no longer have the consequence I had when your sister was with me, but I can show you a very diverting time, I am sure."

Mr. Pellham nodded saying, "To be sure, your aunt is superb at gathering invitations."

"Why, thank you, Randolph!" the matron crooned.

"I am much obliged, Aunt Pellham," replied Beatrice. "Truly. Only I must tell you, at present I have no wish to go to London." Mr. Mornay held his fork in midair. (Ariana was still taking her meals, small ones, in her chamber.)

Mrs. Pellham said, "Oh! I beg your pardon! I understood you desired a coming-out!"

Embarrassed, Beatrice replied, "I meant no disrespect, ma'am." She dabbed her mouth with a linen cloth. "May I have some time to consider your offer?"

"Of course you may," she answered. This struck Mrs. Pellham as reasonable. She no longer felt that strong need to sponsor a gel as she had used to. Marrying Randolph seemed to have filled some part of her that had used to need the attention. Her offer to Beatrice, therefore, was all the more generous in that it was entirely unselfish. She did have a few last words, however, which she lost no time in parting with:

"Do you recall that your sister will now truly be Lady Mornay, as your brother has finally had the good sense to accept the honor of a title. A viscountess! My niece!" she beamed at Mr. Mornay with more than her usual approval.

Mr. Mornay merely nodded. When he finished eating he told Beatrice he needed to speak with her.

When they were alone in the library afterward (so that the Pellhams could sit in the drawing room), he looked wryly at his young relation, and asked, "What has made you think better of a London Season?"

She gazed at him with an odd expression. "I suppose I am merely thankful that my sister is well; if I do go to Town, I should prefer it to be with her and you, sir; not my aunt and uncle."

"Your aunt is likely to put forth a greater expenditure upon you than either myself or your sister."

She nodded, but he could see it did not impress her in the least. *Interesting!*

"I must tell you," he said, "that during your sister's illness I had much time to consider a great many things, one of them being the day you disappeared upon the estate with Mr. O'Brien."

This caught her attention, and she looked up at him with interest.

"Yes?"

"I have come to the conclusion that the incident was sufficiently compromising to your character so that you must wed."

Beatrice's face froze. Her eyes opened wider. She could not help it and had to smile just a little, all beneath the watchful gaze of her brother-in-law. She looked at him, and all he could detect upon her features was relief and joy. By Jove, the girl was in love! No wonder she had given up London!

"I will write to Mr. Barton at once," he started to say, but Beatrice gasped.

"Mr. Barton!" she cried. "Surely you do not think I can wed Mr. Barton!"

He stopped in surprise. "He offered for you, regardless of the incident with O'Brien. It makes an easy escape for you, under the circumstances."

"Escape? To what?" There was silence a moment. "To a life with *him?*"

Here Mr. Mornay had to smile. "Barton has the money to keep you in style; he can buy the Manor House, and you can be neighbour to your sister. Does this not please you?"

Beatrice was suddenly taking deep breaths, too distraught to say anything. She leapt to her feet and walked first this way, then that. Her arms were crossed across her middle. "I can never marry Mr. Barton! Was I compromised by Mr. Barton? *No!* Was I taken care of by Mr. Barton? *No!*"

She looked at Mornay as though he was pigeon-headed. Blinking back tears, she said, "Is he a good, kind man who fears the Lord? *No!* Is he gentle and soft-spoken and wise? *No!*" She stopped before him and opened her arms in exasperation. "Do you honestly think he would make me a good husband?"

Mr. Mornay was trying not to smile. But he said, *"No!"*

"Oh! Then you shan't try to force me to wed him?"

Her startled words brought out the full, handsome smile. "By no means! I only proposed it because I thought you preferred him." How auspicious. He knew that his wife would be delighted to discover that her sister had fallen in love with their young cleric.

Beatrice stared at him for a second. In unison, because he saw it coming, they both shouted, "NO!"

Weak with relief, Beatrice sat back down upon a wing chair in the room. A maid had come in and was building up the fire, but she paid no heed to her. Beatrice looked up at him, smiling through tears of joy, and said, "You are the best and kindest of brothers, sir! You are the best and kindest!"

He was smiling and nodding. "May I tell

your sister or do you insist upon that honour?"

Beatrice looked askance for a moment. "Oh, you may tell her!" she breathed. She was still holding one arm across her stomach while she let this turn of events sink in upon her. But then a terrible thought occurred to her. "Sir!" She caught him before he left the room. "What if Mr. O'Brien does not wish to marry me?"

Mr. Mornay looked at her with mild eyes. "I do not think you will have that problem."

That afternoon, Mr. Barton showed up at the doorstep of the vicarage. He was delighted to discover the good news regarding Mrs. Mornay, and he said just that to the ladies in the parlour. Miss Forsythe was not present, but he would ask about her soon enough.

"And how does Lord and Lady Horatio?" asked Mrs. Forsythe.

"Very well indeed, ma'am, I thank you. It seems that Lady Weverly has decided that she adores my sister; this has put her in the good graces of her new mother and father, and all is as well as it could be for them. For now."

Mrs. Royleforst caught those ending words. "For *now*, sir? What mean you by that, pray?"

"Did I say that? How very foolish of me, for I meant not a thing! What I need to know," he said, looking around the room (and smoothly changing the subject), "is whether it is now safe to call upon the Mornays."

"We think it best, on account of the children, Mr. Barton, to wait a few more days."

"There is always the devilish possibility," said Mrs. Royleforst, "that my nephew may fall ill."

"I see," he said. "And Miss Forsythe? Is she well?"

"She is well, I thank you, sir," said her mother.

"Capital," he said, "Capital, indeed."

"Will you join us for the evening meal?" asked Mr. O'Brien. He did not really wish for the man to stay, but his manners were too good for him not to ask. Mr. Barton, however, declined the offer. With no Beatrice there to amuse him, he would be bored to pieces if he stayed. Even more, while he did not wish to expose himself to any disease, he needed to settle the matter of his wedding. He would write to Mornay, renew his offer, and be done with it. He could return to London a happy man, and

518

stay clear until every last threat of illness was gone. He would then marry Beatrice and buy the Manor House. It was a delightful plan.

Mr. Mornay opened the letter which had just been delivered, by hand, by Mr. Barton. He understood why the man had not wished to come into the house — but it did nothing to raise him in his estimation.

It was a letter asking for the hand of Miss Forsythe.

Having only just come from his wife's bedside, where he had regaled her with the very welcome news of Beatrice's surprising disclosure, he knew exactly how to reply.

Mr. Barton was delighted to receive a quick response to his declaration. But as he read the response — then reread it — he considered that there had to be some way to answer this; to change the girl's mind, perhaps. How could she possibly prefer a country clergyman to him — for he just knew that O'Brien had to be the reason for this rejection. It couldn't be. It lacked sense. He finally concluded that Mr. Mornay, for some inexplicable reason, preferred the "old acquaintance" to himself, but he did not believe it was Beatrice's sentiment. He crumpled the note and threw it into the fireplace. He would see about this. He would not give up quite that easily!

The next few days passed slowly. Mr. Mornay carried his wife downstairs one day; and the next, she came down herself. It was wonderful to see her improving so speedily, but there was a small sadness in the household, nevertheless, for she missed the children exceedingly.

"I cannot stand it for a second longer!" she said, finally on the next day. "Get me my children, this day, sir, or I will go mad!" Mr. Mornay folded his arms and stared for a moment at his beautiful wife. Then he smiled.

"Master Nigel, come, you are to go to your mama!" Mrs. Forsythe's joy could hardly be contained as she summoned the little boy. The child, dark curls bobbing, dropped the wooden toy he'd been holding, in a crouched position, and sprang to his feet. Eagerly, he shouted, "Mama! Huzzah!" The baby Miranda was hastily dressed and made ready and bundled off for Mr. Mornay's carriage which awaited them.

During the drive, Mr. Mornay kept his son upon his lap, and kissed his head, and played with him, and listened to him with endless patience. He feasted his eyes on his daughter too. When they reached the house, the children were brought to the drawing room, where Ariana was seated on a comfortable divan, fluffed with pillows, but she stood as soon as they entered the room, and watched with joy while her son ran toward her. She dropped to one knee and held her arms open for him. The little one flew into her embrace.

"Mama! Mama! Where were you? Where were you?"

"Oh, my Nigel, I missed you!" she said, giving him an almost crushing hug, for she could not embrace him tightly enough. She turned her face and began kissing his head and cheeks, and her eyes were teary, if not closed, as she absorbed this long-awaited reunion. She ceased kissing and petting his face and held him again tightly against her chest, though he began wriggling from her.

"My toy," he said, "do you want to see it, Mama?"

"Yes!" she answered, still beholding him like an angel sent from heaven. Meanwhile, Mrs. Perler brought the baby, and Ariana held out her arms; and this time tears did fall.

"Look, Mama!" Nigel had a complete new

set of exquisitely formed and painted wooden soldiers, and now brandished a few in his hands — they were of the prince's colours, as the Regent had them specially made and sent when he heard of Mrs. Mornay's illness. When Ariana noticed their superior craftsmanship, Mrs. Forsythe said, "A gift from the prince, my love. When he heard of your illness."

"Oh!" She was sensible of the honour and the thoughtfulness, and admired the pieces prettily not just for Nigel's sake, but because they really were tiny works of art. From her apron, Mrs. Perler pulled a few more of the Dragoons, and Nigel shouted, "See how many, Mama? From the king!"

"The prince, my love," she corrected.

"No, he's the king, Mama! He *has* to be the king!" His little face went into a pout. She said, "We cannot make people what we would have them be, but must accept them as they are, my pet."

Some of the toy men were on their knees, aiming a weapon at an imaginary foe; others were on horseback, and the horses were fashioned as carefully and with as much detail as the men. The prince himself was represented by a good, tall fellow (much taller than the Regent, in reality), who held up a sword in one hand, while his other arm pointed forward, as if to direct his troop to the battle. His costume even included a little blue sash across his chest, which, unlike the other painted figures, was made of real silk. And the hat he wore had real miniscule tassels spouting from the centre.

"Has anyone sent a thank-you to the prince?" Ariana asked. "How long ago were these received?"

"Just the other day, and I did send a note of thanks with the messenger who delivered them. At that time, my sweet, we were not certain of your survival" — and here Mrs. Forsythe stopped, her eyes filling with tears just at the thought of how close a brush Ariana had endured with death — "and perhaps it would be a kindness to send another message, telling him of God's mercy upon you and us all."

"Now I think on it," said Ariana, "Mr. Mornay can give our thanks in person, as he is to see the prince after he is ennobled."

"Yes! You will be Lady Mornay, now!" Her mother's eyes were filled with tears, again, though they were happy ones.

Meanwhile Nigel was trying to be patient, but was yanking upon his mother's gown.

"And you," said Ariana, looking fondly down at him, "Will be 'the honourable' Nigel, sir! On paper, at any rate."

Ignoring this, he cried, "Will you play with me and my men, mama? You can be the King!"

"You mean the prince, sir!" she said, playfully.

"Mama, why can he not be king?"

She smiled. "Because the real king is his father! And he lives, still."

Nigel frowned. "Why is he not here? I want the king too, Mama!"

"This is the prince's regiment, sir! You have the honour of being their master, and that must satisfy you."

"I want to show them to Papa again," he said, for they had already been taken out and admired during the carriage ride.

She took his little chin in her hand and made him look up at her. "Today you will stay for tea with the grown-ups! Right in this room too!"

"Tea! Huzzah! An — an — biscuits?" he asked, his dark black eyes large in his face. Ariana smiled; Nigel's eyes were so like his father's.

"Of course!" She nodded to the servants, who left to fetch the tea tray. Nigel had suddenly desired to climb into her lap, however, and so she gave up the baby to Mrs. Perler. Nigel was studying her, and he put his little hands on each side of her face. "You look different, Mama."

"Mama was ill; but I am better, now."

"I'm glad you are better, Mama!"

The tray was brought in with a fresh tea service, and plates of biscuits, scones, and slices of seed cake. Mr. Mornay returned to the room as well.

"Papa!" shouted Nigel. He pulled his hand free from his mother's and charged at his father like a little bull. Phillip was already smiling and received the boy into his arms only to lift him, upside down, and deposit him upon his shoulders, holding tightly to his little chubby legs. The boy's papa was wearing his shirt and waistcoat, but no outer garment, for he had anticipated his son's antics. Ariana settled Miranda once again upon her lap, watching her husband and son with a smile. Nigel's shrieks of delight were blithely ignored by the baby, who snuggled warmly against her mother.

Phillip glanced over from time to time, but he continued playing with his son, getting on his knees and taking the child about on his back. Ariana watched adoringly. Who would have known — not even she — that Mr. Mornay could be so playful and unrestrained with his offspring? It was beautiful to behold, and at times she wasn't sure who was having more fun, the child, or the father. However, as soon as Nigel was removed from a room, her husband reverted to his usual, more sedate nature. She still marveled upon it.

The wet nurse appeared. "I beg your pardon, ma'am," she said with a curtsey; the playing on the floor stopped while Phillip paused to hear what was said. "I believe it's time for the baby to be fed."

"Oh." Ariana paused, sorrow flooding her heart suddenly because she could no longer perform that office. But she lifted up the child, saying, "Of course; thank you, Mrs. Dennison."

At that point, as if aware of the sudden separation from her mother, the baby awoke with a shudder, and let out a muffled cry; then, a louder one. Mrs. Dennison took her with a look of urgency, and disappeared with the crying child from the room, moving determinedly and with rapid strides.

"My sister has to eat? My sister is hungry?" asked Nigel.

"That's right, darling."

"But, Mama, your 'sposed to feed her!"

She smiled weakly. "Mama cannot feed her any longer, but she will be fed, very well, I assure you, by Mrs. Dennison."

"Do you like my men, Papa?" asked Nigel eagerly.

"I do, sir!" he replied, but he got to his feet and started smoothing down his clothing.

Nigel suddenly realized that treats were available and dropped the little men like they had the plague and hurried over to the table. Molly helped him fill a small plate with foodstuffs.

Mr. Mornay sat beside his wife. "I have sent word to O'Brien to see me. Your sister is anxious to settle the matter of her future — though I cannot understand why," he added, in jest.

"Excellent," she replied. "And you will now grant the living at Glendover to him?"

"If he isn't so pigeon-headed as to refuse it."

"Phillip — you are to be brothers now. You must speak well of him henceforward."

Mr. Mornay made a small sound of irritation in his throat. "Must you remind me?"

Twenty-Seven

"When will you speak to Mr. O'Brien?" Ariana asked Phillip. "To tell him that we have decided his fate?" She continued in a droll tone: "He must marry a delightful girl, become a vicar for the first time, reside at Glendover, which is finer and more spacious than even Warwickdon — and live happily ever after, I daresay!" She was smiling at her husband, but a little worry came over her, creasing her brow.

"What, now?"

"If you insist upon the wedding, will Beatrice ever feel he did not desire it? He has made no declarations to her, I think."

He put his head back and frowned at her. "Do not say you are not content with a forced wedding! It is precisely what you hoped for! And we have every right to insist upon it; *and,* Beatrice is in love with the man! What could be more propitious?"

"If he proposed to her without any onus

from us. So that she may never have cause to doubt him."

He smiled down at her, now, amused. "I should say you are quite recovered, are you not? Back to scheming, already."

"Only for the happiness of my dear and cherished sister!"

"And what do you think I can do for her happiness that I have not already done?"

"We must put them alone together again, so that Mr. O'Brien can speak for himself, under no duress, and from his heart."

He looked doubtful. "Who is to say with all the time alone in the world, he will speak for her?"

"He must! I believe he will!" she said, as if there could be no doubt about it.

"Perhaps you can arrange it," he said. "I believe I have had my fill of the matter."

"Very well," she said. "Only, you must give me your word not to interfere."

"Done."

"Thank you, darling!" She settled into his arms and gave him a welcome kiss of gratitude.

Mr. Barton knew that he would have to act quickly. He went by the vicarage first, and found only Mr. O'Brien there. All of his guests, the clergyman told him, had returned to Aspindon only hours earlier.

"Then I must call there," he said, with a look that was faintly challenging.

"By all means," said the cleric. But he had a second thought. "I believe I'll do the same. I have yet to see Mrs. Mornay since her recovery." He paused. "I have an equipage — it comes with the vicarage — but Mr. Hargrove took his horses, and I have yet to purchase new ones. Would you mind terribly if I came along with you?"

Mr. Barton did mind; but what could he say?

Beatrice was feeling happy. Her sister was recovering; the rest of the family had not fallen ill; and now she was to marry Mr. O'Brien! It filled her heart with elation just to think upon it! Yet at the back of her mind was a niggling little doubt. What if Mr. O'Brien did not wish to marry her? What if his thoughts were entirely wide of that mark?

She came upon Mr. Mornay in the corridor while she was en route to the drawing room to sit with Ariana.

"Mr. Mornay, have you written yet to Mr. O'Brien . . . regarding the topic we spoke of earlier?"

Her delicacy referring to the wedding

amused him, but he merely said, "No."

"May I ask you to hold off, sir, for the smallest time? Since we have waited this long already, and no harm has come of it — I should like to see if Mr. O'Brien might himself have . . . that is, if he may wish to . . ." And here her voice fell away. She was embarrassed to speak of this!

"I understand you completely," he said.

Beatrice was surprised, but relieved. "*Do* you!"

"It was Ariana's thought exactly. To give him opportunity to declare himself, is that it?"

"Yes, precisely!"

"It isn't as if I have to worry about him disappearing over the horizon, you know. He's staying put. I have no problem with giving him an opportunity to speak to you himself."

She clasped her hands together. She could almost have given the man a kiss upon the cheek. And then, the next thing she knew, she had done it! She kissed Mr. Mornay upon the cheek!

"Thank you!" she cried, and then took off down the corridor. She stopped after only a few feet, turned, and said, again, still clasping her hands, "Thank you!" He was left looking after her, and he shook his head, but he had to smile. The girl was desperately in love.

Mr. Barton and Mr. O'Brien spoke little during the drive to Aspindon. The first man was thinking that all he needed was a good few minutes alone with Beatrice and he could settle the situation in his favour. All he had to do was persuade Miss Forsythe that she was ready for marriage, and that he was her best hope for the sort of union she desired. He was good at being persuasive, he felt.

Mr. O'Brien had the unmistakable sensation that something was afoot with the man beside him, and he knew only too well, he was sure, what it was about. Barton had very likely made an offer and was en route to find out his fate. Mr. O'Brien had a sinking heart, therefore, and yet he itched to reach the house, to pay his respects to Ariana, and then to see Miss Forsythe. The thing was, it still plagued his mind, the words she had said upon their last meeting. What had she meant when she said that his opinion of Barton had been far too good? And, what on earth was behind her calling him "the most unfeeling man in the world"?

There was a little voice in his head trying to tell him that it meant she cared for *him,*

Mr. O'Brien. But how could that be? She had made it clear what her expectations were, only too well! And he had little to offer her, if compared to Barton's wealth. Which was, of course, what she would do. Here Mr. O'Brien had come into his own, but it wasn't good enough for her. Why, why had his life once again crossed paths with the Mornays, with the Forsythes? But even as he thought it, he was extremely grateful that it had. Not because of Warwickdon, either, or at least, not only because of it. But because he adored Miss Forsythe. He felt rather tragical about it; He was in love and unable to do a blessed thing about it!

As they had turned into the long, tree-lined drive of the estate, the minister turned his heart to God, and emptied it before Him. "Lord, I love her," he said, in his mind. "She wants other things than what I can give her." He thought again about that and considered the situation to be hopeless. "But I give her to You. You have brought us together as neighbours; I pray that if it is possible, if it is *Your will,* that You might bring us together as man and wife!"

There, he had prayed it! He may have lacked the right to speak to her; or the courage; but he had at last prayed for the thing he desired ever more and more, which was to have Beatrice Forsythe as his wife. And he knew that if God was in agreement, He would bring it to pass.

He sat back in his seat with a feeling of expectation. The house came into view, and soon they had pulled up in front.

Mr. Barton said, "Well, here we are, O'Brien."

He looked at the other man. Somehow, he felt that Mr. Barton knew he was there about Beatrice, just as Mr. O'Brien knew that Barton was. As if reading his thoughts, Barton said, "May the best man win." He wore the hint of a smile as he spoke, for it was clear who he considered to be the best man.

Mr. O'Brien responded with, "God's will be done."

At the door, Mr. Barton straightened his neckcloth and his jacket, and put his hat at a rakish angle upon his head, and then used the brass knocker on the door.

There was quite a bustle inside the house.

When the men were ushered into the drawing room, they found it filled with all the occupants of the house saving the children and Mrs. Perler. Mr. Mornay stepped forward to offer Mr. O'Brien a seat — a decidedly unusual greeting, but Mr.

O'Brien was pleased, of course.

Mr. Barton's eyes narrowed.

When his host came up to Barton, he asked, "You haven't come intent upon changing my mind, I hope?"

"Yours, sir? No." His eyes roamed to where Miss Forsythe was sitting, needlework in hand, between Ariana and Mr. O'Brien, who had taken a seat in a wing chair near the settee where the ladies sat.

"But I warn you, I won't have you speaking to Miss Forsythe regarding a matter which is settled, to my mind."

Mr. Barton felt feisty; what did he have to lose? "I have the right, do you not think, to hear from her own lips why she has refused my offer?"

Mr. O'Brien's head spun, for he overheard this remark. His heart skipped a beat. Or maybe a few.

"No, you have no rights whatsoever when it comes to my family." For some reason, it was much easier for Mr. Mornay to be curt in person rather than in writing.

"Mr. Mornay — may I ask if you are fully aware of my situation? My fortune?"

"I am, Mr. Barton. But it is neither here nor there; Miss Forsythe is not to be bartered for; and you have received not only a rejection from her, but from me as well. Let

535

it suffice you, sir. It is my opinion you would do well to leave it alone."

Beatrice was now shooting alarmed looks at the men, for she was overhearing snatches of conversation; words like, "rejection," and "leave it alone." The other women in the room were also gathering that the dialogue was of the juiciest nature. Mrs. Royleforst told her companion to "hush!" and even Ariana lowered her voice and then turned to watch the men.

"Is that what prevents this connexion?" Mr. Barton was saying. "Your opinion? Should it not be the young lady's opinion that matters? Or perhaps that of her mother?" His eyes turned to settle upon Mrs. Forsythe, who also had begun to watch the men, trying to listen, although she felt it thoroughly poor manners to do so.

This was an indirect threat: Mr. Barton was prepared to take his case to Mrs. Forsythe. Mr. Mornay had no problem with the idea, actually. Why not let the girl's mother turn him down? What difference would it make?

"Be my guest, sir."

Mr. Barton's eyes momentarily flickered with something — disappointment? He bowed lightly and turned to Mrs. Forsythe. But he surveyed the room, and saw that many faces were watching his. A maid rushed into the room telling Ariana that little Miranda would not cease her crying. This was sufficient to send Ariana at once from her seat and out of the room.

Mr. Barton looked at Beatrice. "Miss Forsythe — may I join you?" he asked.

She looked uncomfortable, but could hardly deny a simple request. "As you wish," she said, and he took the spot which had just been vacated by her sister.

The man was uncomfortably aware that the eyes of both Mr. Mornay and Mr. O'Brien were settled upon him; but he was not so uncomfortable that he could be put off that easily.

He waited a few moments while other conversations in the room were taken up again. Then, turning to her, he said, in a low tone, "I beg your pardon, Miss Forsythe, but are you aware that I sent a letter to Mr. Mornay? To offer for your hand in marriage?"

She blushed, but kept her eyes averted. "I am, sir."

"You know, then, that he has refused my offer?"

"Yes, I know." She found her courage and met his eyes. He looked injured; she looked away again, staring at the pattern on the rug as though she needed to commit it to memory.

"I had reason to believe that my suit would be acceptable to you, did I not?"

"You never mentioned offering for me, Mr. Barton." She was uncomfortable to the extreme, but realized she would have to finish this conversation. Better to get it over with, in any case, than to leave any lingering doubt.

"You cut me to the quick!" he exclaimed, with a hand to his heart. "Did I not ask if I might court you? Is that not tantamount to declaring my love?" His voice was loud enough for her to hear clearly, but low enough so that no one else could. She blushed afresh.

"I am sorry, sir, truly."

"Please give me your reasons," he said. "What have you against me? I beg of you, Miss Forsythe! I cannot mend my ways if I do not know what is displeasing in them."

She really did not want to get into this discussion, but to quiet him, she said, "You walked out when we were to pray for my sister." She turned her eyes to him.

He saw her dissatisfaction, and thought quickly. "I am a private person, Miss — *Beatrice*. It does not seem so, I grant; but my public appearance is not the same as the man I know myself to be, intimately. I cannot, like some (and he looked briefly at the curate here. Who was staring stonily at him. Which he ignored.), pray prettily, and aloud. I can only think to pray when I am alone."

Despite herself, Beatrice found his answer interesting. "You have only to practice it, sir," she replied. "Praying in a group, or perhaps just a twosome, is no great difficulty once you have practiced it. You must force yourself to try it, perhaps with just one other person at first."

"Miss Forsythe —" and he instinctively went to grasp one of her hands, but saw movement out of the corner of his eye; Mr. Mornay was standing against the wall, arms crossed, watching his every move. He decided against it, returning his hands to his own lap.

"Will you be my tutor? Tell me that you, lovely Beatrice, will teach me to pray aloud, in public, and I will give it practice, with my whole heart." He had turned to face her, so that his whole person leaned in toward her, and suddenly Mr. Mornay was there, in front of him, and with a stony visage.

"I beg your pardon," mumbled Barton, resuming his previous position.

Mr. Mornay retreated, and Mr. Barton

swallowed his pride. He suddenly felt what it must be like to be a chess piece. He was a mere pawn, but Mornay was king! He might only make small moves, but they mattered, utterly.

Meanwhile, Beatrice had thought of more to accuse him with. "When my sister first took ill, you might have put up at least a part of our number at the Manor. You offered no rooms whatsoever! When you have more than you can need or possibly use!"

He was taken aback, but again he thought quickly. "Anne was often ill, you will recall," he said. "She has been better of late, but at that time I feared to compromise her health; I knew she would take it upon herself to play hostess; she would have exerted herself for guests. It might well have prolonged her sickness, rather than allowing her the time and the quiet to recuperate as she has. I think (I am sorry if it offends you), but I still think I was in the right in that decision."

Well! This did seem to answer. But she met his gaze and said, "You mentioned nothing of this at the time, sir."

"How could I? Anne would have counted herself ill-used, and insisted on us taking all of you home with us. Only then, she would have never been able to get her rest. I am her older brother, you recall, and I am responsible for her before others."

She had to acknowledge the truth of that. "I give you my compliments on her marriage, by the way," she said.

"I thank you," he answered, watching her intently with his dark eyes. "I would call myself a happy man, almost — if I could only secure my own happiness in marriage — to you."

Beatrice felt her hair stand on end. How could he dare to say such things to her right there in the middle of a roomful of people? She was blushing afresh, and she looked helplessly around her, and her gaze fell upon Mr. Mornay. He took only a moment to read her feelings. He was a wise and good relation, Beatrice felt. And he was coming to rescue her.

Which he did. With little more than a nod of his head, he had Mr. Barton making his excuses in a minute, and took him away from Beatrice. She let out a breath of relief. In the next minute, Mr. O'Brien sat down in his place.

"I hope you have not had to overexert yourself," he said, as if he knew precisely what sort of conversation had just taken place. Beatrice could only gape at him for a moment, before coming to herself and saying, "No." Inside she was thinking frantically of what she could say, or do, to show Mr. O'Brien that she had not meant any of her earlier foolish statements. She did not care about a fine large house like Aspindon. She did not want to go to London for a Season at all! She could care less about the size of a man's fortune! Oh, how would she ever be able to make him know her, really?

"Has Barton discomposed you?"

She eyed him for a moment, wondering how much to reveal. "I do not wish to speak of that gentleman, if you don't mind," she offered.

"I beg your pardon."

"No, it is just that I have nothing good to say of him at this moment." She hoped that was an explanation. Meanwhile, Mr. Mornay had returned to the room — and there was no sign of Mr. Barton.

"Miss Forsythe," said Mr. O'Brien, "would you do me the honour of accompanying me for a short walk on the grounds?"

"But there is snow on the ground," she protested.

He smiled. "Five minutes of your time would suffice me, if you please. Not nearly long enough to develop frostbite."

Beatrice smiled. "Very well. I shall be happy to."

Mr. Mornay did inquire as to their destination; he could only be expected to be so forbearing, even in this circumstance. As Beatrice went to get her coat and bonnet, Mr. O'Brien spoke to Mr. Mornay a few seconds longer. After thanking him, he went off for his own greatcoat and scarf and hat. When they had both left the room, Mornay peered at his watch fob. It was going on four-thirty.

At the front door, Mr. O'Brien turned to Beatrice. "May I ask you to wait just a few minutes? I have taken the liberty of securing a sleigh for us; Mr. Mornay has been good enough to give us use of it. Do you mind? I'll be only a minute."

But she was already smiling with pleasure. "I'd be delighted! I love a sleigh ride!"

She waited briefly, and then stepped out of doors to wait upon the steps. There was light coming from inside the house, which was just becoming necessary to see well, for the winter day was drawing to a close. There was no moon, and it was still snowing lightly. Beatrice heard a sound and leaned forward, expecting to see the sleigh coming toward her, but could see nothing.

"Miss Forsythe."

She gasped in surprise, but it was Mr. Barton approaching.

"I beg your pardon," he said, "for frightening you."

"My word!" she exclaimed. "You did frighten me. Where did you come from?"

He pointed down the drive, saying, "My carriage is only just over there." She could not make it out, due to the snow and quickly falling dusk, but she looked at him curiously.

"Are you returning to the house?" she asked.

"I was," he said, slowly, watching her. "Are you leaving it?" (with a smile).

"No, not leaving. Just going for a sleigh ride with Mr. O'Brien."

"Ah. The *favoured* gentleman, if I am not mistaken?" He looked around. "And where is he?"

"He is getting the sleigh."

Mr. Barton took in a breath. "Is there any way I can hope to change your mind regarding my suit?" he asked suddenly.

Beatrice felt uneasy, but replied, "I am sorry, sir, but there is not."

"May I know why?" He looked at her with an almost angry expression.

"If you must know, it is because I am in love with Mr. O'Brien."

Mr. Barton said nothing, but merely

rocked on his heels a moment or two, and looked out at the snow falling, in the direction of his carriage.

"I am of a mind to take you for a drive myself," he said lightly.

She looked at him, perplexed. "I am sorry, Mr. Barton, but as I said, I am waiting for Mr. O'Brien to return at any moment."

"The least you can grant me is a short drive," he said, "since you deny me a lifetime with you."

With a sudden feeling of caution, Beatrice turned to grasp the door handle. She was going to wait inside the house and put an end to this pointless discussion. But as soon as she turned, Mr. Barton had her over his shoulder like a sack of flour — just like that!

"Mr. Barton!" she cried, pounding him with her fists. "Put me down this instant, sir!" She dropped her muff and used both her fists against his coat, but he was scarcely paying heed. Instead, he hurried forward carrying her, counting on the snowfall to muffle her cries. Beatrice began yelling the name of Mr. O'Brien, and then, in desperation, *"Peter!"*

Twenty-Eight

Just as he was leading the horses to the sleigh, which had taken far longer than he hoped, for there was no groom in the stables, Mr. O'Brien heard yells in the distance. He had two horses in hand, each by the reins below the head, and he looked around frantically for a place to tie one so that he could mount the other. He hadn't saddled it for riding, and it was slippery from the weather, but he had to get to Beatrice as quickly as possible. He didn't ask himself how he knew it was Beatrice. He didn't stop to think it might have been a sound of merriment, or glee. He wrapped the reins of the second horse quickly around a post, and hurried to mount the first animal.

There was a whinny of protest, and the horse reared up. Mr. O'Brien was at the end of his patience, for suddenly it came to him that Miss Forsythe was in danger, and here this animal had the audacity to give him grief. He stalked to the head of the beast, and spoke very closely to its face, holding it strongly by the reins.

"You listen to me, sir!" he said, through gritted teeth. It was a tone of voice that would have astounded anyone familiar with him, for he had never in his life used it before. "You *will* allow me to mount you and you *will* take me to my bride!"

It was an astonishing thing for him to have said, for he hardly knew that Beatrice Forsythe had to be his bride, but, of course, she did. He left the horse's head and scrambled up a bit sloppily. The horse moved about on its legs for balance, but behaved for him, and he got on!

He turned it at once and went in the direction of the front of the house.

Meanwhile, Beatrice was trying to slow down Mr. Barton at every turn. He had growled at his coachman, "On the double, Jarvey," which told her immediately that the man was a jarvis, a stand-in coachman, not a longtime servant! So she cried out to him, "Oh, sir! This man would have you a criminal for him!"

"Be quiet, Beatrice!" Mr. Barton said, annoyed, as he tried to push her into the carriage.

She clung to the door for dear life. "Do not do his bidding!" she gasped, as loudly as she could. "You'll end up on a gibbet, while he will go free!"

Mr. Barton doubled his grasp on her, while yelling up at the coachman, "I'll pay you fifty pounds for taking us to Scotland! I'll pay you on arrival!"

"Ye'll pay me first, sir," the man replied, in his own low growl.

"I cannot pay you while I must keep hold of this young woman!"

"What are you *doing*, Mr. Barton?" cried Beatrice, in a strained tone that caught his attention. "I am no *prize* for you! Have you lost your senses?"

He hesitated, and the truth came out. "I'll be brother to Mr. Mornay if we wed, and that is good enough for me!"

"Yes, but if you force me to this, he'll be in your life forever, but as a thorn in your flesh! Think of it, sir! No one who incurs his wrath can be happy around him again! Do you truly wish to ruin your life at so young an age?"

She saw more hesitation on his face. In the back of her mind she thought she heard the sound of horses' hooves, lightly, in the snow, but as from a distance. She spoke quickly. "Mr. Mornay will be your brother, indeed; but he will be an Esau to you! You will need to fear him all the days of your life!"

His shoulders slumped. What she said made perfect sense, given who Mr. Mornay was. There had been rumours of the man finding religion, but Mr. Barton could not say they were true. He saw no softening of the features on the man, no difference in the famously caustic nature. Other people, many other people, would have disputed those very claims with utter accuracy and sincerity, but not Mr. Barton. For some reason he had never found favour with the man.

Perhaps it was because he was capable of doing what he was doing; namely, abducting Miss Forsythe to force her into marriage, that Mornay had only extended a cautious friendship. Of course, Mr. Mornay could not have known that he would do this! But the man had never given up a sense of caution he had formed regarding him — Barton could feel it — and now he was giving justification to Mornay's concerns. He didn't mean to be doing so. If Mr. Mornay had only welcomed him as a brother, none of this would have had to happen!

How was it that all of these thoughts could run swiftly through his mind? Beatrice was staring at him, wide-eyed, and darting glances this way and that, seeking a way of escape. She could sense his hesitation, and she said, "Do not make yourself an enemy in Mr. Mornay. You will live to regret it for many a day, sir!" Just as she was shrugging herself free from his grasp, the jarvis, (who all this time was listening) comprehended that his fifty pounds was about to vanish. Suddenly he was very content to be paid on arrival, and in a loud cry to alert the man who had hired him that night, he yelled, "Get 'er stowed, sir!" And, "We're off!"

With a loud crack of the ribbons, they took off, though even the horses were slipping on the icy pavement. Beatrice and Mr. Barton both went tumbling into the carriage to the floor; Mr. Barton was practically upon her. Through the noise of the creaking carriage and the horses in the snow, Beatrice still felt she could make out a different sound, a different tempo, and there, at the window, from her spot on the floor, she saw the face of Mr. O'Brien appear. Oh, that angelic face! He was going to rescue her!

He was looking in, but not toward the floor; Mr. Barton was just getting to his feet and he held out a hand to her, and — apologized.

"I am sorry, my dear Miss Forsythe," he said, above all the sounds. "It seems that the world has decided that we must wed. I promise you, I was going to release you!"

"Turn this carriage around at once!" she cried. Behind his head, through the window, there was only darkness. What had happened to her angel? And then, he was there again, and their eyes met, and she knew that he had some plan. Beatrice took her seat and held on to the edge of it. Mr. Barton noted her action, but did not guess at what was behind it.

"I believe," he said, moving slightly nearer to her, "that you will, in time, learn to love me. And then you will convince Mr. Mornay to do the same. You will tell him how happy you are now that I did this, don't you see? It's all for the best!"

But the horses started whinnying and suddenly the coach was rocking crazily but began to slow down. Mr. Barton looked struck by surprise, for he had no idea what was happening. He reached out and grasped one of her hands, as though to reassure her, only Beatrice pulled it instantly away. Then, to her horror, she heard a report at close range! *Oh my word! What if Mr. O'Brien is killed!*

There was the sound of a thump upon the

road, and the coach slowed to a stop. Unbeknownst to both the occupants of the carriage, the jarvis who had fired off a shot while trying to keep his perch atop the board had fallen instantly backward, and was knocked unconscious by the fall. His shot had missed Mr. O'Brien by a wide margin and gone off harmlessly in the air.

Beatrice was holding her head in her hands. She could not make herself look to see who had been hurt. If it was Mr. O'Brien, she would not be able to bear it. Not when she might have admitted to him far sooner that she held him in such high regard. Indeed, she loved him! She might have had him for a short time only, but now he could be lost forever! Her own foolishness and pride were to blame!

Mr. Barton had a look on his face that was only mildly less apprehensive, for he knew nothing of Mr. O'Brien being about, and assumed it was Mornay. When nothing happened, no one opened the door, he bit his lip and turned, and slowly opened it himself. Nothing. He glanced at Beatrice, and she saw that he was apprehensive. He gave the door a good kick, making it swing wide, and letting in a blast of cold air, but that was all. No sound of anyone being about. No movement other than the wind.

He looked at Beatrice with a puzzled expression. She raised her head, but just sat there looking terribly sad.

"I'll take a look," he said. But as soon as he moved to the door, she started to follow him, only she heard a loud thud, and then saw Mr. Barton stop, rock unsteadily on his legs for a moment, his head tottering, and then he fell forward, knocked out cold, onto the snowy road. Frightened, she stepped back a foot inside the carriage. Outside, Mr. O'Brien nodded in a satisfied manner at the prone body on the ground, for the second Barton ventured forth from the interior, he had given Mr. Barton a quick right jab to the head, using every ounce of his strength.

Now he poked his own head into the carriage, after shoving aside Barton's feet (for they had landed on the steps, which had fallen down by some odd fluke during the chase), and saw Beatrice peering apprehensively out at him. Her look changed into a smile. "Oh! My dear sir!" she cried, moving forward at once. She could hardly come forth speedily enough, and he took her exuberantly around the waist to hand her down. With her feet upon the ground, Beatrice could only continue to stare up at him, at dear, dear, Peter O'Brien, and her eyes watered; and when he said, "Are you all right, Miss Forsythe?" she cried, "No! I am not right! I have been a fool!" The truths she had been hiding came spilling out. "I have said I wanted a man of wealth and standing, when what I really want is *you!*"

And that was enough. That one declaration, in the end, was all she had to say to explain herself to him. He swept her up into his arms and bent his head (and his hat fell off though it had stayed on for all this time) and kissed Miss Beatrice Forsythe upon the lips. For a few seconds, the world was soft and sweet, even warm. They smiled at each other, in the approaching dark, and could see they were smiling because of the snow. Then he kissed her again, and then again. He said, "And I am in love with you. Will you be my wife, Beatrice? Little Beatrice Forsythe, who promised to marry me when you were twelve; will you indeed marry me?"

"Of course I shall!"

"I have little to offer you, I am well aware —"

"Shussh," she said, putting one gloved finger against his lips. "You have everything to offer me that I need. Forgive me for not realizing it sooner."

"There is nothing to forgive!"

Mr. Mornay was glad that he thought to check on his future relation. Somehow he was beginning to feel fond of the man — astounding! After twenty minutes had gone by, he left the house just to be certain that the clergyman and his young sister-in-law had not fallen into any trouble out in the cold. But when he saw the sleigh, abandoned right outside the mews, and a single horse tethered nearby, he had to suppress a groan. What on earth had happened this time? He put the horse into its stall and threw a blanket over it, then mounted Tornado to find out what was what.

He followed the tracks of the carriage wheels and horses' hooves in the snow, slowing only when he spied the vehicle ahead, no longer moving. He slowly clip-clopped his way toward it, cautiously, noting that the carriage was Mr. Barton's. He felt a small apprehension — was Barton up to something? He then saw a man lying on the side of the road. He did not know who it was, but he could also see, on the other side of the carriage, another man face down in the snow. As he came up to the vehicle, he noticed the couple standing close against it. So Mr. O'Brien had finally made his declaration!

It was about time.

EPILOGUE

The wedding was set for the following week.

But today the couple strolled arm in arm, hazarding again the great outdoors on the Aspindon property in the chilly weather. Neither seemed to mind.

"How did Mr. Mornay know that you would return my love?" Mr. O'Brien asked.

Beatrice stopped to look up into the eyes of the tall, handsome clergyman, soon to be her husband — and soon to be the vicar of Glendover, as well.

"I think," she said, "it was when I cried off from wanting a Season in London!"

They both laughed lightly.

He was relishing the sight of her pretty face, the little russet curls peeking out from her bonnet, knowing that they were soon to be man and wife.

They walked on, their steps quickening due to the cold. Beatrice was wearing thick woolen stockings, but even so, could feel the intrusion of the weather. Finally they came out to the clearing, and Beatrice exclaimed, "We've made it! There's the house again!"

It was still the same cheerful cottage, cozy looking, sweet — but small.

Beatrice's smile faltered and she sighed. "I must confess, I know that the glebe here is greater; and the living is double the value of Warwickdon; but I daresay it would be far more comfortable at the vicarage there than at this little house."

He turned puzzled eyes upon hers.

"Than at this house? But of course you know we won't be living *here*?" He suddenly started to chuckle.

"What! Why do you laugh?"

"This house, little Beatrice, is for the circulating warden in these parts. Glendover's vicarage is far more spacious and grand than the one at Warwickdon! The only thing it lacks," he said, with a little smile, "is a family beneath its spacious rafters, which, I dare to hope we will redress in good time."

She blushed, but was shaking with laughter. "You mean that all this time I thought the warden's house was the parsonage? And no one ever set me right?"

"I didn't realize your misapprehension!"

he cried. But he took her into his arms, after taking a quick look around them to make sure they were alone.

He was about to kiss her when she said, "Mr. O'Brien, would you be so kind as to see if that door is unlocked?"

"What, to the cottage?" he asked, in surprise.

"My feet! I can't feel them again!"

"If I take you in there now, Mornay will have my head!"

"If you do not, I will have no feet!" she giggled.

"You are very fortunate, Miss Forsythe," he said with another small laugh.

"Why is that?" she asked.

He bent and lifted her into his arms, and began walking comfortably to the right of the path, along the line of the woods. Their faces were now only inches apart.

"Because this time, I came prepared."

He put her down gently inside a sleigh where blankets awaited, wrapped her feet snugly inside a great thick one; and then climbed in himself, put one arm about her shoulders, and slapped the reins lightly to get the horses moving.

"How on earth . . . ?" she asked, surprised and delighted.

"I arranged it all earlier with your brother-in-law's assistance."

"You were lucky that it snowed again," she said mischievously.

"And you were lucky that Mr. Mornay gave me a set-down for having the audacity to suggest taking you out for a walk in such weather."

"I wondered how you got use of the sleigh!"

He laughed. "He forced my promise to use it coming back, which I desired to do in any case. I owed you a sleigh ride since our last attempt was unsuccessful."

They both knew he was alluding to the evening of Barton's desperate and bungled attempt to whisk her off to Scotland.

After a pause, he said, "Do you suppose we shall ever live in peace with him so close by?"

"Once we are wed, he will put all his attention back to his own family," she said. "I am quite sure of it."

There was a comfortable silence while they glided on, and the world was all beautiful and white.

With an impulsive burst of gladness, Beatrice snuggled closer against him at which Mr. O'Brien thought he might burst with happiness. He had his girl! He had not one, but two livings! *Two* of them! He was no longer a mere curate, but would be a vicar! God was so good! And to think that without Mr. Mornay, none of this would be possible!

Pulling him back from his thoughts, Beatrice said, "Do you know, there is *one* thing I regret?"

With a pang, he wondered if she was going to confess that she did want to go to London after all; or that she had second thoughts about giving up ideas of grandeur. But instead she said, "That you won't have to rub my numb feet back to life!"

He laughed out loud and pressed her closer to his side. "My little Beatrice," he said, into her ear. "I will be delighted to do so; after our wedding, I will be happy to do that, and much more."

The horses pulled them smoothly along the wide trail, and Aspindon came back into view. They both came to attention as the shape of a man upon a horse was suddenly ahead of them.

"Upon my word," said Beatrice, "I do believe he's checking on us!"

"Why hasn't he been off to London yet? To finally accept the title? I would think that gaining a viscountcy would give him reason enough to leave his home for a day."

"And risk having us out of his sight? Out

of his watchful eye? Being a viscount seems nothing to him while we are as yet unmarried, and in need of chaperonage — or so he must think. He takes us for the veriest youths, as though we have no idea of propriety."

Mr. O'Brien gazed at Mr. Mornay getting swiftly closer, and shook his head, but there was a little smile upon his mouth. "Heaven help us. And God bless him!"

DISCUSSION QUESTIONS

1. What aspect of the courtship (romance) between 1. Mr. O'Brien and Miss Beatrice Forsythe did you most enjoy?

2. Do you think Beatrice will make a good wife for a vicar? Why or why not?

3. How did Mr. Barton actually help Beatrice (without meaning to) to realize "what matters most" in life?

4. If Beatrice had stuck to her earliest goals of marrying a wealthy man, of social climbing and pleasure-seeking, how do you think she would have felt in five years' time?

5. If you were to visit Regency England, would you prefer to see London during the Season, or to stay at a country estate like Aspindon?

6. In your opinion, should Mr. Mornay have been stronger during his wife's illness? Or did he react in much the same way you would, given the circumstances? What are God's means of reaching us during times like these so that we can always have hope?

7. When Mr. O'Brien suspects the truth regarding Anne Barton's condition, he is filled with compassion and wants to help her if he can. Would you have shared his reaction? Would you have wanted to censure her? Why or why not?

8. If you had been in Beatrice's shoes, would you have held out for a man like Barton (wealthy and urbane) only with a more honourable character? Or allowed the earnest and kind Mr. O'Brien to "turn your head" as she did?

9. In your opinion, do people today still have to choose between false promises of wealth vs. what matters most? (ie. love and family)

10. How have you avoided the pitfalls of the world's temptations in your own life at times? Have you ever successfully chosen

what is best over what appears "good"?
Share with others how this happened.

A SHORT GLOSSARY FOR *THE COUNTRY HOUSE COURTSHIP*

Advowson — In English law, holding an advowson is having the right to present or appoint a nominee to a vacant ecclesiastical benefice (a church office, such as a curacy, or vicarage, or rectorship) in a parish.

Mr. Mornay holds the advowson to Glendover, and is given "honorary" (ie., fictional) rights to the nearby parish of Warwickdon for the sake of Mr. O'Brien by a big-hearted author.

Benefice — The term benefice, or "living," is used in the Church of England to describe a parish and, literally, its benefits (namely, the church and the parsonage house, a glebe or land, if it is attached, and so on).

The benefice at Warwickdon is replete with a furnished parsonage, a sizeable glebe, and even a carriage for the clergyman's use, as said author could not see leaving Mr. O'Brien high and dry in the country without an equipage. He will, however, encounter the necessity of purchasing carriage horses, himself, which he must do on his own, out of the resources allotted him.

Curate — full title is "Perpetual Curate." An ordained minister, a curate is a person who is invested with the care, or *cure,* of souls of a parish. In the Church of England, a curate was generally hired by a vicar or rector and lived upon a set wage, with no benefit of tithes. He performed all the duties of a parson, and was hierarchically beneath the vicar, who in turn was beneath a rector.

When the book opens, Mr. O'Brien is a poor curate, and poor curates were not uncommon in Regency England (or Georgian or Victorian England, for that matter). By the time of our happy ending, our poor curate is on his way to being a vicar (at Glendover), with an excellent benefice, and also holds a curacy in the nearby parish of Warwickdon. This means he will preside at services for both parishes, unless he chooses to hire his own curate for the second one.

Glebe — The land belonging to a benefice in addition to the parsonage and grounds; a glebe was intentionally assigned to help with the support of the priest or parson, either by his own use in farming, or he could let it (lease it out), and the income from the lease would add to his stipend. At times a glebe could be attached to the grounds of the parsonage, but was not always (in other words, the land might be a short distance from the house).

Magistrate — A magistrate during the regency was commonly a lay justice of the peace who sat voluntarily as a service to the community. In small villages and towns the magistrate was most often the wealthiest landowner or noble of highest rank.

Mr. Mornay is the magistrate at Glendover as he is the owner of the "big house," and the man with the most holdings.

Mama — At this time, the word was always pronounced in upper class society with the accent upon the last syllable (ma-MA). Same for pa-PA.

A regency reader must never refer to a MOMMA! It is always ma-MA!

Nursemaid — A servant who helped in the nursery or schoolroom for the children in upper class households.

Nursery — The room or suite of rooms in upper-class houses used for the youngest members of a household. They spent most of their time here, including sleeping and often eating, as well. Once the children were old enough for tutelage, they either moved to a schoolroom, or the nursery was converted to one.

The Mornay's nursery is actually a suite of rooms including sleeping quarters for both the children and their nurse and nursemaids, as well as toys and other juvenile paraphernalia and furniture.

Ordinary — The Ordinary in a church is generally a bishop of a parish or group of parishes; he must approve all newly nominated beneficiaries (clergymen nominated for a benefice).

Parish — The local church; an administrative (and often geographical) unit within the larger church body.

Fortunately for Mr. O'Brien, the parishes of Glendover and Warwickdon are not more than a few miles apart, meaning that he may preside at services for both if he wishes, without having to travel extensively, and without the expense of having to hire his own curate.

Rector — A rector can be an academic or ecclesiastical title; this book is concerned only with the ecclesiastical (church). A rector would directly receive both the *greater* and *lesser* tithes of his parish, unless he had a vicar who would get the lesser tithes. He also had all the rights to the glebe, parsonage, etc.

Special License — Though there were many legalities concerning marriage by the time of the Regency, the ancient right of the Archbishop of Canterbury to grant "special licenses" for marriage was retained. Thus, for around £5 or so, a special license could be obtained allowing a couple (of proper age) to marry at any time and place, within three months, at which point the license expired. The marriage had to be performed by an Anglican minister unless one was Jewish or a Quaker.

Tithes; *lesser tithes, greater tithes* — Tithes

are the monies paid into a parish church by its constituents, historically 10 percent, which during the Regency was based upon taxing agricultural output. The "greater tithes" were those levied upon wheat, hay, and wood; the "lesser tithes" were levied upon all other farm yields.

Vicar — from the latin word *Vicarius* meaning, "in place of." The vicar presides in the place of the actual rector of a parish, who for any number of reasons has opted to live elsewhere. The rector retained the rights to the greater tithes of a parish, while the vicar was entitled to the lesser tithes.

Warden — The warden was most often in charge of seeing to the upkeep of the church (except for the chancel, which fell to the rector to maintain) and the parsonage. In small parishes, there might be one warden for three or more churches, who was called a "circulating" warden, such as the one whose cottage is found by Beatrice and Mr. O'Brien on the Aspindon land.

Wet Nurse — Generally a lower-class woman who is paid to nurse a child or children of the upper class. In some cases, the birth mother chose not to nurse for aesthetic reasons, or for convenience; in other cases, the mother might have died in childbirth, or was simply unable to nurse successfully.

Ariana Mornay is unfashionably happy to nurse her own children until her illness requires the need for a wet nurse.

ABOUT THE AUTHOR

Linore Rose Burkard lives with her husband and five children in a town full of antique stores and gift shops in southwestern Ohio. She homeschooled her children for ten years. Raised in New York, she graduated magna cum laude from the City University of New York with a Bachelor of Arts in English literature.

Ms. Burkard began writing her books about Ariana Forsythe because she could not find an Inspirational Regency Romance on the bookshelves of any store. "There were Christian books that approached the genre," she says, "but they fell short of being a genuine Regency. I finally gave up looking and wrote what I was looking for myself." She also enjoys writing articles, reading, parenting, family movie nights, swimming, and gardening.

Linore enjoys hearing from her readers.

She can be reached at
admin@LinoreRoseBurkard.com.
**Be sure to visit her on the web at
http://www.LinoreRoseBurkard.com.**
Sign up for her free mailing list and receive
her monthly illustrated
newsletter, as well as news and
announcements about her
latest writing projects or books.
If you aren't online but would like to
contact Linore, please write to her at

Linore Rose Burkard
c/o Harvest House Publishers
990 Owen Loop North
Eugene, OR 97402

The employees of Thorndike Press hope you have enjoyed this Large Print book. All our Thorndike, Wheeler, and Kennebec Large Print titles are designed for easy reading, and all our books are made to last. Other Thorndike Press Large Print books are available at your library, through selected bookstores, or directly from us.

For information about titles, please call:
(800) 223-1244

or visit our Web site at:
http://gale.cengage.com/thorndike

To share your comments, please write:
Publisher
Thorndike Press
295 Kennedy Memorial Drive
Waterville, ME 04901